A Beautiful Spy

RACHEL HORE

A Beautiful Spy

**SIMON &
SCHUSTER**

London · New York · Sydney · Toronto · New Delhi

First published in Great Britain by Simon & Schuster UK Ltd, 2021

1 3 5 7 9 10 8 6 4 2

Simon & Schuster UK Ltd
1st Floor
222 Gray's Inn Road
London WC1X 8HB

Simon & Schuster Australia, Sydney
Simon & Schuster India, New Delhi

www.simonandschuster.co.uk
www.simonandschuster.com.au
www.simonandschuster.co.in

A CIP catalogue record for this book
is available from the British Library

Hardback ISBN: 978-1-4711-8717-9
eBook ISBN: 978-1-4711-8719-3
Audio ISBN: 978-1-4711-8720-9

'She's Olga Pulloffski': Written by Bert Lee and R.P. Weston. Lyrics
accessed at https://www.lyricsplayground.com/alpha/songs/o/
olgapulloffskithebeautifulspy.shtml on 24 September 2020, and
transcribed by Mark McNamara in November 2003.

Typeset in Palatino by M Rules
Printed and bound by CPI Group (UK) Ltd, Croydon, CR0 4YY

MIX
Paper from
responsible sources
FSC
www.fsc.org
FSC® C020471

For David

'... it is curious that in the history of espionage and counter-espionage a very high percentage of the greatest coups have been brought off by women.'

MAXWELL KNIGHT ('M')

Ontario, Summer 1984

She guessed what the envelope contained from the London post-mark, but it was a while before she mustered the courage to fetch a knife from the kitchen drawer and slit it open. With trembling fingers she eased out the newspaper cutting, then sitting down at the table, unfolded and smoothed it out.

The headline struck her at once, taking her breath away. And that awful old photograph. She narrowed her eyes at the text underneath and fumbled for her spectacles. Her sight cleared and the small print came into focus. The words, hateful, sensational, burned into her. She read on, her finger tracing the lines, her lips moving silently. Her eyes prickled, her heartbeat stumbled. That wasn't what she'd told the journalist, how could he have thought ... Her hand flew to her mouth but her eyes remained glued to the dense lines of print. How could he?

When he'd telephoned out of the blue, that soft voice ... it had soothed her, coaxed her to say more than she'd intended. It had all poured out of her, the rancour of years. 'Don't print that,' she'd stopped to tell him at least once. 'It is simply what I felt at the time. Half a century ago. My life is different now . . .'

He'd reassured her, told her not to worry, she could trust him. Why had she believed him? She knew about journalists, but he'd caught her at a weak moment.

An English Sunday tabloid. Anyone might have read it. One of them, perhaps. How stupid of her. They'd know where she was now. Suppose they . . . No!

She let the paper slip from her grasp and sat staring into the distance, allowing the memories to flood in . . .

One

Summer 1928

It all began at a garden party in a leafy provincial suburb.

'Don't dawdle, dear,' called Mrs Gray, hurrying ahead along the front path.

Minnie sighed as she shut the wooden gate then followed her mother round the side of the white-painted mansion with reluctant footsteps. They passed beneath an arch of tumbling pink roses and out onto a sunny terrace overlooking a rolling expanse of lawn dotted with people and stalls selling home-made jam and baked goods.

From here she surveyed the busy gathering with dismay. There were a few people she recognized, but they were mostly her mother's friends, middle-aged women in frumpy hats and floral frocks, some with their husbands in tow. At twenty-one, it seemed that Minnie was the youngest person here. How she wished she'd never come.

'Look, there's Sarah Bowden. Come on, Minnie!' Mrs Gray,

bright-eyed and purposeful, propelled her daughter across the grass to where a willowy lady in navy was queuing by a snowy canopy where teas were being served.

'Betty darling,' Sarah Bowden cried in welcome, carmine lips curving in her foxy face. 'And Minnie. So sweet of you to keep your mother company. I'm here on my own. Ernest had a bowls match, wretched man.'

'I'm not being sweet, Mrs Bowden, there was nothing else to do.' Minnie had never warmed to beady-eyed Mrs Bowden. 'Tennis was called off and Mother wouldn't leave me moping at home, would you, Mother?'

'Really, Minnie,' her mother muttered. 'Do you have to be so honest? I'm sorry, Sarah, sometimes I don't know what to do with her.'

'Poor dear Minnie,' Mrs Bowden murmured, patting Minnie's arm. 'It won't be much fun for her here.' She glanced around and her voice dropped. 'Honestly, Betty, look at the men. The ones that aren't old and married are hardly a young girl's dream.'

Mrs Gray scanned the crowd with a predator's eye. 'Oh, I don't know,' she said briskly, 'there are one or two nice younger ones. Don't slouch, Minnie. It's not attractive.'

They took their turn at the rows of white crockery and there was a pause while they collected cups of tea and finger sandwiches. Minnie slid a slab of warm marble cake onto her saucer then licked her fingers, causing her mother to frown.

Mrs Bowden narrowed her eyes and whispered above the rattle of cups, 'Did you hear that Mr Chamberlain himself is expected?'

Mrs Gray's expression clouded. 'His wife didn't mention it when I saw her at last week's committee meeting.'

'Didn't she?' Mrs Bowden said happily. 'There are rumours, you know, that he's to switch to our constituency in the next election to be sure of a good majority.'

'I know about *that*. Minnie, I've told you how important Mr Chamberlain is becoming in the House of Commons. It would be something for you to meet him.'

'If you say so,' Minnie murmured, long bored by the subject of the Chamberlains, though secretly she supposed that encountering Neville Chamberlain would be special. Not only was he one of Birmingham's MPs, but he was the son of the renowned Victorian statesman Sir Joseph Chamberlain. Now what was wrong? Her mother was inspecting her in a critical manner. *My hair, probably.* Minnie touched a hand to her new blonde crop and worried whether the style suited her.

The sun blazed down. They moved into the shade of a great copper beech, where the older women bought pots of honey from a stall and began to discuss the perennial problem of fundraising. Minnie bit into the sweet, buttery cake and looked up at the house that loomed over them. Their host was the Conservative and Unionist Party agent, Mr Robert Edwards, and his residence was an impressive pile. Freshly painted white shutters gleamed in the sunlight and its six chimneys stood proud against a sky of depthless blue.

A curtain twitched at an upstairs window, drawing her eye. A wizened old man in a dressing gown stood at the open casement, looking down on proceedings. The shrewdness of his gaze gave Minnie an odd feeling. *As though we're all ants in a nest or monkeys in a zoo.* She glanced about at the other guests. Only she had noticed him and this gave her a feeling of delicious secret pleasure.

This time when she looked up the old man returned her gaze, but his stern expression did not alter. Instead he turned back to the room. *He must be an elderly relative of the Edwards'.* The mansion was large enough to accommodate several generations. Certainly it was of a size far beyond the aspirations of Minnie's family, though she felt ashamed for making the comparison.

The Grays' own house a few streets away was modest, poky, if she were to be unkind, but her mother was a widow and everyone said how splendidly she'd managed, bringing up five children on a patchwork of income. To which for the last few years Minnie had contributed a portion of her wages from her typing job at the Automobile Association. 'A respectable position,' Mrs Gray told anyone who asked. 'And will do for Minnie until the right man comes along.' Lately she said this with a sigh because her eldest child was awkward with men and showed no sign of flying the nest. And Minnie, despite loving her mother dearly, had begun to feel stuck. Life should be opening out. Instead nothing seemed to change. Her work offered no path of progress and she couldn't afford to leave home even if she wanted. Also, the two youngest Grays were still at school and her mother needed Minnie's wages.

The distant *whack* of wood on wood broke into her thoughts, followed by a shout of female laughter. Minnie peered down the garden and noticed with interest that an area at the far end had been set up for games and a croquet match was in progress.

'Back in a minute.' She left her half-drunk tea on a table and hurried off, reaching the croquet in time to see a cheerful young man with a cigarette hanging from his lips measuring up for a shot. When his ball hit the hoop and skittered away he gave a cry of mock frustration.

'Bad luck,' she called out on impulse, but when he glanced up to see who'd spoken, she looked away in embarrassment.

'Minnie Gray, isn't it?' A woman's graceful drawl. Minnie turned to meet a familiar gaze. Narrowed hazel eyes in a forthright oval face, powder not quite disguising faint lines around thin, crimson-painted lips. For a second Minnie couldn't place her, then the mannish way the woman drew on her cigarette gave it away.

'Miss Pyle! Sorry . . . I hadn't expected to see you.'

Minnie had occasionally noticed Dolly Pyle at the AA Club and liked her. She must be in her early thirties, her lean figure always elegantly dressed in a tailored suit to which today she'd added a neat round hat. She sported an air of calm confidence, but kindness, too. A couple of weeks ago she'd helped pick up some leaflets that in her hurry Minnie had dropped on the floor of the Members Lounge while restocking a rack. 'You look put upon, dear,' the sympathetic Miss Pyle whispered. 'Are they giving you a hard time?' Minnie had explained how everything was in confusion because of staff illness. Afterwards, she worried that she shouldn't have said this to Miss Pyle, who was a club member after all, but today the woman appeared friendlier than ever.

'Do call me Dolly. Why am I not in the least surprised to see *you* here?' Miss Pyle's eyes twinkled with humour.

'I don't know. It's my mother who's the party member. I just trailed along to keep her happy.'

'What I meant was, well . . . I'd hardly see you as a rabid socialist any more than I am.'

'Certainly not. I'll put my cross in the Conservative and Unionist box when the time comes, but I'm not a rabid anything. If you want the truth, squabbling over politics bores me rigid.'

'And most of the people here, I'll bet my eye.' Dolly sighed, looking round. 'Still, one has to have a social life of some sort. I work in London most of the week, and come up at weekends to look in on my parents. A friend invited me today, but she's off somewhere selling raffle tickets.'

'Everyone here's a bit old and dull for me, to be honest. Not you, of course . . .' Minnie added hastily.

'Oh, I'm over the hill, Minnie.' Dolly smiled. 'On the shelf, too, but I don't mind.' She threw her cigarette butt onto the grass and stepped on it. 'I enjoy my freedom too much to give it up for any man. I hope you're not worrying about that yet.'

'Not much luck in that department.' Minnie sighed. 'Mother's always on about me settling down, but despite that rot I complained about the other day I like working. If I married then my husband would expect me to stay at home. I say, I do envy you living in London. What kind of work do you do?'

There came shouts of surprise from the croquet players. The game had ended, it seemed. When she looked again at her companion, Dolly was regarding Minnie thoughtfully.

Then she leaned towards Minnie and spoke in a low voice. 'I'm afraid that I'm not allowed to tell you about my job. Except that it's something for the government.'

'That sounds mysterious.'

'It is,' Dolly murmured. 'I can't breathe a word to a soul.'

'I promise I won't say anything to anybody,' Minnie whispered back, thinking Dolly was joking, but the woman's expression was perfectly serious. 'Oh, you … how marvellous. I'd love to do something exciting or useful. I'd train as a nurse if I didn't hate the sight of blood.'

'It's not always exciting what I do, but it is useful and important.' Dolly's gaze moved past Minnie. 'Oh, good heavens. I haven't played *that* for years. What fun.'

Minnie followed Dolly's gaze to see that the man who'd muffed his croquet shot was now lifting spiked metal numerals out of a long wooden box. They watched as he proceeded to position them purposefully on the lawn in the shape of a giant clock face, pressing each into the turf with his heel. Finally he worked a hole for a small pot in the circle's centre and attached a tin flag to it before returning to fetch several clubs and balls from the box.

'Anyone care for clock golf?' he cried to the generality.

'Shall we?' Dolly said to Minnie, her eyes dancing.

'I'm up for it!' Clock golf was sedate, but Minnie could never resist a game of any sort.

'Excellent. Two over here,' Dolly called. They went to claim their clubs from the man, who introduced himself as Raymond Mills. The three of them were joined by a plump middle-aged gentleman with spectacles, whose name Minnie missed.

The golf was more amusing than she expected. Both men were only average shots, but good-humoured about it and there was much hilarity. Dolly was competent, potting her ball in two or three shots each time as she worked her way round the numbers. Minnie did better. Even party games like this brought out her competitive nature, a fact that often got her into trouble with her brothers and sisters at home.

'You girls care about the game too much,' Raymond announced after Minnie scored a hole in one. 'You're supposed to flutter your eyelashes and let us chaps win.'

'Why on earth would we do that?' Minnie retorted. 'You don't deserve to win.'

'Dear me, you're as bossy as my elder sister,' he said mildly. He knocked his ball wide and groaned.

'I'm not bossy, just honest,' Minnie replied, worried that she'd been rude. To her relief she caught a twinkle in his eye so she gave him an uncertain smile. He was nice really, with his boyish face and easy-going attitude. She was amused by the way he wore his hat pushed back so that a lock of hair flopped out in front.

Dolly, she realized, was still studying her, a thoughtful expression on her face. *You've done something wrong again,* she told herself. She was always getting into trouble with her mother for saying what was on her mind. In public she tried to be careful, aware that she might upset people. *Men don't like strident women,* Mrs Gray often said. Men were hard work, Minnie had long ago decided. But then Dolly sent her an amused smile, allaying her fears.

'You next, Dolly.'

They continued the game. While Raymond strode off, whistling and swinging his club, to fetch his ball from a flowerbed, Minnie prepared for a tricky shot. Again, she sensed Dolly's eye on her and it made her want to do her best. She gave her ball a sharp tap and it rose, hit the flag and dropped into the pot where, *oh, the suspense*, it wobbled round before coming to rest.

'Phew.'

'Top hole, Minnie,' Dolly cried. 'Excuse the pun.'

Pleasure flooded her. 'Thank you. Sometimes you have to creep up on the ball when it's not looking.'

'Ha, very sinister.' They watched the plump man take his time squaring up for his shot.

'Come on, sir,' Raymond said lightly.

'All right, all right. The sun's in the wrong place.'

Dolly laid a hand on Minnie's sleeve. 'Can I ask you something?' she said quietly.

Minnie looked back enquiringly.

'Would you have coffee with me next Saturday? It would be nice to have a proper talk.'

'Yes, of course.'

'Not at the Club, I think. Do you know the Palace tea room in the park?'

Minnie knew it very well. She felt flattered to be asked, but couldn't think why Dolly was interested in her.

During the winter months the Palace tea room was a welcome place to retreat inside after a chilly walk in the park, but in the summer its doors were thrown open, metal tables and chairs lay scattered across its concourse and families queued at a hatch for ice cream.

When Minnie arrived she spied Dolly Pyle's lean figure already seated at a far-flung table, dappled in sunlight. Dolly was looking out across the tree-lined park, smoking a cigarette in a holder, apparently lost in thought.

'I hope I'm not late,' Minnie said, sitting down beside her.

'Not at all.' Dolly smiled. 'Isn't it a marvellous day?' She signalled to a passing waiter and while they waited for coffee they reminisced about the garden party.

Minnie confessed how embarrassed she had been that her mother had met Raymond later in the afternoon and had promptly invited him for tea. 'He's coming tomorrow. I wish she wouldn't interfere. It's so obvious.'

Dolly laughed. 'My mother used to do the same, but she gave up on me long ago.'

The waiter brought their coffee and Minnie, watching Dolly stir sugar into hers, wondered not for the first time whether this meeting was simply an act of friendliness on Dolly's part. Minnie liked and admired her companion very much, but Dolly was older and wore such an air of mystery and experience that Minnie felt in awe of her.

Finally, Dolly said casually, 'How has work been this week? Better, I hope.'

'Much. I must apologize. That day you helped me ... well, I'd be embarrassed if you thought I was some awful complaining sort.'

'Of course I didn't think that. You were obviously having a hard time, but you remained very professional.'

'Was I? I try to be. Work is usually something I enjoy. It's simply—'

'We all have bad days, but – correct me if I'm wrong – your job doesn't stretch you enough, I think.'

'Honestly, it's fine most of the time, and they treat me very well at the Club, but it's as I told you at the garden party. I'd love to do something really useful and important. I don't know exactly what it is that you do, but working for one of the government ministries sounds interesting.'

'It is, yes, but then mine is an unusual job.'

'You're very lucky, I think.'

Dolly fitted a fresh cigarette into her holder and touched it with a silver lighter that she took from her handbag. She blew out smoke and stared out across the grass. Finally, she appeared to come to a decision and looking directly at Minnie, said, 'This may sound odd, but it's something I've been thinking about. Would you be interested in working for the government?'

This was such an unexpected turn of affairs that Minnie gave a little laugh.

'I'm not being funny, Minnie. No promises, but I could pass on your name, if you liked.' She flicked ash from her cigarette with a stylish movement.

Minnie froze. And now everything fell into place. *The Secret Service. That's who Dolly must work for and why she couldn't speak about it. How thrilling!* She thought of her own job, typing endless letters asking members to renew their subscriptions, the boredom of filing, stacking leaflets, answering the telephone to complaints. She had spoken the truth about liking to work, but the Automobile Association wouldn't do for ever.

Now it was as though a window opened in her mind and light and fresh air rushed in. The Secret Service. What would it be like? Shadowing and spying. Noticing things that others didn't. Like the pictures, perhaps. Excitement rushed through her. Minnie sat straighter and looked Dolly in the eye. 'I'm not sure what to say. Yes, I think.' Immediately the old self-doubt set in. 'Do you really mean it?'

'Of course.' Dolly looked back at her steadily then reached and touched her hand. 'You'd be marvellous, I can tell. I've been watching you for a while. There's something about you they'd like, Minnie Gray.'

Minnie stared at her in astonishment. *Dolly Pyle had been watching her! Why? And who in heaven's name were 'they'?*

Two

1931

For a long time nothing at all happened.

After a few weeks living in a state of high anticipation, then several more feeling let down, Minnie concluded that the opportunity had gone away. If indeed it had ever existed in the first place. All Dolly told her that sunny morning at the tea room was that she'd pass on Minnie's details to her employers. Minnie was fairly certain that Dolly had kept her word – she trusted Dolly – but she also imagined that the older woman had no control over the outcome. Maybe whoever did had not liked the cut of Minnie's jib. Since Minnie approached life half expecting this reaction, she didn't question the idea.

The women remained on friendly terms, but neither spoke about the matter again. A year passed, then two, and Dolly visited the Club less frequently. Minnie almost – but not quite – forgot about that moment when life had suddenly promised freedom and adventure.

On a gloomy Monday evening in November 1931, a letter was waiting for Minnie when she returned from work. She settled at the kitchen table with a cup of tea and slit open the official-looking envelope with a sense of disquiet, rustling open the sheet of paper inside. A government crest was printed at the top, but she squinted in vain at the scrawled signature under the typed message. The letter itself was brief, inviting her to ring Kensington 8128 to arrange an appointment. It was to do with a 'vacancy' in which she had apparently expressed an interest. 'You are requested to keep this matter private,' was the final sentence. Minnie glanced again at the printed crest and the memory of that summer afternoon flooded back. *Would you be interested in working for the government?* A gasp and her hand flew to her mouth.

'What's that you've got, dear?' Her mother was standing at the stove in her apron, stirring a pan redolent with the savoury smell of yesterday's roast lamb.

'It's to do with Dolly Pyle from the Club.' Minnie hastily folded the letter away into her handbag. 'I told you about Dolly. She works in London. From time to time her firm needs another typist and I gave her my address once, ages ago. Perhaps I'll ring them up.'

'Minnie, you don't want to move to London, do you?' Her mother looked anxious and Minnie felt the usual mixture of tenderness, guilt and exasperation that marked their relationship. Boots, their fractious tabby cat, chose this moment to leap up onto her lap.

'I might do,' she said cautiously, waiting for the cat to turn round and settle. 'Not much for me in Edgbaston, is there, Boots?' The cat crouched into a tea cosy shape and began to purr.

'Of course there is.' Her mother clanged a lid onto the bubbling stew and sighed. 'If you'd only try a little harder.'

'If this is about Raymond again, Mother, then please don't.'

'I still don't understand why you were so discouraging of him. I thought he was very patient with you.'

Minnie pressed her cheek into the cat's throbbing warmth. Her relationship with Raymond was the other result of the garden party. It had been her mother's fault, asking him to tea like that and then he'd invited Minnie to make up a four for tennis. For a couple of years they'd met most weeks, sometimes as part of a group to go dancing or to watch motor racing, an enthusiasm of his, sometimes just the pair of them for the pictures. She'd come to love him but in a gentle way. For a long while they were simply friends before things developed. Then she readily succumbed to his kisses, and he kissed delightfully, but all the time the idea went through Minnie's mind that life had something more in store for her and that somewhere there must be someone who'd make her blood race, who'd scoop her up and carry her away, like Errol Flynn in a movie, and she'd be too overcome with desire to resist. Raymond was old-fashioned on that front and she, too, held back, not feeling ready to commit herself to the kind of life marriage with him offered; settling down, leaving her job, having children, endless housework.

In the end she'd had to be honest. She was very fond of him, she told him with a lump in her throat one Sunday when he arrived to see her with a bunch of expensive flowers and a diamond ring in a velvet-covered box. 'I'm sorry, Raymond, I don't feel ready to get engaged.'

'I can wait, Minnie, if time is what you need.'

'It's not fair on you,' she wailed. 'I don't know if I'll ever be ready.'

'I see,' he said brokenly, putting away the little box.

It was with a mixture of relief and regret that she closed the door on his departing figure. She'd always believed that she would be married by twenty-five and Raymond had been her last hope of that.

Although this had happened months ago, Mrs Gray was still upset.

'You're such a lovely girl when you try.'

'You're my darling mother. You would say that.'

'There are some pretty dresses in my catalogue this month. '

'Try them on my sisters, then. You know pretty doesn't suit me.'

Minnie was not happy with the looks God had given her. In her opinion her nose looked like a lump of putty, which no amount of powder could disguise, and she felt dreadfully self-conscious about her hourglass figure. Workmen called after her in the street sometimes, beastly words that made her feel ashamed, but which, perversely, encouraged her to emphasise the curves they clearly admired. Good corsetry helped. As for her peroxided hair, it was a boost to her confidence to see *Hell's Angels* at the cinema. 'I love Jean Harlow,' she told her mother. The feature that pleased her most was her mouth. Raymond had once said she had It Girl lips, so she took special care shaping them when she applied lipstick. She always wore plenty of make-up.

That evening, in the privacy of her bedroom, Minnie read the letter once more and tried to remember what Dolly Pyle had said when she'd quizzed her during that long-ago meeting in the Palace tea room. Something about believing that she'd be good at the kind of work she'd be asked to do. She'd said that Minnie appeared honest, steady and loyal, but also very *individual*. Minnie privately agreed about the first three, but puzzled over *individual*. She hoped that it was a compliment rather than a euphemism for odd or maverick. She pondered this again. Sometimes, admittedly, she felt she didn't fit in. She hadn't any close friends. If her mother was cross she would say that Minnie was being *difficult*, but Minnie didn't mean to be, it was simply the way she'd been made. She sighed. Well, if the Secret Service didn't mind *individual* then it wouldn't hurt to find out more.

She made the call from a public phone box the following lunchtime and was put through to a snooty-sounding girl who gave her a time and a place for an interview. A café on Euston station to meet a Captain King and she wasn't to tell anyone, not even her mother. It all sounded very hole-in-corner, she thought, as she returned to the Automobile Association to eat her lunch. Had she done the right thing?

Three

Minnie had visited London on a number of occasions in her life, but never on her own before and she let her mother assume that it was a proper interview in a London office. Worried about being late, she caught a train that arrived at Euston in good time then paced the sooty, windswept concourse for ten minutes before nervously approaching the restaurant.

When she entered, a warm, smoky fug enveloped her. The place felt cosy, with its cheerful murmur of voices and homely clink of crockery. She glanced about. There were several smartly dressed men sitting alone at white-clothed tables. Which, if any, was Captain King? Then a genial-looking, clean-shaven man at a table in a corner looked up from his paper and met her eye. She walked hesitantly towards him and he rose to greet her.

'Miss Gray,' he said with a friendly, confident air. His handshake was firm and warm and she took to him right away. He was tall with a rangy, athletic frame and though with his irregular features he couldn't be called handsome, there was an ease about him that she found very beguiling.

'What a relief,' Minnie said, smiling uncertainly. 'I was concerned about how to find you.'

'You gave my secretary an excellent description of yourself.' His brown eyes gleamed with good-humour. He whisked her coat onto a hook on the wall while she sat down opposite him at the table.

'I trust you had a comfortable journey?' he asked and she nodded. 'Good, now what can I get you to drink?'

The waitress hurried over at his summons and Minnie observed the charm with which he ordered steak and kidney pie and a pot of tea for them both and made the girl laugh. It should feel odd sitting here with a complete stranger, but the warmth with which he thanked Minnie for coming and the sincerity of his apology for not being in touch earlier reassured her. He was a good few years her senior, she thought, but still in his thirties probably, though the unlit pipe he held and his affable demeanour put her in mind of her mother's older brother, her favourite uncle. He wore his dark hair combed back in the same way as Uncle Simon, too. She wondered if he was married.

The tea arrived and she poured it, then sipped hers as he took a small notebook from his pocket and smoothed it open. Gently, he began to question her.

'Now, Miss Gray, do you still work at the Automobile Association?'

'Yes, I've been there five years.' Minnie explained that though she wasn't unhappy there exactly, the job had its frustrations and she was looking for a change. Something more demanding.

'That's admirable. Tell me about your duties there.'

'The usual secretarial tasks, really.' She described her responsibilities, trying to convey how typing, administration and dealing with telephone enquiries required her to be fast, accurate and efficient. All the while he listened closely, his eyes on her face.

'Excellent,' he said when she'd finished, and he made a note in his book. 'And what do you like to do when you're not working?'

She told him about playing hockey and tennis. 'I read a lot, nothing heavy, novels from the library mostly. Mother's involved with the Edgbaston Conservatives and sometimes I help her by typing newsletters or delivering leaflets.'

The Captain looked up from his notes. 'Edgbaston. That's Mr Chamberlain's constituency now, isn't it?'

'Yes, he moved to us as it's a safer seat, so everything's much busier these days. We have more members. There's a great deal of paperwork.'

'And what do you think of your Honourable Member?' He was looking at her shrewdly and Minnie sensed that her answer to this question was important, though she couldn't think why.

'I've only met him once or twice. I'm sure he doesn't even remember my name. Everybody speaks highly of him, don't they? He's not at all grand, even though Mother says he's becoming important in the Party.'

'Your mother sounds very astute.'

'She's friendly with his wife, so she hears the latest news.'

'Ah.' Captain King wrote another note and underscored it. 'It's delightful that you help your mother in her political endeavours. You share her views, do you?'

'I vote Conservative and Unionist, if that's what you mean.' Minnie shrugged. 'It seems a natural thing for me to do.'

Just then the waitress brought their food and there was a brief pause before he continued.

'Tell me about your family, Miss Gray,' he said between mouthfuls. 'Would you say that you're close?'

'Yes, I suppose we've had to be.' His sympathetic eyes encouraged her. 'You see, my father was killed in action in Flanders. Mother was left with four of us and my youngest brother on the way and there wasn't ever much money.'

His brow furrowed. 'That must indeed have been very difficult. Where do you come in the family, Miss Gray?'

'I'm the eldest. Though I wasn't always . . .' She found she couldn't continue.

A brief moment while she recovered, then the Captain moved on smoothly. 'And the others, do they all still live at home?'

'No, only the youngest, Doug, he's still at school. One of my sisters, Marjorie, got married recently and the other has taken lodgings in the city to be near work. That's Joan. My other brother Richard's a policeman, or rather he's training to be one.'

'I see. That makes the five of you. You started to say something just now . . . when I asked about your place in the family.'

'Did I?' she said. *How thorough he was.* She put down her knife and fork, knitted her hands in her lap and took a breath. 'I had an older brother once but he died when I was little.' *Eddie, bare legs dashing ahead of her through the grass, the breeze ruffling his chestnut-brown hair.* She tried sometimes to remember his voice, his laugh, but it always eluded her.

She looked up to see the Captain studying her and collected herself.

'It still hurts, doesn't it?' he said quietly and she saw with a sudden sense of connection that he knew about that pain. 'And your father. Do you remember him well?'

'Yes, I was eleven when he died.' Minnie couldn't help bitterness invading her voice. The Captain waited for her to go on. 'He was difficult to forget, a strong character.' She described how he had worked for the *Daily Mail* in Manchester, where they'd lived, as their Northern night editor, how the family only saw him at odd times of day and then not at all for long periods after he went away to war.

'Tell me more about him, Miss Gray. What exactly do you recall?' His eyes were searching, though still kind, and his voice had a soothing quality so that she found herself saying more than she intended.

'He was often tired, irritable, to be honest. His work was hard, that was Mother's excuse. We were expected to be silent if he was sleeping during the day and it's not easy for young children to be quiet, is it?' Minnie hesitated, feeling guilty at betraying so much. Mother would be horrified if she knew.

The waitress came and took away their plates and the conversation continued. It was the strangest of interviews,

Minnie thought. She'd never known someone as interested in her life and opinions as Captain King. She even found herself telling him about Raymond, how the pair of them had shared interests in films and sport, though she managed to keep to herself how shy they'd been with one another physically. Instead she talked brightly about keeping an eye out for the right man, and that she'd know him when she saw him, but in the meantime she wasn't concerned. She had plenty of other interests. And friends. She laughed as she described the jolly types she played hockey with. She was fond of them, of course, but, no, she couldn't think of any to whom she was really close.

'Do you still have pals from school?'

'Not really.' Minnie described how she had been sent away to boarding school, where she found life difficult and hadn't got on well with some of the girls. Oh, she could make them laugh with her practical jokes, but then the school accused her of being disruptive and in the end Mother had taken her away. 'Or rather,' Minnie added, feeling compelled to be truthful, 'they asked her to.'

She glanced anxiously at Captain King, expecting him to be appalled by her confession, but instead a smile played round his lips. 'That sounds like my school career,' he said.

'Did you play jokes, too?' she asked eagerly.

'Plenty. In addition, the staff didn't appreciate me keeping pet mice in the dormitory. An injured crow once.'

'Mice? Ugh, I'm not surprised. What about the bird? Did it recover?'

'Yes, though I was made to give it to the gardener's boy.

I used to sneak off to make sure he was looking after it properly.'

Minnie smiled. She suddenly liked this man immensely, wanted to please him.

There was another pause while he wrote in his book. The waitress brought them fruit cocktail in glass dishes. Minnie spooned up the sharp sweetness. She was beginning to feel puzzled about the point of this meeting. Why was Captain King asking all these personal questions and what was the job?

'Could you tell me ...' she asked. 'Your letter mentioned an opportunity ...'

'Of course. You must be wondering what all this is about.'

'I am rather.'

He reached inside his jacket for his wallet and she was puzzled to see a sudden wriggling movement under the material at his breast, as though he kept something alive in his pocket. He smiled as her eyes widened, but did not explain.

Was he preparing to pay? No, instead of coins from his wallet he extracted a folded newspaper cutting. She forgot about the odd wriggling and watched as he moved his empty plate aside and spread the cutting out between them. Minnie leaned in to read the headline. *'Royal Navy mutiny at Invergordon'*. She frowned. What relevance did that have to the interview?

'Did you take much notice of this when it happened?' he said.

'Of course. Everyone talked about it.'

'They did.' He smiled grimly. 'Though you'd be surprised how little interest ordinary people usually take in current affairs.'

'We always read the *Daily Telegraph* and listen to the wireless.'

'I'm glad to hear you're well-informed.' He looked pleased, but still, Minnie wondered, what did the infamous Invergordon Incident have to do with a job?

She squinted at the date of the cutting, September the something. More than two months ago now, but she remembered the event well and the furore it had caused. The crews of several warships at a Scottish port had refused to obey orders following a rumour that their wages were to be cut as an economy measure in the slump. 'The Incident', as it came to be known, had only lasted two days, but its repercussions were far-reaching. The very idea of a Naval mutiny was shocking to people. A national panic ensued. There was a run on the pound and the stock market plummeted. The mood was so serious that a few days later the government was forced to abandon the gold standard, that international mark of financial security whereby Britain's monetary system was underpinned by actual gold ingots piled in bank vaults. The country was still recovering.

Captain King smoothed the paper and murmured, 'I need to explain why this is important. See, here …' His finger traced the lines of newsprint. *'The mutinous sailors sang "The Red Flag", the Communist Party anthem.* This is why we're interested.'

Minnie wondered who 'we' meant. The Secret Service, she supposed, but the Captain hadn't mentioned that yet. 'I see,' she said hesitantly.

'It's a dangerous sign. The Russian Bolshevik revolution in 1917 began with a naval mutiny. There was another in

Germany inspired by Socialists in 1918. Don't think the same thing couldn't happen here. A Communist regime would pose a significant threat to our ancient freedoms. Lead to a totalitarian state, even. There are people among us, connected to the British Communist Party, whom we suspect of having regrettably close ties to the Soviet Union. Our government is exceedingly concerned.'

'That is certainly disturbing.' She understood now and was genuinely dismayed. 'My mother's friends worry about the Communists, but I haven't heard that their type is active in Edgbaston.'

'You wouldn't be able to tell. It's feared they're everywhere, working under cover. And that's our job, to sniff them out, find out what they're planning.' He folded the news cutting and tucked it away in his wallet, then closed his notebook and sat back.

'It's been delightful to meet you, Miss Gray. I'll be in touch once we've both had time to consider. Do you think you might be interested?'

She felt bewildered. 'I'm not sure that I understand what you'd want me to do. Is it something to do with the Communists?'

'Yes, of course it is. You'd be spying on them.' He looked surprised that she'd asked. 'Should you and I decide to take things further, everything will be made clear. At this point I need to know whether in principle you'd like to help. It would only be part-time, at least at first. There would be some recompense – precious little, I'm afraid. You would need to secure additional employment.'

'And I'd have to move to London?' She was struggling to understand.

'Oh, undoubtedly you'd need to be in London. Does that trouble you?'

She took a breath. 'It's a big thing to do, but I'd be prepared to give it a try.'

'Jolly good.' Captain King dropped his pipe in his jacket pocket, then piled some coins on the table for the waitress. 'I won't keep you any longer. Have you other business in the capital, or will you be catching the train back?'

She glanced at her watch and saw to her surprise that a whole two hours had passed. 'I must go back. I promised to be home this evening and the next train is in, oh, a few minutes.'

'Then I'll see you onto it.' He helped her with her coat, then paused while reaching for his own and again she saw the wriggling movement inside his jacket and wondered about it.

'Ah.' He slipped his hand in, but only drew out a small envelope. 'I'll be in trouble if I forget to give you this. It's your travel expenses.'

'Thank you.' She took the envelope gratefully and shut it in her handbag.

Outside, the air tasted of soot. The Captain bought a penny ticket then they hastened to the platform where the train was ready to leave. He handed her up into a carriage and she quickly found a compartment that was occupied only by a matronly older lady. Before sitting down, Minnie lowered the window and he came close to speak to her.

'Remember,' he murmured, tapping the side of his nose. 'Don't even tell your mother.'

'Don't worry. I'll think of something.'

A whistle blew. Doors slammed and the train let off a toot and a blast of steam. The Captain stepped back. 'Goodbye! I'll be . . .' he called, but his words were lost in the snorts and chuffs of the engine.

Minnie waved. 'Goodbye!' He waved back then reached inside his coat and brought out something white and alive with a twitching tail. As she watched in surprise it whisked up his arm and crouched on his shoulder and she realized that the wriggling she'd noticed earlier was a rat, a horrid rat like her brother Doug's. But now the train was moving forward and soon she could see him no longer.

Minnie settled back into her seat with an odd sense that something inside her had altered for ever. The motherly woman opposite stared at her curiously as she knitted, but Minnie hardly noticed because her mind was otherwise engaged. She'd never met anyone like Captain King before. His warm avuncular air must be only one aspect of him, if his job was handling secret agents.

Behind the attentive gaze, the friendly questions and the reassuring voice was a probing mind. And a degree of eccentricity, she smiled, shaking her head as she remembered the pet rat. He'd been observing her all the time, but at a deeper level than at any interview she'd experienced. It had felt as though he was searching for a sense of her, what she believed in, what upset her, who she loved – and what she didn't like. The attention had made her feel wrung out but . . . also special, as though she mattered to him.

She badly wanted to have measured up. Had she met his expectations?

The train rattled on past backyards of endless terraced houses, then the gardens became bigger, with more trees, the dwellings set further apart. At last they were out in the countryside, carving through sodden ploughed fields and green pastures dotted with cows and the stops were at market towns. A mother with a sleeping babe-in-arms joined them in the carriage for a while. Later, the knitting lady unwrapped a sandwich and ate it tidily, using the greaseproof paper to catch the crumbs. Minnie's nose wrinkled at the smell of sardines.

Her thoughts ran ahead. If the Captain offered her a job and she moved to London, she'd need to find somewhere to live and another part-time job to make up her income. The idea was daunting but exciting, too. It would show everyone that she was her own person, purposeful, not simply waiting at home for the right man to come along. It would also mean leaving her mother. That made her sad, because despite their disagreements Minnie loved her dearly and relied on her support and encouragement. She'd have to go home often.

But what exactly would she be doing for Captain King? It was something about monitoring members of the Communist Party, he'd revealed that much. The Communists were dangerous, treasonous, she understood, but he hadn't explained exactly what her role would be and she wished again that she hadn't felt so naïve and overwhelmed, and berated herself for her reticence.

She mulled over the questions he'd asked, wondering

if she'd given the right answers. She'd been steadfast and truthful – she'd sensed from the beginning that honesty was important. There were little things he hadn't asked that bothered her now, such as what her current wages were, and again she wondered exactly what job it was he wanted her to do and what it would be worth. She assumed that her secretarial experience was of value because he'd asked such detailed questions about her typing speed and how she rubbed along with her fellow workers. Had it been sensible to convey that she wasn't much interested in the cut and thrust of politics, but tended to agree with her mother's views? It was the truth, though. Her whole family were loyal Conservatives. If it came to that, most of the people Minnie knew were. The lady opposite, who folded away her greaseproof paper and was now pouring tea from a vacuum flask, she probably was, too. Labour voters were working class, but many of them respectable. Communists would look very different, she supposed. Disruptive, zealous figures one read about in the newspapers but never actually met in real life.

Minnie thought back to what Dolly Pyle had told her, about the value of loyalty to the Secret Service, and it occurred to her now that quite apart from secretarial qualifications and experience, the Captain must be looking for a certain sort of character in his spies.

It had been embarrassing to confess what a rule-breaker she'd been at school, but she'd been reassured by the fact that he'd understood, and even implied that his schooldays, too, had been difficult. Had he not fitted in either? Minnie wished she had asked him more about himself, but it simply hadn't been that kind of conversation and she'd been too nervous.

If she'd lied about anything, though, she sensed that he would have known and it would have told against her.

She didn't think she had lied. Such a thing was against her nature.

It was what she had withheld from him that she worried about. She knew she'd sounded uncertain when he'd asked about her father. She could hardly have told him the truth, that instead of feeling wretched when the news came of his death at Passchendaele, she'd been relieved. A man like Captain King would have had serious doubts about employing a girl like that.

He's probably decided he's not interested in me, she told herself wearily. *I'm too ordinary or too awkward or too something else.* It would have been obvious to him that she was not socially well-connected, apart from the Chamberlain link. She remembered the snooty secretary she'd spoken to on the telephone. No, Minnie couldn't compete with her.

Well. The whole thing had been a little adventure, and now she could sink back into her usual life. Safe, yes, but how dull and frustrating when she longed to achieve something or be someone. To make a difference. She sighed loudly enough for the woman to look up from her knitting, a concerned look on her round face. 'Is anything the matter, dear?' she asked in a motherly tone.

'No. Thank you, anyway.' Minnie hid herself from the woman's scrutiny by taking a library book from her bag and half a bar of chocolate she'd saved from the journey up. The book was a spy story she'd chosen deliberately and she popped a bit of chocolate in her mouth and quickly lost herself in a thrilling world of shadows where every step the hero took might lead to discovery, capture and a nasty death. The spies in these tales were endowed with glamorous good looks and loved to live life on the edge. She looked up misty-eyed each time the train halted, relieved to see the reassuring mundanity of a red-brick station.

Minnie loved spy stories, but they were mostly about men. Were there real-life female spies, she pondered as she dabbed up the last flakes of chocolate. The only one she could think of was Mata Hari, the exotic dancer and seductress, who'd ended up in front of the firing squad during the Great War, convicted of spying for the Germans. The idea of plain, unfeminine Minnie Gray as a latter-day Mata Hari made her snort with laughter, causing the knitting woman to look up in alarm. Quickly, Minnie returned to her book.

By the time she boarded the bus on the last stretch of her journey home she'd got it fixed in her mind that Captain King wouldn't want her and that given what had happened to Mata Hari she'd probably had a lucky escape.

'You're earlier than I expected, dear,' her mother greeted her when Minnie closed the front door and sniffed at the homely smell of sausages. 'It's toad-in-the-hole for supper. Did you have a successful day?' The warmth and security of ordinary life wrapped itself round her and she gave her mother a hug.

'I did my best, Mother, but we'll have to see.'

After several days passed without her hearing from the

Captain, Minnie felt thoroughly unsettled again. As well as loosening her from her mundane routine, the interview had brought up suppressed feelings from her childhood. There came a night when she dreamed of her brother Eddie and her father, of things that she'd half-forgotten because they'd taken place so long ago.

Eddie: the sight of him running through that grassy field as she toddled behind, crying for him to wait. In her dream he ran far away into the distance.

She'd never discovered what exactly had happened. A fall at a funfair that she'd been deemed too little to attend. She'd come into the hall when her father had arrived home abruptly, Eddie a slight, quivering figure in his arms. The atmosphere in the house became urgent, Eddie's bedroom door was shut against her. Minnie stopped her ears to his high, thin cries before a neighbour came to fetch her away.

When she returned the next day it was to a house in mourning. Eddie was gone and nothing was ever to be the same again.

Her father's grief, his guilt, was terrible, a maelstrom, it terrified her. Each time his eye fell upon her it was with resentment that she still existed while his beloved son had been taken.

He expected her to take her brother's place somehow, but she could do nothing right in his eyes. She could not run as fast as Eddie, she could not climb trees, she could not throw a ball correctly. Why wouldn't she wear practical clothes instead of the frilly white dresses her mother made?

More children had come along, two boys her father could

play cricket with, and girls, her two sisters, pretty and fair. Now he no longer needed the tomboy he'd forged, this forth-right girl who answered back. Why couldn't Minnie be dainty and girlish like Marjorie and Joan? 'They look like Bubbles,' she'd sobbed, disdaining the prissy child in the Pears soap advertisement. 'I can't do what you say. I hate you, I hate you,' and then she'd dodge the swipe of her angry father's hand.

Sometimes, when no one else was looking, he would strike her or shove past roughly. Once he shook her after she sobbed that she'd tell. All she could do was to avoid him, especially at any time when his work was stressful and his temper was high.

After the telegram arrived with news of his death, her mother could not understand why Minnie did not mourn her father. The rest of the family had not experienced his violence and they did not believe her when she told them. She'd been forced to bury it all. Until now.

Speaking to the Captain about her childhood had brought all this to the fore. It made Minnie sad and restless, but she'd also sensed that at some deep level he understood her. She wanted to please him, to answer his call, to prove herself to him. This was why when, a week after the interview, he sent a letter offering her a job, she had no hesitation in writing back to say yes, she would be delighted to accept. But after she'd posted the letter the doubts set in. What exactly had she signed up for?

Four

December 1931

On a Saturday morning, two weeks later, Minnie mounted the steps to Number 38 Sloane Street, Knightsbridge. When she rang the bell a dog starting yapping within. After a moment the door opened a crack and Captain King's good-natured face appeared, his hand on the collar of a small brown wire-haired terrier. 'Sorry.' He scooped up the animal, then opened the door wider. 'Come in quickly or the parrot will escape.'

The parrot? What kind of place was this? Clutching her overnight case Minnie stepped across the threshold.

'You found it easily enough?' He closed the door then set the struggling dog on the floor, whereupon it dashed to sniff at her as the Captain took her coat. Sensing she was friend and not foe the animal lost interest and trotted away down a dimly lit hallway that was piled on either side with boxes, bags and packages.

'Follow Bobby,' the Captain instructed. 'Apologies for the mess, but I've only recently moved in.'

Minnie found herself in a large, high-ceilinged drawing room with a view of the street below. It smelled strongly of sawdust.

'Mind the snake.' The Captain's voice came right from behind. 'He can be bad tempered if he's jolted.'

She drew a sharp breath and took care to avoid a glass vivarium on the floor. Its inside had been artfully laid out as a desert landscape with sand, rocks, and a cave-like structure made out of papier mâché, but its inhabitant must have been snoozing out of sight because there was no sign of life.

A low electric hum drew Minnie's attention to a pair of aquariums on stands against the far wall. Fascinated, she wandered across to one and stared at the shoal of bright orange fish darting about in the bubbling water. A sudden squawk from the direction of the window alerted her to a blue-breasted parrot swinging on a perch. It cocked its head at her with half-shuttered eyes, then gave a suggestive whistle that made her flinch, before it flapped its wings and sailed off around the room. She cried out as it narrowly avoided her head.

'I apologize for the bird. I bought him from an old sailor, who taught him no manners,' the Captain said ruefully. 'You look rattled.'

'I simply didn't expect . . . all this.' Minnie swept her hand to encompass the fish, the parrot, the row of feeding bowls on newspaper on the floor and a cage sitting on a shelf between stacks of books where a gold-coloured mouse had begun to scamper on a rattling wheel. Bobby the dog, meanwhile, sat in the middle of the patterned rug, his shining eyes fixed on her beseechingly from under his shaggy fringe.

'Ah, the menagerie. My sister, who owns this flat, is not best pleased by the mess.' The Captain shifted a sack of sunflower seed from one of a pair of shabby armchairs, plumped up a cushion and bid Minnie sit down. Then off he went to brew coffee. There was no wife or maid to do it for him, it seemed.

That meant she was alone with him. Surely she wasn't to receive her training here? Her nervousness grew.

When the Captain had invited her for the weekend, she'd never imagined the Knightsbridge address to be his home. Perhaps after coffee he would summon a taxi to take them to some offices, or a country house training centre? And where was she to stay tonight, she'd like to know? Surely not here with him, that would be improper.

After he returned with a tray, poured the coffee and settled himself in the opposite armchair with a sheaf of papers, she plucked up the courage to ask. 'Will we be here all the time?'

He shot her a guarded look. 'I thought so, yes. Do you mind? My secretary has booked you into a hotel up the road so you'll be quite safe.'

'I didn't mean to imply . . .' she blurted in embarrassment. 'It's simply that I expected somewhere . . . more official, with other people. Do you really work from here?'

'Ah.' The Captain sank back in his chair with a smile. 'You imagined dark-panelled rooms, the smell of old leather and a hushed atmosphere like a spy thriller. No, no, I'm afraid there is some distance between fiction and reality.' He paused to toss Bobby a piece of shortbread. 'The office is not far away, in South

Kensington, but it's too communal for me, like a school staff room, frankly, and it's not easy to conduct classified business. My secretary's there, but personally I like to keep my activities separate from everyone else's. It's the way I work best.'

'Oh, I see,' she said, a bit dismal. So she wasn't to feel part of something big and important after all. How little she had grasped of her situation. Minnie began to fear that she had taken too much on trust. But now this odd man was regarding her most sympathetically with that alarming reassurance of his, so she cradled her warm coffee mug and admitted, 'I still don't understand. Can you tell me more about what I'll be doing?'

He brushed crumbs from his papers and his expression became grave. 'I am sorry, Miss Gray. I haven't been fair and you've been most patient. I'll begin by explaining that you will be working for M Section, part of British Intelligence.'

Minnie's eyes widened. 'I assumed it to be British Intelligence, but M Section – what is that?'

'Actually,' he said, looking a little smug, 'it's me. I am M. M for Maxwell. And here, 38 Sloane Street . . .' He waved his hand. 'Welcome to M Section HQ.'

'HQ? But . . .' She looked about her at the mess.

'I know, it looks a little ramshackle, but I assure you that impression is misleading. We are actually very efficient.' He smiled at her. 'Now.' He turned to his papers. 'I've explained to you the government's concern over the undercover activities of the Communist Party.'

'Its influence on the Invergordon Incident and what that might mean.' Minnie was determined to appear on top form.

'Precisely. Of course the party is not itself outlawed. We're a free country after all, and no one would be prosecuted simply for being a member. No doubt it has its share of well-meaning if misguided people. No, M section's task is to investigate extremists. Those who hold dangerous ideals which they put above loyalty to king and country. We suspect that there are members, British citizens, who are engaged in illegal, even treasonous activities and take their orders from the Soviet Union. It's these we wish to discover and weed out. We don't know for certain yet who they might be, who they are talking to or what they are doing, but we have our suspicions.'

Minnie frowned. 'And you want me to help you find evidence?'

'That is precisely where you come in.'

She was silent for a moment as she took this in. The work sounded thrilling and worthwhile, but she was troubled, too. She didn't know the least thing about Marxist beliefs or how she was to go about her task. Why hadn't she thought about this before?

The Captain must have read the doubt on her face because he leaned closer, his expression serious. 'Let me explain further. We will be starting you carefully and in a small way. It won't sound very exciting, I'm afraid. There's an international organization called the Friends of the Soviet Union, FSU for short. I don't suppose you've heard of it.'

'No, I haven't.'

'There are various branches in London. Its members on the whole do not see themselves as Communists. Indeed from what we can gather, many are good-hearted, if somewhat naïve, folk of a liberal disposition who simply want to help the people of Soviet Russia in their current desperate economic plight. Starving families, orphans and so forth.'

Just then a brass clock on the mantelpiece began to strike. 'Excuse me, would you?' the Captain said, putting aside his papers. 'It's feeding time.' He fetched a small box from a shelf, lifted the lid of the vivarium and tipped the contents of the box inside. Minnie watched in horror as the tank became alive with bounding grasshoppers. Then a thin little black snake slithered out from behind some rocks, where it must have been asleep all along, opened its jaws wide and set about the ghastly work of snapping up its luncheon. Although Minnie averted her eyes, she couldn't block out the repulsive thuds and scraping noises as it did so.

The Captain returned to his chair unperturbed and continued where he left off. 'We have our suspicions about the FSU, though. It's not as independent an organization as most of its members appear to think, and that's why it's a good place for you to start.'

'But won't my ignorance about communism be a problem?'

'Quite the opposite. You will be assumed to be an ordinary, well-meaning and sympathetic enquirer volunteering to help her fellow man. And woman, of course. They're very keen on equality, these socialists.'

Minnie considered the role he'd described. It didn't sound very terrifying and she was sure she could do it. 'And what must I do while I'm pretending to be this wide-eyed innocent?'

A smile played round the Captain's lips. 'Simply wait, my dear. Wait and watch and report back to me about what you see and hear.'

'I see.' So she would be a spy straightaway, even if at a low level. 'That sounds easy enough.'

He looked at her so sternly it alarmed her. 'It is not in any way easy. One false move and that would be the end of your career – I'm afraid I would have no further use for you after that.'

There was no mistaking his seriousness. Minnie sat up straight and said crisply, 'You need have no concerns there. I have often had to pretend in my life. It's like a sort of game.'

He regarded her thoughtfully. 'And you're good at games, from what you've told me.'

He took his pipe out of his jacket pocket and knocked it clean on the grate. 'Now,' he said, beginning to fill it with tobacco from a pouch. 'I shall explain more about what I require you to do. But first there are a few practicalities to discuss. One is your salary. Two pounds and ten shillings weekly is what I can offer you, which is why you must find supplementary employment.'

'I understand.' It certainly wasn't a fortune, but nor had he led her to expect it to be.

'Good. The other is the question of where you are to live. It would be best if you took somewhere by yourself if you could stand it.'

'I'm certainly prepared to give it a try.' Living by herself. The idea did worry her. 'I hope it's all right but I've assured Mother that I'll return home at weekends, at least at first.'

'That sounds eminently sensible. You will need the support of your family to avoid a lonely existence. I must impress upon you once more, though . . .'

'. . . that I must not mention the true nature of my work to them.'

'That's the ticket. Not to *anyone*, in fact.'

Again, that thrill passed through her. 'I haven't and I won't. Mother thinks that I am starting a typing job with an ordinary government department. She suspects nothing, I'm certain of it.'

'Excellent. And you plan to look for a secretarial post?'

'I will once I'm settled. When am I to start working for you?'

Minnie expected him to say in a week or two weeks even, which would give her a chance to look for somewhere suitable to rent and attend a few job interviews. She was surprised therefore when he said, 'The FSU branch I've identified meets on Monday evenings. So shall we say this coming Monday?'

'The day after tomorrow?' she murmured, then added hastily, 'Of course.' There was so much she had to do, but she was determined to manage it all.

He lit his pipe and puffed clouds of smoke. 'Any other questions before we move on?'

'What should I call you? Are you really Captain King?'

A mysterious smile crossed his face. 'It's one of several names I'm known by. If you telephone the office you should always refer to me by my code name, M. In private, well, we can be less formal. Why don't we say Max.'

'Is Maxwell your real name?'

'One of them,' he said with a twinkle.

'Do I have a code name?'

'You're M Twelve. You'll write it like this.' He scribbled on the corner of a page and showed it to her: *M/12*. 'You should use it instead of your name in all communications.'

'M/12.' She wondered wanly who the other eleven were, but dared not ask.

'Now, if you're ready, I'll explain what you should be looking for. Above all, you should not outwardly appear to be looking for anything. Calling attention to yourself in any manner could draw others' suspicion and that would be fatal to our endeavours . . .'

By the following night when she returned, exhausted, to her modest Kensington hotel Minnie had experienced the busiest and strangest weekend of her life. As she readied herself for bed, her head rattled with instructions about what she must or must not do. All delivered by this most peculiar man whom she still thought of as the Captain, but must learn to call Max or M. She climbed into the rickety bed and lay unable to sleep for a long time. The room was chilly and the bedstead creaked each time she moved, but the main reason was excitement. After only two days' training, she was a proper paid-up spy, her first assignment to start the following evening. At last she had the opportunity to prove herself, to the Captain – Max, rather – who saw something worthwhile in her, but also to all the people in her life so far who had underrated her. Life had suddenly become exciting, but would she be good enough?

Five

The local branch of the Friends of the Soviet Union met in a shabby parish hall which Minnie discerned the next day, from a noticeboard outside, was also home to a spiritualist group, an amateur dramatics society and various activities related to health and physical exercise.

She was twenty minutes early, but the doors stood open and there were sounds of activity inside. She hung up her coat in a chilly cloakroom and chose a seat in the dusty hall where several rows of wooden chairs had been arranged on the worn parquet floor before a lectern and a white slide screen. A slight man with a pointed black beard was tinkering with a cine projector in the centre aisle, too absorbed to even glance up at her entrance. Soon, other people began to arrive in dribs and drabs, quite an assortment. One wrinkled old lady dressed in colourful, shapeless garments and rattling with bangles hobbled in on the arm of a swarthy grey-haired gentleman with an impressive curling moustache and hooded eyes. *Straight off the Russian steppes*, Minnie thought, intrigued.

'Are you saving this seat?' asked a tall, angular Englishwoman past her first youth, carrying a large crocodile-leather handbag. She peered earnestly at Minnie through tortoiseshell spectacles.

When Minnie said, 'No, do sit here,' the woman settled next to her and offered her hand.

'I haven't seen you here before, have I? Miss Louisa Armstrong, I'm on the branch committee. How do you do?'

Minnie gave her own name and confided, 'Tonight's my first time and I don't know a soul.'

'I'll introduce you to some people later.' Miss Armstrong went on to ask Minnie about herself and Minnie trotted out the answers she'd prepared. *'Tell the truth as much as you are able,'* Max's voice rang in her head, *'or you'll forget what you've said to whom.'* This sounded sensible advice, so she spoke of how she'd recently moved to London from the provinces to take up a typing job and was to view a flat near Holland Park the following day. Less truthfully, she said, 'I was drawn in by the film advertised for tonight on the poster outside. It's about working life in the Soviet Union, I gather.'

'That's right. It should be most revealing. And Mr Smith, that's him at the projector, is very good. I've heard him speak before.' Miss Armstrong busied herself extracting an exercise book and pen from her huge handbag. 'I always take notes. I don't know why, but facts and figures simply fly out of my head.'

'Oh, that happens to me, too.'

By now the little hall was full and a lithe, stern-looking woman in a cloche hat made her way to the lectern. 'Good evening, everybody,' she said in a cultured voice. 'We've been having a little mechanical difficulty, but I think we're ready to begin, aren't we, Mr Smith?' The bearded man agreed and she went on. 'Mr Charles Smith is a journalist on the *Daily Worker* who has recently returned from an educational visit to Russia at the invitation of the Soviet authorities. After this short film he'll be taking questions about his experiences. Mr Smith, you're very welcome.'

She led the enthusiastic applause and after a few words of introduction in his northern accent the man set the projector whirring, the hall lights went down and a series of fuzzy grey images bounced onto the screen, then steadied and grew sharp. Tinny band music accompanied light-hearted English subtitles beneath jerky footage of factory workers busy on a production line. They were putting together parts of a car, Minnie realized, and appearing a mite too cheerful about it, while their overalls looked too clean to be natural. A subtitle explained that they sang Russian folk songs as they worked and Mr Smith interrupted to point out, 'It's grand to see the women working beside the men in harmony. They're paid the same, too.' Next to Minnie, Miss Armstrong was busy recording production figures in her exercise book.

After the film was over, Mr Smith spoke about how impressed he was by the Soviet economic experiment. 'If this evening has a message, comrades, then it's that Western governments should be supportive of the new modern Russia instead of applying sanctions and plotting war against her.' There were eager questions from the audience about workers' training and education, and whether Mr Smith had met any of the best-known Soviet leaders (he hadn't).

Minnie remembered Max's account of the Friends of the Soviet Union, how well-meaning most of the members were, and she tended to agree with this assessment. She observed carefully the enraptured expressions on people's faces and noted how one particular young man with a beaky nose spoke with knowledgeable ease about rights for British workers when he asked his question. Some of the jargon sounded nonsensical and Minnie didn't understand the 'class struggle' he kept referring to. On the whole, however, there appeared to be nothing sinister going on and she feared Max would be disappointed.

When this part of the meeting was over, notices were given out. A Christmas supper was talked of and a dance was being organized for a Saturday evening in January. Members were urged to buy tickets for both events. Minnie was glad she was committed to returning home at weekends. It provided her with a genuine excuse to keep her distance.

At the end, Miss Armstrong put away her exercise book and asked Minnie what she'd thought of the evening's proceedings.

'Very educational,' Minnie said truthfully, if not for the reasons that Miss Armstrong might have thought. 'I know little about the Soviet Union, I'm afraid.'

Miss Armstrong didn't seem shocked by this confession. 'One has to start somewhere. Let me fetch you a cup of tea and I'll introduce you to one or two people. You'll find us all very friendly and open-minded.'

She was as good as her word. Minnie met the exotic-looking old couple, who, disappointingly, were not Russian after all and spoke perfect English. A pale-faced, restless young man named Kurtz, however, was from the Ukraine. He glowered at Minnie and made his excuses in broken phrases before slinking away. 'Poor boy, he is cripplingly shy,' Miss Armstrong whispered as she steered Minnie on. 'Now, I'd like you to meet our Branch Secretary, Mrs Singer.'

'It's good of you to bother with me.'

'Not at all. It's my job to welcome visitors.'

She guided Minnie over to the woman in the cloche hat who had compered the evening's events and who nodded politely at Minnie. 'I do hope you'll come again,' she murmured.

'I told Miss Gray we're a friendly crowd,' Miss Armstrong said eagerly.

Minnie thanked them then made her excuses and went to collect her coat. She had to stop herself hurrying. Although leaving felt like an escape, it mustn't look like one.

She caught a bus and sat back in her seat, relieved that her first assignment was over and she hadn't made a fool of herself. Then she remembered that Max had advised her to get into the habit of taking notes as soon as possible after an 'encounter' so she rummaged in her handbag for the note-book and pencil she'd bought earlier that day.

At first she fiddled with the pencil, thinking that there was nothing remotely sensational to write about. But since she had to write something she described the people she'd spoken to and the film and found herself enjoying the process of remembering what had taken place and judging what Max might like to know. Would he be able to read her handwriting? She would have to fetch her little Remington typewriter from Edgbaston at the weekend, then she'd be able to present her notes properly.

The next morning, Minnie met the letting agent to view the first floor flat of a house in a Regency-style crescent near Holland Park in West London. It was furnished, one of the things that had attracted Minnie to it, another being that there was a telephone installed, a must, Max had told her. A second bedroom meant that her mother might come and stay, and the freshly painted sitting room overlooking the street was welcoming, bathed in pale winter sunshine.

'You'll have no trouble from your neighbours, Miss Gray,' said the agent, a lugubrious man with scanty, Brylcreemed hair and an ill-fitting suit. 'Gentleman upstairs is a bit of a traveller, you'll hardly see nothing of him. And Mrs Saunders down below, she's a widow, nice old girl.'

As her mother had advised, Minnie cross-examined him about deposits and service charges, made a few mental calculations, then took a deep breath and said she'd take it. It was more than she'd expected to pay, but she had some money saved, and once she'd found a daytime job, what with the £2.10s a week that Max was paying her, she shouldn't be too badly off. It would be her own place, which made her feel very mature. Something told her that with all the work she'd have to do it would be important to have somewhere nice to return to at night. Dizzy with her success, Minnie arranged to visit the agency office later in the day to pay the deposit and pick up the key, then the agent gave her a lift to the main road in his car and she caught a bus to Knightsbridge. She'd promised to meet Max at midday.

An icy wind swept down Sloane Street and Minnie was glad to find herself in Max's untidy hallway. This time he showed her into a comfortable sitting room at the back of the flat that was lined from floor to ceiling with shelves of books and records. A fire leaped in the grate and cheerful jazz music played on a gramophone. Max poured glasses of sherry, they sat in easy chairs by the fire and she felt warm and relaxed. He listened carefully as she recounted her experiences of the previous evening.

'I couldn't decide whether Mr Smith saw how phoney the film was. He claimed to have visited the factory and seen the conditions for himself. He sounded sincere, if that's any help.'

Max rubbed his chin, a thoughtful expression on his face. 'Some of these people want to believe that the things they are seeing are real, even if, like your man Smith, they witness them in person.'

'Because they're idealists?'

'You've put your finger on it. I haven't heard of this Smith. He's on the *Daily Worker*, you say?'

'That's the Communist Party newspaper, isn't it? Yes, he is, according to the Singer woman.'

'And did you speak to anyone else?'

'Only cursorily.' Minnie told him about the eccentric couple and the shy young Ukrainian and again he looked thoughtful, a slight smile playing about his lips.

'The young man, what was he like? A zealous sort, perhaps?'

'I describe him in my report. Just tongue-tied, really, unsure of himself.'

The music came to an end and Max got up to change the record. 'I hope you like jazz,' he said as he lowered the needle.

'I've hardly heard any,' she confessed.

'Haven't you? This is a favourite of mine.'

She was quickly beguiled by the rhythm of the music, then the plaintive tenor voice that began to sing of blackbirds and roses and lost love. Jazz. Max had so many sides to him that she couldn't keep up. He waited by the gramophone, humming along to the song until it finished, and when another started he shimmied stagily back to his chair waving the sherry decanter. He refilled their glasses and then she had his full attention.

'I'm sorry I have so little to tell you,' she said wistfully. 'I've copied out my notes neatly, anyway.' She passed him a folded paper from her bag. 'I hope it's what you're looking for.'

She watched him scan the two pages of her best handwriting and was relieved when he looked up and smiled.

'These are excellent,' he said, tapping the paper. 'You have a succinct turn of phrase. Your Miss Armstrong, for instance. "Bright and birdlike." This is absolutely first class.'

'Do you really think so?' She gave a cheerful smile.

He stood up and heaped a shovelful of coal on the fire. 'The key thing is you are able to distance yourself from your material. To make cautious judgments.'

'I'm so glad.'

He knocked back his last half-inch of sherry. 'Don't worry that nothing momentous happened. It's often the way. It sounds to me that you made the perfect beginning, that you acted exactly as I hoped, my dear, and drew no attention to yourself. There's a meeting next Monday, I take it?'

She nodded. 'With a talk by a visitor from the New York branch. You'd like me to go?'

'Of course. Proceed gently. You're simply "trailing your coat", to use our parlance. Don't do anything to make yourself stand out, but remain open to approaches.' He hesitated, then went on. 'I want to get you into their head office. Organizations like that are always crying out for administrative help. If anyone shows interest in your typing skills, for instance . . . Let's think . . . say that you work for an author with unpredictable hours. Yes, that would give you a solid excuse for having spare time to help them.'

'That's the next step, then?'

'I think so, don't you?' He beamed at her. 'We want to set a cuckoo in their nest! Now, you're looking for somewhere to live, I hope? I'm afraid the office budget doesn't run to many nights in the Hotel Majestic.'

'I've found somewhere already!' Minnie described the flat. He looked impressed.

'A respectable neighbourhood. And not too far out.'

She gave him the address and promised him the telephone number once she knew it. They arranged to meet the day after the next FSU meeting, in a week's time. 'I'll be in touch about where and when,' he said as he showed her out.

She walked back to the bus stop with a light step. Everything was going well so far. The next thing was to find a part-time typing job.

*

Minnie moved into her new flat the following day and the rest of her week passed in a blur of activity. She searched the classifieds for suitable positions, wrote a dozen letters of application and attended one interview, but was pipped at the post by a candidate with more experience and better shorthand. She was hopeful, though. Her particular skills and experience appeared to be of interest in London.

She enjoyed arranging and equipping her own home. The flat with its thick walls felt solid and safe and the faint sound of the wireless from her neighbour's flat below reassuring rather than intrusive. She bought a lamp for the console table she intended to use as a desk in the sitting room. In her bedroom she fixed the sagging curtains to allow light and a view of wintry gardens. The only thing she couldn't do much about was companionship. Eating supper for one by the gas fire was the loneliest thing she'd ever done. She bumped into Mrs Saunders once in the hallway and introduced herself, but Max had advised Minnie to keep neighbours at arm's length. Since the woman had an expression like sour milk and asked Minnie 'not to wear high heels indoors because the clopping noise is so tiring', Max's instruction was easy to obey.

Though energized by her brave new life it was a relief on Friday afternoon to catch a train back to Birmingham. Never before had Minnie looked forward so much to spending time with her family.

Reality, however, didn't live up to expectation. She'd only been gone a week, but already Edgbaston felt provincial, women's dresses looked dowdy, the buses were slow-moving, and no one appeared purposeful. Her mother still complained about the post arriving late and the front gutter still leaked when it rained. If at first the familiarity was reassuring, by Sunday afternoon Minnie was fretting to return to the metropolis. The only moment of interest was that she ran into her old boyfriend Raymond in the street. It was the first time they'd seen each other alone since they'd broken up, but it was easier speaking to him than she'd feared. She told him about her move to London and he wished her luck so sweetly that afterwards she felt briefly nostalgic for their years together.

In London, smog had descended and the walk from Holland Park tube was in choking yellow gloom, but the comforting sound of light music drifting from behind Mrs Saunders's closed door greeted her arrival.

Two letters awaited Minnie in the dim light of the hallway and she snatched them up. In the sanctuary of her kitchen, she opened them and read each quickly. 'That's ridiculous,' she murmured. She'd been called to interview at two different firms the next morning. Since the times offered allowed, she decided she would try her best to attend both.

'My name's Miss Gray,' she told the receptionist. 'I have an appointment with your Miss Baines.'

At nine o'clock sharp the following day, Minnie was introduced to the cool and elegant Miss Baines at the premises of Bulmer & Wyndham, an advertising company in a pleasant square north of Oxford Street. She was the first candidate to be interviewed. It was a large, airy, busy place and the salary mentioned was good. The successful candidate would work exclusively for one of the directors,

Jeremy Wyndham. Minnie liked Miss Baines, with her glossy dark hair and amused green eyes. She was only a few years older than Minnie, but commanded the office with a languid efficiency. After a typing test they chatted amiably about Minnie's secretarial experience while they waited for Mr Wyndham to arrive and be served his first cup of tea of the morning.

Minnie went in nervously to see him. Mr Wyndham was a chubby man in his late thirties with thinning fair hair and cherubic good looks. 'Miss, er ... Gray, I'm looking for someone very specific who'll be able to charm difficult clients.' His eyes flickered over her dismissively and she felt unattractive and uncomfortable and stumbled over her answers.

'Miss Baines will be in touch,' he said, opening the door to show her out. Full of shame and disappointment, she hurried out past several other young women who sat waiting for their turn. How poised and glamorous they looked. Of course Mr Wyndham wouldn't choose her; plain, provincial Minnie Gray.

The second interview was somewhere very different, a Victorian brick edifice at Seven Dials in Covent Garden, where the buildings clustered in a protective circle around a star-shaped junction. The offices were a warren of odd-shaped rooms, but they were warm and the walls were hung with prints of cheerful country scenes. Well-suited, Minnie thought, to the organization, which was a charity for gentlewomen in financial distress.

The atmosphere wasn't as lively as the previous place, but she liked the gentlemanly middle-aged director who interviewed her much better than the obnoxious Mr Wyndham. Mr Meadows wanted someone intelligent and organized, with good secretarial skills, and she knew she fitted the part. Also, the job offered shorter hours, which she judged more sensible given her work for Max. When she was offered the job on the spot she negotiated the terms with confidence and arranged to start in two days' time.

Minnie walked down Shaftesbury Avenue in something of a daze. Coming to a Lyons Corner House, she decided to restore her energies with a celebratory lunch. All by herself, but that couldn't be helped and the sweet girl who served her was very attentive.

An hour later, full of cottage pie and apple tart and custard, Minnie dallied over a pot of tea and reflected how for the last fortnight she'd been living on her nerves. Already she had secured a new typing job, found somewhere comfortable of her own to live and, most important, had begun the secret work that she'd come to London to do. Counting her achievements made her feel as though she'd passed some sort of test, though she'd have been hard-pressed to say who'd set it. Her life finally had purpose.

While she drank her tea she covertly observed a pair of sophisticated young women finishing lunch at a nearby table, and compared their smart clothes to her own plain navy crepe suit. She wondered if her dwindling savings would allow her to buy a new skirt such as one of them wore to pair with a white silk blouse and she thought perhaps they might. So after she'd paid the bill she wandered up Regent Street to Dickins & Jones where she spent a pleasant hour choosing a flattering mid-blue wool skirt, a long white tailored shirt and a pretty belt to cinch in her waist.

Minnie wore her new outfit to the FSU meeting that evening, where she saw many of the same faces. Bright Miss Armstrong sat next to her again, brimming with enthusiasm for the forthcoming guest speaker, and she and Minnie exchanged pleasantries with the eccentric old couple in the row in front while they waited for the meeting to begin.

The man from the New York arm of the organization spoke with a thick American twang about prejudice in the United States against the whole Soviet experiment. He was particularly outraged by the poor conditions of textile workers in the South and glared accusingly round the room as he called for these to be remedied. While Minnie was sympathetic to the workers, she found him tiresome as a public speaker. He kept stopping to clear his throat or sip water and lost his place in his notes. Still, there was respectful applause when he'd finished and he fielded many questions about Washington's foreign policy. There wasn't much new to report back to Max, which disappointed her, but when she visited his flat the following day he didn't seem perturbed.

'These things take time,' he said, beaming at her encouragingly. He was pleased to hear about her job, too.

'Working with genteel elderly ladies. Splendid camouflage.'

Minnie was pleased with his reaction, but feared her spying work wasn't yielding results fast enough. It was hard to tell exactly what Max wanted. He was proving to be an impossible man to read.

Six

Tiny flakes of snow fluttered from a sky of roiling yellowish cloud as Minnie, turning up for her first day, pressed the bell for the Distressed Gentlewomen's Benevolent Fund. After a moment there came a sudden grinding noise from above and she looked up to see a sash window being heaved open by a brown-haired girl with bright red lipstick. 'The door's on the latch, come on up,' the girl called before slamming the sash shut again.

Minnie turned the doorknob and shoved the door open. The stairway echoed to her footsteps, then there was the girl again, waiting in the doorway to the office, hands on hips. Seeing her trim figure in a pretty dress with a Peter Pan collar Minnie remembered how, two days ago, the girl had walked past her while she was waiting for her interview and winked at her. Minnie, judging her to be a couple of years younger than herself, had liked her mischievous expression.

'Miss Gray, shall I call you Minnie? I'm Jenny Moore, the other typist. Come in. Isn't it a foul day?'

'Foul,' Minnie agreed with a smile.

She was glad to be swept into the warmth of the cluttered office. There, in a short space of time, she was divested of her coat, introduced to Mr Jones, a gruff, thick-set older man, and Mr Fisk, a shy, moon-faced younger one in a side room lined with shelves of ledgers, before being taken through to the main office, where a typewriter and a neat stack of papers in a wire tray awaited her on a small desk near Jenny's and within welcome distance of a shimmering paraffin heater. All this time, Jenny rarely stopped talking. 'Mr Meadows will be in later, he's meeting a client. Stanley – he's the office boy – has gone to the post office. Mr Jones and Mr Fisk, you've met, they manage the money and that's all of us. Here's the stationery cupboard for paper and carbons and everything else is in the drawer. There's a whole heap of memos to type, but the letters are to be done first. We're always fundraising and I hope you know your knights from your baronets because we have to get everyone's title right. Absolutely deathly. Here, if I put the addresses between us like this we should get on like a house on fire.'

At that moment the telephone on Jenny's desk began to ring and she snatched up the receiver. While she spoke soothingly to someone at the other end, Minnie pulled the wire tray towards her. She fed a sandwich of paper and carbons into the heavy black typewriter and soon Jenny's bright voice was drowned out by the clack-clack of the machine as Minnie typed the Honourable James Meadows's letters begging the recipients to donate to the charity. She worked slowly at first, but then got into a rhythm, stopping only occasionally to check the spelling of a name.

At lunchtime she left a correspondence book bulging with letters for signature on Mr Meadows's desk in the adjoining office and went out with Jenny to a café up the road for what Jenny said were 'not-bad omelettes'. The café was packed, but the omelettes were indeed not bad. Minnie enjoyed quizzing Jenny about their colleagues and letting her ramble on amusingly. Mr Meadows was the youngest son of Lord somebody. Mr Jones, the older bookkeeper, liked to sing 'perfectly beastly' snatches of Gilbert and Sullivan. Jenny's father was 'something fearfully dull in business'. She lived at home in Clapham, but Minnie gauged that her parents didn't take much interest in her activities. She liked to go out most evenings and asked Minnie to join a group expedition to the pictures that very night, but Minnie said truthfully that she'd be too tired, this being her first day. It was kind of her to ask, she said, and she would love to go another time.

It had been a good day, she thought as she walked to the underground after work. Mr Meadows had complimented her upon a swift and accurate morning's work. She'd taken to Stanley, the office boy, who was amiable in the way of Doug, her youngest brother, and Jenny was the first girl she'd met in London whom she considered might become a friend. It made her feel a little less alone.

Seven

January 1932

Minnie was feeling increasingly frustrated. She'd attended two or three more FSU meetings, during which nothing particularly notable occurred. But then came one when her interest was roused by the man who introduced the speaker, rather than by the speaker himself. When she asked Miss Armstrong in a whisper who he was she was told, 'Mr West? He's a bigwig at head office.'

Minnie perked up. She took care to notice everything about West; his tense wiry figure, his restless hands, the way his gaze roved the room. His eyes settled on hers momentarily and she looked away quickly in case he realized that she was studying him. Afterwards, she was in conversation with Miss Singer, the branch secretary, when West joined them and was introduced. 'Miss Gray is a typist,' Miss Singer explained, as though this was somehow important.

'How long have you been attending meetings, Miss Gray?'

West asked and Minnie explained, trotting out the well-worn explanation of what had attracted her to the FSU, which he appeared to accept, though she was subject to his shrewd eye.

She duly reported West's name to Max, who had never heard of him, and was intrigued to see the man again the following week, though he sat at the back and took no part in proceedings. During tea and biscuits afterwards, however, she was surprised when Miss Singer led him across, looking rather pleased with herself.

'Miss Gray, Mr West would like a word.'

'Delighted to meet you again, Miss Gray.' Despite his intense manner there was a twinkle in his eye and Minnie decided she liked him. 'I'm sorry to prevail upon you so early in our acquaintance, but Miss Singer keeps mentioning you to me. We're in grave need at HQ, falling badly behind with administration, and I wondered whether you might have some spare time to sort us out. On a voluntary basis, mind you, like most of us there.'

Minnie suppressed a spark of excitement, remembering Max's behest not to attract suspicion by pushing herself forward.

'I don't think I should,' she murmured. 'I've only recently started coming to meetings. I don't know much about the organization and won't be much use.'

'It would be a good way to find out more,' Miss Singer said, clasping her hands together.

'Indeed,' West went on. 'And you'd quickly learn, I'm sure. Simply an afternoon or an evening a week would be helpful. Would that fit in with your current employment?'

'I suppose so. I work for an author with unpredictable hours,' she told him, remembering Max's instruction, 'so time shouldn't be a problem. If you're sure, you could try me out.' She did her best to sound doubtful.

'I'd be so grateful. There's a stack of filing and minutes to type up and send out before our next committee meeting. We have a newspaper, too, with a deadline fast approaching. We do our best, but we're short-staffed at present. So if you would . . .'

'I'll come one evening and we'll see how it goes,' Minnie promised. 'Where is the office?'

'Holborn. A cul-de-sac off Queen Square. Ormond Yard, number three. I hope that's not out of your way.'

She thought quickly. It would be only a step from her job at Seven Dials. 'It's not too bad,' she said.

'Good. Can you come on Wednesday, at six p.m.? For a couple of hours, maybe?'

She pretended to consult her engagement diary. 'Yes, Wednesday would be fine.'

'Good, and we'll take it from there, shall we?'

Late the next afternoon Minnie met Max in the foyer of a hotel on the Cromwell Road, near the Victoria and Albert Museum. At first she couldn't see him, but she followed the scent of his tobacco and found him reading *The Times* at a secluded table behind a large painted Japanese screen. His terrier Bobby was with him, lying quietly under the table, but as she approached the little dog scrambled out, wagging his stub of a tail.

Max ordered tea from a passing waitress, then listened

Rachel Hore

to Minnie's news, his eyes widening in delight. Quickly he scanned her typewritten report. 'The speed of your progress is most impressive. When does West want you to begin?'

'Tomorrow evening. Does that sound too obliging?'

'It sounds excellent.'

'I feel awfully unprepared.'

'That's probably a good thing. You'll seem genuine.'

This didn't reassure Minnie much.

There was a pause as the tea arrived and was poured. After the waitress left, Max glanced around to make sure nobody was in earshot, then leaned towards Minnie. 'Now, things to look out for,' he said quietly. 'We believe that the FSU is a front organization under the control of the Soviet Union. You may have heard of the Comintern, short for Communist International. No? It's the Soviet Union's global arm, set up by Lenin in 1919, and its purpose is to plot revolution against the capitalist system all over the world. It wants to rouse the working classes everywhere and that's what it's doing through organizations like the FSU.'

'Can't it simply be stopped?' she asked, feeling naïve.

'The FSU is not breaking any law by existing. This is where you come in. We know that the Comintern has agents everywhere. They're ready with money, advice and expertise to set up national Communist parties and assist with their growth. And we know how dangerous their ideals are to our democracy. Our society would be turned upside down if they succeeded, Miss Gray, and we'd become like Russia, an authoritarian state. What you'll be looking for in your quiet, innocent guise as an FSU volunteer is information about what the Comintern is up to in this country. Anything, even the slightest thing that seems of interest about West or other people's behaviour, their conversation, where they go, who they're going to meet, you must report to me. It might not appear important, but I assure you it could be.'

'I can do that. Should I worry that my new job at Seven Dials is not far from Queen Square? After all, Mr West thinks I work for an author and if he finds out I'm lying ...'

Max chuckled as though at some private joke. 'Don't worry; I shouldn't think they'll be spying on *you*. Not if you play your cards right and carry on acting the innocent.'

'I'll manage that easily!' she said in a heartfelt tone.

He smiled. 'Good luck tomorrow. We'll meet again later in the week then, shall we?'

Minnie would have liked to ask him more about the Comintern and what exactly she should be looking for, but Max was glancing at his watch. She felt wan, wondering where he was going and who he'd be seeing and wished he'd stay longer, talking to her. She was becoming increasingly fascinated by him, but suspected that she occupied only a small part of his life, while he was a large part of hers.

Eight

The following evening, Minnie left work promptly at five, ate a hasty tea at the café she'd visited with Jenny and walked through Bloomsbury to a quiet square of high buildings around a small enclosed garden. Ormond Yard off Queen Square wasn't as easy to find as West had described, but when she eventually pressed the office bell it was West himself who admitted her and showed her upstairs. She saw at once that she'd interrupted something, because in addition to West there were three other men crammed into his shambolic office, all sitting around his desk. She stood self-consciously in the doorway.

'This is Miss Gray, our new volunteer.' Two of the men blinked at Minnie without much interest, but the third, a man of thirtyish with round wire-framed spectacles and a lively, good-humoured face, rose from his chair and nodded politely.

'You're going to shovel up their mess, are you?' he said in his London accent. 'That's smashing. Whoops!' He steadied a stack of files he'd knocked with his elbow. 'See what I mean?'

'It is rather … busy in here.' Minnie felt dismay at the

extent of the chaos. The office was a muddle of paperwork, books and old newspapers. Dirty mugs and plates nestled on West's desk between overflowing wire trays and heaps of cardboard folders. Her interest was roused by copies of the *Daily Worker* and a grim-faced bust of a shaggy-bearded man whom she assumed was Karl Marx that stared at her from the top of a filing cabinet.

'Well, comrades,' West said to the men. 'Thank you for your trouble.' Taking the hint they gathered up coats and paperwork and Minnie was relieved. Although the bespectacled man was friendly, the other two remained silent as they passed on their way out. One, a burly type in early middle age and of East European appearance, was jowly with thick eyebrows like daubs of black paint above glittering brown eyes. The other could have been only a couple of years older than herself, short and rather puny, his small features pulled into an expression of distaste. She was not told their names but committed their appearance to memory.

'Best of luck,' the bespectacled man said to her as he left.

'Thank you. It seems I'll need it.'

When she and Mr West were alone he fetched some tea then showed her into an adjoining office as untidy as his own. Here he shifted a heap of paperwork that had been left on top of a typewriter at a small table, found her a chair and rifled through the pages of a spiral-bound notebook.

'I'd like you to type these minutes, please. They're to be copied and circulated in time for next Tuesday. I'll give you the details.'

'Do you have an example of how they're to be laid out?'

'Somewhere, yes.' While he searched she untwisted the snarled ribbon on the machine.

As she typed she was aware of him at his desk in the next room, periodically sighing and getting up to pace about. From time to time she felt his eye on her through the open door.

West's even handwriting was easy to read and she tried to gauge if any of the information given would be of interest to Max. There was reference to previous meetings, to shoestring budgets and visiting speakers, but none of the names meant anything to her.

The work occupied the best part of an hour. She took the finished pages in to him and while he read them through she looked about and wondered if she should use her initiative and attempt some tidying, but something told her to hold back.

'An excellent job, Miss Gray,' West said, putting down his pencil. 'Only a couple of mistakes, here and here. And then this requires typing. It's the editor's letter for *War*.'

'War?' she said, not understanding.

'The FSU newspaper. Feel free to correct my punctuation. I'll make us another pot of tea, shall I?'

After they'd finished for the evening, West thanked her profusely and begged her to return the following week. As he locked the street door behind them he said, 'Where do you live? I don't mind seeing you safely home.'

Fear leaped in her throat, but she managed to swallow it. 'No, I'll be perfectly all right, I assure you. I live a stone's throw from an underground station.'

Thankfully, he did not insist or enquire further and so they parted, he walking north, she south towards Holborn. It was late and few people were about so she walked as fast as she could, occasionally glancing behind her to see if she was being followed, and was glad to reach the bright busyness of the station.

As her train rushed through the tunnels Minnie wrote hurried notes about her observations, fearing to forget a single detail. *'The foreign-looking man did not speak ... The initials of attendees listed on the minutes were ...'* It was hard to know what Max would think important, so everything had to go down, but was it really what he wanted?

She was too tired to type the notes when she arrived home after the excitement of her evening. It was all she could do to hang up her clothes before she fell into bed, exhausted. Her last thought before sleep overtook her was of the polite man with spectacles she'd met in West's office. She'd rather warmed to him and wished she'd discovered who he was.

Nine

March 1932

Slowly, Minnie adapted to the strains and complexities of her new routine. Work at the charity took up three full days a week, usually Tuesday, Wednesday and Friday. Two midweek evenings were taken up by stints at the FSU office, and weekends she spent with her family in Edgbaston. She continued to attend FSU branch meetings on Mondays when she could, these being important to maintain her cover, but still had no wish to join their Saturday night dances and Sunday hikes. She had no particular objection to many of the people she met. It was simply that they weren't her type. She did not want to spend her weekends earnestly talking about collective farming in the Soviet Union or blackleg labour in Newcastle. Such subjects did not consume her every waking moment and she had different opinions about solving them. Having to keep these thoughts to herself, however, made her feel left out and she was glad that she had Max to confide in.

'All this nonsense about class struggle and proletarian revolution is so misguided and dangerous,' she found herself telling him one evening in early March at his flat. 'It's hard work pretending to take it seriously. Though, of course, I'm pretending away,' she added hastily, seeing his eyes widen. 'I'm sorry to complain. I only have you to talk to about it, you see.'

'Of course, and that's what I'm here for.' Max leaned towards her with concern. 'Yours is not an easy job, Minnie, but you're doing it splendidly.' He smoothed his hair and sat back in his chair.

'Am I? I only hope some of it is useful,' she said wistfully.

'It most certainly is.'

She had been doing her best for him and was surprised how much she enjoyed preparing her reports. Sometimes she typed them up and posted them, but lately she'd started to find that her memory was so keen that if he didn't have much time she was able to recount everything succinctly in a telephone call or at a brief meeting such as this. Max left the room to make coffee and in his absence she glanced around the drawing room, always amused by his ramshackle living arrangements, although she thought his obsession with fauna went a bit far. The little dog had become used to her and sat quietly by her chair. She reached down and gained comfort by stroking his warm body with its wiry hair. Anything in the reptile line, however, made her shudder and she'd taken to leaving the room when the snake was fed. She much preferred the homely back sitting room where they could relax and listen to music and drink sherry and it felt more as though the pair of them were friends.

They were friends, or was this an illusion? She still knew little about Max, but had told him a great deal about herself, for he was the only person she could speak to honestly. No one else of her acquaintance knew she was a spy. Only he understood the daily pressure she was under, appearing to live a normal existence while conducting a parallel secret one.

In the different areas of her life her friends and family, her colleagues at the charity and her comrades at the FSU all saw a different facet of her, but not one of them could know the nature of her most important work. She was beginning to find that her contact with Max was vital to her well-being.

But Minnie still drew a line. She would not reveal to him the true depths of her doubts and fears, for her mother had trained her to keep these private. *'Pull yourself together, Minnie. Stiff upper lip now.'* Whenever she was feeling low, Minnie would whisper this admonition. Holding herself together was a lesson she'd learned well over the years. And Max, she sensed, valued personal resilience.

She was standing by one of the aquariums, studying the fish, when he returned carrying two steaming mugs and humming to himself.

'Mesmerizing, aren't they, the fish? Take you out of yourself,' he said, as though he could read her thoughts. 'Hobbies are helpful in our line of work, I find. And family.'

Did Max have a family life? Minnie had noticed the photograph on one of the bookshelves in the back room of an attractive woman in country tweeds standing before a stout wooden door with wrought-iron fittings. She was tall and lean with short carefree hair, but was not smiling for the camera. A sign fixed on the wall above the door read 'The Royal Oak'. Minnie had asked him who it was and he'd replied, 'It's my wife, Gwladys. We own a pub in Devon.' He'd picked up the photograph, perused it for a moment with a frown, then carefully replaced it before changing the subject. Minnie wondered to herself if theirs was a happy marriage and whether there were children. This was a man's flat but although Minnie had never met Gwladys or Max's sister, every now and then evidence of a woman's presence would appear – a patterned headscarf hanging on the hall-stand, a pair of narrow court shoes under a table – only to disappear again by a subsequent visit. She wondered what kind of person Gwladys was and why the couple lived such separate lives. Otherwise she knew virtually nothing about Max's family background or the work he did. If he ran other agents – and he must do if she was M/12 – he never spoke of them. She was glad. The thought that she wasn't the only one to enjoy his focused attention always brought a painful stab of jealousy.

Stepping out on her lunch hour one day at the end of March Minnie passed a young man selling the *Daily Worker* and, as was occasionally her wont for research purposes, she bought one. A headline on the front page caught her eye: '*Touts and spies*', it read. She stood stock still and as she read on her blood ran cold. '*Efforts are being made to send spies into the Party.*' Her hands shook as she looked for her name. Surely she hadn't been discovered.

But no. The wife of a Communist Party member had been

approached by an undercover Special Branch detective, who had tried to recruit her as a police informant. The relief made Minnie laugh aloud. Later, though, at the safety of her kitchen table, she read the editorial inside and became troubled. *'Vigilance against spies and provocateurs is an essential part of the working class fight . . .'* it said. *'Comrades, be on your guard!'*

She covered her face with her hands and sighed. Even if she was safe at the moment, her Communist co-workers at the FSU head office would now be wary. She'd have to be extra careful. Perhaps Max would pull her out? She knew she'd be deeply disappointed if that happened. The work itself at the FSU, typing, filing, keeping the office in good order, was not scintillating, but the observation work was enjoyable and gave her a tremendous sense of usefulness.

When she met Max at his flat after work the following day, he was furious with Special Branch. He roamed the drawing room muttering, 'Bungling incompetents. They should stay off our patch.'

'Get off, get off,' shrieked the parrot, spreading its wings briefly, and Max shouted at it to be quiet.

'Shut up yourself,' it replied and gave a blood-curdling chuckle.

'What should I do?' Minnie asked, clutching the arms of her chair.

Max stopped and glowered. 'Do? Why, continue as you are. Draw no attention to yourself, show no interest in anything beyond the work they ask you to do. Volunteer for nothing.'

'That's how I behave already,' she assured him.

'Well then. We'll monitor the situation.' It was as though he was speaking to himself. Then he paused, looked straight at her, eyes narrowed, and said, 'Did anyone see you come here today?'

'What? No, I wasn't aware ...' She thought back to the crowds surging up the steps from the underground, the evening street bright with lights, remembered turning up her collar against the cold before setting off down Sloane Street. Shopkeepers had been putting up their shutters. She'd bought a card of matches from a war veteran.

The curtains here in the flat had not yet been drawn across and she went to the window to look down on the street. A burly man loitering on the far pavement glanced up and seemed to meet her eye. How long had he been there? No, he was only hailing a taxi. Minnie returned to her chair. Whether she was being followed was impossible to tell.

'You'd better watch your back,' Max said morosely. His bad mood seemed to pursue her all the way home.

As Minnie predicted, the atmosphere in the FSU office changed. West and other colleagues who came and went were as pleasant to her as ever, but she sensed that they were on edge. Quite ordinary conversations that used to take place in front of her did so less often. Doors that had been left ajar were now closed firmly if a meeting was taking place.

At the same time, West took particular care to say how pleased he was with Minnie's work. 'We're running like clockwork now,' he told her one evening, rubbing his hands. 'I can't thank you enough.'

'I'm glad to be of use.'

'You certainly are. You ought to come to our weekend events. How about a bracing walk on the South Downs on Sunday?'

'Sorry, my sister Joan's getting married in Birmingham this weekend.' *Thank heavens for a cast-iron excuse.* It was kind of him to ask, though. She liked some of the people she met here, if not their beliefs. Part of her wished that she hadn't been planted to spy on them.

West might be satisfied with her, but Minnie sensed with increasing unhappiness that Max was not. It wasn't to do with her or her efforts, she reassured herself, more the limited way in which she could help him in the wake of the Communists' spy panic.

She continued to note what she believed were useful snippets of information, but these were fewer. West announced that he would be going away for a week and didn't say where or why. The man of East European appearance had visited the office again and been closeted with West for an hour. Other meetings were held for which she saw neither an agenda nor minutes. Max always appeared interested in her information, but was clearly frustrated by its paucity.

Life, otherwise, was not all difficult. Minnie was enjoying her job at the charity. As the weeks crept by she felt more and more at home there. The main part of her work involved typing Mr Meadows's copious correspondence, but there was also a certain amount of telephone work. She'd quickly surmised how the charity worked. Well-bred ladies in financial difficulty, or a friend or relative on their behalf, might apply for assistance, and she would arrange for Mr Meadows to visit the claimant to assess the need, which required much discretion. A regular or simply a one-off payment might be the result.

Sometimes Minnie would find herself on the end of the telephone line when one of these ladies called, listening to their problems and doing her best to reassure. These calls might be about money or other practical concerns, or a lonely elderly lady might simply wish to talk. At the same time Minnie was under strict instructions from Mr Jones, the bookkeeper, not to make many calls herself. He liked to run a tight ship. Any permission for expenditure, whether it was on the stationery account or petty cash for sugar, was granted in the most grudging of fashions. 'We're a charity,' he would say. 'The trustees will ask questions.' He was right, of course, costs must be controlled, but Minnie and Jenny thought him ridiculously mean.

'Will the trustees mind if we have a little milk in our tea?' Jenny laughed scornfully. 'Let's set up a union, Minnie; the Distressed Staff of the Distressed Gentlewomen's Benevolent Fund.'

'I'll union you,' was Mr Jones's shirty reply. He didn't approve of disrespect to what he called his 'betters', especially the trustees, and considered organized labour to be the scourge of English society. Despite his miserly nature, however, he could be kind. He had a fatherly manner towards the office boy, Stanley, who needed watching. He was a daydreamer, usually with his nose in a comic and half an inch away from the sack for muddling whatever errand he'd been sent on.

It was Jenny whom Minnie liked most, and their friendship was a shaft of light in Minnie's otherwise sequestered life. Occasionally they went to the pictures together after work. Once and once only did she accompany Jenny to a dance on a Friday night in a church hall near Jenny's home in Clapham.

They'd changed into their dance frocks in Jenny's untidy bedroom. Brown-haired Jenny was pretty in a deep blue fluttery sleeveless georgette gown with a tiered flared skirt and Minnie, pinned into her only dancing gown, a low-cut cherry-red sheath affair that belonged to a previous version of herself, felt blowsy beside her. At least her high-heeled shoes were elegant, if uncomfortable, and the gold thread of the small tapestry bag her mother had given her for her birthday lent a touch of opulence. Jenny said Minnie looked 'very nice', so it was in good spirits that they set out together for the short walk to the church hall.

Minnie, who knew no one and felt awkward, suffered many small humiliations during the evening. Accompanying a pretty and popular girl was one. Jenny quickly had her card marked for every dance of the evening, while Minnie had only two or three and these at the behest of Jenny, who begged her male admirers to dance with Minnie as well until she felt like a consolation prize. Then, although she'd been well taught, Minnie was not a natural dancer and she spent a great deal of time concentrating on the steps. She did not enjoy listening to these rather undistinguished young men talk about themselves with the clear expectation that she should gaze up at them in dumb admiration. If only you knew what I *really* do, she thought furiously, when one fresh-faced boy said sarcastically, 'Oh, typewriting must be an interesting job,' but of course she could not tell him.

There was one partner she did like. His open, good-natured face reminded her of her old boyfriend Raymond, which gave her a pang of tenderness. He held her beautifully and danced with her twice, but then a sulky auburn-haired girl stormed up and claimed him and shot Minnie such a disparaging stare she was left in no doubt of her failure to be serious competition.

The hall grew overheated and the lemonade ran out. Then Jenny disappeared somewhere, and the safety pin Minnie had used to secure the neckline of her dress kept popping open. She was relieved when the music ended and it was time to clear off home.

'What a beastly evening,' Jenny said cheerfully, pink-faced and breathless from a 'little walk' outside with Tony, the partner she'd danced with most. 'Did you enjoy yourself?'

'Very much,' Minnie said tightly, wondering why she bothered with these affairs. Each time she went to one she vowed never to go again, but still the next time she was asked a dreadful sense of duty propelled her to say 'yes'. Well, this time definitely was the last. Her work with Max was more important. It was he above all whom she wanted to please.

Ten

July 1932

Minnie went to the window of her sitting room once more and looked anxiously up the street, which lay tranquil in the early evening light. Max had said seven and he was half an hour late. She hadn't set eyes on him for over a fortnight, the largest gap between meetings since she'd started work for him eight months before, and she'd been worried.

Where was he? She nibbled at a fingernail and wondered whether he was losing interest in her work altogether. Several months had passed since the *Daily Worker* spy panic, but her FSU colleagues still hadn't relaxed their vigilance. They had settled back into their usual routines, but if anything sensitive was going on she didn't hear, because they still took extra care not to let anyone beyond their inner circle know about it. As a result there was little for Minnie to report and this was why, she supposed, Max had been leaving longer between meetings. She'd begun to feel deserted, so when she'd come home to a letter to say he'd be calling on her she bucked up no end and flew about tidying and polishing glasses.

The sky was leached of light by the time a taxi drew up outside and Max's tall, loose-limbed figure disembarked. Minnie hurried downstairs, not wanting the sound of the doorbell to alert her nosy neighbour below, but she was too late. As she admitted Max and he greeted her with an enthusiastic 'Dear girl', Mrs Saunders's door opened and the woman's pinched face peered out, her greying hair in curlers visible under a headscarf.

'Good evening, madam,' Max said to the widow, tipping his hat and smiling in his most charming fashion. The woman harumphed and withdrew. It was all Minnie could do not to burst out laughing as she led the way up the stairs and into the safety of her flat.

'I've told her before that you're my brother,' she said, taking his coat, 'but I don't think she believed me. Especially since my brother Richard came to visit me recently and you don't look like either of us. He's moved to London, you know.' She'd told him before about Richard, the elder of her two brothers, who had finished his police training and was now a bobby on the beat. It had been wonderful to see him.

'I don't mind her assuming I'm your young man,' Max replied, eyes twinkling.

Minnie's face grew hot and she fumbled with the decanter, causing whisky to slop on the tray. He took over, mopping up with a monogrammed handkerchief before pouring drinks for them both.

'Your health,' he said, handing hers over. 'At least don't tell the old girl I'm married,' he added with a smile.

Minnie choked on her mouthful. 'Of course I won't. She'd try to get me evicted!'

'Indeed, not funny. Now.' Max sank into one of the armchairs, looking completely at home, and opened his notebook. 'I feel I've been neglecting you lately and thought we should meet. Did you visit the FSU offices this week?'

'Last night *and* the night before,' she said, sitting on the sofa and smoothing her skirt. 'I'm afraid there's little to report again. Mr West was engaged on the telephone when I arrived yesterday, but when he saw me he told the person at the other end to ask someone else, a woman's name, I think. "It's confidential," he told them and quickly rang off, so I wondered.'

'Wondered what? You didn't hear the woman's name or what it was about?' There was an edge to his voice.

'No, I'm afraid not,' she said miserably.

'Can't be helped.'

There was a pause after which Minnie burst out, 'I'm so sorry. I don't feel I'm much use at the moment.'

'My dear girl,' he said, concerned eyes resting on her. 'The situation is hardly your fault. I've told you before, we must be patient.'

'Nothing changes. There's been so little to report lately.'

'Someone will make a slip, I guarantee it. And when that happens, *voilà* . . .'

She nodded, the kind reassurance sending her close to tears. To hide her emotion she rose and switched on the lamps. As she drew the curtains against the gloaming she caught herself watching a man ambling along the opposite pavement. *Silly girl*. He was only a passer-by, perhaps a little unsteady after a visit to the pub.

'You are jittery today, my dear.' Max missed nothing.

'No, I . . .' Minnie sat down again and studied her hands. 'Sometimes this work is hard on the nerves. I feel I'm getting nowhere.'

He nodded sympathetically, then looked thoughtful. 'I wonder who it was your Mr West was talking to?'

'He's not *my* Mr West,' she said sharply. Something connected in her memory. It was the woman's name. 'Wait. Before he put down the receiver he said, "Ask Isobel." The only Isobel I've heard of is Isobel Brown. I've read about her in the *Daily Worker*. She went to prison once for making some inflammatory speech, didn't she?'

'Isobel Brown,' Max said to himself, then fixed Minnie with a serious gaze. 'Yes indeed. Have you overheard anything else about her? Recent trips to the Soviet Union or anything like that?'

Minnie shook her head, holding her breath for him to tell her more, but he didn't. This was a most maddening aspect of their conversations. Max never indicated how the pieces of information she gave him fitted in to MI5's greater jigsaw. In her turn she rarely dared ask. Something about his demeanour always warned her off.

She reminded herself that she must be humble, perform her duties meticulously, and not worry about matters that were not her concern. That was hard. She wasn't that sort of person.

'Are you all right?' he asked in his most soothing voice, and she realized she'd been miles away.

'Of course I am.' Her voice sounded too bright and harsh. 'I'm tired, that's all. I'll be right as rain after a good night's sleep.' Again she heard her mother's voice in her mind. *Stiff upper lip, Minnie, best foot forward.* She had to trust Max and be patient. If she didn't want him to pull her out altogether, then this was the only way. But it was hard.

Eleven

August 1932

One sultry evening when Minnie arrived at the FSU offices it was to find West's door firmly shut and the sound of muffled voices within. One, she heard, was a woman's, loud, with a northern accent, though she couldn't make out what she was saying. Despite being alone, it was too much of a risk to put her ear to the keyhole, so Minnie raised a window to let in some air then set about her work.

It wasn't long before West's door opened and Minnie glanced up to see a short, stout woman in a black velvet dress emerge. West was just behind, a disconsolate expression on his face.

'Hello,' the woman said, 'you must be Minnie Gray.'

'This is Isobel Brown, Minnie,' West said, looking glum. 'She's been asking about you.'

'I have indeed. Pleased to meet you at last. Phew!' She sank onto a chair, breathing heavily, and fanning herself. 'I do hate this weather, don't you?'

'It's very sticky, typing,' Minnie said cautiously, wondering whether she was in trouble.

'Minnie,' West's voice was brisk. 'Isobel would like a word.' Minnie nodded and he retreated, closing his door a little too loudly.

She focused her attention on the visitor. 'What is it you'd like to speak to me about?'

'Wait, let me get my breath and I'll tell you.'

Minnie fetched the woman a glass of water and she quickly rallied.

'Well now.' She subjected Minnie to her shrewd-eyed gaze. 'You're not what I expected.'

'What do you mean?' Minnie forced a smile.

'I didn't think you'd be so posh. Never mind. Your name has got around.'

Minnie's heart quickened, and she was relieved when the woman said, 'Your comrades here have been boasting. They say this place has been shipshape since you appeared, that you're discreet and trustworthy. I pride myself on being forthright, Minnie Gray, office skills are in short supply among our members. I want to offer you a job.'

It was growing dark by the time Minnie rang Max's doorbell and waited on the doorstep, out of breath from her hurry. She'd telephoned ahead from a call box. Why was he taking so long? When the door finally opened she almost fell inside.

'What's happened?' Max said sharply.

'Don't worry,' she gasped, 'it's good news.'

He showed her into the drawing room where she ignored

his invitation to sit and announced, 'You are looking at the new secretary to the League Against Imperialism and the Anti-War Movement. Two Communist organizations for the price of one!'

Max's eyebrows shot up. 'Good Lord, Minnie, that's smart work!'

'Paid, too. Only part-time, but still.'

'Extremely smart work. Now slow down and tell me properly from the beginning.' He was as excited as she was and this pleased her.

Quickly, she explained. 'The only tricky thing is that Miss Brown asked me to become a member of the Communist Party.'

'What did you say to that?' he asked, amused.

'That I would think about it. She didn't seem to mind, so, anyway, I told her I was interested in the job.'

'Splendid on both counts.'

'So you keep telling me.'

'And you'll say yes?' He looked so eager and she felt so pleased with herself she thought she'd tease him for a while. Especially since she had questions.

'What are those organizations?'

Max picked up his pipe from the mantelpiece and began to polish it with a cloth. 'They're both fronts for the Communist Party, but more so than the FSU. Their purpose is to spread communist ideas more directly. Listen, Minnie, give it a day or two then tell Miss Brown you'll do it, will you? This is a breakthrough. It'll take you deeper into the Party.'

'It'll be more dangerous, won't it?'

'That isn't necessarily the case. Not if you keep your head.'

She thought about it and despite her natural wariness, shared his excitement.

'You can do it, Minnie, I know you can.' Lord, he was pleading with her.

'I think I can,' she said slowly and was rewarded by the smile that played around his lips. She was important to him again.

Then she remembered. 'What should I do about my other job? And the FSU meetings? I can't do it all.'

'No, you probably shouldn't try.'

'The money Miss Brown mentioned isn't a king's ransom.' But with her salary from MI5 she could get by. Oh, blow, she'd miss her work with the Distressed Gentlewomen, and Jenny especially, but it couldn't be helped. The work she did for Max, dangerous and stressful though it was, mattered to her most and must come first.

Puffing on his pipe, Max looked at her with more pleasure and interest than he'd done for months.

From the corner the parrot flapped its wings and gave a sinister, mocking laugh like a cartoon villain, making them flinch, then laugh, too. The tension was broken.

'A drink, Minnie?' Max said. 'A celebration is required, I feel.'

Only when she was back in the quiet of her own flat, contemplating the future, did Minnie begin to wonder along what perilous paths this new job might lead her. She thought of Dolly Pyle and that garden party long ago when everything had started. She'd not seen Dolly for over a year and sensed it wouldn't do to try to look her up. Did she regret saying yes to

Dolly? The answer came. A resounding *no*. Thinking of Dolly made her think of Raymond. Since bumping into him in the street that time she hadn't seen him at all. Her mother, who knew his mother slightly, had reported that he was working for the Post Office and was doing very well, but there was no sign of him getting married. Sometimes if she was feeling low, Minnie wondered about him. It was as though he represented the safe, predictable life she'd lost when she'd chosen to work for Max. But, as difficult and uncertain as that work was, it was what she wanted.

Twelve

The offices of the League Against Imperialism and the Anti-War Movement comprised several musty rooms over a nondescript shop in the Grays Inn Road. On her first day, Minnie stared bleakly at a Soviet propaganda poster taped to the wall above her desk and lamented the nostalgic prints of English country life at Seven Dials, courteous Mr Meadows and droll Jenny, all lost to her now. *Stop fretting, Minnie, you're doing what you want. This is far more exciting and important.* She opened a deep drawer in the desk, intending to stow away her handbag, and her skin prickled with interest to see Communist pamphlets in a box. Removing the cover to the typewriter she dislodged another prize, a Russian dictionary trapped against the wall. She glanced over her shoulder, but the young clerk who'd admitted her had gone off to find a Mr Glading, so she began dusting the desktop with a handkerchief and waited to be told what to do.

'Miss Gray. I thought I knew that name when Isobel told me,' said a voice with a familiar London accent and she looked up to see a man with round wire-rimmed glasses, full lips and a clever, good-humoured face regarding her shrewdly. 'Percy Glading,' he said, shaking her hand. The penny dropped.

'I met you on my first evening at the FSU office, didn't I?' She remembered how she'd liked him then, the only man among the three visitors who'd been polite enough to stand up and welcome her.

'I felt sorry for you – you looked overwhelmed. Whether it was seeing four ugly types like us or the scale of the mess in West's office ... Isobel says you've worked miracles there. You can do the same here, I hope?' All the time his eyes were fixed on her as though weighing her up.

'If someone will show me the ropes.' Minnie folded her arms defensively, but his gaze then moved to her hands with their bitten nails so she hid them behind her back.

He smiled. 'I'd be pleased to do that myself if you don't mind waiting until I've made a call. We take turns to put the kettle on here, has someone told you? And there's a kitty for tea and milk. Young Donaldson here might show you the kitchen,' he said, addressing the clerk who was hovering behind him.

All was friendly and pleasant on the surface at least, but Minnie noticed that when Glading retreated to make his call, he closed his door firmly.

'Percy Glading,' Max repeated. He'd telephoned soon after she reached home and had been about to step into the bath. 'Well, that is a turn up.'

'I take it he's important?' Minnie wrapped her dressing gown more tightly.

'I'll say.' He paused.

'I'm sure it would help me to know more.'

'Patience, M/12. Until our next appointment. I'm away tomorrow, but let's say early evening, Thursday. I'll let you know where.'

She replaced the receiver with the usual sense of frustration. Why couldn't he answer her question straight away? It was like playing a game where she didn't know the rules and he was constantly one step ahead.

'He's one of the most dangerous Communists in Britain. Anything you can find out about his movements, anything at all,' Max said, 'is vital for me to know.'

He and Minnie had met in a bar around the corner from the Royal Opera House. He was wearing a dinner jacket and bowtie, clearly on his way to another engagement.

'In what way is he dangerous?'

Max smiled. 'He won't attack you or anything like that. I shouldn't think so, anyway. No, I'm talking about his political beliefs. He is said to have no allegiance to this country whatsoever. If I tell you a little about his background it might help.'

Minnie sat straighter to listen.

'He's from a poor background, the East End, left school at twelve, the usual thing.' Eventually, she learned, Glading had secured a job as an engineer's turner and grinder at the Woolwich Arsenal, the huge munitions firm owned by the Admiralty that manufactured weapons for Britain's armed forces. Having become an active trades unionist there he had joined the Communist Party.

'He was so hardline in his behaviour, we had him listed as "red-hot" from early on. Then everything went badly for him. Someone alerted the Admiralty to his presence at the Arsenal and got him sacked. There was a stink about that, I can tell you, being fired for your political beliefs. The papers got hold of it, but it did Glading no good, he didn't get his job back. He was very bitter, I'd imagine. After that he disappeared for a while, possibly to Russia, but now that he's back in London there's word that he's even more radical in his politics than before. You must keep a close eye on him. I can't stress this strongly enough.'

Armed with this information, Minnie went to work with a renewed sense of purpose, but progress felt painfully slow. The administrative work Glading and his colleagues gave her to do was of a similar humdrum nature to what she'd been doing for the FSU, namely typing, filing, processing bills and so forth. However, the group of people around her were clearly closer to the heart of the Communist Party and rather than she observing them, it felt worryingly at first as though they were keeping an eye on her. Again, meetings took place that excluded her, and the documents she was filing contained blacked-out passages or oblique references to 'confidential' matters. It was simply because she was new, she assured herself, not because they suspected her of anything. She had to earn their trust.

The hours were not onerous and she was complimented

on her efficiency, but it felt stressful to be formally employed to work among paid-up Communists, to pretend to be sympathetic to their cause and to become privy to their activities. All the time it meant guarding her tongue and never relaxing or being herself. Then there was the guilt. She genuinely liked some of the comrades and they seemed to like her. How shocked they'd be if they discovered she was a spy. On some days it felt like a huge act of bravery simply to get up and go to work.

There was one occasion when she unintentionally let down her guard. Someone had brought a popular newspaper into the office, which had a photograph in it of Neville Chamberlain, who was making his mark as the new Chancellor of the Exchequer. Naturally, this promotion had given rise to much pride among his constituents, including Minnie's mother.

'Don't he look smug?' Glading remarked bitterly to the generality.

'I've met him, you know,' Minnie said without thinking, then seeing Glading's sharp look immediately regretted opening her mouth. 'It's just . . . he's my mother's MP.'

Everyone stared at her.

'Very nice,' Glading said sarcastically and Minnie pretended to be getting on with her typing in order to hide her red face. Max would be furious that she'd drawn attention to herself in that way.

It never occurred to her not to tell him about the incident.

Despite all the difficulties, she was surprised to find how much she warmed to Glading. And he appeared to like

Minnie back. After his initial wariness he set out to put her at her ease and made her smile with his wry comments on life. He was nice-looking, too, with soft fair hair in a side parting, and he'd pull off his wire-framed spectacles when making some serious point and blink at her in a blind, touchingly vulnerable manner. He didn't appear dangerous in any way.

Minnie's mother would have said that he had a 'common' accent, but Minnie liked the lively way he spoke and found him interesting to talk to about politics and culture. She knew from the outset that he was married. His wife, Rosa, would sometimes come into the office with their baby girl. Rosa's parents were Russian, Glading let slip, and she reported this to Max with satisfaction.

As she settled into the job her reports grew longer and Max's eyes lit up when he read them and questioned her. As well as Glading, who popped in and out, there were other people of interest who came into the Grays Inn Road offices from time to time – Isobel Brown and on one occasion the General Secretary of the Communist Party himself, Harry Pollitt, which excited Max enormously. These visitors took little notice of Minnie. They were unaware that while the new secretary quietly continued with her daily tasks she was monitoring them under their noses. One evening, for example, she was able to write in her report:

'IB and PG met with HP today in the inner office, but no information as to what it was about. IB seemed flustered when they came out and mentioned catching a train to Newcastle. PG wished her luck. He said she "wasn't to worry", her duty was to the struggle.'

Because of Max's intense new interest in Minnie's information he often asked her to call in on him, or to meet him somewhere, on her way back from work. She grew used to sitting in his drawing room and telling him about her day.

He'd recently added a bullfinch to his menagerie. She was impressed by the fearless way it nestled in his hands and allowed him to stroke it, though it kept a wary eye on Bobby, who was prone to burst into urgent yaps when unsettled.

'And what did Glading say to that?' Max asked one day a month into her new position when she mentioned a particular conversation she'd overheard.

'That he understood, and of course he would put his name to it if it was policy.'

'But you don't know what it was he and the other chap were talking about?'

'No. And they spoke in an undertone. I've noticed, by the way, nobody ever seems to disagree with anyone. Not openly,' she mused. 'Perhaps they do in their meetings.'

He ignored this observation. 'You don't know who this other man was?'

'No, I told you, he's no one I've seen before.'

She hated it when he interrogated her like this. It made her feel that she'd failed in some way. It was exhausting.

They talked for a while longer about Glading and then Max cut their conversation short.

'I have to leave for an appointment in town,' he said apologetically and seemed in a hurry as he showed her out.

It was a warm evening in late September and a clock from a nearby church struck six as Minnie ambled forlornly back towards Knightsbridge. A pair of young women passed her, laughing and talking so naturally together that she was visited by a sudden pang of loneliness. What had she to do, after all, except go home and eat a solitary supper? She could go to the pictures, she supposed, but it was only fun if there was someone to talk to about the film afterwards. She decided that a walk through Hyde Park might raise her spirits. Then she could catch a bus onward from Bayswater.

Walking beneath fluttering leaves from the swaying trees, observing passers-by, she felt a little better. She'd have to take herself in hand, find something to do that was just for her. Her odd situation meant she was distanced from the sort of people she felt comfortable with. Certainly she had few friends in London. She saw Jenny from her old job sometimes for lunch but it was awkward not being able to speak about the nature of her new work.

Minnie smiled to herself. Her Communist colleagues still thought she worked in her spare time for an author with unpredictable hours. At least this was a useful excuse to bring up if she was ever to be seen en route for Knightsbridge, which so far, to her knowledge, she hadn't been. It was strange to say, but she felt a twinge of envy for the people she spied on, because their entire lives revolved around their politics. Their friends were other Communists. They married Communists and brought up their children to believe their ideals.

She'd first noticed this with the FSU folk, their hiking and fundraising and the dances at weekends. She hadn't wanted to join in and, despite her loneliness, certainly wouldn't start now. Further duplicity would overwhelm her. An activity in which she could be herself with her kind of people, that's what was necessary.

As she walked she pondered her possibilities and thought longingly of the sport she'd played in her old life in Edgbaston. She'd never made close friends, but she loved the sense of belonging that came with being part of a team. Running around in the open air amid shouts of encouragement. Laughing and cheering, being her lively self. Yes, she missed it. Should she try that again? There must be a hockey club near where she lived. Perhaps she should investigate. Still, tomorrow was Friday again and on Saturday she could go home to her mother. If she didn't have Mother to fall back on she didn't know what she would do. It wasn't easy to make arrangements with Richard. Although he was in London his shifts rarely allowed it.

'The Ealing Ladies Hockey Club!' Max spat out the words with distaste. 'Consorting with a bunch of hallooing posh girls? Christ, Minnie, that won't go down well with the comrades.'

'They won't know about it,' Minnie said, jutting out her chin. 'Who will tell them? Not me.'

'There's a risk you'll be found out. It won't look good.'

She folded her arms and shot Max a mutinous glare. It was the first time she had shown him her stubborn streak, but she didn't care. 'I had a trial and they've put me straight into the first eleven at left back.' She hadn't enjoyed herself so much for ages. Running at full pelt through the cold early evening air, the *thwock* of wood colliding with wood then the ball sailing down the field. She'd always played in defence, that was her strength. Resilience, determination. *Nil desperandum* had been her boarding school's motto; that much she had learned before she'd been asked to leave.

And the other girls. Cheerful athletic sorts, but Max was right, they were dyed-in-the-wool traditionalists to a woman. Goodness, though, it was a relief to be among them.

'I have to mix with my own sort more,' she told him, 'or I'll go stark staring mad.'

Max relented. 'You must be careful then. Not being a paid-up member of the Communist Party or selling their newspaper or attending their blasted social events is one thing, but being seen to mix with the cut-glass and pearls brigade is another.'

'You did tell me once that hobbies were important, Max. I promise you I'll be careful,' she said humbly. She'd found his reaction disturbing, but some instinct told her she had to look after herself.

Thirteen

1933

On the evening of the last day of January Minnie arrived at Max's flat to deliver her latest report and was shown into the drawing room. She picked up his copy of *The Times* from the chair she was to sit in and glanced at an article headed '*Herr Hitler in Office*'.

'This is all the comrades talked about today,' she said. 'They're worried sick.'

'I'm not surprised, but if the parties on the left there had buried their differences it wouldn't have happened,' Max observed.

Germany had been the Comintern's big hope for a Communist government. If the Communists and the Social Democrats had worked together and formed a coalition after November's election they would have seen off the Nazis.

'Glading says it was the Social Democrats' fault that they didn't,' Minnie said, 'but I suppose he would take that view. Herr Hitler sounds brutal, though. I can't believe that President Hindenburg's made him Chancellor.'

'The article explains. Hindenburg didn't have much choice. The hope is that Hitler will be held in check by appointments from other parties. And he has plenty of energy and ideas. I know people in London who think he should be given a chance.'

Minnie wondered who these people might be, but Max was in one of his mysterious moods and would not be drawn.

Herr Hitler called for fresh elections in Germany. Early in March, the results came through. A landslide victory for the Nazis.

In the Grays Inn Road offices the mood was very low indeed.

'The British public have no idea what's really going on over there,' Minnie heard Glading bark down the telephone to some unfortunate on the other end. 'The election was a travesty.'

Minnie bent her attention to her work, but she knew what Glading was referring to. In the run up to the vote, the Nazis had deliberately intimidated the other parliamentary parties and the Communists in particular. Police had occupied the Communist Party headquarters in Berlin and Communists had been scapegoated for an arson attack on the Reichstag, the parliament building itself. Many Communists were arrested or went into hiding.

She might not sympathise with the views of any of the German parties, but for once she agreed with Glading. The Nazis were a bunch of bullies.

During the next few weeks the atmosphere in the Grays Inn Road offices was one of permanent unease. Minnie read an article in the *Daily Worker* addressing the need for working class unity in Britain. The hard left of the Labour Party, the ILP, were keen to work with British Communists and the writer tentatively suggested this should be encouraged, though this was not current Comintern policy.

It came as a surprise to her colleagues therefore when on 1 April a letter arrived from the Comintern, which was discussed in front of Minnie.

'What does it say?' she dared ask Glading.

'In short, that we've got to get into bed with the ILP. Moscow wants a united Popular Front against Fascism.'

'Oh, I see,' she said, trying not to sound too interested. 'That does sound a big change.'

She went straight to Max's flat as soon as she'd finished work.

'Everyone is amazed at the news. At first they thought the letter must be an April Fool, but someone telephoned Party HQ to check. Glading says they were all to be liberals now. He was being funny, but I don't think the Comintern have a sense of humour.'

'No, they're far too po-faced for that.' Max's eyes gleamed with interest as he scribbled notes.

'Anyway,' Minnie went on, 'the great Harry Pollitt himself arrived from HQ after lunch and they had a meeting. It went on for ages and they looked nervous when they came out, but nobody said anything. I kept my head down, finished what I was doing and came here. What do you think it all means?'

Max put away his notebook and, rising, began to pace the room. 'I don't know,' he said finally. 'We'll have to see how it shakes down. I think it's probably an overreaction on the Comintern's part. The Russians are very jittery about Fascism in Berlin and now Italy. I don't see the same thing happening here, though.' His tone was clipped and Minnie once again felt there was something he wasn't telling her.

Although he and Minnie agreed that the new German Chancellor was a nasty piece of work, she'd noticed that Max didn't speak pejoratively of the British Union of Fascists. He said he'd known one or two of them in the 'old days' and didn't see them as a threat. He always spoke wistfully of these old days although he himself was only in his thirties. Minnie admired him immensely, but she couldn't understand this attitude. Sometimes she worried if her trust in him was misplaced, but then he'd smile and reassure her in his hypnotic voice so that she felt like one of his animals, special, comforted and safe. It was most confusing.

Minnie was struck by how quickly after the first shock her Communist colleagues settled down to the Comintern's new regulations. She noted how little they disagreed with one another over them, as with everything else. 'I see your point of view, Comrade,' was a common response to a differing opinion. There was never any argument or confrontation. It was astonishing to her that they could be so equable and peaceful with one another, even the men with the women. Sometimes it made her wish that she was truly one of them.

'*Don't argue with me, my girl!*' Her father's voice still shouted from across the years. She remembered her mother trying to mollify him when he was in one of his bad moods. If only communism wasn't such nonsense, like a silly religion, one might even be attracted, Minnie thought as she tidied her desk before leaving one evening. She sighed and told herself not to be ridiculous. What she looked forward to now that the evenings were lighter was a bracing training session on the hockey pitch.

Whatever individual Party members privately thought about the latest orders from their masters in Moscow, the new more outward-looking approach seemed to be working. Larger numbers of people than before were passing through the offices, all purposefully engaged in one project or other. Many appeared to be freshly signed up Party members. Diligent as ever, Minnie noted each of them and Max asked eager questions about names and the activities they appeared to be pursuing. There was one regular, however, in whom he showed no more than polite interest, which puzzled her. This man's name was Dickson. He was a lively, talkative type. He betrayed little sign of what he was up to and kept erratic hours. After a while Minnie stopped bothering to observe him closely. Max clearly wasn't interested in hearing about him. And yet she had a certain feeling about Dickson, that he wasn't all that he seemed and then the answer came to her. He was another of M-section's spies! After that, she left him out of her reports, but regarded him privately with a certain amount of jealousy.

*

Max was delighted when Minnie's job became full-time, but his demands on her grew. 'Now, your Glading,' he announced one day in late April. 'I sense from that recent absence you reported that he's up to something, but he's clever at covering it up. What do you think, Minnie? Any chance of getting to know him better?'

'Better?' she echoed, worried, wondering what he meant, but there was no hint of innuendo in his subsequent explanation. She was relieved. The legendary seductress Mata Hari was not Minnie's inspiration in any way. To her Communist colleagues she was just good old Minnie Gray, efficient, reliable and loyal. Well, she was loyal; simply not to them.

'As I've said,' she told Max, 'he's very amiable. No side at all. I like him. I suppose I could ask for his help. What about asking him to explain his politics to me?'

'Not a bad idea. Go carefully.'

'I know, I mustn't appear eager. Don't worry.'

He smiled at her, satisfied.

When she went into work the following day, she picked a quiet moment with Glading, who was opening post at the nearby desk. 'May I ask you something? It's in these minutes I'm typing. These words you use, "historical materialism". I keep seeing them and wondered what they mean.'

Glading shuffled his chair and leaned over her shoulder to see. 'That's me shooting my mouth off again. Historical materialism is a central principle of communism. Basic Engels. Once you've got it everything else makes sense.'

'But what does it mean? I know what materialism is, but why is the history of it important?'

'No, no, it's totally different to what you think is material-ism, which is an interest in material gain and comforts. It's that history unfolds as a result of material conditions. It's very simple.'

'Is it? You must think me stupid, but it's not to me.'

'I'm probably not explaining it properly. You see, history lies in the constant movement between the proletariat – the labouring classes – and the ruling classes that own the means of production. So, come the revolution we'll have a communist society in England, one in which the proletariat are liberated and history is fulfilled.'

'I think I see,' Minnie said doubtfully. 'Oh dear, there's still so much I don't know.'

'I'd be glad to explain it to you. If I just fetch my copy of Engels . . .'

'That's so kind, but you must be busy.'

'I'll tell you what. Are you free at lunchtime? Why don't we go through it then?'

So that's how they came to be sitting at his desk eating sandwiches and with a dog-eared copy of Engels' *Principles of Communism* open between them. Glading spoke passionately of the history of the labouring classes since the industrial revolution and how the class struggle would finally lead to freedom. Minnie tried her best to follow it and even to argue against it. Glading didn't mind. His short-sighted eyes lit up as he countered her argument with another.

'It's obvious to me,' she said at one point, 'that individuals also need personal liberty. How can one be free to make one's own decisions under the system you describe?'

'That's the whole point,' he said, jabbing his finger at the air. 'We must give up our own selfish desires for the good of the whole.'

'I don't see why one can't have both.'

'Because the wealthy and the strong abuse their freedoms and infringe those of weaker members of society.'

'Not all of them, surely.' She sighed.

On her way to meet Max that evening Minnie reflected on this conversation. Glading's arguments were internally logical, she supposed. If you accepted the basic premises then the rest could be seen to make sense. But it over-simplified human experience and she reviled it in her bones. 'Oh, your little bourgeois heart,' Glading had teased her with a laugh. Minnie's middle-class upbringing was a joke between them.

Apart from jibes about her background Glading was kind to her and she almost felt bad for spying on him. He didn't patronise her or make her feel stupid and she was grateful. For her part she allowed him to believe that her interest in her work had originated in her compassion for the economic plight of the Russian people. Who, of course, she did care about; but Russia was far away and she was more aware of the awful plight of the British hunger marchers, and thought the Communists should concentrate more on policies to help families closer to home.

'He does not love his country as you do,' Max said sternly when she spoke of Glading's humanity. He was feeding crumbs to the bullfinch, which was perched on his finger. 'Idealism takes precedence for him. If we are correct in what we surmise, he looks for his orders from his Soviet masters. Who want the whole world to become like them. Communists wish to do away with private property and with all our ancient freedoms and make everybody look and act the same.'

'Yet he seems to care so much about the working classes. It's very admirable.'

'Trust me, Minnie. He's dangerous.'

'He and I are going to talk some more when we have the time. He's given me some homework.' She waved the tattered copy of Engels at him.

Max eyed it with distaste. 'I hope you learn something useful. Still, well done, you're doing exactly as I hoped.' He chirped at the bird in his hand and smiled when it replied. 'See?' he said, 'we'll both make our birds sing.'

They didn't have long to wait.

'I've been asked to go to France!' Minnie told Max a week later. He looked up from his notebook with guarded surprise.

'To do what, exactly?'

'There's to be a conference in Paris. The Anti-War Movement is sending delegates and they need secretarial support.' It would be for less than a week, but she'd never been abroad before so she was excited.

The most of France that she saw, though, turned out to be the countryside viewed from the train, for the conference itself took place in a large, dingy, echoing hall in a nondescript arrondissement of Paris. Her hotel was in a gloomy side street, her room above the kitchen so she was woken at five each morning by the clatter of crockery and the sound of voices.

Minnie didn't attend the sessions of the conference itself, instead passing most of her day in a shared windowless back office. Here telephones rang incessantly and staff from various countries spoke into them urgently in a babel of languages. The room was noisy and overheated to the point of making her head ache.

She spent the time feeling put upon and terrified that she'd be caught off guard and say something that betrayed her. Some of the Russians hanging about the place made the hairs on the back of her neck prickle. The zealous look in their eyes reminded her of her father's when he had tried to catch her out.

After the meal each evening, she retired to her hotel early to write down the long list of notes on all that she'd seen and heard that day. '*Stocky, clean-shaven Russian-looking man, wide-spaced eyes, flat nose, baggy dark suit, habit of rocking from one foot to the other, spoke to Pollitt for ten minutes. His manner agitated and urgent. Pollitt calm, listens and nods then takes from his inside breast pocket a small manila envelope and passes it to him. The man tucks it away unopened and walks off. Pollitt looks thoughtful.*'

It was a relief to be back on the boat and watch the English coastline come into focus through the misty rain. Minnie couldn't wait to see Max and tell him all that she'd learned. Names she had aplenty, the titles of conference talks and the agenda of committee meetings, but it was difficult to tell how much would be of use to him. Had Glading secretly met with any of the Russians? Had he passed on packages or received them? She would have to admit that apart from the incident involving Pollitt she hadn't witnessed anything like that.

In the end she had nothing to worry about. Max read her notes with avid attention, asked shrewd questions and seemed satisfied by her answers. She'd conveyed a good worm's-eye view of proceedings, she supposed, and he'd eagerly accepted it. She was happy.

After that excitement Minnie endured a period of scant pickings when the days and weeks and months crept by. She continued to conduct her secretarial work quietly and faithfully while noticing her colleagues' comings and goings. She got on well with the regulars in the office, who appeared to like her. She continued her conversations with Glading, pretended to be persuaded by his rhetoric, laughed at his jokes. The most exciting thing to report was when he disappeared from the office for a fortnight. A holiday in Bournemouth, he told everyone, and she had no particular reason to doubt this excuse, but October seemed an odd time of year to go to the seaside.

Eventually, after talking the matter over with Max, Minnie became a paid-up member of the Communist Party, but she still declined to take a turn on the streets selling the *Daily Worker*, which members were expected to do because most retailers refused to stock it. She also kept her personal life private and thankfully her colleagues respected that. So far as she knew no one in the Party suspected her to be anything but what she passed herself off to be, good old Minnie, a sympathetic fellow traveller, who could not bring herself fully to join 'the struggle'.

It helped to have found a kind of social life. Some evenings she met up with team mates from the Hockey Club and their friends, to go to the theatre or out for dinner. At weekends she usually went home to Edgbaston. Then her mother came to stay for a few weeks and although Minnie had to manage Mrs Gray's awkward questions about her comings and goings, she enjoyed coming home to find supper ready and the housework done and an evening of familiar company. She felt lonely all over again after her mother departed.

Whatever she did outside work had to be fitted around her meetings with Max and often she found herself waiting for him in a hotel bar or in the anonymous gloom of a cinema auditorium. It was these meetings that kept her going; he was her anchor in this difficult life that she'd chosen and she'd come to think of him as her friend. Sometimes after meeting him, lying in bed later, waiting for sleep, she pondered the question of what she felt for him. She was not drawn to him romantically and she didn't think he was to her, but she did feel deeply for him. That sense she'd felt early on, that he knew all about her, had never left her. And she wanted to do well for him. Any praise from him was praise indeed.

There came another period when she felt utterly stuck. It was a dry season for information. There were no hints to report of colleagues' mysterious trips, no visits to the office by sinister strangers. Max, as a result, scheduled fewer and shorter meetings. It was very frustrating and lonely for her. During this time her visits home became more important, but it was hard work keeping up with old friends who were used to being without her and to whom she could not confide her hopes and fears. She met Raymond again, at a party. He was with another girl, but his eyes lit up when he saw Minnie and the girl, whose name was Ada or Ida, gave Minnie such a sour look that she didn't speak to him for long.

A whole year passed, a year of patient plodding, waiting for something interesting to happen. She kept going as best she could, but she was desperate for a breakthrough.

Fourteen

1934

One balmy May afternoon, Minnie met Max in a cinema in Leicester Square. The film was a suspense story about a missing woman, but they sat at the back of the near-empty auditorium talking in whispers through most of it. Afterwards they strolled down the grand staircase together and out into the sunshine.

'*Oh!*' A black cat bounded across their path, making Minnie flinch. Then she laughed. 'Does that mean your luck is changing, or mine?'

'Both, I hope.' Max grinned.

'Do you believe in luck?' she asked, quite serious.

'Very much. But you have to prepare for it, make your own opportunities, that's what I find.'

'It's about time I had some,' she sighed. 'I've certainly worked for it.'

'You have indeed,' he said, giving her that look that told her she was special.

She could not see it as simple coincidence when the very next evening the General Secretary of the Communist Party in Britain, Harry Pollitt himself, visited her office and drew her aside. 'Minnie, you're exactly the person I need. I've a job I want you to do.'

She listened carefully to his proposal with genuine surprise. 'I don't know,' she said, when he'd finished, her heart racing. 'It's a lot to think about.'

'I'd like to say take your time, but we don't have that luxury.' Pollitt was a friendly man in his early forties with merry brown eyes, warm and usually smiling. Today, however, his face was drawn and Minnie sensed that he was under strain. 'I need your answer in a day or two. Have a word with Glading when he arrives and he'll explain in greater detail.'

It was hard to stay and finish her work, then to walk calmly to Holborn. Once Minnie reached the underground station, however, she hurried onto the escalator, tripped and almost fell, so eager was she to tell Max her news. When she arrived at his flat she was so agitated and out of breath she could hardly speak.

She felt his steadying hand on her arm. 'What's happened?'

'Harry Pollitt. He wants me ... a special mission. It would involve ... Soon. But I'm not sure ...'

'Minnie, *shh*. Come and sit down.'

In the drawing room he poured her a tot of brandy. 'Now, take a deep breath. What's all this about?'

'Pollitt wants me to go to Bombay for them.'

'India. That *is* a turn-up.' Max sat down opposite, his eyes intent on hers. 'And it's Pollitt who spoke to you about this?'

'Pollitt, yes, but Glading's in on it, too. The Comintern support the Communist Party out in India, don't they? I'd be a courier for the Comintern. But, I-I don't think I can do it.'

Max's expression grew stern. 'It's a challenge certainly, but why on earth shouldn't you go?'

'All the way out there, alone? I've never been further than Paris!' Now that Minnie was recovering from the surprise, doubts rushed to the fore. There would be a long sea voyage, then she'd be working undercover alone in a strange land. There would be no one to protect her. She swallowed a large mouthful of brandy and coughed.

'Alone. Ah, I see.' Max drummed his fingers on the arm of his chair. 'They don't appear to have thought this through.' He leaned forward and waved his hand. 'We'll have to work on it. Pass me my notebook, will you, no, the other one. Now, what did you say to Pollitt?'

'I said it was a great honour to be asked, but wasn't there anyone else, and he said nobody who would fit in well enough. I don't know what he meant by fitting in. Why wouldn't they at least send a man?'

'I think I follow his line of thinking. They and many of their associates would be considered undesirables by the Indian authorities and not admitted to the country. You, on the other hand, have a clean record. Also, a female courier is less likely to attract suspicion. In fact, you must admit, Minnie, you do come from the right sort of background for life aboard ship. What excellent cover. Ideal fishing fleet material – off to the Raj in search of a nice officer to marry.' His smile did not reach his eyes.

'No, thank you very much, that's not the life for me. Anyway, I'd be travelling unchaperoned. That wouldn't make me appear perfect wife-material for your typical "nice officer".'

'I suppose not. And we certainly wouldn't want the Indian authorities to think you're a lady of the night, would we?' He smiled. 'There must be a way to conduct this safely. It's a good chance, Minnie. If you do this successfully, goodness knows what they'll trust you with next.'

She knew that she'd have to go. India. It would be the most thrilling adventure she'd ever undertaken, but it was also terrifying.

Her thoughts ran on hopelessly. How would she manage in a strange exotic place by herself? And what would she tell her mother? For more than two years she'd done everything Max had asked her and nobody, not her family or friends, knew the true nature of her work. 'Just a boring typing job,' was her answer to the usual questions. Now she would have to come up with complicated excuses to justify an absence of weeks or even months. Pollitt and Glading weren't specific, only saying that she would have to start for India soon. She would receive modest payment and her expenses would be covered. Other details were sparse. She was to convey a large sum of money to the Indian Communists. The mission would involve a stop in Paris to convert the money to dollars before boarding ship from Marseilles. She'd have to arrange her own accommodation in Bombay.

The more she thought about it the more the difficulties crowded in. But as she and Max made plans in the days that followed and 11th June, the day of departure, drew near the worries fell away and Minnie began to feel a low thrum of excitement. *This is why you chose this work,* she told herself, *to do something exciting and important.* She'd endured the strain and boredom of the last two years for an opportunity like this. Now she'd be a proper spy at last.

The evening before Minnie was due to leave, she sat on her bed surrounded by neatly folded piles of clothes. A particular box of sanitary towels was the first thing she packed, tucking it into a side pocket of the open suitcase.

It was she who came up with the idea of hiding the stack of banknotes Pollitt had given her inside sanitary pads. If she were to be apprehended and her luggage searched, no official would have the nerve to investigate those. And as Max constantly assured her, why should anyone suspect a respectable English girl enough to search her anyway?

Over the previous couple of weeks Minnie had discovered that there were many ways in which Pollitt and Glading had been, as Max put it, 'not very clever'. They were sending her to India for several weeks not only without a believable cover story, but during monsoon when, because of the terrible humidity, British visitors avoided travel. Also to be overcome was the significant danger that without a chaperone the Bombay authorities might well think she was a prostitute and refuse her entry. They had also not recommended anywhere she could stay. In mitigation, neither Pollitt nor Glading were from the type of family that knew about such things, but, honestly, Minnie thought, they might have sought advice.

She therefore relied on Max who became very busy on her behalf behind the scenes. 'We have to make a success of this mission,' he declared, 'both for your own safety and to be able to continue our activities. Now what do you think of this idea? We'll give you a fictional widowed aunt – let's call her Agatha. She lives in Bombay and you're very fond of her. You've been unwell and your doctor has advised you to visit her for a holiday. That should get you into the country, at any rate.'

'Darling Aunt Agatha,' she said, laughing, then stopped. 'I expect I will look unwell after a couple of weeks at sea. I didn't enjoy the ferry going to France.'

'Most people become used to the motion after a day or two.' Seeing her disbelief, Max added, 'I served in the Navy when I was very young.' Another side of him she hadn't known. 'As for where to stay out there, I'll wire a friend in Bombay. He'll know what to do.'

Minnie packed away some soap and a pretty headscarf that her mother had given her. She'd not told her mother any complicated lies about her intended absence, she'd just withheld the whole truth. She was travelling to France because of her job, she had said, and would be away for a few weeks. Yes, it was to do with the author she was working for.

At this moment she felt very alone. She was excited, but she knew there would be danger. Max's last words to her when they'd parted that day had been, 'And for heaven's sake be careful, Minnie. The Soviets can be ruthless. If you do anything to arouse their suspicions I don't like to say what might happen to you.'

His words still echoed in her mind.

She reached into the bedside drawer for the brown pill bottle that Max had given her, unscrewed the top and gave the contents a cautious sniff. The smell tickled her nose. She replaced the cap then hid the bottle in a pouch in her toiletry bag. Its label suggested it contained 'dry cleaning fluid', but actually the liquid was invisible ink. Max had some complicated idea that she should mark the American dollars she would obtain in Paris, so that they might later be traced, but the fluid stank of onions. Perhaps it would be enough to note down the serial numbers instead.

It was early afternoon when the taxi driver dropped Minnie at the corner of a narrow cobbled street in Paris's Latin Quarter, a stone's throw from the looming hulk of the Panthéon. Most of the shops still had their shutters closed for lunch. The dusty second-hand bookshop was open, however, and when she asked the wizened old bookseller for *mon copain anglais* he showed her through to a back office stacked with books. Wordlessly he pointed out a tiny bathroom behind a sliding door, then left her to lug her case up a tight wooden staircase. At the top she tapped on the door and murmured, *'It's me,'* and so relieved was she when Glading admitted her that she almost hugged him. The first stage of her journey was over.

'Well done,' he whispered, his eyes shining. 'You're sure you weren't followed?'

'Pretty sure.'

He looked past her down the stairs. 'Come in. Sorry it's not posh.'

It certainly wasn't. The flat comprised a living room with a single bed against one wall, and a kitchen. Minnie sat on a ladder-back chair while Glading hunched, ill-at-ease, on the unmade bed. The place smelled of damp and the ill-fitting windows juddered as a motor vehicle bumped over the cobbles below. Grimy, hungry and very self-conscious, she looked round, wondering precisely where she was expected to sleep. Surely Glading would offer her the bed, though her colleagues were not known for old-fashioned gallantry.

'Good journey? Any problems on the way?'

'None to speak of, except the weight of this wretched case.'

Now she was here, Glading didn't appear to know what to do with her. 'May I have something to drink?' she asked.

He leaped up. 'Sorry, I'm forgetting my manners.' She followed him into the tiny kitchen, where she took the chipped tumbler of water he offered and some cherries from a paper bag.

'Look, Minnie, have you got the cash?'

'I'll find it for you.' She finished the fruit and went to open the case, conscious of his eye on her intimate garments as she rummaged in the side compartment for the sanitary pads. At least he was embarrassed enough to look away as she opened the packet and pulled out the banknotes. He took them from her quickly and counted them, then snatched his jacket from the back of the door and thrust the stack into an inside pocket.

'Wait here. Don't let anyone in. I'll be back as soon as I can,' he said from the door. It closed quietly behind him and she heard the thud of his boots retreating down the stairs.

She tried to read, but found she could not concentrate so she straightened the bedclothes, then lay down with her coat over her and dozed for a while.

Maybe an hour passed before Glading returned with a satisfied smile, cradling a bulky paper bag. He withdrew a package from inside his jacket and laid it on the bed. Together they pored over its contents. High denomination notes amounting to thousands of American dollars. She did not ask where he'd made the exchange and he did not volunteer the information. Dollars would be impossible to trace back to London, she supposed, if the worst happened and they were discovered. Glading watched awkwardly, hands in pockets, as she pushed handfuls of the notes inside the sanitary pads and stowed them in the compartment in her case, then smoothed a pile of pretty summer dresses.

'Nice outfits,' he said mildly.

'I have to look the part.'

'It's not the blooming *Queen Mary*, you know that, don't you? No fancy parties or that kind of malarkey.'

Minnie nodded. 'Of course not. I despise that sort of thing anyway.'

'So long as you're not going to be disappointed.'

They smiled at one another and she felt herself blush. She'd never before been alone with a man in a strange bedroom in a foreign city. How odd that now it had happened it should be like this, not romantic at all. She thought of Raymond suddenly, the pleasure of his kisses, and pushed the thought away, focused instead on refastening the straps in the case that held the clothes in place.

'I got us a bit of tea.' Glading took from a paper sack a crusty loaf and some neatly wrapped parcels of what turned out to be cold meat and cheese together with a bag of ripe peaches and they sat with a small table between them and gorged hungrily, washing the food down with a bottle of red wine that he fetched from the kitchen.

She liked the deft way he cut the bread, over newspaper to catch the crumbs, and the quiet, intimate way he spoke about her forthcoming journey. He sounded envious, though he must have travelled a bit himself. To Russia, she remembered, what was Russia like? She was careful not to ask him such things, though, recalling Max's instructions. Instead they rehearsed the brief she'd been given, the number she was to telephone after the ship docked in Bombay, who she was to ask for, but when she wondered aloud what to do if something went wrong he had no reassuring answer. 'It won't.' His grin was humourless. 'It mustn't. It'll be all right if you do everything we said. Give them the money and our messages. It's easy.'

'I hope you're right,' she said, her voice tight in her throat.

'Try not to worry,' he said, more softly.

As she'd hoped, he insisted that she take the bed. He would sleep rolled up in a blanket on the floor. When she lay down she must have fallen asleep right away, because the next moment Glading's hand was shaking her shoulder and she opened her eyes to see the light of dawn pushing its way under the shutters. The room smelled of fresh coffee.

When she was dressed and ready to go, he stood before her, hands in trouser pockets in that way now familiar to her, and smiled gravely. 'I'll wish you luck, Comrade,' he said. Then, carefully, he withdrew one hand and touched her cheek. 'See you back in London. Look after yourself, won't you?'

Minnie nodded, then bent to pick up her case, glad to hide her face in case he saw her fear.

'Here, let me,' he said gently, taking the suitcase from her, and she followed him downstairs. He opened a door on to a courtyard, with the glimpse of an alleyway through an arch beyond, and let her out into the early morning air.

'Goodbye,' she whispered huskily, but the door was already closing. He was gone. Minnie set off alone.

Fifteen

The train to Marseilles was busy and Minnie was thankful to have a reservation. In her compartment a tall, bespectacled young priest lifted her case onto the luggage rack and smiled as he took his place next to her, by the window. Terrified that he might engage her in conversation, she found the book in her bag and tried to read, but the endless activity of passengers settling in around her put paid to her concentration.

Eventually the train jerked into motion. Minnie closed her eyes in silent relief then tried to master a rising unease that something was missing. Surely not. The dollars were safely in her case and her tickets, passport and personal money were stowed in the bag on her lap. She'd bought pastries, fruit and lemonade at a stall so that she wouldn't need to leave her case untended to visit the dining car.

Once she felt calmer, she became aware how warm the compartment was getting. Peeling off her cardigan she folded it on her lap. More comfortable, she began to take note of her surroundings.

The view from the window was of the backs of buildings, higgledy-piggledy and with lines of washing strung between them. They passed the occasional green park, then through a long cutting where the wild embankment was studded with poppies.

Beside her the priest read a letter written in thick black handwriting. Opposite, two stout elderly women in black spoke in a French too fast and incomprehensible for Minnie's schoolgirl grasp. One brought out a box of cakes, leaned across and offered one to the priest, who took it with a word of thanks, causing the woman to beam with pleasure.

The suburbs gave way to countryside now, fields of green crops, pastureland dotted with sheep and cows. Not very different from home, Minnie thought, though the farmhouses were distinctive with their coloured shutters and it took her breath away to see gracious chateaus with their fairy-tale turrets.

From time to time the train stopped at a station and more passengers climbed on. Soon the corridor was filled with people and assorted luggage. Two soldiers in uniform slid open the glass door of the compartment, causing Minnie to freeze in fear. One caught her eye and winked before they moved on and she relaxed. Time to unwrap her pastries. The sticky sweet custard and almonds comforted her.

It was mid-morning now and the compartment was heating up even more, the countryside ablaze with sunshine. The further south they travelled the worse the heat became. The priest and the old women left the train at Dijon to be replaced by two schoolchildren in the care of a severe lady with pince nez. Minnie panicked briefly after she returned from a visit to the lavatory to find that an elegant gentleman with a twirled moustache had taken her place. It was with some difficulty that she made him understand that he should move.

The afternoon heat grew sultry, hardly bearable. Minnie sipped her lemonade and stared at the changing view. Serried rows of vines, the houses here were sun-baked, with terracotta tiled roofs. For a time there were fields of sunflowers, then lavender. At Lyons a matronly woman with grey hair piled up on her head like a cottage loaf took a seat in the compartment. She held on her lap a large basket containing two plump hens. Minnie watched, fascinated, as the birds jerked their heads accusingly and chuckled to themselves.

Already she was further from home than she'd ever been before, yet it hadn't been as bad as she'd feared. Apart from the conductor who'd checked her ticket no one had questioned her or even looked at her with suspicion. She dared think ahead now, to Marseilles, still an hour or more away. The port, Max had instructed, was a short journey from the railway station and a taxi would be best.

It was after four when they drew into Marseilles and she was limp with exhaustion. Minnie paid a porter to carry her case and he took pity, finding a cab for her and negotiating a fare to the docks.

'The *Mélisande*,' she repeated to the driver as they passed through a labyrinth of shadowed narrow streets, and read him the ship's location from her papers, but he still had to stop at the Harbour Master's office to ask directions. Eventually he pulled up on a remote quay where the sea lapped at the black hull of a sooty packet steamer moored there. It was silent, apparently deserted. *This can't be right*, she thought as she got out and fumbled for coins, but then she glimpsed the name on the boat's prow and saw that it was. She'd known it was only one of P&O's mail boats, not a grand passenger liner, but surely this disappointing vessel wasn't fit for the high seas. The vessel was even smaller than she'd imagined, and it craved a decent lick of paint.

Minnie climbed the gangplank, her nose wrinkling at the smell of oil and coal, and a sleepy French steward appeared who took her case and preceded her down a steep stairway to a stuffy cabin in the stern. A porthole threw daylight onto a matted floor and a double bunk. She learned upon enquiry that she had the room to herself and though this pleased her, she thought to ask if there were other ladies on the voyage.

'*Non, mademoiselle,*' the steward said gravely. '*Vous êtes la seule.*' And she sighed, her fears confirmed.

After he'd left, she quickly visited the bathroom along the corridor, then lay down on the lower bunk, feeling its hardness under the rough blanket and thin mattress and trying to accept that this narrow room would be her home for a fortnight. After a while, she sat up, worrying what to do with the money in her case. Unable to think of a safer place than the sanitary towels, she rose and set about unpacking, stowing her dresses in a wall cupboard and everything else in a wooden crate underneath the bed. Feeling happier, she locked the cabin and went up on deck to explore.

Siesta was over, now, the ship bustling with activity. She walked the deck, admiring the blueness of the Mediterranean and a picturesque view of islands. Then she located a dimly lit but comfortable lounge where the barman was opening up, and asked for a gin and tonic to celebrate her safe arrival. Choosing a deck chair outside, she amused herself watching the arrival of supplies and boxes of mail as she sipped her drink.

Twenty minutes later a battered khaki-coloured truck rattled onto the quay and screeched to a halt. Half a dozen lads with English voices leaped out, laughing and jostling each other as they gathered up kit bags and holdalls and strode up the gangplank. Ordinary soldiers, Minnie supposed from their savage haircuts and cheerful banter. One looked up and pointed her out to his friends and she turned her head away, blushing. The truck drove off to be succeeded soon after by a dusty taxi, from which emerged a sinewy ageing gentleman whose luggage included a collection of butterfly nets. She watched with interest as these and a box labelled 'Fragile' were conveyed below deck with much fuss and instructions to 'be careful'.

While Minnie was thinking about when and where dinner might be found, a fair-haired young man with rosy cheeks walked up the gangplank. He wore a cream-coloured linen suit that suggested the best of English tailoring. Liking the brightness of his expression, the guileless blue eyes spaced widely apart in a round, good-natured face, she returned his 'Good evening' politely when he tipped his hat to her.

Dinner was served in a functional dining room in the prow, where she was relieved to find that the Tommies were gathered on a table of their own and that she was seated next to the ship's captain, a grizzled Scot named Briggs. He introduced the elderly naturalist, a Mr Hibbert, and Mr Hugo Hill, the blue-eyed Englishman, the only one of the company to have dressed for dinner.

Captain Briggs was an old sea dog, laconic, but civil enough. From him Minnie learned that the *Mélisande* was to sail on the morning tide.

'What is the route?' She wanted to check, although she'd seen it on Max's atlas.

'We head east through the Mediterranean,' Briggs informed her, 'then south through the Suez Canal and the Red Sea, before crossing the Arabian Sea.' They were to stop at several ports along the way to deliver and take on mail and at Aden for refuelling. After Bombay the ship would continue on to Australia and New Zealand.

'Australia's where I'm going,' Mr Hill said. 'Melbourne eventually.'

He was a well-spoken man of Minnie's age, friendly but not too much so, and she warmed to him.

'Quite a journey,' she said politely. 'Have you been there before?'

'Never. I'm to take up a position in my uncle's wholesale business.' He didn't sound very happy about it. 'You're disembarking at Bombay, I gather?'

Minnie explained as casually as possible that she was visiting an aunt.

Shy Mr Hibbert barely opened his mouth except to eat, but in answer to direct questions said that he was bound for New Zealand because he was writing a book about the insect life there. His words were difficult to hear owing to raucous laughter from the Tommies' table.

As soon as dinner was over Minnie retired to her cabin, worn out by the day's events. She changed into her night-clothes, but before she climbed into bed she took out the stash of American dollars and copied the serial numbers into a notebook, in case it was possible for them to be tracked.

Very early the next morning she was torn from sleep by clunks and shouts and vibrations from the boat's engines firing up. She rose groggily and dressed, then went out on deck to watch the crew weigh anchor and cast off. Black smoke billowed from the single funnel as they motored out to sea in the pale dawn light. The water was smooth and tinged with gold and it felt like the beginning of a great adventure to leave the islands behind and strike out into open sea. Late in the day the waves became choppy and Minnie staggered to her cabin and lay down on her bed. She felt too wretched and giddy to get up for dinner and passed a broken night, fighting the roll and pitch of the boat, and the jolts from waves slapping on the hull.

The following day the sea was calmer and she felt much better. After breakfast she settled herself on deck with a book, but with half an eye on the antics of the young soldiers who climbed onto the side rail and started horsing about with a stolen cap. As soon as the bar opened mid-morning they crowded into the lounge where they sat drinking beer most of the day and playing cards. Occasionally one or other would saunter out to engage Minnie in conversation, but she gave short answers and refused all offers of drink or joining their entertainment. She was very glad when Hugo Hill arrived on the scene, still a little green round the gills, and asked respectfully if he could sit with her. After that the Tommies let her alone.

Hugo, as he asked her to call him, proved an amusing companion. In his stories about the minor public school he'd attended, the attempts he'd made to hold down jobs, the girls he'd failed to impress, he portrayed himself as the innocent abroad, tricked or beguiled at every turn, yet never sorry for himself. It was restful, too, that he accepted Minnie's usual account of herself at face value and did not ask intrusive questions.

'You're very brave,' he did say, 'being the only lady on board. I like a girl who can look after herself.'

'I didn't plan it to be this way. But I am used to looking out for myself.'

'Any problem with those chaps in the bar, let me know.'

'They're no trouble really, but thank you.' She suppressed a smile. Physically speaking he was no man of action, but it was kind of him all the same.

She was particularly glad of Hugo's company because she soon discovered that Glading had accurately predicted the humdrum nature of the voyage. Captain Briggs's priority was to deliver the mail. He took scant interest in his passengers. There were no arrangements for deck quoits or egg-and-spoon races, no dancing – everyone simply repaired to the bar after dinner. It was here, though, that she began to realize Hugo's limitations, for after a few whisky and sours a bewildered look appeared in those guileless blue eyes and she noticed how he repeated his stories to the assembled throng, but with different endings to the ones he'd told her. He was still good company, but definitely needed watching.

The following day the *Mélisande* reached Port Said at the mouth of the Suez Canal, and her passengers disembarked. It was Minnie's first glimpse of Arabia and she was enchanted by the palm trees and the dress and grace of the people. The Tommies threw pennies into the harbour for brown-skinned boys to dive for. In the busy market magicians performed tricks for the visitors with ropes and coins.

There was a notable change in the climate, too. As their voyage continued, Minnie chose to wear her lighter summer dresses and the passengers sat under awnings erected over the deck.

The narrow canal was busy with craft of all kinds and full of interest. At Suez, she was excited to see her first camels, but the unrelenting vistas of greyish sand quickly became tiresome. Gradually, though, she accommodated herself to leaving western life behind. She began to feel that she was somebody different, someone less inhibited by the petty observances of English life. Was this new person the one she really was underneath, she asked herself. Even so it would not do to drop her guard.

As they crossed the Red Sea, which she saw was not red, but blue, the heat intensified. Nights tossing and turning in her cabin became unbearable, so eventually she gave in to Hugo's invitation to join the rest of the passengers sleeping out on deck. She felt perfectly safe doing so with him snoring gently beside her and was enchanted by the tropical stars burning overhead.

At Aden, the *Mélisande*'s passengers were ordered to leave the ship for the day, closing portholes and doors tightly behind them in preparation for the filthy business of recoaling.

Mr Hibbert the naturalist, more animated than they'd seen him, bore off Minnie and Hugo to visit some botanical gardens a few miles away. For several hours in the heat they wandered through an exotic landscape of tropical trees and magnificent flowers and listened to the songs of strange birds, until darkness began swiftly to fall. Returning to the ship, they were awestruck by the scene that greeted them. Flares lit up the quay and outlined the silhouettes of porters who were carrying coal up the gangplank in bags and baskets, chanting as they went. Each emptied their load into the hold then passed back down to the quay for more. 'It's like a nightmare picture out of a book,' Hugo whispered and Minnie agreed. She and her companions had to wait until the recoaling was finished and the decks scrubbed down before trudging warily back on board.

After Aden the heat grew sticky, the skies boiled with cloud and the atmosphere was ominous. There were moments of great beauty in the flashes of sunlight on the sea. One morning a cry went up and Minnie rushed to the rail to see a school of flying fish that leaped like glittering rainbows. Her heart soared. She had never seen anything so marvellous. If the night was clear, a waxing moon hung low like a Chinese lantern, thronged by pulsing stars in the soft hot darkness.

On the evening before they were to dock at Bombay, the moon reached its fullness. Minnie and Hugo took their drinks out on deck after dinner and leaned over the rail to watch the quivering pattern of the ship's lights on the water. Hugo, who had drunk far too much, had spent dinner bragging about his plans for a new life in Melbourne, how he'd make his fortune and build a mansion overlooking the sea, but now he turned wistful.

'Of course, I suppose everything will be very different from England,' he said, swirling the brandy in his glass. 'It'll take me time to get used to the climate, for a start, to make friends and so forth. Don't you think?'

'I imagine so.' Minnie was only vaguely listening. She was brooding about the following day, haunted by dread of the tasks ahead.

Hugo took a large gulp of his drink. 'I say,' he said, conversationally, 'I don't expect you'd fancy it there, would you?'

'Fancy what?' She glanced up, bemused.

He moved closer and she could see sweat beading on his forehead. 'We could get married after we dock in Melbourne,' he went on. 'They say it's a good life there.'

She edged away, repulsed, then saw the dismay on his face and felt guilty for disappointing him, while annoyed at herself for feeling guilty.

'No, you wouldn't want someone of my sort,' he said abruptly. 'I can see that.'

'Hugo dear, we hardly know each other.' Minnie tried to cheer him up. 'You can't really mean it. It's only this awful heat and the effect of the moonlight.'

'You're a sensible girl. I'm not much of a catch. Got into a bit of trouble back home, to tell the truth.'

'What sort of trouble?' she asked cagily.

'A spot of bother in the City. I'd got myself into debt, you see, and one thing led to another. I was lucky to avoid prison. My family clubbed together for my ticket. Said I'd best start again somewhere else.'

'That's awful. How had you got into debt?'

He shot her an embarrassed glance. 'Bad luck, really. I lent a pal some money and . . . let's say it didn't work out.'

Horrified by Hugo's confession and relieved that he didn't press his suit further, she finished her drink, then murmured her excuses and escaped below.

After another sleepless night Minnie rose exhausted, packed and was up on deck early to look for the first signs of India. She'd never seen a vista so striking. The boat passed a scatter of densely wooded islands glowing like emeralds and fringed by white sand. Where the water around them became shallow, the navy blue of the deep sea lightened to turquoise. Sunlight flashed off other craft as the *Mélisande* slid onward: a great cruise liner, tiny bobbing fishing boats, a Chinese wooden junk with jagged sails. Ahead, above the distant line of land, the sky was thickening with dark cloud. Soon Minnie could make out the shapes of buildings. As the ship drew near, a distant oblong shape transformed into a towering imperial portal. 'The Gate of India,' someone near her said. Next to it was a broad-shouldered domed affair that looked like a palace. A sense of the city coalesced, its vast expanse of flat roofs, towers and pinnacles like a giant patchwork blanket draped over the landscape. And now at last the wide-stretched arms of a great harbour came into focus, shimmering in the haze.

Was it the sound or the aromas of the vast city that reached Minnie first? What began as a faraway murmur separated itself into shouts, the rattles and clangs of cranes and anchors from the docks, a blare of horns, the rumble of cartwheels and, winding above it all, the hypnotic wailing of a musical pipe and the urgent beat of a drum. All this was accompanied by the ripe odours of spices and sewage mixed with an acrid smell like burning rubber.

A tugboat led the *Mélisande* to her berth and details of the scene before Minnie came more sharply into focus – the delicate filigree decoration of buildings, the quays a panorama of vibrant colours as the crowds jostled and flowed. Minnie stared and stared, caught up by the cheerful dazzle of it all.

She waited with her case as the gangplank was lowered and tried to think of practicalities: the money hidden in her case, the name of the hotel she needed to find, and urged herself to stay calm. Max had trained her well. When it was her turn she repeated her story to the official clearly and forcefully, her gaze direct, her stance upright as he examined her passport. Yes, she'd been unwell and had come to stay with her aunt in Bombay. A widow, who lived in . . . and here she consulted her engagement diary and named a road in Malabar Hill. The man nodded and stamped her papers without any questions and she was free to enter.

So here she was on the quay, alone in a strange land, exhausted already by the humidity and the assault on her senses. Eager Indians surrounded her with reaching hands, offering their services in bright voices, but she clung onto her case and waved them away. Then, thank heavens, one of the young soldiers from the ship appeared at her side.

'Need a hand, miss?'

'I'm looking for the Taj Mahal Hotel.'

'That's easy. It's that huge place we saw from the boat. Now which of you chaps speak English?'

He selected one of the rickshaw drivers, who assured her that the hotel was *very very* close, but *no no*, it was too hot for the memsahib to walk. Minnie yielded up her suitcase reluctantly, worried as ever about the money inside, and the soldier handed her up into the back of a rickshaw hitched to a battered bicycle. As it forged the short distance through the busy streets she was in a state close to terror. It was the cacophony, the putrid smells and strange sights. Bony buffalo quite unlike English cows lurched along, their patient faces buzzing with flies, but, most of all, she was shocked by the desperate eyes and grasping hands of the beggars they passed. She'd never seen such wretches. How dirty the streets were, actually running with stinking sewage. Ragged children, mangy dogs and chittering monkeys fought over food scraps thrown away in the gutter.

The broad expanse of the Taj Mahal Hotel occupied the seafront near the great Gate of India. The soldier was right, Minnie did remember seeing its handsome dome and little turrets from the boat.

By now giddy with heat, it was wonderful to enter the quiet and shade of the large reception area with its cool tiled floor and turning ceiling fans. She approached the Indian man behind the desk hesitantly.

'Good morning. I'm to meet a Mr Crickett Smith here. Do you know him?'

'One moment, memsahib.' The man turned and conversed in his own language with someone unseen in the office behind him, then spoke briefly into a telephone.

'Someone is looking for Mr Smith,' he told Minnie. 'If you would like to wait in the bar. You may leave your suitcase here.'

'Thank you, but I will take it with me.' Crickett Smith was an old friend of Max's, an American musician who simply 'happened' to be working as the hotel's jazz band conductor. In the absence of other accommodation arrangements Max had wired ahead to ask him to help her.

The receptionist directed a young boy to carry her case and she followed him into a grand lounge studded with exotic greenery where she gave the boy a few coins and sank wearily into a rattan chair. Here she ordered a cold drink from a waiter, mopped her brow and wondered what on earth she would do if Smith couldn't be found. She had nowhere to stay and little money of her own. Certainly not enough to stay in this luxurious hotel.

She was gulping down lemonade and torturing herself with a dangerous whimsy involving being caught by the authorities with the Communist dollars, when a man in a white linen suit strolled up and introduced himself cheerfully as Smith. She'd never actually met a black man before, but was immediately engaged by Smith's easy manner, his rich drawling voice and the generous way he offered his friendship. He insisted on calling for cocktails, which arrived in elegant glasses clinking with ice. As she sipped hers, they talked about the coincidence of Smith knowing Max and about his work as trumpeter and jazz band conductor at this hotel. 'Max said you'll be wanting somewhere to stay,' he said eventually. 'Though what he's doing letting you arrive in monsoon I don't know. A friend of mine has recommended a boarding house for you. Inexpensive, but I think it'll be all right.'

'Thank you. Can we go there at once? I think after that cocktail I need to lie down.'

Outside, Smith handed her into a waiting rickshaw and climbed in next to her. As they pulled away into the traffic, he talked all the while about the sights they passed, but she was so hot and tired everything muddled together in her mind. Their journey took them inland through busy streets then up a hillside into a more tranquil area with trees. Halfway along a road of higgledy-piggledy small residences, he bid the driver pull up beside a neat squarish building edged with pots of brilliantly coloured flowers. He helped her down with her case and instructed the driver to wait. At a wide-open doorway where a muslin curtain waved in the breeze he called inside and soon a trim grey-haired Indian woman in a red sari came out and welcomed them with her palms pressed together and a little bow. Smith introduced Minnie to her, then touched his hat in farewell. 'You know where to find me, Miss Gray, if you need further assistance. Promise me you'll ask.'

'I will,' Minnie said faintly. By now she was almost passing out. 'Thank you so very much, Mr Smith,' she managed to add. 'I'm only here a short while, to visit my aunt in Malabar Hill, so I should be all right now.'

Smith chuckled. 'Ah, the sainted aunt. Max did mention her.' He obviously thought the whole thing an immense joke, but Minnie was disturbed. If Smith didn't believe her cover story perhaps others wouldn't either.

'You've been most kind,' she said sincerely, and shook his hand. A young man appeared and took her case and she followed her new landlady into the welcome gloom of the building. The woman smiled with kind eyes and indicated a communal dining room before leading Minnie up a flight of stairs to a small shuttered bedroom at the back with a single bed, a chest of drawers and a matted floor. Here she was left to arrange her belongings and rest before lunch.

It was much cooler here than outside, but the air still felt thick, oppressive, so unthinkingly she opened the window and pushed back the shutters only to be knocked back by a wave of heat. When she recovered enough to look out, she caught her breath. Below, a mosaic of roof terraces rolled out towards the distant sea. Colourful lines of washing hung everywhere like bunting and coils of smoke and spicy smells suggested cooking fires. The heat was growing unbearable so she shut out the view and in the gloom turned her attention to her suitcase.

She was keen to change, but when she unpacked her clothes she found them already damp with the humidity. She hid the sanitary towels with the bank notes at the back of a drawer. Tomorrow, if all went to plan, she'd be rid of the money. After that, exhausted, she drank some water left for her in a jug then lay down on the bed and fell at once into a deep sleep.

When she awoke it was late afternoon and she sensed a change in the atmosphere. The heat had become tense, ominous. She rose, groggy and heavy-limbed, and stumbled over to fiddle open the shutters. In the sky ahead, moving swiftly towards her, surged a band of thick, blue-black cloud. Birds were flying for the trees, calling in alarm. Down below, women and children were reeling in washing. As she watched, the first raindrops fell. They built quickly to a downpour that drummed on the roofs and obscured the view. She closed the shutters and stood listening to the deluge, wondering how long it would be before she could leave this hateful place and go home.

Sixteen

Minnie telephoned from a public box the number Pollitt had given her and was eventually put through to her Communist contact, who told her to meet him at the Tea House café in the old city. The next morning, after a breakfast of savoury porridge and fruit, she left the boarding house. The houseboy gave her an umbrella and secured the services of a passing horse-drawn cab. The rain had ceased for the moment, but the air was still muggy. Minnie felt tired and limp and her head ached because she'd spent a troubled night.

As they reached the main streets, distant sounds of shouting reached her ears and when they entered a grand square edged with banks and modern offices they encountered an ugly scene. A great protest march was underway. A few of the banners were in English and it was with concern that Minnie read slogans demanding higher wages and better working conditions. Gathered nearby to challenge the marchers was an alarming phalanx of Indian policemen armed with batons and, as Minnie's cab drew near, an urgent whistle sounded and the police charged in among the demonstrators, striking right and left with their clubs. The horse shied, the cab driver shouted something incomprehensible and the vehicle lurched away towards a side street, Minnie gripping the side and her belongings. She'd never seen such violence and chaos before and it shocked her. The driver apologized and the journey resumed, but it was a while before she was able to calm herself.

The site of the rendezvous was nicely public, she was relieved to find, a large canopied café in a part of the old city where the streets were full of shops and market stalls. Adventurous Europeans were to be seen inside eating and drinking, along with wealthy locals. Minnie sat at a table by herself for an hour beyond the meeting time, watching the rain come down outside and growing increasingly worried as she clutched her bag containing the bank notes on her lap and tried to make her pot of tea last as long as possible.

A departing customer left an English-language newspaper on a nearby table so she snatched it and perused the front page, her eyes widening as she read about the strikes and protests that were afflicting Bombay and other Indian industrial cities. An editorial inside posited that the Communist Party was behind the unrest and hinted darkly at 'the hidden hand of Red Russia'. Minnie felt herself prickle all over. What if the authorities were on to her? Had her contact not turned up because he'd been apprehended – or worse? She thought of the violence she'd witnessed.

She was caught in this new agony when she became aware of someone hovering nearby, a thickset, middle-aged

Indian in traditional dress who was fastening his umbrella and casting her guarded glances. Minnie folded the paper, sat up straight, and met his eye with a direct look of her own. Immediately he came across, wiping his face with a handkerchief.

'Mr Popat?' she asked.

'You are Miss Gray?' For simplicity she was using her real name here.

'You're very late.'

He jiggled his head. 'I must apologize. It is a difficult time. Will you come with me, please?'

For a moment she couldn't decide what to do. She'd expected the meeting to take place here, that she'd slip the money to him and murmur the message Pollitt had given her. Popat was a complete stranger. Where did he intend to take her?

He must have understood her hesitation because his face softened. 'It's all right, I promise you,' he said in a low voice, 'but we cannot stay here. There are police spies everywhere. I have a comrade with a business nearby. In the room behind his shop we may speak more freely, and you will feel comfortable because his mother will be there.'

Minnie nodded reluctantly. Leaving some coins to pay for her tea, she followed him out into the street, where thankfully the rain had eased.

Mr Popat's comrade's sari shop was a few hundred yards along a narrow side street and when they entered she gazed with astonishment at the bales of fabrics in jewel-like colours that were piled up to the ceiling. Popat threw a greeting to an elderly man they passed who was unrolling a length of glittering cloth for two lady customers, and led Minnie through a bead curtain at the back of the shop into a cluttered stock room beyond. Here they exchanged greetings with a wrinkled old woman in a white sari who sat sewing at a table. Popat pulled out a chair for Minnie and called up a narrow wooden staircase. A distant voice answered and after a moment a slight, balding young man with a wary expression clattered down to join them.

'Very happy to meet you, comrade,' he said to Minnie, pressing his palms together.

The old lady brought Minnie a glass of water, then continued to sew, and the men paid her no attention. Instead they focused on Minnie. 'You have the money, Miss Gray?' Popat asked. Minnie looked from one eager face to the other before opening her handbag and extracting the precious notes from a cunning compartment hidden in the lining. She felt the men's interest intensify. It was a large sum of money. She'd counted and recounted the notes in her room that morning.

Now she pushed the pile over to Popat. 'I will need a receipt.' She made a scribbling motion. He stared longingly at the money for a second then swept it up and counted it carefully. Next he spoke excitedly in his own language to his friend. When he looked up at Minnie his eyes were soft with emotion. 'Thank you,' he said in a low voice, very sincerely. 'This will help our cause very much. Many, many respectful greetings to our British comrades.'

'They send you theirs too,' Minnie replied, and she recited the formal message of support from their British counterparts that Pollitt had drilled into her. The men smiled and bowed, then Popat's friend went to an embroidered picture on the wall of a lady with too many arms and pushed it aside to reveal a safe. He stowed the money inside before returning to the table with a notepad on which he wrote out in neatly printed English the receipt she would need to give to Pollitt on her return to London.

Popat thanked her again and asked her where she was staying. She should expect to hear from them again shortly, he said. 'I am sure there will be something you must take back with you, but I don't know when it will be ready.' This was because of the strike. Their officials were being watched and it was not easy for members of the cell to meet. Perhaps in a few days the trouble would die down.

Wondering what on earth the 'something' might be, Minnie gave them the address of the boarding house then Popat showed her out through the shop.

Outside, the rain was starting once more and she was glad of the umbrella. She made her way back up to the main street as quickly as she could, dodging puddles and wishing that she'd accepted Popat's offer to accompany her, because she was subject to lascivious male glances and clutching hands at every turn of the short journey. Near the café where she'd met Popat she spotted the cab that had brought her and hailed it at once.

She sank back into the seat exhausted and closed her eyes briefly, allowing relief to flood through her. She had got rid of the money. Her mission had been successful! If only she didn't have to wait in Bombay for whatever it was the Indian

Communists wanted her to take back to England. Otherwise she'd have been able to make arrangements to depart immediately. Oh, how she *longed* to go home.

The rest of the day passed slowly. Whenever the rain ceased the heat intensified further, the air thickening so that it became difficult to breathe. It was all Minnie could do to lie on her bed and mop her brow. If she rose to sip water or to visit the bathroom the effort sapped all her energy. Her face in the square scrap of mirror above the basin was puffy, blotched with grey.

At dinner that evening she felt nauseous and could do no more than nibble at a piece of bread. The sight and the smell of the strange food was too much for her. She smiled a weak apology to the young woman who served her and retreated to her room with the bread. Later she lay watching a line of giant ants walk across the floor bearing the crumbs she'd dropped. She slept fitfully, longing for morning when she hoped to hear from her Communist contacts and be able to leave this place.

All the next day Minnie waited, but no message came. Still unable to eat much and drained of energy she could not have left the house even if she'd wanted to. In the early evening, after she'd pushed open the shutters to air the room, a feral monkey leaped in. She retreated with a gasp as it bared its teeth at her. She watched it from the bed, frozen in terror, but after tipping over her handbag in an apparent search for food it stole her comb and went on its way.

At first light the following morning Minnie woke with her stomach churning and had to stumble to the bathroom. She was ill for several days, hardly able to leave her room, her belly cramping with a terrible pain, ingesting only lemonade that the landlady brought her. After the attacks eased she continued to lie low, barely managing to creep down to the dining room at mealtimes to eat what little she could face. But still no message came.

The days passed and life remained the same, the sky glimpsed between the shutters a surging mass of blue-black cloud, the rain relentless when it came, the air as humid as ever after it cleared. She could not focus on her novel, she had no sight of a newspaper, and she did not dare to go out.

There came a day when she stared up at the ceiling to see a speck of black mould had appeared. The next morning this had grown and soon there was another and another. Day after day she lay there and the burgeoning pattern of dots and lines arranged itself into the features of a face, a snarling face of a man with a moustache who went on to haunt her dreams. Sometimes she'd wake in the night and her thoughts would chase themselves round her head. Why hadn't these people been in contact? Had they forgotten about her? She'd given them the right address, she was sure that she had.

Then another thought came to her, and the more she resisted it the more she became certain that it was the truth. Mr Popat must have been arrested. That was why he hadn't been in touch. Would the authorities torture him for the truth? Perhaps he'd be forced to name her and her identity would be exposed. They'd come for her. Perhaps they were outside now, waiting for her to emerge. Then they'd strike. Max's words came to her: *The Soviets can be ruthless. If you do anything to arouse their suspicions I don't like to say what might happen to you ...*

The days became a week, two weeks, and still she waited, increasingly desperate, alert to every sound. She thought about contacting Mr Smith at the Taj Mahal, but what could she tell him and how could he help? He could relay a message to Max for her, but how long would that take and what would Max be able to do anyway? No, she must manage on her own. There would be a point, surely, when she'd simply have to admit defeat and take a boat home, but she had no idea when that point would be. She'd never felt so frightened or alone in her life. Spying was no longer a game, or the excitement she had once craved. It was dangerous, life-threatening.

One afternoon, three weeks after Minnie's arrival in India, the landlady brought her an envelope limp with damp. Minnie waited until she was alone to slit it open, fearing what it might contain. The handwritten message from Mr Popat was short and to the point. There was nothing she needed to take back to London after all. She sank down on the bed, stunned by this anti-climax. Then she burst into sobs of relief. She was free to go home.

Minnie boarded the *Mélisande* on its journey home. On the boat she stumbled about, a shadow of her former self. After her illness her summer dresses hung loose on her and for a while she could muster little energy to do anything except sleep and lie around on deck. The humidity was still intense, but this time there was an occasional breeze and Minnie craved the coolness of it on her face. *You are safe*, she kept telling herself, *safe and on your way back to England*. Once she felt a bit better she would write up her notes. For now she drew the shreds of her sanity around her and lay low.

Thankfully there were no Hugos to distract her on this journey. If she wanted company she found it with Amy Cotton, an army officer's wife called home to look after her sick mother. Amy was in her forties, but seemed younger, for she'd been blessed with a good figure and a positive disposition. She was also used to the climate, for she'd lived in India most of her life. Minnie enjoyed the normality of their conversations. She was also jealous to learn from Amy of another side to India that she'd missed, the pleasures of summer in the Himalayan foothills, the sheer beauty of the country and the vigour and grace of its people. She described moonlight picnics in the gardens of Delhi, amid the tombs; dances, parties, tiger hunts. The contrast with Minnie's own experience was stark and she wished she'd taken more interest in the attractions of Bombay. Instead the memories she'd taken away were the unpleasantness of the monsoon period, the strangeness of the food, her own illness and lassitude. Other than that, dirt and poverty had been her main impression.

'You must come back another time,' Amy insisted. 'And see it all properly.'

'I don't think I can,' Minnie mumbled. 'Poor Aunt Agatha is not expected to live long.'

After Aden the climate was more manageable and she began to feel better. The heat was a dry one from which it was possible to find shade. They still had to cross the Red Sea and the Mediterranean, but once they docked in Marseilles home and civilization would feel within reach. Dear old England. Minnie thought with fondness of its soft green landscapes, the smallness and cosiness of it all. There would be proper English tea with proper milk and solid butter instead of rancid oil and, importantly, everyone would speak the same language.

She parted from her shipboard friend at Dover, full of relief at being home. She'd been away for nearly seven weeks. On the train to London she nibbled at a bar of milk chocolate, watched country stations, hay meadows and pretty villages fly by, and made her decision. She would not spy for Max anymore. She'd had her measure of danger and learned that the whole thing was not a game. She'd known what it was like to be a pawn in international politics, to have been in a strange country with no safety net and no real friends, where no one would have cared if she'd been thrown into prison, far from home and the people who loved her. No, she would report back to Max then break the news to him. That she wanted to find a normal job, live a humdrum life and not seek adventure anymore. She was fed up with lies and pretence, with watching her back. She ate another square of milk chocolate with contentment, leaned back in her seat, closed her eyes and slept.

Seventeen

The following morning Minnie spoke to Harry Pollitt on the telephone to tell him she was home and promised to meet him the next afternoon. In the meantime, her meeting at Max's flat did not go as expected.

On the one hand it exceeded her hopes, because Max was delighted with her.

'All this about Glading,' Max said, looking up from her handwritten notes, a gleam in his eyes. 'There's solid evidence here that he's taking orders from abroad.'

'From the Comintern, you mean, or India?'

'Russia. You've given me the names and descriptions of Glading's contacts, the serial numbers of the American bank notes, the address of your meeting place in France. The very fact that he was in Paris with you and changed the money is enough to give us reason for further investigations.'

Further investigations! Minnie felt exhausted all over again. She had hoped that the evidence from her trip would have enabled some sort of line to be drawn under

Glading's activities and it would be the moment for her to stand down.

'Is there not enough to arrest him?'

'Not yet, no.'

'Listen,' she said, drawing a deep breath. 'I don't think I can go on. It was awful out there, you can't imagine how it felt. I was so ill and frightened and ... and alone. I could never do it again. Ever.'

'We're immensely grateful to you. *I* am immensely grateful. But let's discuss the matter after you've had a rest. One question, when you were with Glading in Paris, did he talk about having visited Russia again?'

'No,' she sighed, but she remembered Glading's 'holiday in Bournemouth'. 'There wasn't the opening.'

'Never mind. We now have other information to suggest that he has, so you must be even more careful in his company. If he suspects you, I've said before, he and his sort will not be forgiving. The Soviet regime can be brutal. They "liquidate" people they regard as traitors – the word is theirs, not mine.' He went on to describe how there was a new brand of activist being trained in Russia to have absolute loyalty to the Soviet Union. The Comintern were losing faith in regime change via the ballot box. Instead they were discussing secret subversive activities in Britain and elsewhere to prepare for revolution.

Minnie gazed at him dumbfounded. She'd spent the night alone with Glading. He'd been kind, she liked him, but here was Max, whom she had trusted absolutely, revealing that the man was an extremely dangerous revolutionary and that even back in dear old England her life might be in peril!

She twisted her hands in her lap, then lifted her head, intending to tell him again that she could not go on. But Max had risen from his chair and begun to pace the room, deep in thought. Finally he turned to her, his face bright and determined. 'Yes, we must move on to the next stage now. You have achieved much and now you have the trust of Pollitt and Glading. Who knows what they will let slip in your presence or what tasks they may give you?'

'You're not listening. I don't think I can go through with it.'

He was swift to sit down beside her again, to take her hands in his and to reassure. 'Of course, poor Minnie, you're exhausted. You need rest. They'll give you a few days off, surely . . .'

'A few days? Is that all you think it would take? Max, surely you can see what this mission has done to me.'

'Longer then, if you need time to recover.'

She sighed.

'The fact is that you're in a prime position. If they sense you're less keen that might endanger our whole operation. I believe we're not far off obtaining really important information. We need evidence of actual espionage. What might Glading be plotting? Who might be helping him, that sort of thing.'

She returned home and slept for the rest of the day. The next afternoon she met Pollitt and Glading in a café in Holborn to report on her meeting with Popat and what she'd witnessed of police violence. Pollitt was full of questions and appeared as puzzled as Minnie was about her unnecessarily delayed return, but he praised her resourcefulness and gave every impression that he was fully satisfied with her conduct. Of course she should have a few days' holiday before returning to work. She'd earned it.

The successful outcome of this meeting gave Minnie much to think about. What if she did resign from her spying activities? Would she leave not with relief but with a sense of disappointment, that she'd left something important unfulfilled? She imagined how life would be: an ordinary typist's job, playing for her sports team, maybe returning to Edgbaston. What had seemed on the boat back to England to be cosy and safe now sounded plain dull. And she'd no longer sit in the ramshackle flat in Sloane Street or wait in the gloom of a cinema auditorium and enjoy her conversations with Max. Maybe she should continue for a while at least. She could always leave if things became stressful again.

Over the following few days, though, all her doubts swarmed back in. She still felt drained and her appetite had not fully returned. The effort required to resume her office duties the following week simply could not be found and she had to telephone to say that she was sick. She could not sleep and instead lay awake rigid with anxiety, forced to relive the traumatic weeks of her stay in Bombay and to brood on Max's latest warning. Any noise brought her instantly to full wakefulness. She began to feel desperate.

In the end she came to an agreement with Max. She would resign from her job with the League Against Imperialism and the Anti-War Movement, but she promised him that she would stay in touch with Glading and Pollitt who regarded her as a good comrade. It would be a difficult balancing act, but she hoped it would satisfy everyone, including herself. She would still be a spy and she would still see Max, but she had to think of her health.

My life is my own again, Minnie reflected several weeks later. She drew back the sitting room curtains in her London flat and stood for a moment with eyes closed, basking in the morning sunlight. She couldn't remember when she'd last felt so content.

After handing in her notice, she'd decided to temp for a while and was enjoying the anonymity of working a week here and a few days somewhere else. There was no need to pretend anything and few people were interested enough in a temp to ask personal questions. She simply had to be pleasant, efficient and keep herself to herself. That didn't mean, however, quelling her powers of observation and she found she often saw things that others missed. In her latest job, behind the scenes at Selfridges, she noticed how one of the unmarried typists developed the same pale and fragile look that Minnie's sister Marjorie had when she was expecting. When she found the girl in tears one day she made her a cup of sweet tea and discreetly finished her work for her. The downside of being a temp was that she remained isolated because she could never take part in office gossip or share confidences. Her undercover work, however, had made her used to this.

Something that distressed her was that she hardly saw Max; she supposed this was to be expected, but she'd come to believe that they were close friends. She'd shared so much of herself with him. Now theirs would be the occasional rushed rendezvous in a secluded corner of a hotel bar, or an art gallery. If she'd been to an FSU meeting or had lunch with Glading she'd tell Max anything that she thought useful, but this didn't amount to very much.

In those early weeks, waking up in the peace of her flat Minnie was happy, but as the months went by she began to wonder, was this enough for her? Was this selfish, pleasurable London life all she was worth? There came a time when she realized that the answer was no.

Eighteen

Autumn 1934

One afternoon in November Minnie walked to the local library to change her books. Inspecting the titles on the 'new publications' shelf, she saw a book called *Crime Cargo*. A bolt of shock passed through her. The author's name on the spine was Maxwell Knight. She picked it out, knowing it had to be Max. It was a detective thriller about a kidnapping on a cruise ship, his debut the flap copy informed her. Minnie flicked through the opening pages and wasn't impressed. Still, she borrowed it and read it quickly at a sitting, though her first reaction was confirmed. The writing style was clichéd as though an enthusiastic schoolboy had written it. On the positive side she admired his knowledge of American slang.

When she'd finished, she turned the pages again, wondering how much the book revealed about its author. Max's wry sense of humour was much on display, but she was more interested by his fictional hero, who was courageous, dogged and, above all, loyal. These were attributes that Max valued in her, but presumably aspired to himself and now she felt she knew a little more about his inner life. Or did she? Max was a writer and he'd never mentioned it; he was a man of many parts and she felt disappointed that she knew only one or two of these.

Who was this man who'd become so important to her? When she was with him he gave her his full attention and made her feel special. Now she was reminded that he had a whole other life – or other lives – that didn't involve her. There was the mystery of his relationship with his wife, his friendship with an American jazz musician, his one-time acquaintance with British fascists – and now this book. It struck her, as she put it aside, how neatly he had underpinned her cover story. She really had been working for an author with unpredictable hours.

Christmas 1934 came and went enjoyably enough at home in Edgbaston with her mother and Richard and Doug, both of her sisters being married now and with arrangements of their own. When would she settle down, her mother's friends asked after the morning church service, but with false brightness. Minnie had recently turned twenty-eight, and was in danger of 'missing her chance', as her mother put it. Sometimes she worried about it herself, especially when she felt lonely and isolated. But she had watched Joan and Marjorie with their husbands, how they did so little without recourse to male opinion, the way they gave up their jobs to tend their houses and she believed she had the better option. The man of the romantic fiction she'd read, the one for whom she'd give up everything, had never turned up.

'I suppose it's not always the way of things,' her mother sighed as she glanced at her husband's faded photograph on the piano, more upright and distinguished in his officer's uniform than Minnie remembered him in life. 'Your father and I, well, we were friends long before we realized that we loved one another. Our families approved and getting married seemed the right thing to do. There was no great passion about it. I do feel your generation expects too much. These silly films have a lot to answer for.'

She'd not heard her mother speak so openly about her own marriage before. It was an honesty that came with age, perhaps. Mrs Gray had been a widow for nearly twenty years and if she wasn't a merry one no one could say that she hadn't made the best of a bad job. Given that her mother had made her own decisions for so long, Minnie thought it a bit much of her to criticize her daughter for her independent spirit.

Minnie enjoyed spending the brief time with her brothers. Doug, the youngest Gray, had left school now. A friendly, nice-looking lad, he'd started work as a trainee bank clerk in an Edgbaston branch. And Richard, tall and broad-shouldered with cropped, curly brown hair and a direct blue-eyed gaze, had gained a pleasing air of confidence. He was full of stories about life policing his London 'manor' and hopeful of early promotion. Minnie felt proud of them both, while envying the easy expectation that as men they might follow a proper career.

Someone else who was following a proper career was

Raymond, whom she came across at a Conservative New Year's party. There was no sign of Ida or whatever her name was. 'I've applied for a position in London,' he told her. 'It's a big step for me, but there are no openings here, or at least, not one that's right for me.'

'I hope you're lucky,' she told him. He appeared more certain of himself these days and as friendly as ever, and she felt a little sad when they said goodbye.

Nineteen

February 1935

Minnie was washing up after supper in her kitchen one winter's evening when the telephone rang. She dried her hands, then answered with a cheerful 'Hello', thinking it was her mother, who often called around this time.

'Is that Minnie?'

A man's voice, familiar, with a northern accent. 'It is,' she said cautiously.

'Harry Pollitt here.'

'Mr Pollitt!' A prickle of anxiety. 'What a surprise.' It was months since they'd spoken.

He chatted affably, asking how she was, and said that Glading had suggested her name to him. Would she mind calling in to Party HQ later in the week? There was something about his tone that suggested this was a summons, not a request. Warily, she agreed to see him in her lunch hour the following day.

After she'd replaced the receiver she paced the room for a while, gnawing at a fingernail and thinking furiously. Then she went to the telephone again. No one answered at the Sloane Street flat and she returned to the kitchen sink feeling distinctly uneasy. And yet her curiosity was once again piqued.

The best thing about the offices of the Communist Party in King Street, Covent Garden, Minnie always thought, was that they were central, in the heart of theatre land and only a short walk from the National Gallery in Trafalgar Square. She opened the door into the small waiting room that was decorated with posters about meetings and rallies, gave her name to the receptionist, then leafed through the *Daily Worker* while she waited to be called.

'Mr Pollitt's ready to see you now.'

Inside, the main office appeared deserted apart from a young man with oiled-back hair who sat behind an untidy desk. He wore a woollen scarf and could only nod at Minnie, as he ate a pork pie from a paper bag with little regard for crumbs.

'Miss Gray!' Now she saw, silhouetted against the pale light from the window, the solid, tweed-suited figure of Harry Pollitt himself. He was rooting half-heartedly through a heap of paper but quickly abandoned his task to come and shake her hand in his enthusiastic, friendly fashion. 'Everything's such a mess. My assistant has left and I can't find a thing. Hang your coat up there, that's it.'

He showed her into his office and shut the door. Minnie sat

on an uncomfortable wooden chair and waited while he settled himself behind his desk, which was decked with files. A
stern photograph of Lenin frowned at her from the wall above.

'Miss Gray – Minnie,' Pollitt said, leaning forward. 'To
come straight to the point, I have a great favour to ask. I'd like
you to come and work for me here.'

She was stunned. Whatever she'd expected it hadn't been
this and her spontaneous reaction was defensive.

'You know I can't . . .'

He stayed her with a raised finger. 'Let me explain. I don't
simply want someone to type letters and deal with this bumf.
I need a proper secretary like the capitalist bosses have.' He
chuckled at his own joke. 'You're the only woman I've come
across with the right abilities and whom I can trust. Glading
agrees with me. Minnie, it has to be you.'

He gave her an appealing look and she drew a tight
breath. She could not deny that it sounded an intriguing
role. And Max . . . a sense of thrill passed through her. He'd
be beside himself with excitement. She knitted her fingers as
she prepared her answer. Time to think about it, that's what
she needed. And to speak to Max. 'I'd like to, Harry, I really
would, but those weeks in India finished me.'

'I know. We hadn't foreseen the difficulties there, and I'm
sorry. It must have been a trying experience, but it was a
great achievement. And you're better now, aren't you? You
look very well, if you don't mind me saying. Bit o' pink in
your cheeks.'

'Flatterer. I suppose I do feel more myself again.' Minnie
was secretly pleased at his concern.

They talked some more about the nature of the job. It would be full time, Pollitt warned her, and busy. She promised to think about it over the next few days and to telephone him with her decision.

She walked out into the busy street so caught up in thought that she hardly noticed the freezing sleet on her face. This, she knew, was one of the big decisions in her life. She had always liked Pollitt. She might not agree with his views, but he was a warm person and she respected his sincerity. It was well known that his beloved working-class mother and her struggles to feed the family had been his great inspiration. He'd be a kind employer.

She must contact Max. Though she guessed already what his reaction would be. She'd be inside what he called 'the Kremlin', the heart of the British Communist Party itself, working for its General Secretary! The offer was a terrific mark of success for her and she was delighted about that. Still, something stayed her. It made her heart beat in panic and the palms of her hands clammy. It was fear. Fear of the enormity of the task, fear of the pressure on her that everything could go wrong.

She telephoned Max from a call box in Trafalgar Square and was thankful that this time he picked up straight away. 'Something important has come up,' she told him. A shadow fell across her hand and she glanced round. A man was waiting impatiently outside. She shielded her mouth as she whispered into the phone, 'I need to meet you after work.'

'I'll be here.'

She caught the warmth in his voice and felt limp with relief.

*

Max's reaction when she told him was as she'd predicted. 'Good Lord, Minnie.' He half rose from his chair, causing Bobby to leap up quivering. 'You must say yes.'

'You know what you're asking,' she said. She was standing with her back to the fire, feeling shivery. 'It's too much for me, all the pretending.'

'But it's the opportunity we've both worked for, surely you see that. His secretary, Minnie, think about it.'

She folded her arms, hugging herself, and said miserably, 'I *am* thinking, that's just it.'

'If you want to know everything about a man's work you ask his secretary. And that would be you. He's the most senior-ranking Communist in Britain, Minnie. Imagine what we'd find out.'

'Yes, yes, but at what cost to me? It's all very well, but it's good old Minnie Gray who takes the risks.' She hated the whine in her voice.

'I'll be here to support you. Minnie, think how you'll be serving your country.' The way Max looked at her, pleading with her, the persuasive tone of his voice, these were difficult to resist. She would meet him regularly again and enjoy his friendship.

Minnie sat down, arms folded, and stared dully into the fire. Tears threatened but she blinked them back. 'Ouch.' Sharp claws dug into her knee. Max's little dog. She put out her hand and he bounded into her lap and lay down. He'd never done such a thing before and she stroked his oily hair, comforted by his warmth.

'Minnie,' Max said gently, 'you shouldn't decide right away, but I urge you to think seriously about this offer. All the work you've done for us to earn these people's trust. You can't give up now.'

'Us,' she echoed. Us, she supposed, was not just the two of them, it was the secret service, M-section. Just who were these people? She only knew Max, unless she counted the series of well-bred girls at MI5's office who fielded calls and passed on messages. She sometimes wondered if anyone else there had ever heard of her existence and if they had, whether they were the slightest bit interested in her. Max had often told her that in this business agents and staff were only told what they needed to know. It was more secure that way.

She helped the dog onto the floor and stood up slowly, heavy-limbed, brushing hairs off her skirt. 'You know I want to help, but . . .'

It was his belief in her that buoyed her up during the sleepless night that followed. She'd be working for her country, that's what she told herself. She was being offered the chance of a lifetime, the opportunity to uncover secrets that no one else had cracked. *Why can't you do anything right?* Her father's words rasped in her head. They were followed by Max's: *You can do it, believe me.* Max needed her. He'd begged her. She'd be important to him again and he'd promised to support her.

In the end what decided her was the awareness that if she turned down this challenge she might regret it for ever.

Twenty

Minnie folded the sheet of paper into a narrow wad, which she tucked under the hem of the heavy greatcoat where she'd unpicked the stitches. Then she threaded a bodkin and began to sew, stopping every couple of stitches to check they were as neat and exactly spaced as the others. All this time the coat's owner, a burly young Russian seaman, was sprawled on a chair, watching her with brooding eyes under black brows.

'That should do it,' she said. She examined her work then bit off the thread and passed the coat over to him.

The man felt the hem, nodded, then rose, shrugging on the coat, and buttoned it. 'Thank you,' he said in accented English and swung his kitbag onto his shoulder. 'Goodbye.'

'*Bon voyage.*' After he'd gone Minnie dropped the sewing kit into her drawer, exultant. She had gained first-hand experience of a secret method of communication. Pollitt had briefed her. The report she'd sewn into the coat would be smuggled to the Soviet Union and passed to an agent of the Comintern. The information it contained, she understood, was routine rather than treasonous – minutes of a meeting – but it was solid proof that Pollitt had covert lines of communication with Moscow. Max, Minnie knew, would be eager to hear about it.

She'd worked at the King Street offices for a month now and found the work harder than anything she'd done before. It was the sheer amount of it, though she shouldn't have been surprised, knowing something already about the bureaucratic nature of the Party. Thankfully, Pollitt was efficient, with a reputation for running his diary 'sharp on time', but he had a huge weight of correspondence and a relentless schedule of meetings, including editorial meetings for the *Daily Worker*, that involved masses of paperwork.

The fact that there were often key British Communists in the meeting rooms delighted Max. Minnie was able to supply him with detailed information about people's behaviour, their opinions, their comings and goings and the names of several of their Russian contacts. Typing Pollitt's letters was another fruitful task, as was sorting and filing his correspondence. It wasn't long before she was able to create a picture of his activities, not simply the day to day business of the political party, but other more covert aspects that might be considered by MI5 to compromise the security of the nation and require further investigation. Sewing secret messages into the clothing of Russian sailors was the latest.

It was the British Communist Party's reliance on links with the Soviet Union that most intrigued Max. Minnie noticed how in their aims and outlook Pollitt and his colleagues did not consider the interests of the British state. Instead they took their orders from a foreign power, and many Western governments regarded Russia as their biggest enemy.

Minnie had several discussions with Max about differing attitudes to the Soviet Union, but she was confused about where his personal allegiances lay. From the newspapers she knew that many people were anxious about developments in Germany and Italy, where popular leaders of an extreme right-wing disposition were being voted into power. Germany in particular was a worry because of Herr Hitler's expansionist national ambitions. There was talk that his aim was to unpick the terms of the Versailles Treaty, drawn up by the victors in 1919 to punish Germany after the Great War.

Still, it was the Soviet Union, with its desire to spread communist revolution worldwide, that was generally seen as the greater enemy of the West. Until recently, Minnie had gathered that Max had supported this judgement and his comments about British Fascists such as Oswald Mosley and his Blackshirts were dismissive. 'Mosley's simply posturing.'

Recently, in the wake of Blackshirt violence, she'd noticed that his attitude was changing. He never divulged much, but when she asked him directly about whether he was worried about British Fascism he said, 'There's danger from both sides, Communists and Herr Hitler's style of Fascism. That's all I'll say on the matter. Your job is as important to us as ever, please don't doubt that.'

Minnie was seeing Max more frequently these days. Her reports were longer and more regular and many evenings were taken up preparing them. Sometimes she lay awake at night trying to remember supplementary details. All the time, at home or work, she was watchful and wary of being watched. The only times she felt she could be herself were when she was shouting encouragement while chasing a wooden ball across the freezing grass.

Even at home in Edgbaston she could not relax, never being able to give her family a true account of her activities if she was asked.

Once or twice she snapped at her mother, 'I've been doing the usual things. Work, hockey, seeing friends. I don't know why I'm not sleeping well. Don't fuss so.'

'It's only because I worry about you. You are very touchy these days.' There were tears in her mother's eyes at the sharpness and Minnie felt ashamed of herself.

'Well, don't worry. If it makes you happier I'll ask at the chemist for some sleeping pills.'

'It's not about making me happier, Minnie. It's you. You're not yourself since taking this new job.'

Who am I then? Minnie wondered. Working undercover full time, she wasn't sure anymore.

It was early on in the job that she noticed that Pollitt kept a book in a desk drawer that he would occasionally take out and use to cross reference against some fairly harmless-looking note or letter she'd brought to him. He did not explain what he was doing and Minnie pretended not to be interested. It wasn't long before the opportunity arose for her to satisfy her curiosity. The chance came during her lunch hour. Pollitt's office was empty and she pushed the door to and tried the drawer. It was locked, but she quickly found the key in a bowl on the windowsill.

The book was a slim volume written in English. It was a political treatise, an extremely dull one. Minnie turned its pages in puzzlement for a moment before an idea occurred to her. If she balanced the book on its spine it fell open at a certain page. Hearing voices beyond the door she quickly glanced at the page number, shut the book and replaced it. Her fellow workers did not turn a hair when she emerged calmly from the room with a folder of correspondence. Pollitt's efficient new secretary was going about her legitimate business.

'The book is part of a kind of cipher,' she told Max that evening, when they met in a hotel bar, 'but I don't know how it works.'

'We'll obtain a copy and set our codebreakers on it.' Judging by the gleam in his eye she knew she'd stumbled on something important. 'If you notice anything more about this matter, let me know at once, will you?'

'Of course.'

Though the work was arduous, Minnie settled in easily with her fellow workers. Glading was there more and more and his company was enlivening. They sometimes discussed films or plays that they'd seen. Occasionally Rosa, his wife, called in with their little girl and Minnie enjoyed talking to them.

She liked it that her male comrades didn't find anything unusual in conducting proper conversations with women. They didn't belittle her opinions or try to flirt and instead treated her with respect. This she valued, but there were also times when it was hard to look them in the eye. *You think I'm your friend, but I'm not, I'm your betrayer.* Did this mean she was a good or a bad person? She felt it worst with Glading. *Here I am smiling at your daughter, laughing with your wife, but I'd turn you over to the authorities tomorrow if I had to.*

Minnie had been working at the King Street offices for a few months when, arriving one morning, she was greeted with a grin from Duncan, the pork pie-eating clerk she'd first met at her interview. He started to hum a tune, then gaining in confidence, broke into a squeaky tenor voice.

'*Olga Pulloffski, the beautiful spy . . .*' he sang.

Minnie stared at him, sure that her cover was blown. Several others milling around the office burst out laughing. She stared round, scared out of her wits. Duncan sang on and she tried to stay calm. The tune was vaguely familiar. Only this time there was no missing the words.

> *She's Olga Pulloffski, the beautiful spy*
> *The gay continental rapscallion*
> *Some say that she's Russian*
> *And some say she's French*
> *But her accent is gin and Italian*

They know about me, they know. The realization was a torment. She trembled and felt sick. *Don't let them see.* Somehow she recovered herself, licked her dry lips and managed to breathe. Finally, she pulled a piece of paper towards her with unseeing eyes and croaked, 'You'll crack the windows with your caterwauling, you will!'

Pollitt arrived like a cheerful breeze and everyone quietened and returned to their work. For a while Minnie sat terrified, sure that Pollitt would confront her, but everything went on as usual. Just as she was starting to concentrate on a report she was supposed to type, he emerged from his office. 'A word, please, Minnie.'

She froze in terror, then swallowed and forced herself to stand. *Notebook*, she told herself. *Pencil. Act normally.* She entered his office, the blood running cold through her veins.

'Close the door behind you.'

She did as she was bidden and stood, uncertain, but when she raised her eyes and looked at him he smiled.

'What's the matter? Take a seat. It's just some dictation.'

She sat down shakily. 'Sorry, I've a bit of a headache today,' she managed to murmur and was touched when he poured her some water.

The rest of the morning passed without incident.

When she returned from her lunchbreak, though, Duncan looked up from his newspaper and began to croon, '*Olga Pulloffski ...*' This time she ignored him, but as she slit open some letters she gave her attention to the words. The song was about a female spy, a femme fatale who lured men to their fates. She remembered now why the tune was familiar. She'd heard it wending up through the floorboards from Mrs Saunders's wireless.

All day she was on edge and was still shaken by the time she arrived home. She drank two glasses of sherry, one after the other to calm herself, which was a mistake because it made her maudlin. She'd have to tell Max about the song in her report, but it sounded foolish that it had scared her so badly. Nobody had accused her of anything. The worst thing about the whole episode was that it accentuated her sense of isolation. Her colleagues thought the song a huge joke. *I don't belong there. Where do I belong? I have friends, but they don't know me*, she reflected as she scrambled some eggs for her solitary supper; *my family don't know me, not really.*

Shortly after her lonely meal her mother rang and, in the way of mothers, could tell immediately that something was wrong.

'A bad day at work?'

'Just some silly teasing,' Minnie told her, frustrated that she couldn't explain.

'You must give as good you get, darling. Don't let the bullies win.'

After her mother rang off Minnie sat quietly by the gas fire, reflecting sadly that the most important person in her life was no longer her mother, it was Max. She relied on him entirely for her sense of self. Only he knew who she really was. Only he gave her validation for the lies and deceit. The game she was playing was his. She fed off his praise and reassurance, was soothed by his voice, given strength by his encouragement. *But the work I do is important*, she told herself fiercely. *I have to go on.*

She swallowed the first sleeping tablet that night and the following morning stumbled into work in a daze. When she entered, Duncan's ferrety features lit up to see her and he began to sing quietly.

'It was funny the first time and possibly the second,' Minnie snapped, snagging her coat onto a hook. She plumped herself in her chair, blinked tiredly, then ratcheted paper noisily into her typewriter.

'She doesn't like it, comrade,' a young typist told Duncan in a crushing tone and he looked crestfallen.

'All right, keep your hair on.'

For the time being he shut up, but over the next few weeks, if the staff of 16 King Street were in a devilish mood, he might start up the refrain once again. Eventually, Minnie accepted that no one really suspected her of anything. The song, though, was still torture to hear.

In due course a different kind of rumour started to float about, a vicious one which no one spoke out loud in her presence, but which the ever-observant Minnie picked up from people's glances and silences.

It came about because she and Glading formed a habit of taking lunch together occasionally. He first asked her to join him when he wanted some stylistic advice on an article he'd written for the *Daily Worker.*

He took her to the same café that she'd frequented when she'd worked at the Distressed Gentlewomen's charity and she was on tenterhooks the whole time that they would bump into Jenny. Then she'd have to introduce her to Glading and the different parts of her life would collide horribly and who knew what might happen.

While they waited for the tea and fish and chips they'd ordered Minnie read through the typed sheets Glading passed her. As they ate she observed that it read well and after they'd finished she tactfully corrected some of his grammatical shortcomings.

'Thanks, it's as well not to make a fool of myself,' he said, tucking the article away in his pocket. He beamed short-sightedly at her and she smiled back.

'You wouldn't do that,' she said, 'but I'm happy to help.'

'We're lucky to have you,' he said, stuffing a last chip into his mouth. 'But don't you feel it's all a bit much? Pollitt never lets up, does he?'

'I must admit it's a faster pace than I'm used to. Even so, I'm enjoying it. It's nice to be at the centre of things.'

'He's a good man to work for.'

'Everyone seems to like him, don't they?' She poured them both the last of the tea. It felt so natural and friendly to talk to Glading like this, but she knew she must be guarded in her remarks so that he shouldn't think she was digging for information.

'Oh yes, he's well thought of. Exactly the man you want in the job. You know his history, of course?'

'You mean about the family being very poor?'

'Yes. He worships his mother. She was a cotton weaver near Manchester and his father a blacksmith's hammerman. Six children, three of 'em died. Mrs Pollitt worked like stink to keep things going. She's the one who got him interested in politics.'

'Her experience is why there needs to be change,' Minnie said, genuinely moved by this account. What Glading didn't know was that Minnie's views about how to change the world were different to his.

'Which we're working for every day. It's a war, Minnie, that's what it is, and you're a soldier in that war. We'll have you selling the paper at the factory gates one of these days.'

Minnie still refused point-blank to take her turn hawking the *Daily Worker* or canvassing. The thought of doing either absolutely horrified her. She'd be 'making an exhibition of herself', as her mother would say, and she'd never be able to persuade others of an ideology she loathed. 'I'm not that type,' she'd told Glading and Pollitt briskly.

'I'm doing what I do best, in the office,' she said now and gave Glading a challenging look.

He smiled and instead began talking about a comedy he'd seen at the theatre, making her laugh. And then, realizing the time, they split the bill and strolled back to the office. It had been an enjoyable as well as a useful interlude; and when Glading suggested they do it again, Minnie agreed and soon it became a habit.

She understood why some might think she and Glading were having an affair, but didn't allow it to put a brake on their friendship because Max needed her to gain Glading's trust. Gossip didn't bother Minnie much, except she wouldn't like the rumour to reach the ears of his charming wife.

The truth was that she wanted Glading to see her only as a friend. He probably wasn't attracted to her, but just in case, she was careful not to do or say anything to encourage him. It wasn't simply that she would not do anything to hurt his wife Rosa, whom she liked and felt secretly sorry for. She knew that Max would not approve of an affair because it made the job more complicated.

'After a man has his way with a woman he loses interest in her,' was a view he'd expressed more than once about the activities of female spies. Minnie wondered what on earth she'd have done if he'd asked her to seduce Glading. He was not handsome, but there was something attractive about his manner, his charm, intensity and friendliness. Still, she'd like to think that she would have refused.

As the weeks crawled by there came a time when the sleeping tablets no longer worked and Minnie would lie awake until first light then fall into a doze from which her alarm clock dragged her. There were mornings when she surfaced with a sense of desperation, as though she were clinging to a cliff edge with her fingernails. On such mornings on the way to work the roar of the train through the tunnels reminded her of the rain in India beating on the roof and she had to remember to breathe.

There were times at the office, too, when she did not seem able to concentrate. In meetings, her pen would hover over the paper as she tried to record the ebb and flow of some complicated discussion.

Concentrate, Minnie, she'd tell herself, aware that her thoughts had been floating away.

It didn't help that it was a period of change in the Party. The nature of campaigning was shifting. There were still to be the usual membership and fundraising drives, but orders were to move away from hunger marches and workers' demonstrations in favour of members' conferences and petitions. To make sense of everyone's confusion required total concentration.

Minnie found her thoughts returning constantly to the question of who she was and where her loyalties lay. To Max, yes, but she felt little loyalty to MI5, the organization he represented. And what did they know or care about her? Hardly anything, she imagined, beyond sending out her pay cheque.

On the other hand, the flesh and blood Communists she saw every day, with whom she worked and shared jokes and friendship, she was directed to regard as the enemy. She did not agree with their politics, but she badly wanted to belong. All her life she'd wanted to belong, to feel needed, important. *Why can't you be like your brother was?* Where did loyalty to herself, her health and well-being and personal happiness come in? Nobody except her mother worried about that and increasingly Minnie felt cut adrift from her. A dirty stream of dishonesty ran between them, impossible to bridge.

Her meetings with Max became more and more vital to her sanity. Only he understood the pressure of what she was going through. He praised and encouraged her. Lately, he also pushed her to her limit.

'You write about Glading's absences,' he said on one occasion. 'Where do you think he goes?'

'He meets people, but I haven't the faintest idea who they are.'

'Keep your ear to the ground, then. See if he will tell you.'

'Sometimes I worry he suspects me.'

'They're clever, these people. And you have to remember they're under orders to be discreet.'

'He certainly keeps a great deal to himself.'

'Don't ask questions or he'll suspect you.'

Minnie nodded impatiently for he hardly needed to remind her. He too was secretive, she often thought. She wondered if he was still writing novels and whether one day she'd pick one up and read about herself. Would he describe accurately how spying sapped the spirits and left one feeling isolated? She'd never mentioned that she'd read his book in case he asked her what she thought of it and he'd see through a lie.

Sometimes she resented the fact that she was so tied to him. The mere sound of Max's voice on the telephone pleased and soothed her. If she arrived home to a letter from him about a rendezvous it brightened her evening. Was this love, she sometimes wondered? And if so, what kind of love? And how did he feel about her? It was all so confusing.

One day Minnie showed up on time for a rendezvous at the hotel in the Cromwell Road and after an hour passed without Max appearing, she gave up. *I've got the date wrong*, she told herself as she paid for her drink. She was so tired these days that she didn't always pay attention. By the following evening, however, she had still not heard from him. She telephoned his flat. No one answered.

Twenty-one

'He's very ill indeed,' said the young woman who answered the telephone. 'Rushed to hospital yesterday. We understand that it's pneumonia.'

After another day of silence Minnie had rung Max's office from the call box in Trafalgar Square and spoken to the latest snooty secretary.

'Pneumonia? I'm so sorry to hear that.' She'd never known Max to be ill. 'How bad is it?'

'One simply can't be certain.'

'What should I do? About my reports, I mean.'

'I'm waiting for someone to tell me. It's an absolute shambles here.' The secretary sounded put out. 'Look, I don't mean to be rude, but I'm rushed off my feet and ...'

'Yes, of course. I'll wait to hear.'

Minnie hung up and walked slowly back towards King Street, feeling gloomy. Pneumonia, that was serious. A cousin her own age had died of it last year. Poor Max. She wondered who was looking after Bobby and the other animals. His wife, maybe. Her thoughts rushed on. *What if he were to die?* No, she mustn't think about that, she must concentrate on the here and now. Carry on as usual and wait to be told how to proceed. If she hadn't heard from MI5 in a day or two she would telephone again.

The letter from a Miss Roberts arrived the following day. She was a colleague of M's and would be standing in for the time being. Since the weather was clement for May she proposed a lunchtime meeting in a park near Embankment underground station.

Miss Roberts was already waiting on a bench when Minnie showed up. A striking brunette, elegantly dressed, she drew Minnie's searching gaze. Their eyes locked and the woman's perfectly painted lips curved in a polite smile.

'Miss Gray,' Miss Roberts said in a graceful, cultured voice.

Minnie shook hands warily, envious of this woman's thoroughbred poise and style.

'Isn't the blossom delightful? Shall we walk?'

They strolled round the little park, where office workers were eating their sandwiches or sitting on the grass in the May sunshine.

Minnie thought the officer pleasant, if somewhat on the frosty side. 'Do you know how M is?' she asked her anxiously.

'Not good. If his sister hadn't found him and called the ambulance who knows what might have happened.'

'Poor man.'

'Yes, poor old M.'

They were quiet until they found a more secluded area

behind a low wall where there was less likelihood of being observed.

'It's an awful bore for you, but I suppose I must ask how everything is going?'

Here Minnie pulled a manila envelope out of her handbag. 'Nothing very exciting at the moment. Just my latest report. I hope that it's clear enough.'

'I'm sure it will be.' Her companion folded the envelope in half and tucked it into her pocket without inspecting its contents.

Minnie was surprised and not a little hurt by this casual attitude, but supposed that Miss Roberts knew her job. She hoped she would be able to understand the minutiae of Minnie's observations and how they formed part of a bigger picture. Indeed she'd have to trust this to be the case, for now Miss Roberts was putting out her hand.

'Goodbye. I'm very glad to have met you at last. I'll be in touch again shortly.' And she was off, her long legs tripping in high heels towards the station, leaving Minnie to stare after her. Then she walked slowly back to King Street, feeling quite unsettled.

The days and weeks passed and Minnie met up with Miss Roberts several more times, each time giving her a written report on recent events at Party Headquarters in King Street. Once, when rain threatened, they met in the rather smart bar of the Meridian Hotel, but Miss Roberts appeared to prefer the outdoor life, because more often than not she'd arrange to meet in a park or public square, places where there was little chance of private conversation.

All this time, the news about Max was meagre. He was still very poorly and unable to receive visitors.

Once, Miss Roberts remarked, 'What do you think of him?'

'I like him, if that's what you mean.'

The woman regarded her thoughtfully. 'Bit of a dark horse, isn't he?'

'I suppose he is.' Minnie was bemused. That appeared to her a desirable quality in a spymaster.

'He's not everyone's cup of tea, you know.'

'I wouldn't know about that,' Minnie said icily, hating to hear him being run down. 'But we can't all like everybody, can we?'

'Quite,' Miss Roberts said enigmatically and threw away her cigarette.

It was hard working with this woman who seemed to have little empathy. Minnie mourned Max, his warmth and reassurance, his useful suggestions and guidance. Without him to report to she felt lonelier and more lost than ever.

And then something happened that made her question everything.

Twenty-two

Summer 1935

It was a warm Sunday afternoon later in May and Minnie was loitering on Birmingham station for the train back to London when a man's voice behind her spoke her name and she turned.

'Raymond! What are you doing here ... No, that's silly. Catching a train, like me.'

She'd always loved his easy laugh. 'I could be meeting someone off one.'

'Are you?'

'No. I'm living in London now.'

'You got the job you applied for. Mother didn't say.'

'Not the one I told you about. Another. It's quite recent.'

'Congratulations.'

'Thank you. Is Mrs Gray well? And the rest of the family?'

'Everybody's very well indeed, thank you. My brothers are working. Both my sisters are married with children, I expect you know that?'

'Yes. I'm not surprised, they were pretty girls. And you?'

'I'm well too, thanks,' she said, deliberately misunderstanding his question.

'You're not engaged or anything? If you are, my mother has slipped up and not told me.'

'Not since we met at New Year.'

'Me neither. There was that girl, but it didn't work out.'

Minnie was saved from replying by the rumble of the heavy engine surging in, steam whistling, brakes screeching. Raymond held a door open for her to climb on to the train. Oddly for a Sunday, it was nearly full, but they found a less tightly packed compartment. While Raymond swung their bags onto a rack, someone moved up to allow them to sit next to one another. Minnie was acutely aware of the warm firmness of Raymond's thigh against hers.

'You still look just the same,' he whispered in her ear. His breath was scented with peppermint.

'Pish, I bet I don't,' was her automatic reply, but she glanced at him and was pleased by the admiration in his eyes. Her bathroom mirror told her daily that she looked older and more strained. It required particular care to disguise the shadows under her eyes.

Raymond, she thought, had put on a little weight over the years and it suited him. His face was fuller and there were laughter lines at the corners of his eyes, but these merely added to the impression of kindness and enjoyment of life. He was a good-looking man and she was surprised that he hadn't found a girl. Maybe his old diffidence held him back.

They talked easily, all the way to Euston. The new position

was with the Post Office and he had his eye on a managerial job. He lived in Highgate, not a fashionable part, but he liked it. The suburban feel reminded him of Edgbaston. He played cricket for a local side in the summer and had taken to the game.

In turn Minnie trotted out her latest story about her secretarial job for a government department. 'The hours are long, but I like it all the same.' As they talked, in greater depth than they had for years, she remembered everything that she'd loved about him, the steady friendliness, the sense of responsibility towards work and family. She'd missed this easy closeness.

At Euston she was delighted when he suggested that they should meet again.

'I'd like that. Here.' She scribbled her telephone number on the back of a receipt.

For the first time in months she passed the Sunday bus journey home with optimism instead of dread of the week ahead. Raymond might not be exciting, but she liked him very much and was heartily tired of excitement – at least of the kind she endured while working for Max. She yearned for more soothing company.

When the telephone rang later, she promptly answered it, half hoping that it was Raymond. Instead, she was surprised and relieved to hear Max's voice, very weak.

'I've been awfully worried,' she breathed.

'Sweet of you to send me that card.'

'How are you?'

'On the mend.' He brushed away further enquiries about his health. 'More importantly I want to know about *you*.

Would you come to see me? I'm home now, but the blasted doctor won't sign me off for work. I had a rather pretty nurse to look after me for a while, but now there's only my sister.'

'I'm sure that cheered you up,' she said, having heard him complain about her bossiness before. And where was his wife, she wondered.

He laughed. 'How about tomorrow? Ethel will be here, but we can send her off to feed the menagerie or something so that I can give you my full attention.'

When Minnie arrived at the flat in Sloane Street after work the following evening a youngish woman with a sharp face and a look of Max admitted her. 'I know who you are,' Ethel said, 'and I disapprove. My brother is still extremely unwell.'

'I completely understand, but popping round now was his idea. I promise I won't stay long.'

Minnie was shown into a dimly lit bedroom, which was at the back of the apartment and imposingly furnished with dark mahogany. Here Max lay propped up on pillows in the double bed, with Bobby curled up at his side and a heap of paperwork strewn across the eiderdown. A jumble of books and newspapers lay on the floor.

'Minnie,' he said, giving her a faint smile, 'Excuse the mess.' Max looked thin and his voice rasped more than it had on the telephone. 'Ah, grapes,' he said, inspecting the contents of the bag she gave him. 'Very nice. Kind on the old throat. Now, as you can see,' he said, gesturing to the paperwork, 'I'm trying to catch up on what I've missed. Pull up that chair, will you?'

Minnie sat gingerly by the bed. 'Are you sure you're not pushing yourself too hard?'

'Have I missed anything terribly important?' he asked her anxiously. His eyes were sunken and had lost their spark and she realized with dismay how ill he must have been. 'I haven't made much progress in catching up with all the case notes. It might be easier if you simply talked me through what's been going on.' He stopped to cough and catch his breath. 'What's our friend Mr Glading been up to?'

'Oh, nothing important, or at least I don't think so. He's keeping his cards as close to his chest as ever.'

'We'll just have to bide our time. How are you getting on with that Roberts woman?'

Minnie hesitated. 'She's very professional,' she said finally. 'I have no complaints.' She could hardly say how abandoned she felt. After all, the illness wasn't his fault.

'You don't like her?'

'I didn't say that. It's simply that she isn't you.'

Max looked pleased. 'I'm sorry,' he said huskily. 'It must be a difficult time.'

'Not as difficult as for you, but yes, it has been hard. One feels so alone. But don't worry about me, Max. Concentrate on getting better. That'll perk me up no end.'

He fixed her with his rheumy gaze.

'We'll talk properly when I'm up and about, yes?' He closed his eyes briefly.

'Of course.' He'd obviously had enough, but she must hide her disappointment. As if at some signal, the door opened and an irritable Ethel put her head round. 'Max, you know what the doctor said.'

'Yes, yes. We're finished now, old thing.'

Minnie took up her bag reluctantly and rose. 'I'll wait to hear from you then.'

'That would be best. Chin up!'

'Isn't that the kind of thing I'm supposed to say to you?'

As Ethel let Minnie out she said crossly, 'It's very wrong of his office to send people round. Tell them, will you?'

She shut the door rudely on Minnie without waiting for an answer. Minnie stood angry and dejected on the step then said, '*Tell them yourself,*' as loudly as she dared to the closed door.

Feeling not in the least bit triumphant she went on her way. She'd had such hopes of their meeting. That her relationship with Max would be restored to how it had been before, that he would be warm and reassuring. That the deep reservoir of dread which had banked up in her during his illness might be released, that she might explain how difficult she found her situation. Instead her confession had been stymied by pity for the wasted figure on the bed and Max's inability to engage. For the moment she'd have to endure, to continue to teeter along her mental tightrope, inch by inch, day by day, and hope for success and her release.

Drops of warm rain began to splash on her face, bringing her back to the quiet of the street, where the last of the shops was lowering its shutters and a portly businessman in a bowler hat was hailing a taxi with his furled newspaper. In the time she'd been inside the summer sky had clouded over, but only now, halfway to the underground, had she noticed.

*

The telephone rang soon after she reached home and when she answered it in a dull voice she cheered up to hear Raymond.

'Is that you, Minnie? Thank God. I lost the paper you wrote your number on.'

'Oh, Raymond! That's not flattering.' By that confession he had encapsulated why she had always found him appealing and exasperating at the same time. An attentive man would not have lost the number of a girl he liked, or if he had would not have admitted to it. Raymond had always been transparently honest. That might not be romantic, but at least she had always been able to trust him.

'I'm sorry. I thought you'd be impressed that I remembered it.'

'I am, I am.' She sighed.

'Actually, it's because your number is the date of my mother's birthday. I noticed that at once.'

'A chap should always remember his mother's birthday,' she said, with a smile in her voice.

'I still know yours,' he said quietly. 'It's the twenty-eighth of November.'

'And that's your father's birthday,' Minnie laughed. 'Come on, you must try harder than that.' She sank into a chair, relaxing, enjoying the old banter. 'Now, yours is next month, isn't it? The thirteenth, is that right?'

'It is, well done, but I've given up having birthdays. Once you're thirty you might as well be dead.'

'Thanks for that. It's on my horizon.'

'I suppose it must be. Sorry. Listen, this isn't why I

telephoned. Minnie, I can't believe we shared that train journey. I ... I've been thinking about it ever since. I wondered if you'd like to go out with me one evening next week. Have supper, maybe, in one of those little places in Soho, and I could look in the paper for what shows are on.'

'That's a wonderful idea. Yes, let's do that. Thursday's not bad for me.'

They bickered briefly about the relative merits of French or Italian food before he rang off. Minnie replaced the receiver feeling much happier than she had for a long time. It would be lovely and comforting seeing her old flame. Raymond was someone she wouldn't have to impress or circle around while they got to know each other. Had he grown in confidence? Yes, she thought he had, and it suited him.

'Oh, blow!' While she was turning bacon under the grill for supper she remembered that she was meant to be seeing Miss Roberts after work on Thursday. Her memory was as bad as Raymond's. She'd jolly well ring to cancel the lovely Miss R. She was fed up with work running her life. The thought of this minor act of rebellion was cheering.

The cosy restaurant in Soho Raymond booked tried hard to persuade its customers that they were in Paris, with bright prints of the Eiffel Tower and Nôtre Dame on the walls and a pervasive pong of sautéed onion. The head waiter sported a magnificent Gallic moustache, which Raymond could hardly take his eyes off as he showed them to their table and pulled out the chairs with a flourish.

'Everything sounds much more exotic in French,'

Raymond said, as he perused his leather-bound menu. It was the kind of place where the English translation of the dishes was provided. '*Escargots*, and I'll have the roast chicken, but it sounds a bit ordinary compared to *poulet* however you say it.'

'*Poulet aux aromates et gratin dauphinoise, monsieur*,' the waiter said. '*C'est delicieux*.'

'We'll both have that then,' Minnie said. 'But I'll have the soup first.'

The waiter brought the bottle of white Burgundy requested, which Raymond tasted, a formal expression on his face. 'Very nice,' he declared. The wine was poured, cutlery arranged just so, a basket of rolls placed between them.

'Bread is very different in Paris,' Minnie said, tearing a piece from her roll. 'Light and more flavoursome.'

'You've been to Paris?'

'Twice, for work,' she said, regretting that'd she'd mentioned the wretched bread. 'Not that I saw much of the city.'

'I've never been abroad.' Raymond sounded wistful. 'London is the furthest that the Post Office has taken me. What *is* this work you do? Paris sounds very glamorous for the civil service.'

'I assure you it's not at all glamorous,' she said, primly. 'Just the usual secretarial chores. My employer had some meetings in Paris and needed someone to look after the paperwork, that's why he took me.'

'Is he married, your boss?'

'Oh, Raymond, don't be silly. There's nothing like that goes on, I assure you.'

He grinned and said sheepishly, 'I wanted to be certain.'

It was at that moment their first courses arrived. Raymond had asked for snails, but now he was faced with the reality of half a dozen of them in their shells he gazed longingly at Minnie's soup. He managed to spike one, but was defeated by the garlic and gulped half a glass of wine to take the taste away.

'Shall we swap?' Minnie changed their plates round then speared a snail, dipped it in sauce and popped it in her mouth. 'Mmm, now we'll both smell like Frenchmen.' She licked her buttery lips, aware of Raymond's admiring expression.

She'd forgotten how endearing he could look. With his honey-coloured hair that still flopped at the front and his large, warm brown eyes, he had an open, friendly appearance, but there was an edge to him, too, that hadn't been there before. Why should she be surprised? They were both older and he would be on his guard, wouldn't he, since it was she who had ended their relationship those four or five years ago. Minnie blushed at the thought of her gauche younger self and busied herself blotting her lips, leaving an imprint on the napkin with her lipstick.

'Like a kiss,' he said, seeing it.

'Oh, don't be soppy.' She laughed.

After their main course arrived, the chicken surprising them by its tastiness, they exchanged more news about their families. Their conversation was hardly earth-shattering, but Minnie was able to relax with him through a haze of good wine. She'd liked his older sister and was pleased to hear that she was happily married with children.

There wasn't time for dessert, so Raymond settled the

bill and they left in a hurry for the Coliseum, where he had bought tickets for a variety performance. They weren't very good seats, it turned out, but apart from a trio of daring Spanish acrobats the show wasn't worth more expensive ones. Minnie liked the closeness of Raymond murmuring in her ear and enjoyed his attentiveness, helping with her jacket, and being bought chocolates and generally made to feel that he cared about her.

'Thank you,' she said afterwards as they made their way through the labyrinth of red-carpeted corridors out to the foyer. 'It's been an absolutely marvellous evening.'

'I'm sorry about the show. All things considered it was pretty grim.' Bathed in a pool of neon light Raymond looked strange, exotic even, but also rather tender and uncertain, and she took pity on him.

'Honestly, I've enjoyed myself.'

Outside, as they walked towards the underground, she said, 'Perhaps ... would you like to come to supper next week? I'm still a perfectly frightful cook, but I expect I can rustle up something straightforward.'

His face lit up. 'I bet it would beat anything my landlady serves up. I've taken to eating out on Thursdays when it's liver. It's like chewing india rubber.'

'Next Thursday, then, and I promise it won't be liver!'

They'd reached the underground now, where she pecked his cheek in farewell. 'Don't forget my address!'

On the train Minnie became fascinated by a young couple who sat comfortably leaning into one another, sharing a book, the girl checking to see if he, the slower reader, had finished before she turned the page. They appeared perfectly content and Minnie felt a stab of envy at their togetherness. She wondered whether there was a book that she and Raymond might both enjoy, but couldn't think what it might be. She'd never seen him reading anything but a newspaper.

Glading and some of the others read a good deal, political books and magazines mostly, and then talked about what they'd read and Minnie found this interesting, though she tended to rely on their opinions rather than bothering to read the books herself.

The couple left the train at the station before hers and she liked the way the man took his girl's arm, but then she saw the cover of the book the girl held and stiffened. It was by Max. What must have been mere coincidence felt like some spectral message: *You cannot escape me.* So anxious did Minnie become that she hardly noticed the train start up again, then almost missed her stop.

The following Thursday Raymond arrived a few minutes early and Minnie saw him from the open window, clutching a bunch of flowers, then glance at his watch before he rang the bell. 'It's not locked,' she called down.

'I think I've upset your downstairs neighbour,' he said, when she let him into the flat. 'She peered round her door and gave me a look like this.' He mimed Mrs Saunders's po-faced expression.

Minnie laughed as she led him into the sitting room. 'Don't worry about her. Whenever a man visits she smells immorality.'

Raymond's face fell and she rushed to add, 'I assure you it's usually my brother Richard or someone to do with work.'

He looked relieved, then said, 'That's a bit rich of the department, isn't it, bothering you at home?'

'It's only messages,' she said vaguely, but this still made him frown so she changed the subject.

'Are those for me?'

He glanced down at the flowers. 'Good Lord, yes,' he said and handed them over. 'I hope they're all right. I'm no good at this sort of thing.'

'I adore carnations. I'll put them in water. Be a darling and pour us a drink while I find something to put these in,' she called as she went. 'Sherry will do for me.'

Supper was indeed straightforward; haddock that she'd bought in her lunch hour and kept cool in the office basement, peas, potatoes and a parsley sauce that had gone lumpy.

'I hope the fish is all right,' she said as she dished up. 'It didn't smell to me, but a cat followed me all the way back from the tube station.'

He tried a mouthful and pronounced it delicious. He even said he liked the parsley sauce. Buoyant with success she piled the empty dishes, then brought out of the larder a bowl containing a dozen precious strawberries drenched in sugar and a tin of biscuits she'd baked the night before. These they consumed in comfortable silence in order to savour every mouthful.

Raymond finished his third biscuit with a sigh of satisfaction. 'Food of the gods. I could become used to your "frightful" cooking.' He looked at her mischievously, one eyebrow raised. Minnie laughed and touched her fingers to her hair.

'You've exhausted my stock of recipes. Unless you count scrambled eggs and beef stew.'

'I love a good stew.'

'Hint taken.'

'Let me help you with the washing up.'

'There's no need for that. I'll leave it to soak.'

She brewed a pot of coffee and they moved into the sitting room where she showed him the latest photographs of her family and they talked easily of the different directions in which life had taken them. Minnie asked encouragingly about his new role at the Post Office and discerned that he worked harder now than he had when she first knew him. He was ambitious, too.

'If I can rise above supervisor then there's no knowing where it would take me. I'd be happy to stay in London or move to another city if that's what they want.' A manager's work was well paid, too, from what he heard. 'I've started a little nest egg,' he said, 'for a deposit on a house when the time comes.'

All the time she sensed that he was laying out his stall. He didn't actually speak of searching for the right woman to share that house with, but he spoke wistfully about his sister's husband and children back in Birmingham and she saw the meaning in his eyes.

'I've been surprised that you haven't met anyone,' he said, switching the conversation.

She was annoyed to find herself blushing, and examined her

nails as she considered her answer. 'I work too hard. I rarely meet anyone. Or if I do, it doesn't seem to lead anywhere.'

He was silent for a moment, then he said quite suddenly and all in a rush, 'Minnie, I don't suppose you'd like to come out with me again sometimes, would you? To cut to the point, maybe we could see ... If we might pick up where we left off. I'm different now, you know. Back then I wasn't sure of myself, didn't know about the world, or girls or anything ...'

He trailed to a halt and looked across at her for help and she experienced a leap of affection. Dear old Raymond. 'I'd like to go out with you,' she said, slowly. 'I think I may have behaved a bit badly to you back then, but I didn't know what I wanted. I thought life should be more exciting than it was. It all seemed to be about settling down and having babies and I didn't want that then. I wanted to do something in the world, something that mattered.'

'And have you?'

'Sort of, but it's been harder than I imagined. I see now that there are many ways to be useful, but still, Raymond, I can't imagine ever being content simply to be a housewife.'

'Can't you?' He looked a bit disconcerted, but then rallied. 'Well, I always say if a husband is happy and the children looked after then there's no reason a wife shouldn't carve out something for herself. As long as it doesn't make him look a fool in front of the other chaps who think he can't afford to support his family. Don't roll your eyes, Min. I don't agree with that way of thinking, but it's just how people are.'

'Do you read, Raymond?' she asked suddenly. 'Books, I mean.'

'Sometimes.' He sounded wary, so she told him about the couple she'd seen on the tube the previous week and how it had made her think about shared interests. They discussed the types of book they'd read, but couldn't come to an agreement about ones they both liked, except for *Little Women*, which Raymond's sister used to read to him when he was small. Raymond's tastes were conventional. He'd left fiction behind after the boys' school stories and action adventures of his teenage years.

'I like books about things that have actually happened, Min. Real-life stories about war and adventure.'

As they'd discussed the reading she enjoyed, Minnie realized how the people she spied on had opened her mind to the world of ideas. She might not agree with those ideas, but they'd been an education of a sort. She no longer chose spy stories in the library; her life had little in common with the glamour and high living that their heroes indulged in. Romance, too, she'd abandoned in favour of more realistic novels.

'I mean stories of ordinary men and women muddling their way in office jobs and dingy lodgings, people who set out with dreams that they end up having to modify. Endings are not always happy, Raymond. Sometimes they involve a compromise . . . Oh, when did I become so cynical?'

'You're not. It's how life is.'

She smiled at his sincere, open face, the dear tuft of hair, thinking what a good man he was, steady in his opinions, uncomplicated. A man she'd be safe with, but happy? Perhaps.

It was half past eight and still light so they went out,

planning to walk in the park, but when they arrived the park-keeper was locking the gates. Instead they wandered the leafy streets and admired the white stucco houses of the rich, turning shades of peach and mauve in the sunset. Raymond glanced shyly at Minnie and tucked her arm in his and for once in a very long time Minnie felt at peace. Darling Raymond. When they said goodbye at the end of her road, he drew her into the privacy of a narrow cut-through and kissed her deeply. They stood quietly together for a minute with their arms round each other, she resting her head on his shoulder, enjoying the sensation of warmth and safety.

The following Saturday, instead of going home to Edgbaston, they borrowed bicycles and took them on the train to cycle in the Hertfordshire lanes. That Sunday afternoon she watched him play cricket, though she turned down a suggestion that she help with the teas. She knew he already looked upon her again as 'his girl', but she wasn't ready for that label and the curious questions that the cricketing wives and fiancées might throw at her. Instead she sat alone in a deckchair behind dark glasses, apparently watching the game, but in actuality gripped by worry at the approach of Monday, a busy day of meetings at King Street. Later, over tea and meat paste sandwiches, she had to pretend to everyone that she'd witnessed Raymond's extraordinary catch behind the wicket that had won the match.

Twenty-three

Minnie's anxiety about Monday drove out all memories of her lovely weekend. She woke early with a throbbing headache, still in the clutches of a frightening dream, and it was a minute or two before she could steel herself to stumble from her bed in search of aspirin.

Her hand shook as she poured tea and she felt too nauseous to eat breakfast. She toyed with the idea of reporting sick, but rejected it. The postponed rendezvous with Miss Roberts was due to take place after work and the day's Party meetings were important ones. She'd be letting everyone down if she went back to bed, the people she was spying on and most of all, Max. She thought about the bizarre nature of these opposing loyalties as she applied an extra layer of powder to disguise her drawn features. The aspirin had dulled the headache and she managed to nibble on a biscuit before leaving home.

Minnie was exhausted by the time she left the office to meet Miss Roberts. The day had been physically and mentally gruelling, and her headache had returned with full force. Several times she'd had to interrupt a meeting to check what had been said, and she hated the way everyone had stared at her as she blurted out an apology.

She met Miss Roberts at six in the noisy anonymity of the Corner House on Shaftesbury Avenue. Having fallen behind with written reports, she recounted her recent observations and picked at a teacake while the woman took notes.

As the meeting drew to a close and Miss Roberts packed away her notebook, Minnie asked, 'Please, do you know how M is?' She had not liked to telephone in case Ethel answered.

'He's still off sick, that's all I know,' the woman answered. She sounded tetchy, as though Minnie had no business to be asking, but Minnie didn't care. Being cut off from Max made everything much worse. Her work had begun to feel pointless.

'Pointless, pointless,' she repeated to the rhythm of the dripping tap as she lay in a hot bath later, feeling sorry for herself. It was Max she wanted, his advice and encouragement, not the cold professionalism of Miss Roberts who listened to everything she had to say and wrote it down but offered nothing, no gratitude or direction in return. She made Minnie feel worthless, nobody.

'They do seem to expect a lot of you,' Raymond said when she was late to meet him after work two days later. Out of breath from hurrying, she slipped into her seat at the table of the hotel bar. 'What was it this time?'

'Oh, a meeting ran over.' This wasn't a lie, but she could

not tell him that the meeting was at the *Daily Worker* or what it was about and when he asked, she brushed his question aside. 'Don't let's talk about it. I'm here now.'

She hated this subterfuge. There was so much of her daily life that she could not share with him. When he let off steam about the difficulties of his working day, she listened and asked questions and wished she could do likewise. He seemed unconvinced one time by her shamefully vague attempts to describe a situation which had caused her boss to send her across town with a confidential letter only for her to find that its recipient had left the country in a hurry. She could hardly tell Raymond that her employer was leader of the British Communist Party and that she suspected the departed was on Special Branch's wanted list.

'I still don't understand what you do all day, Minnie.'

'Some of it is confidential. Please don't keep asking or I'll get into hot water.'

'It sounds most odd to me.'

He became exasperated, too, by her unavailability some evenings. 'You're working again? I hope they pay you well. I must say, it's a bit hard on a chap when he wants to see his girl.'

'It's not long until Saturday, Raymond.'

Several weeks passed and Minnie had still not told her mother that she was seeing Raymond again. She could not have endured her eager expectancy. If the relationship became serious, she assured herself, that would be the time. Mrs Gray still sighed over her eldest daughter's single state, even though she was far from the only young woman they knew who had not found a husband.

Still, she had difficulty persuading her mother that remaining single was not a sign of failure. 'I'm not like my sisters,' she snapped once when her mother brought it up again. 'I like working and being my own person. Can't you see that?'

'But you don't seem very happy to me.'

'It's only because you keep going on about marriage.'

'You'd be a lovely mother, Minnie. It seems such a shame.'

'No, I wouldn't. I'd be bored and frustrated.'

'You don't know that. When your little ones arrive, Mother Nature takes over. Oh, Minnie, if you didn't work so hard I'm sure you'd find someone. You do yourself down so. A nice girl with a good figure like yours shouldn't have any difficulty. And once you get past thirty . . .'

And on she went. Minnie put up with it because she knew her mother had her best interests at heart and to be fair she didn't know about the important work Minnie was doing. If she did she might have been proud of Minnie's vocation. More likely, though, she'd have been horrified. Either way, the issue wouldn't arise, Minnie knew, because she could never tell her.

It was early July, she'd been seeing Raymond for nearly two months and matters were becoming increasingly difficult. Her work was stressful and so was their relationship. He was puzzled and hurt that she could only put aside a small part of her life for him.

'I have to meet someone after work,' she would say or,

'There's a report I have to write up.' Then there was hockey training, which she was loath to give up, and evenings when she was simply too tired or needed to do chores.

At King Street her workload grew. The trouble with being organized and efficient was that people asked her to take on even more and it was hard to say no. She was also becoming increasingly suspicious that Glading was secretly meeting someone of interest to MI5 and needed to keep a close eye on the matter.

The way it had happened was this. She was taking a short cut through Soho one lunchtime when she glimpsed Glading through the window of a restaurant. He was sitting at a table across from a dark-haired man with a monocle and a small pointed beard. Glading was listening to the man intently, an expression of awe on his face. Minnie hurried on by in case he saw her, but managed to glance at the name of the place, The Pavement Dining Rooms. It was one she would never visit, for its exterior was run-down and the clientele solidly male, probably office clerks. Glading did not return to work that day.

The following morning she became convinced that he had seen her, for as soon as she arrived at the office he made a point of engaging her in conversation, telling her enthusiastically about a film he'd seen the previous afternoon. It was a story about a man who was mistaken for a spy and made to flee. She listened with growing unease. There must be some reason he was telling her this. Was he warning her that he suspected her of subterfuge? His face showed only amusement as he recounted the plot, but she was left shaken.

When the day proceeded as usual she calmed down. *You're getting paranoid,* she scolded herself and remembered when her colleagues had sung that awful song. That hadn't meant anything either. Perhaps Glading was simply being friendly.

That evening, Minnie typed her report on the last couple of days' events, making sure to describe Glading's companion as accurately as she could – '*The dead spit of Lenin'.* Just as she was checking her work Raymond telephoned.

'I can't, Raymond,' she said, when he asked her to meet him and another couple the following evening for dinner.

'I wish you would.'

'So do I but I have a meeting after work.' She was due to see Miss Roberts.

'What time will it finish? Can't you come along afterwards?'

'Yes, I suppose so. I don't know what's wrong with me at the moment. I'm dog tired.'

'You're working too hard,' he said, disgruntled.

'I'm not sleeping very well.' This was true. Lately she'd found it difficult to drop off, then she'd wake in the night and lie there for hours.

'That's because you're overwrought.'

After they'd made the dinner arrangement he rang off and she wandered the flat, tidying up as she went, unable to settle to anything.

Finally, she sat down at the console table that she used as a desk, drew a pad of writing paper towards her and wrote a letter to Max.

'*I apologize for disturbing your convalescence, but I have come to a decision and must notify you immediately. I'm unable to continue* this work ... I find it burdensome beyond measure ... cannot be myself ... terrified of being discovered.' Her deepest feelings poured onto the page. Finally she wrote about Raymond, though she did not mention him by name.

'There's a man I've met. The one I spoke to you about in our first interview. He and I were once close and I think that we could be again. I cannot tell yet if this relationship will lead to anything, but I'd like to see if it does. You will appreciate how difficult it is for me. My time is taken up by this work. I'm unable to divulge to him the reasons for my unavailability or to be truly honest with him about myself ... I beg you to consider releasing me from our arrangement.'

She did not sleep well, worrying that it was overemotional. Despite her doubts, she pushed the letter into the postbox on the way to work the next morning. Expecting a sense of relief at her decision, she felt only disappointment in herself and dread. She ought to feel happy, she told herself, thinking of Raymond and second chances. Why, instead, did she feel she'd failed?

Raymond's friends, a colleague and his wife, were very sweet, but they were newly married and the woman hung onto her husband's words at dinner in a way that Minnie found cloying. If Raymond had arranged the outing in order to persuade her into marriage he hadn't succeeded. Afterwards, she said goodbye to him rather perfunctorily, then felt guilty and wrote him a note of apology. 'My dear Raymond, I'm so sorry ... I was so tired ...' In bed she fell asleep at once, but woke at two and after that she tossed and turned until dawn, worrying what Max would think of her letter. At six o'clock she gave up on sleep and made herself a cup of tea, which she drank in bed, bleary-eyed, before dragging herself through her morning routine, all the while wondering how she'd get through the day ahead without falling asleep at her desk.

Minnie no longer visited Birmingham every single weekend, and there was no hockey at this time of year, so she met Raymond in town on Saturday afternoon. It had rained solidly all day and for the sake of something to do, he took her to a tea dance at a hotel near Bond Street. A waitress brought plates of beautifully arranged food on paper doilies to the table. Raymond wolfed sandwiches as they watched the other couples dancing, but Minnie picked pink icing off a Chelsea bun and wondered why she still hadn't received an answer from Max.

The music was the kind Max liked and the saxophonist had a similar build to his friend Crickett Smith, which in turn brought back memories of her Indian ordeal. Raymond, too, seemed wrapped up in his own thoughts, because he hardly spoke. Was this what they'd come to already? Nothing to say to one another, a silence that could hardly be called comfortable.

'I was thinking of going home to Birmingham tomorrow,' he said finally, choosing an éclair that oozed cream. 'Perhaps you'd like to come with me.'

'I told Mother I wouldn't. I'm absolutely shattered.'

'It would do you good, then. I asked my mother whether I might bring someone to tea.' He gave his sheepish smile. 'They've always liked you, Minnie.'

'I'd like to. Just not tomorrow.'

'Righto. I'm sorry that you're tired.'

He couldn't help letting a note of impatience creep into his voice. *Oh, blow, I've hurt his feelings.* 'I'm sorry, too,' she added, reaching to touch his hand. 'I'd love to meet your family again, really. I was fond of your mother. It's ... I suppose I don't feel ready. We've not been seeing one another very long, have we, and I don't want to give your parents ... well, false hope.'

Raymond put down his sandwich and scanned her face with anxious eyes. 'I can understand that. It's simply ... I didn't know you felt like that. That we weren't going to give things a proper go. I still feel the same way about you, Minnie.'

'I didn't mean it like that. Oh, I don't know what I think about anything. Raymond, life's very difficult for me at the moment.' Minnie bit her lip, then went on. 'You don't understand.'

He stared down at his half-eaten sandwich, then back at her. 'You are a funny girl. I can't tell what you're thinking or feeling a lot of the time.'

'No, nor me myself ...' The band was striking up a tune she recognized. One Max had played her, surely. 'Shall we try a dance? I rather like this tune, whatever it is.'

They joined the half dozen rotating couples in the gentle blues song, then a lively ragtime hop, but when that faded and the band struck up the next number, Minnie froze in horror. She clapped her hands over her ears and hurried from the floor.

'Minnie, what's wrong?' Raymond said, following her to

their table. She reached for her wrap and her umbrella and turned to him. 'I have to go, Raymond. I . . . I don't feel well.'

'Why don't you sit down? You haven't eaten much.'

'No, it's not that. I must go. Please . . . a taxi . . . I must go home.' She was beginning to gabble and the room was going round. The dancers spun. The music played on, louder and louder. No words were sung, but she didn't need reminding, she knew what they were and they clanged in her head: *Shame on you, shame on you / Oh fie fie! / Olga Pulloffski, you beautiful spy.*

Outside, Raymond flagged down a taxi and took Minnie home, where he poured her a brandy, then sat and soothed her as she sipped it, the glass clinking against her teeth. 'There, there,' he said desperately. 'What's wrong?'

She shook her head.

'I could telephone for a doctor.'

'No, don't.' The warmth of the brandy coursed through her veins, and with a tremendous effort she managed to calm herself.

'Look, is there anything I can do to help?'

'Nothing, Raymond, thank you, you're so kind. I'm better now, honestly. It must be exhaustion.' She put down the glass and stood up. 'I'll go and lie down, sleep it off.'

'What about a bite to eat? Some toast, perhaps. I could manage that if you show me how the grill works.'

Minnie shook her head tiredly, wanting him to go so that she didn't have to hold herself together anymore. But he wouldn't.

'I don't like to see you like this.' He rose and came and put his arms round her and kissed her face. 'Can't you tell me what's wrong?'

'I ... It's silly really. The pressure of work. It's all been building up and then that song set me off.'

'I can't remember what it was.'

'It doesn't matter. Oh, I'm not making sense, Raymond, I really *must* go to bed. I just need to get to sleep, then I'll be right as rain.'

Tucking the bedclothes round her he sat on the bed, holding her hand and watching her with a worried expression on his face.

'You don't need to stay, honestly,' she said, yawning. 'I'll be all right.'

Still he didn't take the hint. 'Why don't you get the train home with me tomorrow? Your mother can look after you then. Surely you can take a few days off?'

She considered this and rejected it. Her mother would ask questions. There would be a fuss. 'No. I could do with having a quiet day to myself.'

'If you're sure.' Raymond smoothed the bedclothes where he'd sat and said, 'It's difficult if you won't let me help you.'

He looked so forlorn that she pushed her hand into his. 'Raymond, you've been a great help already. I'll manage.' *I always manage.* Her eyes began to flutter, then they flew open again as a thought occurred to her. 'Raymond,' she said urgently. 'Don't try to speak to my mother about this, will you? I don't want to upset her.'

The indecision in his expression told her that he had been considering contacting Mrs Gray.

'Raymond. Promise you won't?'

'If you're ill, Minnie . . .'

'I'm not ill.'

'I'll stay here if you like.'

'No. Darling Raymond.' She pulled him to her for a kiss, then turned onto her side and closed her eyes, but only when she heard him quietly withdraw and the click of the flat door shutting did she begin to relax.

But then a thought occurred to her and she groaned. After a moment she summoned the energy to push back the bed-clothes, shuffle out to the hall and slide the bolt across the door. Feeling safer, she went back to bed.

At first light a brief rumbling sound woke her and for a long moment she lay tense, wondering what it was. It came again and now rain began to patter against the glass and she real-ized that the rumbling was thunder. Relieved, Minnie closed her eyes and sank into sleep once more. When she woke next the storm had moved on and the only sounds were someone whistling in the street and the ticking of her clock. It was after nine. She sat up, surprised. She never slept this late.

All of Sunday she stayed inside, snuggled in bed, eating scraps from the pantry. With the rain pouring down and the front door locked she felt safe and the sound of Mrs Saunders's wireless turned up loud downstairs was reassur-ing. The ability to concentrate eluded her, though. She tried to read a novel, but didn't remember what she'd read. Instead, that sense came to her again of clinging on to a cliff face with her fingernails and dread washed over her in waves so that she had to remember to breathe. Sometimes she sank into a fretful doze.

She was woken late in the afternoon by the ringing telephone and staggered out to answer it, thinking it would be Raymond. But no, it was Clara Jameson from the hockey club wanting to discuss teams for the autumn. Minnie listened to Clara chat away for a minute or two, and did her best to make sensible interjections.

'Are you all right, Minnie?' Clara asked. 'You sound very faint.'

'I'm all right. Go on, you were saying about the away matches.'

She felt better talking about ordinary things and after Clara rang off she went to the window and saw that the clouds had cleared. Her dark mood had, too, so that she was able to think and make plans again. Raymond was right. A day off from the office would do her good. She'd ring in sick tomorrow. Perhaps next weekend she'd go home to her mother to be spoiled.

It was later, while she was washing her hair, that the telephone rang again. *It must be Raymond this time.* She wound a towel quickly around her head and went to answer it.

'Hello, Minnie.' Not Raymond then. It was Max. *At last.* His voice was strong, full of life. 'I've been away for a while. Only just arrived back and seen your letter.'

'Oh.' So that was it. She sat down. 'Where have you been, somewhere nice?'

He sidestepped the question. 'I must apologize. All those weeks of silence. I've let you down.'

'You've been ill, it's hardly your fault.'

'No, I blame myself. Will you ever forgive me? I didn't realize that you felt as badly as this ... what you say here in the letter ... that you can't bear it anymore. If only I'd been here to help you you'd never have got yourself into this dreadful state.'

'Your illness hasn't helped, but it's not the only—'

'I'm returning to my desk tomorrow. Not a moment too soon. We must meet, Minnie. May I come round right away, this evening?'

'No. No, you can't ...' She was incensed that it was all about him. And she wasn't ready. The flat was a mess, she was a mess. Suddenly she felt so weak she was frightened she might cry.

'Tomorrow, then?'

'Yes, maybe.' She didn't want to tell him that she planned to miss work. 'In the evening.'

'Come here then. Six o'clock. We've much to talk about. And *don't worry*, Minnie, we'll sort everything out.'

When she replaced the receiver she sat for a moment with her face in her hands. He hadn't listened to her, he didn't care. He'd ignored the content of her letter and instead had spoken about himself. This did not augur well.

As she finished washing her hair a deep-seated sense of duty reasserted itself. She'd have to go to work the next day after all. It was the only way she would be able to hold herself together before doing battle with Max. She'd feel on the wrong foot if she had to start by confessing to him that she'd missed a day's work.

When the telephone rang again at eight o'clock she was sewing a button onto a blouse for the morning. It was Raymond, back in London. She assured him that she felt much better and they agreed to meet one evening later in the week.

'We'll go somewhere special,' he told her. 'My girl deserves a treat.'

'That's so sweet of you. I must be an awful disappointment.'

'You're not, darling, but you must let me take care of you.'

You've no idea, have you, poor dear Raymond?

All she said was, 'I'm not usually this pathetic. I'll be all right, you know.'

She hoped with all her heart that this was the truth. Max or Raymond, that is what it was coming to. Both of them wanted her, but in different ways. It was becoming clear that she couldn't have both.

Twenty-four

Max looked much better than when Minnie had last seen him. Sipping sherry in his small sitting room, he listened without interjection as she explained why she wanted to return to ordinary life.

'I feel so alone, unable to speak honestly with anyone except you.' She described what it was like to feel cut off from him during his illness, how she'd disliked Miss Roberts's bloodless professionalism. When she glanced at him, he smiled but said nothing, and she wondered whether he secretly agreed with her about his colleague.

'The work for Pollitt is relentless, there's too much of it. And I have this feeling they know who I really am, and any moment I'll be frogmarched into his office, or something worse, thrown out onto the street. You know, sometimes I think I'm being followed, but I've never been sure, then I think I'm being silly. I can't sleep for the worry. There's the other thing, too . . .'

'Go on, I'm listening.'

He replenished her glass and she told him about Raymond and how she thought he wanted to marry her.

'It's hard that I can't speak to him about my work, that he doesn't know who I really am and what I do.'

Max regarded her, frowning. 'And you're fond of this man. Yes, I see. The secrecy takes its toll on one's relationship. It's probably easier for the male agent.'

Minnie considered this. 'How do you manage?' she dared to ask.

'My wife ... is understanding. We have an agreement.' He shifted impatiently in his chair. 'Now, Minnie, you won't have to do it for ever, but I must ask that you continue a while longer. The importance of your reports is incalculable to me, to the government. For you to stop now would be most damaging. The safety of these isles is at stake. Your great personal sacrifice hasn't gone unnoticed by the bigwigs, and I urge you strongly not to give up on us now.'

She felt warmed by his praise, the importance of her work, the trust he vested in her. Tears threatened, but she bit her lip and forced them back. *Chin up, you can do it!* 'I see,' she said, her voice dull. 'How long would I have to go on? I thought I could manage, but it doesn't seem to end. The tension is awful. Every moment I fear that I'll be exposed and then, oh, the shame. It's not simply the danger. These people I'm spying on, I like them, they're my friends. If they discover I've betrayed them I'd feel ...'

'They may be friendly, but they are *not* your friends.' Max's voice was no longer velvet, but steel. 'You must preserve distance.'

'I don't mean that I'm on their side,' she cried. 'You don't think that, do you?'

'Of course I don't, but these people, the worst among them, are our bitter enemies. Please remember that. As for how long, I can't tell you. But Glading's recent activities are deeply concerning. It is imperative that you find out more about this man he met, the one who you say looks like Lenin. Only you can do this, Minnie. You have Glading's trust.'

'You don't know what you're asking of me.'

'I do, you've explained. You're strong, Minnie, resilient. I've always known it. You can do this. Just for a tiny bit longer.' His voice was softer again, almost purring. And the way he leaned towards her, his kind eyes upon her made her prickle with ... not desire, no, but pleasure. For a moment, the room swayed, the effects of the alcohol, perhaps. Her eyelids fluttered and she sighed.

'Minnie?' She opened her eyes. He was studying her, a smile playing about his lips.

She sat bolt upright. 'Have I been asleep?'

'Almost, I think. Catching up after your broken nights. Have you finished with your glass?'

'Yes,' she said, passing it to him. Taking the hint, she rose to leave.

After Max showed her out into the golden evening, Minnie walked slowly home through the peace of Hyde Park, wrapped in a dreamy sense of puzzlement. Max's charm, the balmy air, the twitter of birds roosting in the trees, all conspired to restore her. Perhaps it was possible to go on with her work a bit longer. A few weeks wouldn't hurt, she supposed; a month, maybe two. That would surely be long enough to find out what Glading was up to. And then she could address herself properly to Raymond, see if things could work out between them.

But what if a few weeks wasn't long enough, her inner voice whispered. *How long would your strength last? Is Max pushing you too far?* And, more desperately still, *Can you trust him?* The very question shocked her.

Twenty-five

The restaurant in Piccadilly Circus where Minnie met Raymond on Thursday night was bigger, grander and busier than any he'd taken her to so far. She took it all in as they were shown to their table. Gently glowing lamps hung low from a high ceiling. The walls twinkled with blue and gold mosaics depicting Greek gods and girls dancing with garlands. Everywhere tables shone with spotless white linen, silver cutlery and candles. Scents of roast meat and caramel fought for dominance and somewhere above the hum of cultivated voices floated the tinkle of a distant piano.

Theirs was a small square table against a partition with a good view of the room. 'Is it awfully expensive?' Minnie asked, once they'd ordered drinks, as she looked round at the other diners, many in evening dress, the women sparkling with jewels. She felt out of place in her pretty blue and white frock and was annoyed that Raymond hadn't warned her that she needed to dress up.

'I wanted to treat you,' he said over the top of his menu, his eyes shining. 'Thought it would cheer you up a bit.'

'That's so kind.' She smiled. 'I am rather tiresome at present, aren't I?'

'Never tiresome,' he said, his eyes crinkling. 'Just not ... yourself. Now, what'll you have? There is a set menu, I believe.'

She consulted the larger menu and, seeing no prices, dutifully chose dishes from the set menu, Windsor soup and grilled chops, worried that Raymond was being recklessly generous. The same thought must be going through his mind because he asked for soup, too, and the fried fish and settled for a house wine.

'Frank brought Sally here when they got engaged.' He spoke in a casual tone, crumbling his bread nervously. 'He said it was jolly good.'

'It seems very nice indeed.' Her voice wobbled. Was this what the dinner was about, then, a proposal? She should feel happy at the idea, but suddenly she didn't, she felt rotten. Her gaze drifted to the door, where a well-dressed couple had just entered and were handing over their coats. She froze in shock.

The woman looked familiar and very attractive, a redhead in her late thirties with a healthy complexion and a lively expression. She wore a long emerald green dress that showed off her tall athletic figure. It wasn't her, though, that had drawn Minnie's stare, but her escort. She'd know that charming smile anywhere, that loose-limbed grace. It was Max. And the woman, she remembered now from the photograph, was Gwladys, his wife.

Max surveyed the room and Minnie lowered her face quickly, hoping he would not see her, but when she raised it again, she saw with horror that he was being seated directly in her line of sight. When he glanced up his eye was drawn to Minnie's across the room like a magnet to iron filings. Did she imagine the flicker of acknowledgement in his face before he looked away to engage in vivacious conversation with his wife?

'Minnie, what's wrong?' Raymond followed the direction of her gaze. 'Who's that you're looking at?'

'No one,' she said brightly, snapping her attention back to him. 'I wondered if I knew them, that's all.' She took a gulp of her gin and tonic and the ice rattled against her teeth.

'You look as if you've seen a ghost.'

She smiled at him. 'I have a slight headache, that's all. Perhaps I'd better not have the wine when it comes.'

'It might relax you, Minnie. You need to relax more. You're overdoing it, that's my point . . . I say, is this our soup already?'

The waiter placed warm fragrant dishes before them and poured red wine with a flourish. As they ate, Minnie hardly noticed the taste of the broth, so aware was she of Max across the room. She glanced across at him from time to time, when she thought Raymond wasn't looking, and once caught him looking back at her, but as a stranger might, accidentally, because his uninterested gaze flicked to Raymond, then back to his wife. It felt like rejection, a blow. Why was he here? Was he spying on her? She could hardly concentrate on what Raymond was saying, something about his mother having toothache. She forced herself to listen and made sympathetic noises, but now her headache was worse and the pleasure had gone out of the evening. This was awful, because Raymond was going to such expense.

'Are you sure it's just a headache? You seem peaky to me.'

'I'm fine, really. The soup is delicious, Raymond, you do spoil me.'

He smiled delightedly. 'You're worth spoiling, my dear.'

The waiter appeared as soon as they'd put down their spoons and whipped away their dishes as though in a hurry for them to eat and leave. Raymond leaned towards her. 'I'm so concerned about your nerves, Minnie. Can't you give up your work, or at least find a job that doesn't weigh so heavily?'

'Raymond, I wish I could.' Involuntarily she glanced across the room to see Max in a pose familiar to her, stroking something he held in his cupped palm, a small bird, she realized, surprised that he'd bring it into a restaurant. She had the sudden fancy that it was she in his hand, that he was stroking and comforting her, the sound of his voice in her head as he coaxed her to go on with her mission. Was that why he was here, to remind her of her duty to him, to keep her close?

'Minnie? Are you listening?'

'Of course, Raymond, please go on.'

'So why can't you?'

'Can't I what?'

A ripple of exasperation crossed his face. 'Find a new job. You'd feel so much better, have more energy. I was thinking we might go away together for a few days and we could talk about it then. We could talk about everything.'

'What a lovely idea. Where would we go?'

'Oh, I don't know. The sea. Lyme Regis is nice.'

'I've never been there.'

'We went on holiday when I was ten or eleven. You can walk out on the Cobb, that's a famous long sea wall, and when you reach the end it feels as though you're right out at sea.'

For a moment Minnie was filled with a wild joy. 'I'd like that.'

'Let's do it then.'

The waiter brought their main courses. Her chop glistened, the peas were scented delicately with mint.

'Raymond.' She picked up her fork, then put it down again and studied his dear, kind face, so full of hope. 'I can't.'

'It doesn't have to be right away.'

She glanced across the room and sighed. 'Not Lyme Regis. I mean my job. I can't give it up at present. I'm sorry.'

He looked bemused. 'Why on earth not? You're not in any trouble about money, are you?'

'No, it's not anything like that. It's ... duty. No one else can do the work I do.'

'Surely that can't be true. I expect you're very good, but typing and filing and things ... lots of girls can do that.'

'Yes, of course. I can't really explain in a way that would make you see.'

'It's jolly odd, that's all I'll say.'

'I'm sorry.' She could not eat another mouthful now. Their evening had been spoiled. She kept feeling that Max was staring at her, though when she looked quickly now he was concentrating on his food.

'You are looking at someone.' Raymond's voice seemed to come from far away. 'Is it the couple over by the wall?'

'It's all right, Raymond.'

'Is it? I must say you're behaving quite unexpectedly this evening. I feel I've done something wrong.'

'No, it's not you. I think I'm still not myself.'

'Do try to eat.'

'Yes.'

If only, she started thinking in panic, *if only Raymond would make me decide. If he asked me to marry him, I would have to decide if I loved him enough to say yes. And Max would have to go hang then, wouldn't he?*

She glanced up to see Raymond still staring at her. Was that pity in his eyes? Her resolution fell. *Perhaps she had put him off.*

'I am sorry, Raymond.' She laid down her knife and fork. 'You've brought me to this lovely place and I'm being awfully disappointing.'

'I'm worried about you, that's all.'

'You mustn't be worried. It's something I must sort out myself.' She reached for her wine, but her hand shook and she knocked it over. The ruby liquid splashed over the cloth and she jerked sideways to avoid it. A waiter appeared and deftly restored order, but if the evening had been strained it was ruined now. Everyone around was staring at her, or so it felt.

'I think I'd better go,' she said to Raymond in helpless tones. She felt hot, it was so hot in here and her head throbbed.

While he paid the bill Minnie stumbled to the powder room and dabbed her face with cool water. A sudden sound and in the mirror she saw the door swing open and Gwladys enter the room. Their eyes met and Minnie's heart began to race, but the woman merely nodded politely. Minnie snatched up her handbag and returned to the restaurant. Max sat alone sipping coffee. There was no sign of Raymond, then she saw him by the front desk, collecting their coats. She walked quickly in his direction, intending to ignore Max.

'Good evening, Minnie.' She halted. 'I trust you've enjoyed your meal.' He was smiling at her and anger welled up.

'No, to be honest. Not one bit.'

His smile vanished.

'But that's what you want, Max, isn't it? That's why you're here.'

He frowned. 'I can assure you it was coincidence. Gwladys was in town and this is her favourite restaurant.'

'I don't believe you.'

'Minnie, please, this isn't like you.'

'I thought you cared about me.'

'Of course I do. What's wrong?'

'You must know.'

And with that she swept on by.

Outside, Raymond tucked her arm in his and they walked to the underground station in silence. There he turned to her and said gently, 'Are you sure you'll be all right getting home?'

'Of course. Raymond, I'm sorry . . .'

He looked past her for a moment, then he smiled sadly at her. 'There's nothing to be sorry for. I'd wanted this evening to be special, that's all.'

'It was special. The meal was lovely.'

'When you feel a little better call me up, will you, Minnie?' He sounded pleading.

'Yes, of course I will.' Her voice was unsteady.

'I'll be going home this weekend, I expect. What about you?'

'I don't know yet.' How could they suddenly be so stiff with each other? He looked so unhappy and she felt like weeping, but the silence was widening like the wine stain that had spread through the tablecloth.

'You'll take care of yourself now.'

'Yes, yes. And you, Raymond.'

He touched her shoulder gently, then turned and left her. She stood watching him walk away until the corner took him from sight. At the top of the steps a youth in a flat cap was selling the *Daily Worker*. Minnie recoiled as though struck and, feeling for the hand rail, fled down the stairs into the station.

Gripped by indecision, Minnie hardly slept that night. Did Raymond love her for herself? Did she love him enough? Should she give up her job and if she did what would that mean? All her hard-earned experience lost, all usefulness to her country gone. She'd be ordinary Minnie Gray – or rather ordinary Mrs Raymond Mills. Did she want to be that, helping with cricket teas, tied down by young children, not being able to work outside the home. Or was Max and her work for him more important, more in tune with the real Minnie, hard and lonely though it was. Which was it to be, Raymond or Max? Her head ached and her thoughts spun, each one contending with the others, all powers of judgement gone. The rising moon shone through the curtains and cast shadows on the wall. Shapes of nightmare creatures with deformed faces and gnarled hands. A trapped fly threw itself against the window. Finally she got up and let it out, then switched on the light and scrabbled in her bedside drawer for her sleeping tablets. One would not be enough. Two, then. With stale water from a bedside glass she swallowed them down. The next morning she woke late and woozy and telephoned in sick.

She passed a quiet day by herself. In the evening, when she was curled up on the sofa reading an old newspaper, the telephone rang. After a moment's hesitation she reached for the receiver.

'We were due to meet this evening.' It was Max. His voice was icy.

'I'm sorry, I forgot. I'm not well. I haven't been to work.' There was silence. 'Hello?' she said.

'Listen, about last night at the restaurant. That was your young man, I presume?'

'Raymond. I'm not sure he's my young man anymore. You spoiled our evening.'

'I told you, it was a coincidence.'

'And I told *you*, I don't believe a word of it.' They'd never spoken to one another like this before. Something profound had changed last night. It felt as if both Max and Raymond wanted control over her and she'd exasperated each of them. She must choose, but she couldn't. Her head still hurt. If only everyone would go away and leave her in peace.

'We need to talk,' he said, more softly. 'It's important. Shall we say Monday? Maybe you'll have recovered by then. A good rest is what you need, then everything will look straighter. Do that for me, Minnie. I need you. Your continued work is absolutely vital. Don't let me down.'

That caressing voice, that reassurance, what should she do? Keep going as she was a little while longer. 'Monday, then.' She agreed to go to his flat after work.

She stayed off sick the whole week and felt better. On Wednesday she left a telephone message with someone at Raymond's digs to say she wouldn't be joining him in Edgbaston. It would have been awkward, she told herself. Instead she spent the weekend in London. Dinner out with hockey friends, a long conversation with her mother, who had news of another forthcoming grandchild, an absorbing novel. But on Sunday night as Minnie was bleaching the roots of her hair it occurred to her that she hadn't heard from Raymond for days. Had he taken her refusal to return to Birmingham as a rejection? She rinsed out the peroxide and stared at her face in the mirror, thinking how tired and drawn she looked. Should she telephone him? He'd probably be back in London by now. What would she say, though, after that last awful evening? She'd be embarrassed. He'd ask questions she couldn't answer. Tomorrow. She'd ring him tomorrow after she'd had it out with Max.

'Minnie, calm down. How many times must I say this? I was not there to spy on you. My wife and I often visit that restaurant. How could I have known you'd be there? Think about it.' Max was leaning in one of his habitual poses, one arm on the mantelpiece, the other gesturing with his unlit pipe, a despairing expression on his face.

'It felt as though you were spying on me. You pretended the whole time not to recognize me, yet you kept glancing my way. How do you think that made me feel?'

'I could hardly introduce us all to each other. It wouldn't have been suitable.'

'You mean we weren't good enough to meet your wife.'

'Of course that's not what I meant.' He sounded flustered.

'You could have found some clever explanation for how we knew one another.'

'It seemed easier not to try. As you know, I never speak about my work to Gwladys.'

'It would have been easier for me. You can imagine how it affected my evening. I couldn't relax.'

'Well, I'm sorry. Your Raymond appeared pleasant. And fond of you, I think.'

Was there a tone of sarcasm there, or was she imagining it? Heavens, why did it matter what he thought of Raymond? And yet it *did* matter. It mattered very much and Minnie was ashamed of that.

'He's important to you, this man,' Max continued.

'I . . . I'd like him to be, I think.'

He regarded her thoughtfully. 'What have you told him, about your work.'

'Nothing very much, of course I haven't. That's why it's so difficult for me. I feel I'm lying to him all the time. Don't you feel that with your wife?'

'Not really. She takes little interest. It's other things we have in common.'

It struck Minnie how different his situation was from her own. For a start he wasn't undercover as she was. His position was administrative. Of course, his work was confidential, but he didn't have to pretend to be someone he wasn't. And he was right, it was easier to be an agent if you were a man. A woman would not usually expect to know all about her husband's work. It was his sphere. He might complain about aspects of his job, or share news of success, but his wife's role would be one of emotional support, not to ask questions or to understand exactly what he did and why. When the situation was reversed, the same was not true. Raymond would expect his wife to be transparent. If she were to continue working for MI5 she could not, she saw now, be the person he expected her to be.

'How did it feel being back at the grindstone?' he asked, changing the subject.

'Not particularly interesting.' She realized that her reply must have sounded evasive, but she was telling the truth.

On the way home Minnie thought about Raymond, recognizing still more clearly that she would have to make a choice between her work for MI5 and her relationship.

She rang him after she'd arrived home, but the confused old man who answered said that he was out so she asked him to leave Raymond a message. She stayed up, waiting for him to call back, but the phone remained resolutely silent. The old man hadn't bothered with the message, she imagined.

That night she lay awake, struggling with her dilemma.

Even if she gave up her work she'd never be able to tell Raymond about it. There would be a hole, a large part of her life that was closed to him and which she'd never be able to fill. Wasn't it kinder for her to step away, to set him free? But why should she? She didn't want to. She felt paralysed, as though something was sitting on her chest, squeezing the breath out of her.

The following lunchtime, knowing she would be out until late in the evening, Minnie rang Raymond at his work. When a brusque male voice informed her that he was out, some impulsive, self-destructive urge made her supply her office number. She'd never given it to Raymond before, her excuse being that it was difficult for her to take personal calls at work. Now that she'd done so she knew that matters between them would come to a head.

Pollitt was away for the day so she had to field his calls. Each time she answered the ringing phone she steeled herself, but it was never Raymond. Finally, towards the end of the day, she heard his voice at the other end of the line. 'Minnie? Is that really you?'

'It is.' She glanced round, but the office was emptying and she didn't think she'd be overheard.

'The receptionist said . . .' and here Raymond spoke in a whisper . . . '*the Communist Party.*'

'Yes, it's where I work.' She spoke more sharply than she intended.

'Well.' His voice returned to normal volume. 'I can't pretend I'm not shocked.'

'I . . . I'm sorry I didn't tell you before. We can meet up and I'll explain. Not tonight, though. I've got something on.'

'I see.'

'Don't be like that. It's only the flicks. Oh, I suppose I could cancel it.'

'I'd be glad if you did.'

They agreed to meet at six. When Minnie replaced the receiver she was shaking so much that it slipped from its cradle, tipped off the edge of the desk and hung swinging. She snatched it up, hoping no one had noticed her agitation.

Raymond was a quarter of an hour late, but it felt twice as long. Minnie waited at the corner of Trafalgar Square near St Martin's-in-the-Fields, watching the evening sunlight flash on every bus that went by and hoping he would be on it. And suddenly there he was, his upright figure, so dear and familiar, crossing the road towards her. When he reached her side she was shocked at the expression of misery in his wide-spaced eyes.

'You look fed up,' he said in dull greeting and she knew that something had changed between them.

'Do I?' She hugged herself defensively. They began to walk together, slowly, aimlessly, across the square.

'I never know where I am with you, Minnie. The Communist Party.' Raymond shook his head, dejected. 'Why couldn't you tell me before?'

'I didn't know what you'd say.' She'd taken the risk and made things worse by telling him. 'It's just a job, you know.'

'How can it be "just a job"? It's like . . . I don't know, going to a mosque when you're not a Mohammedan. Or joining another country's army. Are you really a Communist or do you only pretend to be?'

'I have to be a member, but I don't believe it all.' Minnie stopped, then said in a rush, 'Don't ask me any more, please, Raymond.'

He shook his head in disbelief. 'A paid-up Commie. I simply don't understand.'

It's not what it seems, she wanted to cry out. 'It's like any typing job, Raymond.'

'More than that, surely. Quite a commitment, I'd say. All those late evenings. And Paris. It explains so much but ... not you, Minnie. You're like me. I thought we had the same views.'

'We do.' She clutched herself tighter, finding his confusion unbearable, but was too proud to beg him to understand.

A daft-looking lad with ragged sleeves revealing bony wrists approached. 'Got any change, mister? Ain't eaten today.' Raymond glared at him, but Minnie felt for her purse, gave the lad sixpence and brushed away his thanks.

'Come on,' she said. 'We ought to go somewhere. It's a lovely evening.'

They walked towards The Mall then up a broad flight of steps to Haymarket where they found a café that was still open. It was busy with cheerful diners eating a quick supper before going on to the cinema or a show and Minnie and Raymond were led through to a table at the back. As they ate Welsh rarebit and sipped strong tea Minnie tried her best to field Raymond's questions. What did she do in her job?

What were the people like? How on earth had she got into it? When he called her colleagues 'filthy revolutionaries' it was too much.

'Some of them are my friends. I like them,' she blurted out.

'Lord, now I've offended you.' He shook his head. 'But you've sprung this on me. I'm deeply shocked, to tell you the truth, Minnie. You can be mysterious sometimes, but I thought I knew you. Now you behave oddly and tell me all this and I see I don't know you after all.'

She touched his hand. 'I'm still the same person underneath, Raymond. In the important ways.'

'Are you, Minnie? Are you? It doesn't seem like it to me. I'm an ordinary sort of chap, I won't apologize for that. I need a girl I can trust. Show me you're that kind of girl, Minnie, please show me.'

'I ... I can't show you that,' she burst out. 'It's too complicated. I'm sorry, I have to go.' She felt close to crying and she hated anyone to see her cry. She fumbled for some coins. 'Here, let me pay my half.' She could hardly focus on his dear, confused face. 'I wish I could tell you everything, but I can't.'

'Minnie, wait.'

'Don't follow me, please, it would do no good. I'm very fond of you, Raymond, but we must leave it here for a while. I thought I could do it, but I see at the moment that it's simply not going to work.'

With that she pushed her way between the tables to the door. When she stepped outside she found it was raining heavily and she had no umbrella. By the time she reached the underground she was wet through. So deep was her misery she hardly noticed the journey home. She'd hoped that by revealing some of the awfulness of her situation she'd draw Raymond closer. Instead, she'd pushed him away. Now she thought of the things she should have said but hadn't. She could have begged him to forgive her, assured him that she loved him. Instead she'd been stupid, stiff and proud.

She managed to hold herself together until she got home. She ran a hot bath and sat in it for a long while, going over everything, tears slipping down her face. Then she went to bed with a cup of cocoa and reached for the bottle of sleeping tablets. She shook one out and swallowed it with a mouthful of water and a grimace at the bitter taste.

The pill only gave her a few hours' sleep, but this was enough to get through the next day and several after that. Going into work, day after day, pretending all was as usual, filing her reports for Max. All the time, trying not to think about Raymond. And suddenly, one afternoon, she wasn't able to cope anymore. Her hands shook, she could not type or answer the ringing phone. Her head ached, she was ill again, she told Pollitt, and he sent her home, worried about her. In the cab she rested her face against the cool of the window and wished, *If only I could sleep.*

Twenty-six

Minnie was whirling through darkness, distorted voices calling her name, then the darkness brightened and the voices cohered into one voice, a voice she knew. The whirling slowed and she opened her eyes and blinked. A tumble of images fell into focus, but made no sense. She blinked again. Daylight. A high-ceilinged, narrow room.

'Oh, thank goodness,' came the voice. 'Minnie, it's me.'

A face moved into her line of vision. Anxious dark eyes, reddened lips twisted with anguish, curls of honey-coloured hair, a familiar perfume. Her sister Marjorie. She felt warm breath as Marjorie's lips moved: 'Minnie, can you hear me?'

She closed her eyes and felt herself falling, but the voice called again. 'Minnie! Wake up!' Marjorie was shaking her arm. Minnie forced her eyes open. 'Minnie, listen. It's time to come back.'

Back, back from where? Marjorie's face withdrew and a stranger's appeared instead. It was broad and motherly and topped by a nurse's cap. A nurse? Minnie felt a grip on her wrist as her pulse was read and wondered why her throat hurt.

'We've been frantic, frantic, I tell you.' She moved her eyes to see Marjorie huddled on a chair. 'They said you might not pull through. Those pills you took, Minnie, how could you have been so silly.'

Minnie tried to shake her head, not understanding about the pills. The effort made her dizzy and still she could not speak. She was aware of her body, blissfully warm and heavy between stiff sheets, but it was as though it belonged to someone else for she'd lost the power to move. She let her eyes flutter shut and sank into sleep once more.

When she next came to consciousness, no one was there, but apart from her sore throat she felt quite tranquil. The air was full with a heavy sweetness and she felt as though she was lying dreamily on a sun-baked lawn. Yet she knew she couldn't be because instead of a summer sky there was a white ceiling above. She stared at a jagged crack, which stopped dead where the pale green of the wall began. A tall, thin window with a view of clouds. This time her head moved when she told it to and her gaze travelled down the wall. Now she saw the source of the sweet smell. A vase of yellow roses on a cabinet. She shifted her gaze. The room was full of flowers. A tumble of lilac, pink and white stock, a tall blue-blossomed plant, whose name escaped her. She was wondering where they'd all come from when she heard a knock. The door opened and her heart leaped as her mother entered the room.

'Minnie, you're awake. My darling. I was only gone a moment . . .'

Minnie raised a feeble arm and Mrs Gray bustled across to embrace her daughter. Oh, the familiar powdery warmth. 'My darling, my darling girl,' Mrs Gray murmured into her ear. 'I feared we'd lost you, I truly did, but here you are. So pale, my love.' She sat down on the chair and gripped her daughter's hand.

'I . . .' Minnie cleared her throat. 'I don't remember . . .'

'You're in the nerve hospital, I'm afraid, Minnie, but they say you'll be all right. You'd become overwrought . . . a very kind gentleman rang to tell us . . . a Captain King . . . you'd missed a meeting with him so he called by that evening and when you behaved strangely, he realized you were in a bad state. Then you told him you'd taken some pills. Are you sure you don't remember?'

Minnie shook her head. She was still in that lovely dreamlike place where nothing troubled her very much. Funny that she found it so easy to sleep here when she didn't at home. Perhaps they'd given her something.

'And he's sent such gorgeous flowers, so kind. Look, these roses are from him and the lilac. The card with the carnations says "from your friends in King Street". That's the office where you work, isn't it? Marjorie chose the lilies. I don't care for lilies myself, the pollen gets everywhere and they remind one of funerals . . . Oh my dear Minnie, I'm sorry to have said that . . . I've been so worried.'

Her mother's voice finally cracked, she gave a sob and fumbled for her handkerchief. Minnie squeezed her hand, and managed a soothing, 'Don't, don't.' Despite all the sadness and difficulty in her mother's life, she had rarely seen her cry.

At that moment a bosomy nurse in a crisp blue uniform marched into the room and said in a stern voice, 'Visiting hour is over for today.'

Mrs Gray rose, still dabbing her eyes, bent and kissed her daughter. 'I'll be back tomorrow, darling. Marjorie and I are staying in your flat. Your Mrs Saunders downstairs has been most kind, finding the spare key, showing us how the water heater works.'

After she'd left, the rush of annoyance at Mrs Saunders that cut through the dreaminess was interrupted by the nurse poking a thermometer sharply under Minnie's tongue. She refilled the water jug on Minnie's table and snapped a dead bud from a carnation, before whipping the thermometer out again, frowning as she read it.

'Back to normal. You're a lucky girl,' she said severely, then her eyes softened. 'You mustn't frighten us again.'

'How long have I been here?'

'You were brought in the night before last.'

'I don't remember,' Minnie whispered.

'Doctor will see you tomorrow morning and he'll no doubt explain. Now, could you manage a little soup?'

Minnie realized she did feel hungry. After the vegetable soup she was left alone, watching the sky turn slowly to dusk and trying to think back. Something very sad had happened that made her want to cry. She was grieving, but for what? She'd shut it away in her mind, though her body remembered it. Her thoughts roved over the different areas of her life, but it was like that parlour game where one tried to identify small objects hidden inside cloth bags.

Her illness had upset her family, but she couldn't recall what she had done to put herself here. The sight of the flowers saddened her. Yellow roses, everyone knew, stood for faithlessness – was that what Max meant by them, that she'd betrayed someone or something important? 'The staff at King Street' had sent her flowers, which suggested that they didn't know her secrets. That was a relief. There was something else, though, or someone else, that was the source of her pain, and now it came to her. It was to do with Raymond. Minnie had blotted it out, but now it returned to her in a rush of agony. They had quarrelled. He no longer trusted her and she'd done nothing to reassure him. Her decision had been made. And now her memories slipped back. The cool of the cab window after Pollitt had sent her home, the relief of shutting her flat door behind her and crawling into bed although it was only mid-afternoon, and simply lying there, shaking. Later, she'd taken more pills than she was meant to in order to sleep, but Max had arrived … And now, two days later, here she was. And there were no flowers from Raymond. Maybe he didn't know.

Minnie closed her eyes and struggled against the threatening tide of grief, but she was too weak and at last the dam broke and she cried and cried. After her tears were spent, she sank into a deep sleep.

'A few days' rest and you may go home.'

The doctor was the sort who, in another set of

circumstances, she might have confided in. Quietly spoken and with a gentle demeanour, he was more like a saint than a medical man. He fixed her with his mild hazel eyes and she wanted more than anything to pour out her whole story to him. But she knew she couldn't so she simply said, 'I didn't take those pills to kill myself. You do believe that, don't you?'

'Of course I do. But you mustn't keep any more in the house. They're addictive and then you need more and more of them to have the desired effect and before you know it you'll be in here again.'

'Yes, Doctor.'

'And this job you do.' He consulted his notes and said with some distaste, 'You work at the Communist Party office, it says here.'

'Yes, don't tell my family, though.'

'Sounds like a health hazard to me. You know what the Commies would do with us medics? Have us work for nothing. You'd be better off out of there.'

Minnie nodded wearily. If only he knew how much she wanted to take his advice.

After he'd gone she found it easy to sleep once more. When she awoke there was a man sitting quietly by her bed, his hat on his knees, watching her. It was Max.

'Good afternoon.' He smiled at her and she smiled back sheepishly.

'How long have you been there?'

'Only a few minutes. Did you know that you snore?'

'I do not.'

He laughed. 'Lost none of your spirit, I see. That's the ticket. Actually, I lied. You don't snore. Anyway, you're in a better state than when I saw you last.'

She felt herself blush. 'I must thank you.'

'Not at all. When you didn't turn up again I was concerned. You haven't been ... yourself recently. That was the second meeting you'd missed.'

'I left you a message the first time.'

'So you did. No need to apologize, Minnie, in this business it can happen to the best of us.' He ran his hands around the brim of his felt hat and she realized he was hiding strong emotion. She waited, hoping that he might apologize for his part in her breakdown, but he did not. Instead he cast his eye over the flowers. 'It's like Kew Gardens in here. A lot of people care about you, Minnie.'

'I know, it's lovely,' she murmured, moved by this thought, and trying not to think about Raymond. 'Thank you for yours. Why yellow roses?'

'I don't know.' He appeared surprised. 'Because they're pretty and have a scent.'

'I love them. It's ... no, it doesn't matter.' Perhaps he didn't know the language of flowers after all and didn't think her unfaithful. She gave a quiet sigh, then explained to him what the doctor had said, that she would soon be out of hospital and needed a rest. Max studied his hat, with lips tightly pressed, then looked up at her and said, 'Your work is valuable to me, Minnie, incalculably valuable, and I'd like you to stay in place, but clearly that is no longer possible. There's too much risk.'

'That I might break down again and blurt out everything?' she said with heavy sarcasm. 'That would indeed be inconvenient.'

'I didn't mean it like that. The risk is to your health. There must be another way. I'll have to think.' It was as though he was talking to himself. Then something occurred to him.

'What have you said to the doctors?'

'Said? Nothing about my work for you, if that's what you mean.'

'You're sure?'

'In my *ravings*? I would not have said anything, Max.' Nothing indicated that she had blurted out anything in delirium. No nurse or doctor had mentioned it. She shivered at the idea.

'Don't say anything, even to a doctor. I know how sympathetic they can be.'

'I think you should go now, Max. I'm awfully sleepy.'

'Of course.' He rose and took her hand and his expression was concerned and warm. 'Don't worry about anything. We care very much about you and you must get better soon. Then we can talk.'

He spoke with such warmth that she believed him. Then why, she thought after he'd taken his leave, did she feel such unease?

Raymond and Max. By being unable to choose between them she was in danger of losing both.

After being discharged from hospital a few days later, Minnie shut up her flat and returned to Edgbaston with her mother.

There she lived quietly, sustained by regular meals and short walks. She slept badly still and her concentration was too poor to read, but she often sat in the garden, sipping lemonade and leafing through the pages of her mother's magazines. The newspaper, as ever, was full of bad news, but fashions, crafts and recipes were soothing material for an invalid wishing to avoid reality. Minnie ignored her mother's suggestion that she look up old friends and begged that everyone should leave her alone to recover, so they did.

This withdrawal from the world could not last for ever. A fortnight after her arrival she woke one morning visited by a familiar feeling of dread. It came as no surprise, therefore, when, after breakfast, her mother called her to the hall telephone saying, 'It's that nice Captain King.'

She had to force herself to take the receiver and say hello.

'How are you, Minnie?' The familiar purring voice had her once more in his grip. She rubbed her eyes and leaned back against the wall for support.

'A little better, thank you.'

'Good. You're taking it easy, I trust.'

She assured him that she was and they exchanged banalities before, as she'd feared, he moved on to business. 'You must take as much time as you need, but do you have a faint idea of when you'll be ready to return to London?'

When, she noted, not *if* she'd return. 'I don't know.' She watched a spider weave its web across a corner of the ceiling as she spoke and began to twist the telephone cord round her fingers. She would go back. This at least she felt sure of. Edgbaston was a necessary interlude, but it would quickly become boring. She might have lost Raymond and be unable to continue her work for Max, but her life was in London now. Minnie had come to love its busy-ness, its energy. The city had changed her and claimed her for its own.

'I won't go back to King Street. I'm sorry, but there it is. The mere thought of it. I can't do it anymore.' There was a heartbeat of silence at the other end of the telephone. The spider lost its balance and plunged suddenly, but quickly recovered itself.

'No, I understand.' Max's voice sounded flat.

Her eyes widened in surprise. He'd accepted her decision without argument. She expected relief to flood through her, but instead felt only emptiness and a reluctance to let him go. 'I'll help in any other way I can. I mean I won't simply disappear.'

'I'm pleased to hear it. When you return to London we should meet, but for the moment you must rest. Let me know how your friends in King Street react when you resign. Bear in mind that it would be useful to keep the door open. Would you do that for me?'

'Of course.' The idea pleased her.

'What will you tell them?'

She'd already thought about that. 'The truth. That the work's too hard for me and it's made me ill.' She still prac-tised one of the most important lessons he'd taught her – to use the truth whenever possible, so there wouldn't be lies to catch her out.

'Good. I'm sure they'll accept that without question.'

'You may think this odd,' she rushed on, 'but I'll miss

them. You call them "my friends", and actually they are, Glading and Pollitt. I'd like to go on seeing them.'

'Then that suits my purpose exactly.'

'Max.' She took a deep breath. 'We'll still see one another, won't we?'

'What a silly question. Of course we will,' he said and his voice was wonderfully warm and sincere. 'I look forward to continuing our meetings.'

That was a formal way of putting it, Minnie worried as she replaced the receiver. She went upstairs to rest on her bed and think. Despite everything she longed to see Max again. If he'd ended their relationship outright she'd have been devastated. She tortured herself wondering if she was important to him because of the information she gave him, or whether they really were special to one another, but told herself not to be foolish. Of course they were friends. He knew so much about her, how she responded to different situations, what made her frightened, what helped her be strong. She'd often confided in him. But what did she know about him? Only the side she needed to, that he allowed her to know. Theirs was not an equal relationship, but she could not bear for it to end. And now, knowing it wouldn't, finally, relief washed over her.

Max was right. When she rang Harry Pollitt he understood completely why she was resigning her post. 'I feel responsible, Minnie,' he said. 'I've been a slave driver, haven't I?' It was he who suggested that they keep in touch and he sent her a cheque to cover her unpaid wages and a little more besides.

Twenty-seven

September 1935

Down the street the leaves on the horse chestnut trees were turning gold and schoolchildren scrambled for new-hatched conkers that bounced on the pavement. Minnie, drinking tea in her dressing gown, watched them through the sitting-room window of her mother's house in a thoughtful mood. Summer was over and life was starting up again. It was time for her to return to London.

She considered the practicalities. Although she was no longer in employment she had regularly squirrelled away a portion of her income, her rent was paid up and she had enough to live on until she felt well enough to look for a job.

The rest of August had passed in a haze. She'd lived each day as it came and gradually became calmer. Recently she'd spent a few days with a spinster cousin of her mother's who lived in a country town outside Birmingham, a pretty place on the tourist trail with a ruined castle and antique shops and a babbling river overhung by willows.

Now, back home in Edgbaston, she felt cocooned. It was safe but extremely dull, and she was ready to emerge and discover what she'd turned into. Definitely not a butterfly, she thought. Maybe a plain moth. She certainly hoped that life would be different, better, now that she'd given up her stressful job.

And for the moment there would be no Raymond. She thought of him with sadness. In a particularly tearful moment in early August she'd confided in her mother about seeing him and how they had quarrelled. On Mrs Gray's eager advice she wrote, telling him she'd been unwell, but would be glad to hear from him now that she felt more herself again, that she was sorry about everything. She'd been disappointed by the formality of his reply, though it had been solicitous enough. He was concerned that she'd been unwell and hoped to see her shortly, but he hadn't been in the pink himself and had been granted a week's holiday. He was off to Lyme Regis and would send her a postcard.

Lyme Regis. Where he'd asked her to go and she'd demurred. There was something barbed about his 'not in the pink'. She'd been so full of her own suffering that she hadn't considered his. His heart must be sore, and his pride probably, poor Raymond. She felt a rush of warmth for him and had looked out for the postcard. It never came. She wrote him one from Warwickshire, with a picture of the castle. That was two weeks ago and there had been no reply.

As she was upstairs dressing she heard the rattle of the

letter box then the thud of the post hitting the mat and felt a rush of hope. From the top of the stairs she watched her mother bend stiffly to scoop up the letters, flicking through them as she returned to the kitchen. Nothing for Minnie, then.

'Shall I ask Raymond's mother how he is?' Mrs Gray said when Minnie came downstairs. 'I need to send her the latest Conservative newsletter and could pop a note inside.'

'Don't you dare!' Minnie said, horrified at the indignity of such an approach. Really, the way her mother hovered over her was becoming annoying. It was like being a child again. The thought confirmed her decision to go back to London.

As she unlocked the street door of the house in Holland Park she felt a frisson of anxiety. *Buck up, Minnie. Life in London will be different now you're free.* There was a neat pile of post waiting for her on the hall shelf. Bills, she supposed, gathering it up on her way.

Upstairs, she opened the door warily, but apart from a stale smell of disuse all seemed as she'd left it. In the drawing room she threw open a window and swept a couple of dead flies outside, then sorted through the pile of post. Amid newsletters from the hockey club and the Communist Party, the predicted bills and a postcard from her pal Jenny, she found two envelopes that caused her surprise. She sat down and stared at them, knowing what each contained before she carefully slit them open. Two cheques. The latest monthly retainers from MI5.

She laid the cheques beside her on the sofa and sat biting a finger nail. So Max had been serious when they'd last spoken back in July. She was still on his books. She'd believed she was free, but she wasn't. She was still officially his paid-up spy. She rubbed her arms, feeling suddenly chilly.

He telephoned the following evening, though how he knew she was back she didn't ask. 'How are you?' he asked, his voice as warm and solicitous as ever.

'Much more myself, thank you.'

'Well enough for work?'

'I'll be looking for a job when I'm ready.'

'I meant for me.'

'I don't know, Max.'

'We should meet up, though, don't you think?'

'Yes, I'd like that.'

'How about cocktails at the Ritz?'

'I've never been there before.'

'Tomorrow at six?'

When he'd ended the call, she dropped the receiver onto its cradle thoughtfully. She looked forward to seeing him, and she was charmed by the thought of the Ritz Hotel. He was obviously trying to butter her up.

Entering the hotel, Minnie was captivated at once by its hushed pink and gold opulence, the rolling expanse of carpet, the high painted ceilings and glittering chandeliers. She felt ordinary and out of place, at first, nervous that someone would challenge her presence, but nobody did and she followed the sign to the Palm Court with growing confidence.

Max was already waiting at a table on the edge of the Palm

Court, sipping whisky from a crystal tumbler. When she approached he rose at once to greet her.

'Dear Minnie.' He grasped both her hands and studied her face with his warm brown eyes. 'It's so good to see you. You look much better.'

'I should hope so,' she said shortly, freeing herself and sitting down. Then she softened and smiled, realizing how much she'd missed his familiar scent of tobacco, the way he made her feel special. 'You look well yourself, though, Max.' He'd recovered the weight he'd lost through his illness, though perhaps his face was leaner, the angles more sharp.

'Never felt better.'

A waiter arrived and Max ordered her an exotic-sounding cocktail, while he stuck to scotch.

'So you've never been here before. What do you think?'

'Very swish.' She looked about at the murals of cherubs and nymphs, a pretty fountain. In the distance a piano tinkled away. The cocktail arrived with a slice of lime in a wide, shallow goblet, its rim frosted with salt.

'This is *such* a marvellous place for people-watching,' she whispered, peering around at the beautifully dressed women, the polished young men in elegant suits. 'That gentleman over there, for instance.' She nodded covertly towards an elderly, regal-looking man with a hooked nose and fierce eyes, like an eagle's. 'He looks as though he's left over from the French empire.'

Max smiled and picked up his drink. 'What a vivid imagination you have. Now, here's to a new Minnie,' he said, by way of a toast.

'I don't feel new,' she sighed. The cocktail surprised her by tasting sweet and sour at the same time and she made a face. 'A bit old and battered, more like.'

'But up for a few light duties, I hope.'

'What duties do you mean?' So she was bought and paid for, she thought in dismay.

He leaned towards her and spoke in a low voice. 'I meant what I said. I want you to keep an eye on your so-called friends in King Street. So far as you can.'

'I'm not off the hook then?'

'Not if I can help it. Minnie, I shouldn't have to remind you how important your work has been to us. In the last few years our understanding of Russia's meddling in British affairs and its relationship with the Communist Party here has been transformed by your information. Sorry about the lecture, but we can't let you go now. I insist that we continue to meet every now and then.'

Despite everything she felt a warm swell of pleasure inside. She was needed, she was important. But still she hesitated. Then she opened her handbag and withdrew the cheques she'd brought with her. 'I will do my best to help, Max, but I don't need these.' She placed them on the table in front of him.

He frowned and pushed them back to her. 'Please accept them.' Beneath the apparent altruism his voice bore a hint of steel. 'You are still worth every penny and I need to know I can rely on you.'

'You can always rely on me.' Minnie stared at him levelly. 'You don't need to pay me for that.'

She couldn't ever imagine not seeing him. He made her

feel ... valuable. And he was the only person she could confide in, who knew everything about her. She could not deny it. He'd become her anchor. Yet stuffing the cheques back into her bag made her feel a little dirty, as though their relationship was simply a transaction.

Although Minnie had let Max believe the visit to the Communist Party offices to be his idea, she'd planned to do it anyway. From the receptionist to Harry Pollitt himself, everyone was pleased to see her and wanted to know if she had recovered. She felt touched and overwhelmed.

'Miss Gray! We've missed our beautiful spy,' a familiar voice said behind her and she turned, her heart racing at the old jibe, but Glading was smiling all over his round face and she laughed as she shook his outstretched hand.

'I've missed you all,' she assured the assembled throng.

'We can always find a job for you here,' Pollitt said. He was standing in the doorway of his office watching proceedings with a benign air. Behind him the portrait of Lenin glared at her and she had to hide a shiver.

'No, I'm sorry. I'm much better, but I need a quieter life.'

After half an hour catching up on office gossip, Minnie took her leave, promising to call in again, and was on her way out when Glading caught up with her. 'You're not free for lunch, are you?' he asked. 'I've a meeting now, but it finishes at twelve. You know Pollitt's punctuality. I could see you at the usual place at a quarter past?'

'I should like that.' Despite everything, she felt the old thrum of excitement. 'I'll do a little shopping first.'

When she arrived at the busy café with her purchases Glading was already sitting at a table in a corner, reading a book and smoking with an expression of intense absorption. She'd always admired his quick intelligence, his passion for learning. At her approach he closed the book and rose to greet her.

'Buying fripperies, eh?' he said jauntily, pointing to her carrier bag. 'Nice to have money to spare.'

'Your wife never buys herself anything, I suppose?' Minnie shot back, enjoying their old repartee.

'Not if I can help it.'

'I'll pay for lunch if you're that strapped for cash.'

'No, no. We'll go halves as usual, shall we? Now where's that waitress gone?'

This was something else she liked about him, that he didn't insist on paying for everything. It didn't stop her reminding him from time to time that women typically earned less than men, but then he'd answer that he had a wife and child to feed. She'd never had this sort of conversation with anyone else. Raymond, for instance, would have been shocked. A man should always pay, was his view, and that was that. The thought of Raymond hit a tender spot, but now the waitress had reappeared and Minnie concentrated on ordering poached eggs on toast.

While they waited for their food, Glading enquired after her health and asked what she'd been doing with herself. 'I'm well again, but I must be careful not to overdo things. There's no question of me returning to the office.'

'Pollitt can be a slave-driver.'

'You all work so hard for the cause.'

'It's the only thing worth working for.'

She remembered what Max had told her. That Glading and his sort would do anything, absolutely anything, to implement their ideas. From Glading's tone, she knew it to be true. Her eggs arrived and a pot of tea and she fastened her eyes on her food, hoping he'd not noticed her fear.

A party of young men in cheap suits arrived and sat round a table close by and the noise of their cheerful conversation meant that Glading had to lean closer to make himself heard.

'We do miss you in the office, you know. The new girl's not the same. Efficient enough, but can't say boo to a goose. Still, young Duncan's taken a shine to her. She laughs at his jokes.'

'I'm glad he's found someone who does.'

'What will you be doing with yourself, then? Sell your silver spoon to pay the rent?'

'Very funny. I'll have to look for something, though. My savings won't last long. Anyway, I need to keep myself occupied.' This was the truth. It wasn't simply money, she was already starting to get bored.

'We always need volunteers. What would you say to that?' Glading's intent look belied his casual tone.

'How do you mean?' Her knife and fork stilled in her hands.

'Oh, there's always this and that.'

'You know I'm no good at campaigning. I hate that sort of thing.' Thinking that the moment, whatever it was, had passed, she continued to eat, but Glading ate a last fragment of steak pie and pushed his plate away.

'So you've told me many times, and I wasn't meaning that.

Something might come up, Minnie, and I'd like to think I could count on you.'

'Such as what?' Her heart began to beat faster.

'We're friends, you and I, aren't we? We should meet like this from time to time. That's all.'

'Of course we're friends.' Her interest was piqued. 'And yes, you can count on me.'

After they parted Minnie wandered along Oxford Street, staring into shop windows but hardly noticing the displays. Her old life already dogged her again. Max still held her on a string, now it seemed Glading did, too. What was stopping her cutting these ties? A sense of duty, perhaps, to the England she knew and its quiet conservative way of life. To Max, whose approval meant so much to her. How, she pondered, could she want a thing and resent it at the same time? It was this that had ruined her relationship with Raymond. What a pile of contradictions she was.

When she reached Marble Arch she caught a bus back to Holland Park, because she always found it more calming than the underground. By the time she closed the door of her flat behind her she'd stopped worrying so much. She would write to Max to report the day's events, but warn him that nothing might come of Glading's heavy hints for the moment.

She poured a cup of tea, kicked off her shoes and put her feet up on the sofa as she opened the post. There was still nothing from Raymond, but she must stop brooding about that, she told herself fiercely. Looking for a job she liked with hours she could manage should be her next priority. She would buy a paper in the morning and search for vacancies.

Twenty-eight

The following week Minnie went for an interview at the office of a trade magazine in Manchester Square, north of Oxford Street. On arrival, she realized it was only a few doors down from Bulmer & Wyndham, the advertising company she had applied to several years before and where she had been belittled by the director for whom she would have worked.

This magazine wanted a typist, but though the interview went well the job wouldn't do because the money was so poor. Minnie was leaving, cross about her wasted morning, when a sound made her look up and she noticed an elegant woman clutching a huge portfolio emerge from the front door of Bulmer & Wyndham and glance, frowning, up and down the street. As she drew near their eyes met and she saw with a jolt that it was the woman who had interviewed her all that time ago. Minnie even dredged up her name. On an impulse she said, 'Miss Baines?'

'Yes. Do I know you?' Miss Baines said, her eyes narrowing. She was much the same as Minnie remembered.

'I'm Minnie Gray. You saw me about a typing job once. I say, do you need help with that thing?' A gust of wind had almost blown the portfolio from Miss Baines's grasp and she ran across to help. While they secured it, Minnie said, 'I'm ever so sorry if I distracted you. I've attended an interview a few doors down and seeing you took me by surprise.'

'No harm done,' Miss Baines said, 'though the wretched cab hasn't turned up. Look, I don't remember you, to be honest, but you're looking for work, you say?'

'Yes. I was offered the job just now, but I'm afraid it didn't suit.'

'Ah. Did I think you were any good?'

'I passed the tests all right, if that's what you mean. It was the gentleman I'd have been working for that was the problem, the fair-haired one with the signet ring ...'

'Mr Wyndham. I know what you're about to say. His assistants never stay long.' She looked at Minnie quizzically. 'By coincidence, I had to sack a girl this morning. She turned up late for the fourth day in a row and was rude when I ticked her off. Listen, if you ...'

Her words were drowned as a black cab roared up and pulled in at the kerb. The driver leaped out, came round and opened the rear door. 'Sorry, ladies, the traffic's something else this morning.'

'Come with me, if you'd like,' Miss Baines said to Minnie. 'I have to take some designs to Mr Wyndham. He's at a meeting in Regent Street. We can talk on the way.'

Minnie, who had nothing else to do, climbed into the cab.

By the time they returned to Manchester Square an hour

later where she successfully performed a couple of short tests, Minnie had secured employment as a part-time typist reporting not to the dismissive Mr Wyndham, but to Miss Baines herself. The salary was generous and the hours suited her perfectly. She began the next morning and quickly felt at home. The office, big airy rooms with pale, beechwood furniture, felt clean and modern, and since Minnie worked efficiently and cheerfully, she rubbed along well with Miss Baines and even impressed Mr Wyndham with her knowledge of cricket.

The weeks passed and she did not hear from her old friends at King Street and the single meeting with Max was a pleasant quiet drink. At last she was beginning to feel more like her old self before the stress and anxiety had begun to bite so hard.

This brief period of peace was shattered when Minnie arrived home one evening in October to find a letter from her mother. She hung up her jacket and put the kettle on before opening it, looking forward with pleasure to her mother's gossipy warmth. A familiar name in the second paragraph immediately caught her eye. As she read, her pleasure drained away. '*I met Mrs Mills today in the lift in Debenhams,*' her mother had written. '*I had bought that winter coat with the Persian lamb collar I told you I wanted. My dear, it'll come as a bit of a shock for you if you haven't already heard, but Raymond's getting married.*' Minnie's hand flew to her mouth. '*He met the girl in Lyme Regis. She was on holiday there with her parents. Quite the whirlwind romance, apparently. I hope you're not too put out by this news, but I fear . . .*'

Minnie drew a sharp breath. Lyme Regis. That was where she and Raymond would have gone if she hadn't been unwell. What a bitter twist. She scrunched up the letter without reading the rest and shoved it into a drawer, then began to pace the kitchen, trying to absorb the news. A small, tender part of her had been clinging to the hope of Raymond and now she must let that hope shrivel and die. There was nothing more she could do.

The kettle began to whistle and reaching for it, her hand shook and she cried out as boiling water splashed her. She held her hand under the cold tap, but the pain was such that she could not hold back the tears.

Her scalded fingers took a week to heal. Her heartache much longer.

Twenty-nine

Autumn 1936

A whole year passed without much incident and Minnie came to assume that her spying days were over. She felt much stronger in herself. She enjoyed her typing job, being Secretary of the hockey club and seeing friends and was glad to be sleeping much better. Only occasionally, when she was alone in her flat or passing one of her old haunts, the café she used to frequent with Glading or the cinema where she'd meet Max, did she feel a restlessness, a pang of regret. Usually this would fade, but sometimes a sadness would come over her and she would wonder what everything she'd done was for, a sense of something unfinished. *Buck up, Minnie,* she'd tell herself then. *Life might be less exciting, but think how much happier you are.*

Bulmer & Wyndham took the main national newspapers so that its staff could keep up with the trends. One Friday at the end of November Minnie unwrapped her lunchtime sandwich and pulled the *Daily Mail* towards her. As she bit into cheese and pickle her eye rested on an intriguing headline: *'Riddle of Dying Woman in Club'* and she quickly read on. A woman had been found unconscious in a bedroom at the famous Overseas Club in St James's earlier in the week and despite the best hospital treatment had subsequently died. When she came to the dead woman's name she almost choked. It was Mrs Maxwell Knight. Max's wife, Gwladys. Minnie pushed the sandwich aside and read the article again, trying to take in the details. Mrs Knight had come up from the country on the previous evening, but instead of staying with her husband she had checked into the club where he was a member. It was thought that she'd taken an overdose of barbiturates, though whether on purpose or by accident would have to be decided by an inquest.

Minnie checked to see that no one was looking before she tore the article out and folded it away in her handbag, a lump of distress swelling in her throat. Poor Gwladys. She'd only been thirty-eight, the paper said. Very young to die. Poor Max, too. The *Mail* described him as an author, with no mention of his day job, which was interesting. Minnie wondered idly why Gwladys had not stayed with her husband in his Sloane Street flat, but on reflection it confirmed what she'd long suspected. Mr and Mrs Knight largely lived separate lives.

Minnie could hardly think of anything but this tragedy for the rest of the day and Miss Baines was quite sharp with her when she made a mess typing columns of figures. What should she do? She badly wanted to see Max to say how sorry she was, but at the same time recognized that she couldn't. Now would be a time for family and close friends. Although she and Max were close in many respects and her heart ached for him, no one else really knew this. She'd be treated as an outsider.

In the end, she wrote him a short letter. It took several false starts to hit the right note and still she thought the result seemed bald, but she hadn't known his wife and anything other than simple polite warmth would probably appear intrusive.

She blotted the letter carefully and put it in an envelope, then took it out again and wrote a PS. 'I hope that we may be in touch once this most difficult time is past.'

That was that for the moment, she thought as she went to the corner of the street and pushed the letter into the post-box. There was actually no burning reason why she and Max might meet in the near future because she had nothing to report to him. Walking back to the house she was once again dogged by loneliness.

All Minnie received in response to her letter was a black-edged printed card that arrived in the post two weeks later. It read simply: 'Mr Maxwell Knight thanks you for your condolences on the death of his wife Gwladys and appreciates the kindness shown.'

It was a Friday near Christmas and Minnie had taken the day off to buy gifts for her family. Despite apprehension of accidentally bumping into Max, she chose Knightsbridge and Harrods because good old Auntie Minnie was expected to sprinkle a touch of London glamour at Christmas and she didn't want to disappoint.

Harrods was beautifully lit up like a fairy palace and she wandered the bright departments admiring all the lovely things she could never afford, in search of something special but reasonably priced for her mother. She spent a long time examining shawls, especially a warm woollen one of midnight blue embroidered with tiny white stars, but it was quite beyond her budget so she reluctantly replaced it on the pile.

The prettily packaged soap and talcum powder she chose would suit her sisters and she tracked down silk ties for Richard and Doug. Exhausted by the decision-making, Minnie treated herself to coffee in one of the restaurants and puzzled over the problem of what to buy her mother. She would really love that shawl, she thought, and doodled a quick sum in her diary. If she restricted the amount she spent on her little nieces and nephews, who were too young to mind anyway, she could just about afford it. She was wondering how much exactly she had in her bank account and when the next lot of bills might arrive when she noticed a woman sitting at the next table engrossed in *The Times*. Her cool demeanour, the immaculate make-up, the glossy thoroughbred look, all were unmistakeable. It was Max's colleague who'd temporarily been her MI5 contact when he'd been ill. She was so caught up in her reading, a little frown playing on her face, that Minnie wondered whether to pretend she hadn't seen her, leave money for her coffee and simply slip away, but her curiosity got the better of her. The woman might have news of Max.

'Miss Roberts?'

The woman glanced up, still frowning. When she saw Minnie, recognition sprang into her eyes. 'Minnie Gray. Goodness.' She glanced round the restaurant as though to check that they weren't being observed. Then she pointed to the newspaper and said to Minnie in a low voice, 'I suppose you've been following the case?'

'The case,' Minnie echoed, misunderstanding. 'Do you mean the King's abdication?'

'No, I'm fed up to the back teeth with hearing about that dreadful American woman. I mean Mrs Knight's inquest,' the other woman said. 'It's been all over the papers. Look.' She handed *The Times* over, folded to the article she'd been reading. The headline was *'Death of Author's Wife'* and Minnie began to read. She'd been looking out for news, but hadn't seen today's paper.

'Of course, it's done his reputation no good at the office, no good at all,' Miss Roberts started to say, though Minnie only half-listened. She was caught up in the account of Gwladys Knight's death, which the newspaper called 'mysterious'. The facts were concerning.

Max, it seemed, had not given a true statement of his actions to the police. He had initially claimed that he visited his wife at the Club the night she arrived, but it turned out that he hadn't. This obfuscation had led to Gwladys's mother and brother accusing him of murder or, at the very least, of driving his wife to suicide in order to get hold of her money. The Coroner, however, believed that there was nothing to demonstrate Max's involvement in his wife's death. The medical experts were unsure whether Gwladys had taken too many barbiturates by accident, mistaking them for less harmful aspirin, or deliberately meaning to kill herself. The Coroner went on to declare that it was impossible to say which. He delivered an open verdict.

'I don't understand why M lied about visiting her,' Minnie said, looking up from the paper. She felt bewildered and dismayed by what she'd read. There was so much about Max that she didn't know.

Miss Roberts assumed an expression of disdain. 'He neglected the poor woman, that's what I've heard, installed her in the country, miles from London, and hardly visited her. I expect he lied because it would be embarrassing for him if it came out in public' – here she lowered her voice even further – *'that he and Gwladys weren't living together as man and wife.'*

'Oh.' The nature of the marriage, which Minnie had puzzled about for so long, suddenly came into sharp focus. Max and Gwladys had indeed lived separate lives, but this hadn't been Gwladys's choice. Max had neglected her, which sounded awful. And, yes, she could imagine him attaching importance to keeping up appearances. She'd noticed that streak in him herself. As she handed back the newspaper Minnie remembered what Miss Roberts had said a moment ago about the whole business doing Max 'no good at all'. She supposed that must be true. The last thing MI5 would want was the private life of one of its key spy-masters splashed all over the newspapers, especially when it involved a suspicious death. The press described him as an author, but she imagined that behind the scenes his real job must be known.

Poor Gwladys, she thought, remembering the striking, vital woman she'd seen in the restaurant. And poor Max. Whatever the truth about his marriage, he surely didn't deserve to be the subject of gossip at the nation's breakfast tables.

Beside her, Miss Roberts finished her coffee. Minnie asked her quickly, 'How is M, do you know? I haven't seen him for a while.'

The woman shrugged. 'Nor have we. At least, not much.' She looked hard at Minnie. 'You've been useful to him. He'll be back in touch, I imagine.'

She rose and pushed back her chair. 'Good luck with your shopping,' she said, eyeing Minnie's Harrods bags, and swept away in a cloud of scent before Minnie could even draw breath to say goodbye. She watched the woman's departing figure thoughtfully and the words from that hateful song came to mind, *'the beautiful spy ...'* Miss Roberts with her glamorous hairstyle and her sinuous walk looked more the part than Minnie ever could.

As she took the lift down to haberdashery to buy the shawl for her mother the tune kept playing in her head and she was thankful to escape with her purchases out into the frosty air. The meeting with Miss Roberts had shaken her. Still, she'd thrown Minnie a scrap that she'd pecked up eagerly. *You've been useful ... He'll be back in touch ...*

Thirty

'It's beautiful, darling,' her mother sighed, shaking out the shawl, a splash of rich colour in the room. 'Really lovely.' She stroked the soft material and examined the tiny embroidered white stars. 'I'll have to think of an occasion to wear it.' She looked doubtful and Minnie, sitting next to her on the sofa, stroking Boots the cat, couldn't help an impatient laugh.

'You don't need a special occasion, Mother. If you're cold in the evenings wear it round the house.'

'Oh, I couldn't, darling. It's far too lovely for that.'

She watched her mother replace the shawl in its box and carefully fold up the wrapping paper – 'to use again next year' – feeling a sense of hollowness inside. She'd tried so hard and spent a great deal of money on something that would, she saw now, spend its life unworn in a bottom drawer because it was too precious to use.

Her mother must have seen her disappointment because she said, 'I know, I can wear it to the Conservatives' dinner in March,' and Minnie felt a rush of warmth towards her.

'That's a good idea.'

'Now, we'd better see how the birds are doing, hadn't we, or everyone will arrive and no dinner.' Mrs Gray rose stiffly and re-tied her apron. 'There'll be seven of us, won't there, including the baby? Such a shame that Richard has to work. I suppose it's because of his promotion. Would you be a dear and fetch my bedroom chair? I asked Doug to do it before he went out, but he doesn't have a sensible thought in his head these days.'

'Young love,' Minnie said with a sigh, lifting Boots off her lap. Even her youngest brother was getting married. He was spending Christmas Day with his fiancée's family. Marjorie, who was coming to lunch with her husband and family, was recovering from giving birth to her third child. It was a shame about Richard, though he was doing well and talking about moving to Special Branch. She smiled to herself, remembering its sensitive relationship with the Secret Service and how annoyed Max had been when it had tried to recruit its own spies.

Everybody else was settling down, procreating. Well, if she hadn't done, it was her own fault. She felt a prickle of sadness thinking of Raymond, but brooding was pointless. Raymond was a chapter closed to her, married now and, her mother had discovered, with a child on the way.

Marjorie's family arrived half an hour late and lunch, two roast partridges, a mountain of vegetables, plum pudding and custard, with tinned fruit cocktail for the toddlers, was served up and eaten. Marjorie, pale and heavy-eyed, ate with one hand as she cradled the grizzling baby, but the older children, rosy-cheeked, bright-eyed, at four and three, were the perfect age for Christmas. They understood enough about the specialness of the occasion, but not too much, so that the ceremony of presents after lunch was a source of wonder, the emergence of the pretty doll and the clockwork train from the parcels Minnie gave them something magical rather than greedily evaluated.

The adults sat around eating chocolates or cracking nuts, tossing the shells into the fire, taking turns with the baby and swapping stories of past Christmases. All perfect, Minnie thought, but why, then, did she feel so restless? Honestly, these days, if she was in London she wished to be at home in Edgbaston with people she knew through and through. And now that she was here it felt dull and cloying.

As the pale mauve afternoon sky darkened to purple and the shadows crowded in she went to the window to draw the curtains and paused to look out at the sodden front garden and the stumpy shapes of the pollarded chestnuts beyond. Tiny snowflakes danced in the air and when she touched the glass it felt icy. Here she was in the warm, but the dangerous chill of the outside called her. She stepped over Marjorie's husband, setting out the new toy railway on the carpet, slipped past Mrs Gray and Marjorie, bent over a knitting pattern on the sofa, and out to the hall. Coat, scarf, hat and gloves all donned. Minnie closed the front door quietly behind her, clutching her key for warmth in her pocket.

The snow wasn't coming to anything, but still the evening air was sharp with frost and smelled of gunpowder. Cruel gusts caught up dead leaves in eddies round her ankles and she shivered as she walked slowly up the road. There was no one about, but here and there, neighbours had not yet drawn their curtains and she glimpsed candle-lit trees and cosy scenes in sitting rooms. As she turned the corner a tiny dog crouching on a windowsill barked at her soundlessly through the glass. Out here, with the whirling snowflakes burning her cheeks, for the first time today she felt truly alive. What did life hold for her, she wondered. Whatever it was she was ready.

Thirty-one

February 1937

Minnie didn't have long to wait. One squally dark evening she returned home from work and a gust tore the front door from her grasp. A cheap brown envelope sailed from the hall shelf onto the floor at her feet. She wrestled the door shut then picked up the letter and turned it over. It looked entirely uninteresting so she stuffed it into her coat pocket and forgot about it.

The next morning, waiting in the underground, she pulled out her handkerchief to blow her nose and the envelope fluttered onto the crowded platform. 'Excuse me.' She bent to rescue it from between a lady's feet. This time she tore it open and peeped in at the printed letter inside. '*Dear Comrade Gray . . .*' The annual request to renew her Communist Party membership. She thrust it into her handbag with a feeling of disquiet, but now a train was rushing in. She held onto her hat as the crowd surged forward.

Each time Minnie looked in her bag that day she noticed the envelope and bit her lip, wondering what to do. She loathed the idea of renewing again, hating what the Party stood for, but something told her she should. There was Miss Roberts's comment before Christmas about her continuing importance to Max for a start. Then, if it came to anyone's notice at King Street that she'd allowed her membership to lapse, the wrong kind of reason might be attributed. The simplest thing to do, she decided on the way home, was to be upfront with Pollitt about the matter. And seeing Pollitt would offer the excuse she needed to make contact with Max. She'd still not heard from him since the death of his wife and she was concerned.

When she telephoned Harry Pollitt from a public box the following lunchtime his voice boomed warm and friendly down the line. 'Of course we must meet. Your half-day, you say? Why don't you stop by after lunch?'

Minnie arrived at the King Street offices early in the afternoon to find it as busy as ever. Some things were different. There was a poster up in the entrance area advertising a meeting about the civil war in Spain and when the receptionist let her in it was to see two earnest young women, needles flying as they stitched letters onto a red banner. An anxious-looking scrawny youth sat clutching a cloth cap. As she waited for Pollitt to see her, the young man explained in a whining voice that he'd come to volunteer to fight the Fascists and why wouldn't anyone see him. Pollitt's door was closed and there was no sign of Glading.

Minnie had to wait twenty minutes before Pollitt opened

his door. The would-be volunteer stood up hopefully, but to his chagrin Pollitt ignored him. Instead he beamed at Minnie. 'Miss Gray, come in, I'm sorry to have kept you so long.'

In his gloomy office he bid her sit down and gestured at the papers scattered over his desk. 'Drafting a speech for the fundraiser tomorrow night,' he explained. 'Conditions are dire out there for the brigades. No ammunition, precious little food and a trail of innocents like that one outside coming through our offices thinking we'll give him a rifle and send him out to save the world. Now, it's good to see you, Minnie.' He twinkled at her. 'We can't persuade you to come and stuff some envelopes, can we? It's all hands on deck here at present.'

'I'm sorry, no. It's quite the opposite reason I've come for.' She opened her bag and took out the brown envelope. 'I felt I must tell you in person. I can't renew. I . . .' she said in a bashful whisper, 'I have a boyfriend I'm rather fond of. And he doesn't like me being a member, you see.' It wasn't quite a lie, only in that the boyfriend was no more. She had the grace to blush, but to her relief Pollitt mistook the nature of her shame.

'A boyfriend, eh? Never mind,' he said gently, taking the letter from her. 'You can only do what you can do. And you can always change your mind if the boyfriend doesn't work out. Though I hope he does for your sake.'

'So do I.' She answered his smile with one of her own. 'Thank you for understanding.'

She glanced round his office, judging it less tidy than when she worked for him, but otherwise noticing nothing out of the ordinary amid the dark furniture, the rows of books and the stern portrait of Lenin. Nothing to interest Max, she thought, disappointed. They chatted for a few minutes inconsequentially about what each had been doing, then Pollitt looked at his watch and Minnie took the hint and rose from her chair. The air was freighted with the sense that something was coming to an end and she felt a lump swell in her throat as she shook his hand.

When she'd left Pollitt's office, closing the door behind her, she saw that the pale-faced lad was now addressing his whining to a fair-haired man who stood with his back to her. A man who was at once familiar. As she passed him their eyes met and his face lit up with pleasure. 'Minnie Gray, this is a surprise.'

'A good one, I hope. It's wonderful to see you.'

'And to see you.' Glading shook her hand eagerly. 'It's been far too long. How are you?'

'Well, thank you. The quiet life suits me.' Behind Glading the pale-faced man she'd interrupted had slumped into a crestfallen gloom. 'I needed to speak to Mr Pollitt about something ...'

'Ah, I'm waiting to see him myself. Perhaps ...' He looked thoughtful, and Minnie held her breath, but then Pollitt's door opened and he called Glading in, so she said a hasty goodbye.

Well, she told herself as she stepped outside on the street, and stopped to button up her gloves. *I suppose it's all over.* She felt a bit flat. She'd achieved the first object of her visit, but she didn't really have anything to report to Max. With slow reluctance she walked away.

Thirty-two

Two evenings later, Minnie was sitting at her kitchen table rubbing polish into a pair of court shoes when the telephone rang. Hastily peeling off her rubber gloves she went to answer it.

'Minnie Gray,' the voice said down the line. Glading had an irritating habit of never revealing his name on the telephone, in case the line was bugged.

'Oh, it's you.' She straightened, instantly on her guard. It went through her mind that Pollitt must have told him the reason for her visit to King Street and he was ringing to persuade her to change her mind.

Instead he said, 'Can we meet for lunch? Tomorrow, if you're free.'

Tomorrow. She couldn't think straight for a moment. 'Yes, I think so.' She would finish work at one.

After they'd made the arrangement she returned to the kitchen to continue polishing her shoes, but hardly noticed what she was doing. What on earth did Glading want? An underlying urgency in his voice had told her it wasn't to be a conversation about membership.

Minnie left the shoes to dry on a sheet of newspaper and went to the telephone. She'd not spoken to Max for months, but his number was emblazoned on her mind. He answered straight away and caught her excitement. His voice was as warm and reassuring as ever. 'Come here,' he insisted, 'as soon as you've seen him.'

The café Glading had named wasn't their usual one, a bus ride from Manchester Square to Clerkenwell. With its simple wooden furniture and oxblood painted walls it felt modern in a dull utilitarian way. There were Soviet posters on the walls and the other customers were serious-looking men of Pollitt and Glading's ilk. Minnie, though soberly dressed in her navy skirt and jacket, didn't feel at ease there. Fortunately Glading was already there, sitting at a table in a corner writing in a notebook. 'Minnie.' He welcomed her warmly.

'What an odd place,' she confided, sitting down opposite.

'Is it?' he said, glancing around without interest. 'At least they're our sort. Mine, anyway, but you're with me so that's all right.'

Food was ordered and quickly brought, a meat and vegetable pie, rather salty. Minnie described her new job when he asked and he listened without saying much. She wondered what was distracting him.

'Listen, Minnie,' he said finally, when they'd finished eating. 'I want your help.' He wiped his mouth with a napkin then leaned in closer.

Her every nerve stood on full alert, but she forced herself to speak calmly. 'My help doing what exactly?'

'Can I trust you?' He kept his voice low.

'Of course you can, but what do you mean?'

'I can't have you keep asking me questions, you see.'

'Now you're making me anxious.'

'Don't be. It's something very easy I want you to do.'

'I can't agree if you won't tell me what it is.'

Glading drank a mouthful of tea and gave her a level look. Finally he said, 'All right. I need you to rent a flat and live in it.'

'Rent a flat? But I already have one,' she said, puzzled.

'Pipe down, will you?' He glanced about. 'I know you do. This would be a different one. You'd have to move.'

'I like my current one, thank you. Why would I move?'

'It's for the cause, Minnie. Will you or won't you?'

'Glading was very specific,' Minnie told Max later. 'It must be at ground floor level and not in a block because there must be no porter. All I have to do is let him use the place occasionally to meet people. I must live there, but he'll pay the rent. Otherwise I can carry on with my usual life.'

She was sitting in one of the armchairs in the drawing room in Sloane Street. Max's face, which she'd thought rather sad and old, was becoming happier and younger-looking by the minute and his eyes showed that old sparkle.

'What else about it?'

'Nothing yet. He's particularly cagey and I'm not to ask questions, remember?'

'Yes, yes.' Max began to prowl the room, his hands in his pockets. There were fewer cages, Minnie had noticed. The vivarium had gone and even the parrot was subdued. Bobby, who was an ageing dog now, dozed by the fire, but when his master said in a definite voice, 'It's to be a safe house, obviously, but I wonder who else knows about it,' he raised his head briefly.

'Everything's to be in my name,' Minnie said, misunderstanding.

'Yes, yes. My question is whether Glading is acting on his own initiative.'

'There's no hint that Pollitt knows about it, if that's what you mean.'

'What's Glading up to, then, I wonder?' He spoke in a whisper, as though to himself, but then he swung round to confront her. 'You'll do it, of course, Minnie.'

'I . . . I only said I'd think about it.'

He nodded. 'A good answer.'

'I meant it though, Max. I haven't decided yet.'

Exasperation leaped into his eyes. 'Minnie, you must do it.'

'I don't know if I have the strength.'

'Of course you do.'

There was a dullness to his voice and her heart went out to him. Whatever the state of his relationship with Gwladys, the manner of her death, the investigation and the inquest that followed, the public exposure, all this must have taken the stuffing out of him. She'd asked him earlier how he was, but he'd brushed the matter aside.

He folded his arms and stared at the floor. A silence followed.

She said, 'I thought about saying no to Glading and not telling you.'

He raised his head and she saw hurt and surprise in his face and felt a sort of triumph as well as a certain amount of guilt.

Finally he said, 'But you didn't. Why didn't you, Minnie?'

She looked away. 'I don't know,' she mumbled. 'The usual nonsense, I suppose.'

'Nonsense? Duty to your country?'

'Yes.' She picked a blonde hair from her dark skirt then looked up at him. 'And loyalty to you. Hasn't it always been like that? You look so sad, Max, and I'm sorry. Sorry about your wife and everything that happened. I bumped into Miss Roberts, did she say? She told me that it's made life difficult for you at the office.'

His expression hardened and she regretted her words. 'Miss Roberts,' he snarled, 'knows nothing.'

'Still, it must have been awful. Your wife, she was very lovely.'

'And I feel guilty every day that I didn't spend more time with her. But never mind the office, Minnie, this would show them. You must do it. This is the opportunity we hoped for, to finally pin something on Glading. What does he need a safe house for? And why isn't he telling Pollitt? It can only be for a nefarious reason. And he trusts you, that's a trust you've earned.'

She mulled over this and felt the old thrill, faint, but growing in strength. 'I do feel better in myself,' she said finally. 'I think I could do it. For the time being, anyway.' Now she'd come to a decision she felt more energized.

'Good. Well done, Minnie. Now, we must get to work.'

We. They were working together again, she and Max. An older, sadder Max, but then she had changed, had become guarded, more protective of herself. The old naïve Minnie had relied on Max completely. Now she was more wary. It felt good to bask in his attention again, but he would have to earn back her trust.

It took a couple of weeks of visiting properties for Minnie to track down the right place. Then one evening she met Max in the hotel on Cromwell Road and showed him the details of a flat she recommended. It was in Holland Road in Kensington, a short distance from where she currently lived.

She'd viewed it with the agent that afternoon and immediately liked the quiet street with its handsome lines of terraced houses, their neat stubby front gardens and red brick frontages piped thickly with white stucco. The flat in question was the ground floor of one of the houses, as Glading had specified, and the upstairs neighbour apparently spent most of his time at his country home. It felt spacious, with two main rooms and two bedrooms, and was being let unfurnished. This didn't matter as Glading had spoken about funds being available for furniture and curtains, and, anyway, she wanted room for the few special items she'd acquired over the years that would help make it feel like home.

Minnie looked out of the front window and was satisfied by its clear view of the street and opportunities for parking, which had been Max's specification. MI5 could easily set up a surveillance operation to record comings and goings to the flat. Max had told her that photographs and a log book would be crucial evidence in any prosecution.

She wiped a finger across the dusty windowsill and looked about the room, imagining how her two easy chairs might be arranged on either side of the gas fire, and wondering whether her bookcase would fit in the alcove and what Glading would still need to buy – a coffee table, a sofa, perhaps, and curtains. Bedroom furniture. She could imagine herself living here comfortably, but the idea of someone outside in a car training his eye on the place made her shiver. Perhaps it would be better if she used the gloomier back room for relaxing in and left this one for Glading's activities, whatever they might be. That would give her more privacy.

Yet Glading would undoubtedly have an opinion. She glanced across the road and froze. An Indian man in a turban and carrying a suitcase was knocking at the door of a house opposite. Perhaps he was looking for her. But no, she was safe, he was only a salesman. Was it too late to say she couldn't do this job after all? Yes, it was. She'd only antagonize both sides, Glading and Max, whom, of course, she'd need to bring separately, without alerting the agent, to see the outside of the property.

Despite all the difficulties, once she'd signed the tenancy, Minnie again sensed that little spark of joy she'd first experienced all those years ago when Dolly Pyle had asked her whether she'd be interested in working for the government.

Thirty-three

An exceptionally busy few weeks followed. The tenancy took effect at the beginning of April and Minnie cleaned the place thoroughly before moving in. As predicted, Glading had strong opinions, and the front room became her sitting room. Since it was by far the pleasanter and lighter of the two rooms, despite her worry about being overlooked she was satisfied.

Soon afterwards, she and Glading went shopping. They attracted some queer looks in Heal's because in a number of ways they appeared an ill-matched couple and she wasn't wearing a wedding ring. Also, Glading kept butting in and offering unusual requests, which bemused the sales assistants. The curtains had to be fully lined, for instance, even though the weather was growing warmer. Minnie imagined that this would be so no one could see in. Less understandable to her was his awkwardness about a shabby gate-legged dining table left in the flat by the previous inhabitant. Minnie was puzzled that he was so preoccupied by it. She would simply have thrown a pretty cloth over it and have done. He examined half a dozen different tables in a catalogue before sighing and pronouncing that the old one would have to 'do the job for the moment'. Why he might need anything different he didn't say.

Indeed, he hadn't explained anything much to her. This was frustrating, but not surprising. Glading had always behaved in this way. Everything with him was a shade secretive. She'd learned that lesson during their meeting in Paris when he'd given away nothing about the broader context of her Indian mission, or about his own visit to the country, even though they were alone together in a room in a foreign city, a time of closeness when one might have expected him to reveal more about himself.

Minnie was sad to leave her old flat, but at least the new one was bigger and the hot water geyser in the bathroom more efficient. And there was no Mrs Saunders. Instead of her busybodying, there would be MI5 watching the house instead.

Glading had promised Minnie that he would always call ahead before he visited. Day after day she expected to hear from him as April passed but there was silence. She wasn't worried exactly. After all, he'd given her money to cover the rent and the credit payments on the furniture, and she lived her life as usual, but it was uncomfortable to be on tenterhooks, waiting for something to happen. When she left home in the mornings or returned from work, she was sometimes aware of a flicker of movement at a window of the house opposite. She never saw anybody come or go and Max said nothing about having set up an operation there, but she couldn't shift the prickly sensation of being watched.

It was early evening almost three weeks after she'd moved in that Glading telephoned. In the background she heard the hum of a busy pub. He apologized for the short notice but could he bring someone round to meet her? 'He's with me now.'

'Yes,' she replied, in as calm a voice as she could muster, 'if you could hold off for half an hour.' After he rang off she tried telephoning Max at Sloane Street, and was surprised when some mysterious woman – not his sister Ethel – answered and told her he was out. Unsure whether to identify herself, she said that she would ring his office and leave a message, which she proceeded to do. By now very flustered indeed, Minnie rushed around tidying up, then frowned at her reflection in the bathroom mirror, ran a comb through her hair and slicked on some lipstick. Would she pass muster with Glading's friend, whoever he might be? It was too late to worry.

Her first impression of the man looming behind Glading on her doorstep was how very tall he was. When she invited them in he had to duck under the lintel.

'Miss Gray, this is Mr – er– Peters,' Glading said. He seemed tense, his forehead beaded with perspiration, and he smelled of beer.

'Very pleased to meet you, Miss Gray,' Peters said in a heavy East European accent, extending his hand to shake hers. *Such long, cold fingers,* she thought, *and I'm certain your name isn't really Peters.* It wasn't simply his height and pallid face. The long, dark swept-back hair, black suit, shoes and tie completed her impression of a cod Hollywood Dracula. Peters examined her critically through small heavy-lidded eyes and she forced herself to stare back. The only dash of colour about him was a glint of gold in his teeth when he spoke. He gave off an air of coiled-up energy and his nostrils flared as he exhaled as though he were about to pounce. In all, he looked like the popular notion of a Russian spy and she wondered at his Soviet masters' naïvety.

She showed the men into the front room and offered them sherry, which they refused, although Glading looked long-ingly at the decanter. Peters folded his lanky figure into one of the easy chairs and rested his hat on his lap as though he might need to leap up and leave at short notice. Glading slumped unhappily into the other chair. Minnie perched on the new sofa, all attentive. Peters cleared his throat, but nobody said anything.

'These dark evenings are hard to get used to, aren't they?' Minnie murmured. She rose and switched on the lamps, but this proved a mistake because at once Glading asked if she would draw the curtains. When she went to the window, though, there was no sign that they were being watched. The curtains safely pulled across, Glading and Peters watched her sit down.

'Shall I leave you both to talk?' Minnie said brightly, but Glading said there was no need for that.

After a short pause Mr Peters said, 'This is indeed a pleasant room.'

'Thank you. Shall I light the fire? The evenings are still so chilly.'

'No, I am warm enough, thank you.'

Glading gave a nervous cough. 'Miss Gray hasn't lived here long. Tell Mr Peters where you were before, Minnie.'

'Only a mile away. Near the park. D'you know the area?'

'No, I do not.'

How long have you lived in this country? She couldn't ask that. Casting around for something neutral to talk about, she was put off by Glading's unease. She was being tested, she supposed.

'You have a job, Miss Gray?' Mr Peters asked finally. He began to drum his fingers annoyingly on the arm of the chair.

'Yes,' she said, relieved at a safe topic. 'At an advertising company in Manchester Square, near Oxford Street. I'm a typist there.'

'It is a nice place to work?'

'Very nice. The people are friendly.'

'And the pay is good?'

'Not bad.'

These banalities continued for the best part of an hour with Glading's occasional nervous interjection.

And then, suddenly, it was over. Whether Glading felt that his companion had seen enough, or they had another engagement, Minnie didn't know, but he stood up and said, 'We'd better be getting along, don't you think?' After she and Peters shook hands again she showed them out into the moonlit evening.

As she was closing the door, relieved, but already thinking of what she would write in her report for Max, she glanced at the house opposite and caught a pale face looking down from the upstairs window. It quickly withdrew. So there *was* someone there. She shut the door and leaned against it, feeling that everything was too much.

While she was typing she suddenly remembered the mysterious woman who had answered the telephone at 38 Sloane Street. If she hadn't been Ethel, then who was she? A housekeeper, perhaps, or another relative. It was only four or five months since the death of Max's wife and although Gwladys hadn't lived there much he might well require domestic help and companionship. That must be the explanation.

Another week passed and Glading telephoned to say that he was visiting again, but this time he'd be alone. Minnie informed Max straightaway.

Glading turned up after Minnie had finished supper and sat companionably with her at the kitchen table drinking tea and talking while she tidied up. He seemed more relaxed tonight, his normal chatty self.

'What did you make of our Mr Peters?' He lit a cigarette and she passed him an ashtray.

'He seemed all right. Russian, I presume.'

'No, in fact, he's Austrian. I don't know how, but he ended up in the Russian Cavalry during the war.'

Minnie considered this and laughed.

'What's funny about that?'

'I was trying to picture him in Cossack costume on a galloping horse with a knife tucked between his teeth.'

'Very amusing. He was a brave and ruthless fighter, if what I hear is true.' Minnie saw that while she'd found Peters sinister and even a bit ridiculous with his formality and lack of small talk, Glading admired the man.

'Sorry, my brother had a picture book . . .'

'I bet he did. Minnie, there's another bloke I may need to ask you to meet, but I'm putting him off for the time being. The less either of us have to do with the likes of *him* the better.'

'Oh?' she asked, trying not to sound as interested as she felt.

'He's a small man. Thinks a lot of himself and there's not much for him to think a lot about.'

'Not my type then,' she laughed.

'Nor mine.' Glading finished his tea and went to put his cup by the sink, then smiled at her. 'You're doing fine here, Minnie. Peters seems to think so, too. Well done. I'll be off now. I expect I'll be along again soon.'

'You'll let me know beforehand?'

'In case you're *entertaining*, you mean?'

She folded her arms. 'That's for me to know and you to wonder.'

'You're an attractive woman, Minnie, that's all I meant.' He blinked at her bashfully through his spectacles and edged closer.

'Don't.' This was a new development and unwelcome. She sidestepped him and swept into the hall to show him out.

Minnie met Max in the usual Cromwell Road hotel. 'So Glading didn't hand over any documents to Peters?' he asked.

'Not at the flat, I'm certain he didn't.'

'Then it sounds as though this Mr Peters simply wanted to size you up. I've an idea who he really is – your description of him is excellent, by the way – and Glading telling you he's Austrian fits exactly. If I'm right, then you've done well to impress him.'

After this period of activity Minnie was left alone by Glading for a few weeks, which was stressful in itself. Each time the telephone rang she was sure it must be him. Instead it would be a friend or her mother. Mrs Gray had entirely swallowed Minnie's explanation for moving, that she'd wanted a garden and a bit more space.

May turned to June, the weather improved and early one evening Glading turned up at her door. He slid inside, looking furtive. He was paler than usual and roughly shaven, as though he hadn't slept. Shocked by the change in him Minnie showed him into her sitting room, where he readily accepted some sherry. After a couple of mouthfuls the colour returned to his cheeks.

'I've been thinking, Minnie. There are things happening and ways you could be useful, if you're game for it.'

She frowned. 'I don't know. You'd better explain.'

He opened and closed his mouth as though uncertain of how to broach his subject. Eventually he said, 'It would take up more of your time. A big thing to ask, I know, but it would involve giving up your typing job.'

'My job? But why? I have to eat.' She didn't have to pretend her annoyance.

'Hold your horses, will you? I'd make it worth your while.'

'I don't understand. I like Bulmer & Wyndham. What are you asking me to do?'

'It's important work for the cause. Listen. Do you know anything about photography? Taking proper photographs, I mean, not holiday snaps.'

'That sort of stuff's too fiddly for me. Photographs of what, anyway?' she added cautiously, though her interest was roused to full pitch.

'Only some documents. Things I'll be *borrowing*. There's a bloke I know who could teach you, then you could do it here. It'll be a piece of cake.'

'I'd like to help, but I've never done it before. Why don't you ask this man, whoever he is?'

'Because I can't. I'll pay you, Minnie. I've worked it out. If you get another job with just a couple of mornings or afternoons then I can make it up. How about five quid a week. You can't say fairer.'

Minnie bit her lip. Five pounds a week was a decent amount. If she found a job with the reduced hours he suggested she'd be very comfortable, especially since he was paying the rent. His Russian friends must regard him seriously if they were subsidizing him to this level. It would be a wrench to leave Bulmer & Wyndham, but Max would be delighted about the reason. She had no knowledge of photography, but the idea of 'documents' spurred her interest.

'Well, I don't know,' she said, brushing biscuit crumbs from a cushion. 'I worry that I wouldn't be any good and you'd be disappointed.'

'It can't be that hard, can it, Minnie, photography, and I need someone I can *trust*. The work must be done here and I can't ask any Tom, Dick or Harry. Think about it, will you?

Hang about, I've an idea. Why don't you give in your notice and have yourself a holiday. Two weeks off. Go home to your mother, or take her to the seaside, I don't mind. Then you can come back and I'll have sorted everything out ready for you to start afresh.'

'I'll think about it.' It was so hard to keep excitement out of her voice.

After Glading had departed she hurried to the telephone and arranged to meet Max the following day. To her surprise he told her to come to an address she hadn't visited before.

Dolphin Square was a huge new modern residential development that had been recently completed overlooking the Thames in Pimlico. Minnie had seen photographs in an illustrated magazine at work, but was still overwhelmed by the reality of the vast complex, the towering red-brick apartment blocks looming above a freshly planted garden square. It took her a few minutes to find the right door.

'Is this M-section now?' she asked, smiling, when Max invited her into a clean bright space that smelled sharply of paint.

He chuckled. 'Sometimes. It's very up to the minute, isn't it?' Although compact and sparsely furnished the flat was luxurious, hushed by its thick wool carpet and with a glorious view of the gardens. He'd made himself at home. Papers were strewn across an artfully lit desk and he had to remove a plate bearing half a ham sandwich before she perched on a hard, but stylish sofa.

'We were becoming very cramped at Sloane Street.' He

settled in a scallop-backed chair opposite her, his notebook open on his knee.

'More animals?' She remembered the sad lack of them on a past visit.

'More animals and more people. This place is owned by my new brother-in-law. He's away a great deal and suggested I borrow it. Very good of him.'

'A new brother-in-law?' Had a sibling got married – his sister Ethel, perhaps?

'Yes. Some might say it was a little soon.' He looked bashful. 'But I couldn't let the luck of meeting Lois go by.'

'Oh, I see. Congratulations,' she stammered. So he'd married again, already – she was stunned. Her mouth felt dry and she could not find more words. He'd not thought to tell her before. *But why should he? Ours is a business arrangement. Yes, but we're friends – aren't we? Of a sort. You're in a compartment, Minnie, one of his many compartments.*

Then it occurred to her that he was breaking the news to her in the only way he was capable of, a funny, sidewise one. She remembered the unfamiliar woman who had answered the telephone to her recently, and berated herself for not twigging then. Not his sister or a housekeeper, but his new wife. Lois.

'Are you all right, Minnie?' He broke through her thoughts. 'Now, tell me what Glading is up to.'

She tried to recover herself, but felt like a swan paddling furiously underwater while on the surface conveying that all was serene. 'Glading. Yes. Um, he wants me to spend more time working for him. I'm to give up my current job and find another with shorter hours. Oh, and I'm to be taught how to photograph *documents*.'

'Documents?' Max sat up straighter and could hardly contain his excitement. 'You know what that means, Minnie? If they're classified then we'll have him!'

'But I like my job and I know nothing about cameras. My brother has a Box Brownie, he develops the pictures himself, but he's never let me use it. What if I'm no good?'

Max gave her a long hard stare and she sighed. Of course she would agree to Glading's plan, but she sensed that she was walking further into danger.

In July, with great regret, Minnie handed in her notice at Bulmer & Wyndham. To her relief, they accepted her reason, that she needed a change of scene, without question. Miss Baines took her out for lunch on her last day and promised to stay in touch. Minnie left with a large bouquet from the directors, a roguish handmade card of herself as Jean Harlow, signed affectionately by all the staff, and many happy memories. *That was it, then*. She felt quite forlorn returning to the silence of her flat.

Two evenings later as she prepared to leave for Edgbaston, where she was to spend the 'holiday' Glading had granted her, he arrived at short notice. It was late and his voice had sounded slurred on the telephone, so she opened the street door warily. He lurched inside in a miasma of beery fumes and muttered apologies. Much concerned she marshalled him through the kitchen to the bathroom beyond, then hastened to put the kettle on. *He's alone, that's a good sign,* she comforted herself as he shuffled past her back down the hall. *But still, something must be wrong.*

She piled a tray with tea and toast and took it through to the sitting room where she found him slouched on the sofa, his eyes red-rimmed and unfocused, his face tinged green. She sat down next to him and poured the tea, but it was a good half an hour before he'd sobered up sufficiently to string two words together. Even then what he said made little sense.

'Six of the bastards tonight.' His words were indistinct. 'Questions, more questions. They put the wind up you, all right.'

'Which bastards do you mean?' she asked, her mind alert.

'Ah, you know ... my ... people. Keep you waiting, too. Can't do this, won't do that. Drives me up the wall. Wish you weren't going away, Minnie. Wish ... Need you here. You're sensible, you are.' She felt his hand wander onto her knee. 'Know where I am with you.'

'Stop it.' She pushed him away firmly. 'I'm sorry about going away, but it was you who told me to go. Can't you have a bit of holiday yourself? Take the family to the seaside. Or is it too busy at King Street?'

'Dunno. Hardly been there. Too much else going on.'

'Oh.' He *must* be acting without Pollitt's involvement. That was interesting news and Max would be glad to hear it, but it worried Minnie. The stress of it was clearly getting to Glading. If he was becoming a loose cannon anything could happen. She struggled not to panic, but it was difficult. Suppose he cracked? The 'bastards' would be ruthless with him. She shivered, remembering the word 'liquidate' that Max had used, and how would that affect her? She had to be careful, very careful indeed.

She went to the window and made a show of closing a gap between the curtains while glancing out at the house opposite. It lay in darkness, but there, a glint of silver at the upstairs window. Someone was watching all right. She shivered. Suddenly she wanted Glading gone.

She began to reload the tray. 'I need to go to bed,' she told him crisply. 'I have an early start.'

He looked up at her pleadingly. 'Can't I sleep here? I'll be no trouble.'

She shook her head vehemently and glanced at her watch. 'Rosa will be anxious. If you leave now you'll make the last train. Go on. Please.'

After she'd sent him grumbling into the night she cleared up, then continued packing. By the time she'd finished it was midnight and she felt bone weary, but she couldn't go to bed yet. She switched on the desk lamp, fed paper into her typewriter and tapped out a quick report of the evening's events. Only when she'd stuffed the envelope in her handbag ready for posting did she wash and change and sink wearily into bed.

In her dreams she was walking down a long, narrow street, with towering, red-brick buildings closing in overhead. She woke in stifling darkness, her heart pounding, gasping for breath. For a long time she lay awake, alert for any strange sound, but all she heard was the distant dripping of the kitchen tap.

Thirty-four

The two weeks Minnie spent in Edgbaston with her mother were enjoyably mundane, but she found herself unable to relax. The memory of Glading, drunk in her flat, was a worry to her. If he annoyed his Russian contacts perhaps she wouldn't be safe. Then she wondered how she was supposed to learn photography for, so far as she knew, he'd recruited no one to teach her.

Her younger brother Doug still lived at home, his new wife having moved in after their wedding while they saved up for a place of their own, so Minnie asked him to show her how his Box Brownie worked.

'Why are you so interested all of a sudden?' he asked, with his boyish grin.

'Oh, it'll give us something to do,' she'd replied, with a shrug. 'I might sign up for an evening class.'

She had no intention of doing any such thing. Evening classes were not to her taste and, anyway, she mustn't appear too keen in Glading's eyes. Nor, however, did she want to make a fool of herself with his Russians.

After overcoming Doug's suspicions she persuaded him to share the secrets of the darkroom he'd set up in the garden shed. She discovered she loved the glowing intimacy of its red-tinged gloom and seeing the images bloom like magic on the paper. He gave her the job of rescuing the prints from the fixing solution and pegging them up to dry. 'You're not bad,' he said with condescension.

'This is Mr Stevens,' Glading muttered, looking shifty.

'How do you do, Miss Gray. Enchanted to meet you.'

Apart from his stiff formality, foreign accent and unconvincingly English name, this man Glading brought to see Minnie several weeks later was as different to tall, vampiric Mr Peters as was possible to be. The newcomer was short in stature, with fairish curly hair and no neck to speak of. He also had an unjustified air of self-importance, which quickly identified him as the agent Glading once referred to as 'small'.

'Delighted to meet you, too,' she murmured as she led them inside. From the nervous glance Glading shot her as he passed into the sitting room she understood that it was important that she impress this visitor. Both men accepted sherry, though Stevens sniffed at his suspiciously before taking a sip and making a face.

While Peters's small talk had been distinctly lacking, Stevens had none at all. Instead he asked intrusive questions as he strutted around the flat, sherry glass in hand, inspecting all the rooms and even poking about in the kitchen drawers. Minnie followed, quietly furious. Glading trailed behind them with an expression of sheepish acquiescence.

In the dining room Stevens stood in the doorway and tutted, then advanced towards the gate-legged table, currently occupied by Minnie's sewing basket and a new dress she was in the process of altering. He planted a plump hand on the open leaf, which duly wobbled.

'No good,' he pronounced to Glading. 'You need a stronger table. Bigger, too.'

'Of course,' Glading mumbled, looking harassed.

'And you'll buy the equipment as we discussed.'

It was not a request, but an order.

'Yes.'

Stevens then turned on his heel and addressed Minnie, who stood quietly behind. 'I think we will start soon once everything is in place.'

She nodded, but tried to keep her face blank. Questions, she sensed, were strictly not required.

During the second week of October a van arrived and two cheery Maples delivery men manoeuvred a refectory table into the dining room. The gate-legged table was folded away and banished to the tool shed.

The sturdy new table filled the room. Minnie stroked the polished wood and thought of boarding school, but Glading had bought no benches and she only possessed two kitchen chairs. He had not, it seemed, acquired it for people to sit around, so what in heaven's name was it for? She had her suspicions and these were confirmed two days later when a heavy cardboard box and several supplementary odd-shaped packages arrived and she helped Glading unwrap what turned out to be a set of photographic apparatus that included a Leica camera on a tripod and arc lights.

They both stared at it all in bemusement. Minnie made a half-hearted attempt to read the instructions, but the camera was very different from Doug's Brownie so she tossed them down. 'What now?' she asked.

'Don't know. We're expecting visitors. They'll deal with this stuff.' The table and the camera had made Glading twitchy.

The visitors arrived half an hour later, the bumptious Mr Stevens accompanied by a neat, dark, furious-looking woman he introduced as his wife. They made an odd couple. Mrs Stevens said something in French to her husband and looked Minnie up and down in a way that made her feel that her petticoat must be showing or she was wearing too much lipstick. Although she had become used to the charmless nature of Glading's new friends, she thought this woman was the limit.

'Do you have coffee?' Mrs Stevens said in heavily accented English when Minnie offered them tea. 'I do not like English tea.'

'Oh dear. Coffee. Yes, coming up.'

She had shown them into the sitting room, but while she waited for the coffee to brew she heard them move into the dining room, draw the curtains and switch on the light. Mrs Stevens's high heels clipped impatiently on the floorboards and her gravelly exclamations suggested that she was not entirely happy. 'What is this? *Mais c'est trop difficile . . .'*

When Minnie entered with the tray it was to find a grim-faced Mrs Stevens still in her outdoor coat attempting to fit parts of the equipment together under the dim ceiling light while her little husband translated the instructions into strangely accented French and Glading looked on miserably, his arms tightly folded.

Mrs Stevens managed a *'Merci'* for the coffee, winced when she tried it, as though Minnie were trying to poison her, but drank it anyway. After that it was back to work with the photographic apparatus, Mrs Stevens calling orders and assembling everything with much tutting and sighing until finally she was satisfied.

'Bon. Demain?' she addressed Glading. 'We come back tomorrow?'

'Would that be all right, Minnie?' Glading looked embarrassed at the woman's briskness.

Minnie swallowed her annoyance. 'Yes, of course. The afternoon would be best as I have a job interview in the morning.'

'A job?' Mrs Stevens looked suspicious.

'Yes, I'm a typist.' Minnie mimed with her fingers and Mrs Stevens's expression cleared.

The Stevenses, accompanied by Glading, arrived at two o'clock the following day and spent the afternoon closeted in the dining room experimenting with the camera. Glading skulked about, jumpy as a cat. Minnie waited in the sitting room, pretending to read, but ready to leap up each time something was wanted. Coffee was twice ordered and provided. On the second occasion she was required to stay in the dining room and hold a flash bulb while Mrs Stevens photographed a map of the London underground network for practice. After that

Minnie was instructed to empty the walk-in broom cupboard in the hall and turn it into a makeshift darkroom where Mrs Stevens developed the negatives before taking them through the kitchen to hang up to dry in the bathroom. Most of the time the woman appeared unsure of what she was doing. The first batch of pictures was declared a failure and tempers ran high. Mr Stevens was subjected to a torrent of angry French by his wife and did his best to soothe her.

After they all left, Minnie sank onto the sofa and covered her eyes. She was physically and mentally exhausted. The dining room felt barred to her now, the camera and the arc lights staring at her menacingly. The brooms and mop cluttered up a corner of her kitchen. An air of threat had settled over her little flat. It felt less and less as though it belonged to her, hardly a home. And since that morning's job interview had not gone well she'd be here every day for a while yet.

Minnie had no idea what would happen next or if she would be asked to help, no sense of the size and importance of the work Glading was dragging her into. Or how dangerous it might be.

Strung out as she was she forced herself to write a report for Max and took a walk in the chilly October evening to post it and clear her head.

As she was returning to the flat she noticed a light on downstairs in the house opposite, the curtains not yet drawn. A man was standing in the window looking out at the street and smoking a cigar. He raised the cigar to her in friendly greeting and she nodded coolly. He must simply be a friendly neighbour, she realized, not anyone sinister. This should have been a relief, but instead it plunged her into despair. She was under so much strain that she suspected everyone.

Nothing of interest happened for several days, then early on the evening of 21 October, Mrs Stevens arrived on the doorstep bearing a large rectangular package and an air of agitation. Minnie stiffened. Something serious was happening at last. As she stepped aside to admit her visitor she noticed a black car parked up the road on the other side. She couldn't see the driver clearly, but the knowledge that Max's watchers were there added to the sense of high drama.

Once inside the flat, Mrs Stevens's behaviour became odder than ever. She marched straight into the dining room as though she owned the place, swished the curtains across the window and switched on the light. Minnie followed her only to be hustled out. 'Please, you go in here.' She ushered the astonished Minnie into her own sitting room before returning to the dining room and shutting the door. Minnie sat on the sofa clutching a cushion for comfort and wondered what to do.

After several minutes, the doorbell rang again and Minnie was allowed to admit Glading and, later still, Mr Stevens. The three visitors spent a long evening in the dining room with the camera and then Mrs Stevens in the makeshift darkroom developing negatives. When coffee was requested, Minnie made it, but was not allowed to take it in. Glading was sent out to fetch the tray. Whatever was being photographed must be of vital importance and Minnie's frustration at not knowing became immense.

At nine-thirty Glading interrupted her reading in the sitting room to tell her that he and Mr Stevens were leaving, but Mrs Stevens hadn't finished. Half an hour later Mrs Stevens put her head round the door. Her normally sallow face was grey and there were deep shadows under her eyes.

'I am still busy, but you can go to bed if you want,' she said. It sounded like a command, not a suggestion.

'How very kind,' Minnie replied with sarcasm. The woman glared at her and withdrew. Minnie sighed as she got up, picked up her book and turned off the gas fire.

In the hall her nose wrinkled at the stink of chemicals from the darkroom, the door of which had been left ajar. Outside the dining room, which was shut, she paused and listened. A shuffling sound came from within, then a metallic clang, as of something dropped, followed by an exclamation. She stepped away quickly, in case Mrs Stevens caught her snooping.

In the safety of her bedroom Minnie switched on the reading lamp, sat down on the bed and thought for a moment. She would need to use the bathroom and if tonight's negatives were drying there, she might be able to examine them.

It would be natural for her to go and wash, but it meant going through the kitchen and Mrs Stevens might hear her. Her every move would have to appear normal. Quickly she worked out her plan. She changed into her nightclothes, and slipped a pencil stub and a sheet of paper torn from a pad into her dressing gown pocket.

Cautiously she opened the door, then padded out through the dark kitchen in bare feet. In the bathroom she pulled a cord and the light flickered on. She blinked at what she saw and gave a quick intake of breath. Over the bath, pegged to a string like a length of sinister bunting, several dozen photographic negatives glistened blackly in a row. The occasional drip from them plinked unmusically into the tub. Swiftly Minnie closed the door and drew the bolt across, then fished the paper from her pocket, clamped the pencil stub between her teeth and leaned over the bath. With a shaking hand she turned the first negative towards her and studied it. The image on it involved a pattern of thin white lines on a black background. Part of a diagram of some sort. The next one showed a different section of the same diagram, or so she guessed. A number was printed underneath in tiny type and she had to step into the bath to read and copy it down. On the third and fourth pieces of film she made out parts of a caption: '14 inch naval gun'. A strange tingling feeling ran through her as she wrote this down and she hardly dared breathe.

She'd just stepped out of the bath when she heard the sound of a door opening. High heels tapped over the kitchen floor, and Mrs Stevens's voice called, *'Ma'mselle?'*

'Coming,' she called back, stuffing paper and pencil into her pocket. She pulled the lavatory chain, ran water noisily into the basin, then found some cold cream in the cabinet and smeared some on her face. After a quick glance at the photographs to check all was as before, she unbolted the door.

Mrs Stevens was waiting outside, the oblong parcel tucked under her arm. She looked past Minnie to the negatives with narrowed eyes, then, distastefully, at Minnie's shiny face. 'I am finished now,' she said. 'Please leave the films to dry. Do not touch, eh? Monsieur Glading will fetch them tomorrow.'

'I understand,' Minnie murmured, pleased that she had more time to examine them, and followed Mrs Stevens to the front door. Outside a taxi waited, its engine chugging. Mrs Stevens climbed in with her package and Minnie watched the vehicle move away. She was about to close the door when she heard another engine start up and the car she'd noticed earlier slid away from the kerb in pursuit. Whatever Mrs Stevens's destination, it would soon be known. Relief at the thought flooded through her. She shut the door and leaned against it to recover, then trudged back to the bathroom to complete her observations before collapsing into bed.

First thing in the morning, exhausted and nervous with excitement, she managed to track down Max, hoping to hear good news. Surely her work was over at last.

'We must meet,' was all Max said down the telephone. She'd have to wait until the afternoon.

Thirty-five

'I don't understand,' Minnie stormed, pacing the room. 'She had stolen plans for the gun with her, Max, actually with her. There could have been no defence.'

She'd arrived at the flat in Dolphin Square and handed over her report only to be given bad news. The watchers had followed Mrs Stevens, who had met her husband and returned the plans to an unidentified man, but Max had not given orders for their arrest.

She stopped pacing and watched in disbelief as he sat filling his pipe and reading her typed report, apparently unmoved. 'Calm down, Minnie, please. Take a seat and let me explain.'

Arms folded, she sank onto the sofa and frowned at him. He took his time, finishing the report and lighting the pipe, then leaned back, puffing out smoke as he contemplated her.

'I understand why you're angry,' he said finally, 'but you must believe me when I say that there's a bigger picture than you know. If we'd nabbed your Mr and Mrs Stevens last night, you're right, we'd have cooked her goose without difficulty, but what about the others?'

'Glading collected the negatives from me this morning. Surely he'd be—'

'Listen, Minnie—'

'Everything I've told you . . .' she went on.

'Yes, it's useful, but not quite good enough. If we'd arrested the Stevenses the whole operation would have closed down and you'd have been exposed, in danger. And it's not just your safety I'm thinking about. We're in it for the long haul, we have to be. Glading is starting to talk to you now. He's cracking and that will make him reckless. He'll make a mistake sometime and then we'll have him. And not simply him, all the others in his network.'

Minnie supposed this made sense. She sighed. 'The plans that I described in my report. Where do you think they come from?'

'I'll put someone onto it right away. If the blueprint was indeed for a new Royal Navy gun then my suspicions will be confirmed. But there's still work to do. Who is the insider supplying the plans? Who else might be involved? We have a description of the man the Stevenses met last night to return the plans, but it proved impossible to follow him as well as them. No, we must wait till we know everything about this operation and have the evidence nailed down. *Then* we'll pounce.'

Minnie covered her face briefly with her hands, then looked up. 'I don't know how long I can go on doing this.'

'Be brave.'

'I can't get away from it. It's my home, for goodness' sake. I have no control over my own life, when Glading will next come, what state he'll be in, who he'll bring with him. I feel invaded. And that at any moment it might all go wrong and then ...'

'I can only imagine how difficult it must be.'

'How long will it take? No, of course you can't answer that, but I can't do this for ever. No one could.'

'My dear.' Max leaned over and took her hand, enfolding it in his. 'You are doing marvellously. No other girl I've come across could do what you're doing.'

Despite everything she felt a rush of pleasure at the compliment.

'However, I've something important to point out to you. You cannot back out now.'

She pulled her hand away and stared at him, stunned by the warning note in his voice.

'You know too much, don't you see? If you let Glading down now he will suspect you. I've told you that he and his friends are desperate people. Some of them would do any-thing – *anything* – for their ghastly cause. And the Soviets have no scruples. They use special poisons. They murder their own people. It's a brutal regime. I must warn you, dear girl, that your life could be in danger.'

'What if I promised Glading that I'd never tell,' she moaned. 'He knows how ill I was last time. Surely he'd understand.'

'*He* might, but *they* won't. Now that you've met some of them and know what they're doing you're a risk. He's powerless, Glading, just their instrument. That's the saddest thing about what he's doing. He thinks he's important, but he's not, he's merely a pawn in their game. And you, dear girl, are another.'

Minnie's shoulders slumped because she saw suddenly and clearly that what Max said was true. There was no backing out now. 'All right,' she muttered finally, not looking at him.

'You'll continue for the time being?'

She nodded.

'I am glad, Minnie. I value our friendship.'

She blinked at him, confused. Was that how he saw their relationship, that they were friends? When he gave so little of himself? And yet he made it sound like a transaction, that they were only friends if she continued to work for him. Despite this she was comforted. He wanted to see her. She meant something to him.

Thinking about this later, she recognized that Max was still her anchor. She could not operate without him. And wondered anew whether this was a kind of love. No, she told herself fiercely, she certainly wasn't in love with him in any straightforward romantic way. His getting married again hadn't bothered her, it had been his tardiness in telling her that had. He wasn't a replacement father, either, she was too astute to believe that. However, she did want to please him by her efforts, her loyalty, as one might a father.

Minnie did not see Mrs Stevens again, but not because the woman was apprehended. Instead, a few days later, Glading visited the flat and told her that the Stevenses had returned to Moscow in a hurry.

She stared at him in shocked disbelief.

Glading explained: 'They heard their little girl was ill, poor kid, and had to leave right away.'

'Oh, that's ... sad,' she managed to say. Sometimes she wondered if Glading thought her stupid. The Stevenses had spent an evening photographing secret blueprints, then left the country. Was she supposed to think this a simple coincidence? Obviously they'd returned to Moscow because they had the photographs of the plans for the naval gun, which must by now be in the possession of the Soviet authorities. Why bother with this lame excuse about a sick daughter back in Russia? It took a supreme effort on her part not to say something biting.

Your job is simply to watch and listen. Max's voice whispered in her mind. She'd done that and now the Stevenses had escaped British justice. It was MI5 that she was most angry with. And specifically Max.

Thirty-six

Winter 1937

Following the disappointment of the Stevenses' escape it was more gruelling than ever for Minnie to continue her double life. She couldn't help feeling let down, despite understanding the logic of Max's position. How long she could continue, she didn't know. As long as it took to close the net around Glading, but that was impossible to predict. She was taking temporary employment through a secretarial agency again to keep herself sane.

Glading meanwhile was appearing more jittery than ever. One afternoon in the middle of November he arrived at the flat in Holland Road and stood chain smoking, looking out at the street where the wind was blowing the last of the autumn leaves into untidy swirls. He looked dishevelled, Minnie thought, as she glanced up from mending a tear in a cushion cover. His hair needed cutting and he hadn't shaved properly.

'I hate all this hanging around,' he said, stubbing out a

cigarette. 'They're supposed to be sending someone to replace the Stevenses, but they're taking their time.'

Her hand with the needle hovered for a second. There was no need to ask who 'they' were. Whoever it was running the show back in Moscow. 'It's frustrating for you,' she murmured and forced herself to calmly resume sewing.

'For both of us, it seems. There won't be any work for you to do either. Not for a while, anyway, till they sort things out. After Christmas, I reckon. We can practise, I suppose, with the camera.' He sounded half-hearted and Minnie's lacklustre response to the idea was genuinely felt.

She snipped the cotton and wondered how Glading was filling his hours. He'd told her he no longer had much time to work for the British Communist Party, so what was he up to?

'There is something you could advise me on,' he said gloomily, 'and that's Christmas presents for my contacts. That's almost a dozen. What am I supposed to buy?'

'I didn't think they believed in Christmas.'

He laughed at that. 'I don't, but they do. Or they want the *presents*, anyway. Rosa and the child, I don't mind getting gifts for, but I need ideas for the others.'

She told him that he couldn't go wrong with beautifully packaged foodstuffs. 'Fortnum and Mason or Harrods are the best places.'

'Give over. I can't be seen in there. They're where the rich capitalists go.'

'I bet your *friends* wouldn't mind that. They'd love a few little luxuries.'

'Minnie ...' He moved to sit next to her on the sofa. 'Will

you get them for me, huh? I'll repay the money.' His hand crept onto her lap and began to rub her thigh through her skirt.

'Don't do that. I've told you before.' She gave him a shove and stood up. 'Think of your wife. She'd be so hurt. And don't say she wouldn't know.'

She was taken aback by the hard look he shot her, but added coldly, 'Of course I'll get the wretched presents. Tell me your budget and how many you need. Then get off home to Rosa.' Poor Rosa. She wondered how much the woman knew about her husband's work. What would happen to her and the child if Glading ever got caught? Minnie felt a prickle of guilt at the thought.

There was no further talk of practising photography and Minnie extended her hours of temping work. She found herself under the supervision of a Miss Tomms in the typing pool of an import/export company in Bayswater. The work was tedious but the pay was good.

As the days passed Glading visited the flat twice more, but looked increasingly tense and unhappy. Then, one evening when he arrived she saw in him a new sense of purpose. He held himself straighter and there was determination in his eye. 'I need to borrow the camera stand,' he announced and went at once to fetch it from the dining room.

'I suppose it's only gathering dust,' she ventured, watching him pack it up.

'Well, I've a use for it. I can't take all this waiting around.'

She raised her eyebrows, but didn't dare ask what he'd be photographing.

Later, she met Max. 'I don't know what he's up to. I thought he needed me to help, but he must have decided it would be easier at home using his own camera.'

Shortly before Christmas, Glading was back at the flat to collect the Leica camera. 'Mine doesn't fit the stand properly,' he told her. 'And it's tricky balancing it on a pile of books.' His earlier optimistic mood had vanished and he seemed more on edge than ever. His hands shook as he packed the camera into its case and his gaze skittered around the room as though he'd forgotten something. Finally he said, 'I don't know when I'll see you next, Minnie. Bloody Russians, I wish I knew what was happening.'

After he'd gone she drew a deep breath of relief. Perhaps she'd be left in peace for a while.

Christmas provided a welcome dose of normality. *Other people's* normality, Minnie thought, as she watched her nieces and nephews eagerly open the gifts she'd brought with her.

'You're good at choosing presents, Minnie,' her sister Marjorie said with a sigh. 'And so generous. Money's awfully tight at the moment.'

'I don't have any kids of my own to splash out on, do I?' Minnie smiled down at the baby, who sat calmly tearing wrapping paper with his chubby fingers, then bent and removed a piece of string from harm's way.

Peter, her eldest nephew, sat at the table with her brother Richard, laying out the contents of a box of metal shapes and screws.

Minnie loved how Peter was in awe of his handsome uncle.

Now a junior officer with Special Branch, Richard had managed to secure two days' leave. How calm and assured he looked these days, she thought, feeling proud of her brother. Doug, too, was doing well at the bank. He and his wife had been with them for lunch, but had now walked round to see the in-laws nearby.

As she teased Boots the cat with the piece of string she wondered if this was real happiness, being with people who loved you and whom you loved, content to be yourself. *But I can't be myself. They don't know what I do and I can't tell them.*

'I wish you'd move back here, Minnie,' her sister sighed. 'Don't you get awfully lonely in London?'

'No more than Richard does. Do you, Richard?'

'I don't have any time to be lonely,' he said, looking up from fitting a toy wheel on an axle. 'Wish I could see you more often, Minnie.'

'There's no point in asking Minnie that again, Marjorie,' their mother said, setting down a loaded tray. 'She's chosen her own life and if it suits her we must respect that.' She frowned at her eldest daughter as she poured tea into cups. Despite the irritation, Minnie felt guilty that she caused her mother so much worry. Mothers knew, didn't they, when something wasn't right. She wished she could tell her everything and reassure her how important her work was to the country her mother loved.

She thought about Glading then and wondered what kind of Christmas he'd be having with his wife and daughter and what Rosa knew of his latest activities. Did he fear any moment the knock at the door, the arrival of the police, the effect it would have on his little family? However difficult Minnie's life was, his must be worse. Most of all she felt deeply sorry for Rosa, who was very sweet and kind.

Glading had sent Minnie a card and a gift, a box of the same luxury chocolates she'd bought for his Russian friends, and she cynically wondered if it had been a leftover. She'd been glad to bring them home, however, and pass them round after lunch – they were deliciously creamy. She'd bought Glading a bottle of whisky, Rosa an embroidered handker-chief, and for their daughter a clockwork mouse.

Minnie stayed in Edgbaston until new year. 'Let's hope this year is better than the last,' Mrs Gray murmured when the newscaster on the wireless wished them a prosperous one.

'You always say that,' Minnie said, rolling her eyes.

'Do I? But don't you think it right to look forward with optimism?'

'I suppose so,' she sighed, appreciating that her mother's life had not been easy. Privately she doubted how much there was to be positive about in the world beyond the window. Everywhere you looked these days there was conflict. *As for me, I don't want much*, she thought, *only for something in my life to change. To get out of this mess I'm in.* The end was coming, it must be. At some point Glading would take a wrong step – surely – and then it would all be over.

Max had sent a Christmas card to the flat showing a painting of the Houses of Parliament in the snow. In it he'd written, 'A peaceful Christmas and a successful 1938, with best wishes, your old friend Max.' She wondered what

Glading would make of the Establishment picture if he saw it, but in an act of daring displayed it on her bookshelves all the same.

The happiness of Christmas evaporated as soon as Minnie stepped down from the train at Euston and the sense of routine returned. When she let herself into her cold and musty flat the reality of her London life closed round her in a suffocating grip. Once she had lit the gas fire, drawn the curtains against the foggy dusk and switched on the lamps, she felt more cheerful. She relished the prospect of the cold ham and Christmas cake her mother had packed. She'd have a bath first, she decided.

Over supper, which she ate in the warmth of the sitting room, she opened the post. A hastily inscribed Christmas card from her hockey club friend Clara made her smile at the girl's well-known scatty lateness. Bills she put to one side unread for when she felt stronger. That left a flimsy brown envelope on which her address had been unevenly typed. She slit it open, withdrew the single sheet of paper it contained and frowned. It was from Glading.

'Something's cropped up. Will call on your return,' the typed note read and was signed simply 'PG'. Beneath he'd added as an afterthought, 'Thanks for the gifts. I hope you've had a peaceful Christmas. With expectations of a successful new year.' She froze. Peaceful. Successful. Those were Max's words. Glading must have seen the card. Her eye went to the picture of snowy Westminster on the shelf. But he couldn't have done. Had he come to the flat in her absence and inspected all her Christmas cards? He possessed a key so it was theoretically possible.

It took her a while to calm down, to reassure herself that the words were nothing more than a coincidence. Uncanny, though, that both sides in this game thought the same way. Neither man had expected Minnie to be 'happy' or 'merry' at Christmas time.

Thirty-seven

January 1938

Minnie waited in that evening and the next, but by the time Glading telephoned, whatever might have 'cropped up' had gone away for when she mentioned his note he simply said, 'Oh, that.' He told her he'd come round the following night.

He arrived after supper and helped himself liberally to her sherry.

When she asked him in a roundabout way how his work was going, she was subjected to a litany of complaint. Nothing was happening. No one had arrived to replace the Stevenses, he was running out of money and didn't know what he was supposed to be doing. 'It's a shambles,' he complained. 'Everybody's too cautious to do anything. Somebody needs to take charge and do something.' The implication was that the 'someone' should be Percy Glading.

It was unusual for him to confide so much. Minnie

considered how best to respond. It might not be to MI5's advantage for Glading to do anything seriously rash, for the Russians might close the operation down. 'I'm sure you're right,' she said carefully, 'but isn't it sensible to be patient?'

'Patient, oh, I've been patient all right. I'm fed up with being patient. I've done what I'm supposed to and everything's in place.' There was a dangerous look in his eye that alarmed her. Perhaps he was becoming unstable.

She said nothing in reply and was rewarded.

'Next weekend for instance.' He gave a bark of laughter. 'Ask me what I'm doing next weekend, go on.'

'Tell me.'

'I'll be at home photographing a book. Two hundred pages, it is. Quite a job, don't you think?'

'Two hundred pages,' she echoed in genuine amazement.

She hoped he'd say more, but he seemed to realize he'd already told her too much because all he said was a gloomy, 'Let's hope they appreciate it.'

It was at this moment that she began to suspect Glading was taking a whole new direction. Her mind worked quickly. Whatever he was up to it might not be with the knowledge of his Russian contacts. He was boasting of it to her because there was nobody else. He was branching out on his own.

'M, it's me,' she whispered later into the telephone.

'Yes, what is it?' He picked up her excitement straight away.

'I think something else is about to happen.'

'Photographing a book,' he said thoughtfully, when she'd told him what Glading was up to. 'Thank you, M/12.'

'Please listen. If he's starting to act on his own he might be putting himself in danger and me, too.'

'I'm aware of that. Didn't we discuss it?' His voice was calm, assuring. *As though I'm one of his animals*, she thought miserably. 'But you must trust me.'

'You'll act on it? M, he must be stopped.'

'And he will be. Now please don't worry. We're looking after you. All will be well.'

He rang off then. She slowly replaced the receiver and sat lost in thought. What would Max do? Surely it was time to close in on Glading. Despite the warmth of the sitting room Minnie shivered.

She stayed indoors all the following weekend, too frightened to go out. From time to time she went to the window and scanned the street anxiously. There was no car with watchers, unless they were being unusually discreet. She was on her own. What was happening at Glading's house in North London? She'd never been there, but she closed her eyes and tried to imagine the police arriving, breaking down the door, catching him red-handed photographing the book and taking him away. Then it would all be over. *The spy, the spy, the beautiful spy.* She opened her eyes. The flat was silent, but for the hissing of the gas fire. She'd never felt so alone.

On Sunday night the telephone rang. She snatched up the receiver. It was Max.

'Yes?' she gasped. 'Have you got him?'

'Listen.'

'You haven't.' She sat down, disappointment flooding in.

'It wasn't the right time. Trust me.'

She sighed. There was no other option. She arranged to meet him the following day in the hotel in Cromwell Road.

They sat close together with their drinks behind the Japanese screen.

'I ... look,' Max said, 'it's most irregular, but I feel I need to explain. Yesterday our men saw Glading leaving his house in the early afternoon. Wait a minute.' He shuffled some papers then read out, '"He returned three hours later with a folded newspaper under his arm. This appeared to contain a small book or magazine, but they couldn't be sure. Then, today, Sunday ..."' He read on. Glading had left the house with the same paper pinned under his arm. He was followed as far as Charing Cross station, where he descended the steps to the gentlemen's lavatories. There he ran into a young man coming the other way carrying an attaché case. The MI5 men witnessed Glading handing him the folded newspaper with its contents. Later, they trailed the young man to a house in suburban Plumstead.

'We've already identified *him*. He's an assistant chemist. Works in the Woolwich Arsenal.'

'The Arsenal? Wasn't that where the plan of the gun came from?'

'Yes, how did you know that?'

'You mentioned it at some point and I put two and two together.'

'Brooks of Sheffield, you are.'

'Don't talk about knives.' She shivered. 'Why weren't they arrested?'

'Not enough evidence. We've only got your word about the book and its likely contents. Our men couldn't be sure what it was. We could have made fools of ourselves and that would have been the end of the whole operation. No arrests, Glading goes scot-free.'

She gave a moan of frustration.

'Keep going, Minnie. We're learning fast, building up evidence. We now have the shape of a Soviet spy ring. There's the chap the Stevens handed their plans to, George Whomack, and the young man tonight, Charles Munday. Both of them work for the Woolwich Arsenal, where Glading himself was once employed. Whomack and Munday are stealing secret material, Glading is photographing it, you're looking after the safe house. Glading may be getting careless, if what you say about him going solo is right. Chin up, Minnie. It may not be long now.'

She could not sleep that night, alive as she was to every sound, to the strange shadows of trees that the moonlight cast across the bed. Somehow she must go on with this life, step by step, trusting Max to strike when the moment was right; but if she projected her thoughts any further than the following day, she felt only despair.

Thirty-eight

It was lunchtime a few days later. The receptionist at Minnie's latest workplace put her head round the door of the main office. 'Call for you, Miss Gray. Wouldn't give his name. I'll put him through on line one.'

'Thank you.' Minnie, at the filing cabinet, pushed the drawer shut and walked quickly over to the telephone on the supervisor's desk, currently unattended, and picked up the receiver.

'Hello?'

'Minnie?' Glading sounded furtive. 'Can you talk?'

She cast a glance round, but only one of the other typists had returned from lunch and she was wearing headphones. 'Yes, briefly.'

'Meet me for lunch tomorrow?'

'I'm supposed to be seeing a girlfriend.' She had been looking forward to seeing Jenny.

'Well, put her off. It's important, very important. Meet me at the Windsor Castle, one o'clock sharp.'

The line went dead.

As she replaced the receiver, Miss Tomms returned from her lunchbreak, and glared at Minnie suspiciously through the raindrops on her spectacles as she untied her headscarf. Personal calls were not encouraged.

Minnie adopted a serious expression. 'I'm afraid my mother isn't very well again,' and Miss Tomms's expression changed to warm sympathy, because she, too, had an ailing mother.

Cancelling the arrangement with her friend Jenny and ringing Max would obviously have to wait. All afternoon Minnie could hardly concentrate on her work.

The Windsor Castle pub in Notting Hill was convenient for her office and Minnie knew Glading liked it. She had teased him because its recent refurbishment had lent the interior a very feudal Olde Worlde appearance. Oak-panelled rooms opened into one another and she finally glimpsed him in the saloon bar sitting at a corner table near a blazing fire. Above the arched brick fireplace hung a painting of Windsor Castle and Minnie smiled to herself. Somewhere less representative of Glading's republican values would be difficult to find. No one except her would look for him here.

He didn't see her come in. He was looking towards a different entrance, nervously smoking a cigarette. Minnie's eye was drawn to a large battered leather suitcase on the floor at his feet. What might that contain?

'Sorry I'm late,' she said. She hung up her coat and slipped into the chair opposite.

'I'll fetch you a drink,' he said shortly, by way of hello. 'Keep an eye on the case, will you. Glass of dry sherry?'

'You spoil me.' She smiled. 'And a nice bit of fish, please. I haven't got long.'

While Glading was at the bar she gave the suitcase an exploratory nudge with her foot and was rewarded by a metallic rattling noise. Not clothes, then, or books.

He returned with a glass of pale sherry and another whisky. Two plates of fish and chips duly arrived and in between mouthfuls, he explained the purpose of their meeting in low, urgent tones.

'This is really important . . . I need your help this evening. No time to explain properly.' He stopped to gulp at his whisky then went on. 'Someone can get the papers out tonight, but we have to get 'em back before tomorrow. I've got the camera apparatus here.' He reached down and patted the case. 'You're to be home by six and I'll join you. We'll set it up together then I must be off to Charing Cross station.'

Minnie nodded, not able to trust her voice. She put down her knife and fork. 'Of course,' she managed to croak finally. Half the food still lay on the plate but she'd lost all appetite.

Glading stabbed a chip, put it in his mouth and chewed it quickly. 'This'll properly show them.' His eyes gleamed. Maniacally, she thought, alarmed.

When she left him, saying truthfully that she had to be back in the office, she tried to act in a leisurely fashion, but her heart was beating so fast she couldn't think straight. Max, she had to ring Max right away, but she mustn't let anyone see her do it.

Once out in the cold air, she set off in the direction of Notting Hill Gate, as though she were returning to work, but kept darting quick looks behind to make sure she wasn't being followed. At the underground station she bought a copy of the *News Chronicle*, then walked slowly down the steps, glancing at the headlines. Instead of heading through the barrier to the stairs down to the platforms, however, she went straight to a telephone booth. The coins slipped in her nervous fingers, but finally she heard Max's voice at the other end of the line.

'M. It's me.'

'Yes. What's the matter?' He'd caught her urgency.

'It's tonight.' She could hardly get the words out. 'He'll be at the flat. There'll be documents, I don't know what.' She stumbled out details and he asked terse questions that she answered till he had what he needed.

'Ring me at once when he goes out to meet this person. Charing Cross station, that's what you said?'

'Yes, but I don't know when it'll be.'

'Never mind. I'll deal with it.'

'M ... you will get him this time, won't you? I can't ...'

'Calm down.'

'Please.'

'We'll do our best.'

'Because I ...'

'Keep calm, I said. There's a good girl.'

He hung up. Her hand shook as she replaced the receiver, then she took a deep breath, tucked her newspaper under one arm and walked calmly to the ticket barrier.

It was dark when she left work at five and as she walked home from her bus stop she found herself trembling. Here and there in her street the lights were on and ordinary people returned home to their ordinary families and ordinary lives. Tonight she envied them. She was relieved to see a familiar car parked almost outside her address, the silhouettes of two men just visible inside.

Her flat lay in darkness and she was pleased, thinking she'd have a little time to herself before Glading arrived, but as soon as she entered she smelled tobacco smoke. She pushed open the door to the sitting room and gave a little scream when she saw the orange glow of a cigarette and someone slouched on a chair. It was Glading.

'Sorry,' he said, sounding weary. 'I've set up the apparatus. It took no time at all.'

'Oh, you must be used to it. Why are you sitting in the dark?'

He shrugged.

Minnie bustled about switching on lights. As she pulled the curtains across she glanced out at the watchers, but saw mostly the reflection of the room in the window glass with Glading staring morosely at her. The air throbbed with tension.

Turning to him she said, 'When are you supposed to be at Charing Cross? I'll make you something to eat if there's time.'

'Not for another hour, so that'd be perfect, thank you.'

She prepared a supper of bacon and eggs, which they ate in the kitchen. After that he went into the dining room to replace an arc light bulb, he said, then he pulled on his coat.

'I'll go now. It's eight-fifteen at the station, but I don't want to be late. I'll be straight back.'

After he'd gone and the black car slid away in pursuit she telephoned Max to report the time of the meeting. Once she'd done that she pushed open the dining room door and switched on the light. There the equipment lay ready, the camera on its stand, the arc lights looming dead-eyed over everything. She hugged herself. The room was freezing, but it wasn't the cold that made her shiver. The aftertaste of supper was metallic in her mouth. She retreated, closing the door, and returned to the kitchen to wash up. Anything to pass the time. The hands of the kitchen clock reached eight-fifteen. He'll be there now, she thought, slowly drying a plate. She pictured him meeting a man dressed similarly – dark overcoat, a peaked cap pulled over his eyes. The station would be quiet now, so Max's men could easily point them out to police.

Eight-twenty. There would need to be several policemen, she supposed. Special Branch officers. Glading would be taken by surprise. *But face the worst, Minnie. Suppose the arrest hadn't happened?* Why, then he'd be on his way back to Holland Road by now, a tightly wrapped parcel under his arm. Would he take the underground or a bus? She should have asked. Eight-thirty, eight-forty-five. If he were coming he'd arrive by nine-fifteen, surely.

She felt her throat swell in panic, sending her rushing to the bathroom to be sick. Afterwards she swilled water from a tooth mug and stared at her reflection in the mirror. Her eyes were huge in her ashen face, mascara smudged on her cheeks.

Taking a towel she dabbed it away. She could not afford to look wild and dishevelled; it might invite his suspicion.

The minutes ticked away. She returned to the kitchen and sat at the table, staring at the clock. Nine-ten, twelve, fifteen. She could hardly bear it.

At twenty past nine the door buzzer sounded, urgent, repeated, and her heart plummeted. Glading was back. She gripped the table for support. The arrest hadn't happened. She must open the door. She stood up. Her knees threatened to buckle under her. The buzzer sounded again and she forced herself forward. Down the hall, swallowing against rising nausea, out into the common hallway, over to the street door where Glading's silhouette darkened the hatched glass. She opened the door to admit him. Then stepped back in alarm as a tall uniformed figure entered and said, 'Minnie, dear, don't be frightened.'

It was her brother, Richard.

Thirty-nine

'What are you doing here? Oh, Richard.' She fell against him in relief and his arms enfolded her. She started shaking, but not with sobs, with laughter. She laughed and she laughed, and after that she cried. It didn't matter why Richard was here. It was over.

'You must pack at once,' Richard said. 'Everything you need. Quickly.'

There followed a fever of activity. Clothes, shoes, toiletries, books, all tumbled into a case. She picked up her little typewriter.

'You won't need that.'

'I might do. I can't leave it.'

A sleek car gleamed outside, the young man in the driving seat rubbing his hands together against the cold. Richard helped her lock up, then the driver fitted her luggage into the car's boot while he assisted her into the back seat. He slid in beside her and clasped her hand as the car set off along the dimly lit deserted street.

Minnie sat back and closed her eyes, her mind distracted, her brother's warm hand the only thing linking her to reality. Then she opened them and said, 'Did they get him?'

'Yes, they got him.'

'And he had the plans?'

'I don't know, I wasn't told.'

'I thought you were him.'

'I know, I'm sorry. Someone should have telephoned ahead.'

'It doesn't matter now.'

'No, I'm here. Listen, Minnie, I'd no idea . . . I don't know anything. They said you're . . .'

'What?'

'A spy. That you've been awfully brave.'

She smiled at him in the gloom. 'Not brave. I simply did what I was told. I must have been stupid.'

'No. Brave is what Captain King said. But – this is rotten – I'm not to ask you about it. Not yet.'

'I see.'

They passed Wimbledon station, heading south.

'Where are we going?'

'A safe place.'

'Richard . . . where?' She suddenly felt terribly frightened.

'Minnie, don't worry. The driver knows. He'll get us there.' He squeezed her hand. 'Your Captain King has arranged everything. I don't know how he knew about me. My inspector called me to the telephone this afternoon and there I was, speaking to MI5 about you. You, Minnie! I'm still pinching myself.'

'So am I,' Minnie whispered. 'I'm so glad you came.' She

silently blessed Max. How had he known about Richard? She must have told him.

They drove on, beyond the suburbs and through the icy darkness of the countryside, where the road snaked through towns and villages. On a stretch of empty road headlights dazzled from behind. Richard's driver checked his mirrors and his hands tightened on the wheel. The other car drew up close behind and hooted, then it swerved past them. Minnie caught sight of the thickset driver and for a moment her heart skipped a beat, but the vehicle skidded away into the distance and the road was empty once more.

Her head ached and she felt sick again. 'How far now?' she mumbled.

'How long, driver?'

'Almost there, guv. Two or three miles.'

The road dipped to a narrow bridge over a glittering stream, and the car engine strained as it climbed a hill the other side. A few minutes later the winding road brought them to the outskirts of a small town. Soon old buildings crowded in on either side, then the street opened out into a silent market place dominated by a clock tower. The head-lights caught an inn sign bearing an image of a bear and the car braked, and, turning sharply, passed under the sign and through an arched entrance. The driver parked by some old stables in the dark yard beyond and switched off the engine.

'This is it?' Minnie was puzzled.

'Yes. Come on, we'll find our rooms, then order supper.'

Inside were wood panelled rooms, uneven floors with creaking boards, the scents of lavender polish and home cooking. Quiet, comfortable, in normal circumstances the Bear would be a relaxing place to spend a weekend, but this wasn't normality.

It was late. They ordered sandwiches at the bar, but Minnie couldn't eat for exhaustion. She was troubled by the sight of a man of foreign appearance seated at a table near the fire, but he hardly glanced their way.

Her bedroom, the four-poster bed hung with drapes, soft rugs underfoot, was at the back of the inn and when she slipped into bed and turned out the lamp a thick country darkness enveloped her. She lay with eyes open, her heart thudding, her hearing acute. Each new sound was a threat. The creak of old wood, an owl hooting, the rush of the wind.

She must eventually have slept, because something wakened her, a shuffling noise as though someone was in the room. Her every muscle tightened. After a while she realized the sound came not from within the room, but from behind the wall, an animal or bird, perhaps, and her mind whirled off in other directions.

She thought of Glading, wondering where he was, locked in a police cell, probably, huddled on a bunk under a rough blanket or sitting with his head in his hands, like her unable to sleep. He probably didn't know yet how he'd got there, who had betrayed him. But others might. *Liquidation.* She shuddered.

Finally, she fell into a doze and when she woke next a pale light was pushing its way between the curtains and the cheerful clatter of breakfast preparations rose from below. She lay for a while listening, trying to take comfort from its mundane reality, but she still had to clutch the bedclothes to stop her hands from shaking. Only when Richard tapped on the door and called her name did she muster the courage to leave her bed. She could hardly believe it when he said he'd come to say goodbye, because he'd been summoned back to London.

After breakfast, Minnie spent most of the morning in her room with the door locked, before being called to the telephone. Downstairs, she was shown into a small private side-room.

'Hello?'

'I rang earlier,' Max's voice purred, 'but they said they couldn't find you.'

'How strange. There's no telephone in my room, but I was there all the time.'

'Never mind. How are you?'

'Fine, I suppose. Well, no, not really. M, what happened? Richard could tell me practically nothing. I know you caught Glading or I wouldn't be here. Please explain, I feel so frightened.'

'You're perfectly safe there. Yes, we got him all right. They picked him up at Charing Cross station with one of his cronies, an insider from the Woolwich Arsenal. This fellow had just handed Glading a brown paper parcel and that's when the police moved in on them. As we suspected, the parcel contained blueprints. Special Branch are searching both men's addresses. It's too early to say what they've found, but, yes, we've got him.'

'So it's over. It's finally over.' Minnie sat back in the chair, relief washing over her. Then she remembered. 'Does he know? That it was me?'

'I shouldn't think so.' Max was hesitant. 'Not yet, anyway.'

'Does he need to know? Oh, I can't bear the idea.'

She was met by an impatient sigh. 'He will have to some-time. There'll be the trial. Surely you understand that.'

'I won't have to attend, will I?'

'I'm afraid you will. You're our main witness.'

She'd guessed this, but hadn't wanted to believe it. 'I don't know if I can do it. Testify against him. He'll be there, watch-ing me from the dock, won't he? He'll know. Everyone will know. I can't do it.'

'You will do it.' His voice was low, persuasive, underscored by menace. 'You must. It's not enough to have caught him red-handed with stolen secret documents. We have to prove what he intended to do with them, that he's a traitor. Your evidence will be crucial. And even that may not prove to be enough.'

She gave a little gasp. 'Not enough? But everything I've been through. I thought at least ...'

'We'll make sure your real identity doesn't become public. No name, no photographs in the press.'

'But I'll still be in danger. Glading will know, won't he, and he'll tell all his friends. Pollitt, everyone.' She shivered and wrapped her cardigan tighter.

'Everything possible will be done to protect you. That's why you're where you are. A country town in Surrey. No one will look for you there. Is your brother still with you?'

'No, he's had to go back to work.'

'Gone? I'd requested ... blow them. Never mind. Well, hang on there and don't tell anyone where you are. I'll be in touch again shortly when I have more news.'

After he rang off Minnie sat for a moment with the receiver in her hand. She felt abandoned, desperate. If Richard were here it might be bearable, but once again she must fend for herself.

She found the strength to call the secretarial bureau to inform them she was ill and not able to work till further notice, then made her way to the bar where she ordered a large sherry and sat sipping it in a quiet corner, grateful for the comforting country Englishness of the place. There was no sign today of the foreign-looking man she'd found so sinister the night before, only a couple of old codgers playing dominos over pints of beer.

The drink warmed her all the way down and she began to feel calmer. When she'd finished it she asked for another, and thinking she'd better soak it up with something solid, ordered roast beef for lunch. After eating she felt better and went upstairs to her room and lay down on the bed.

Still, she could not sleep. Her thoughts acquired a life of their own. Her work as an undercover agent, pretending to be someone she wasn't, might be over, but now her whole life was suspended. Where would she live? Surely she couldn't stay here for more than a few days and she could hardly return to the flat in Holland Road. She tried hard to focus on the present, to reassure herself that Max would look after everything, that she'd be all right, but she could not prevent a renewed sense of panic. There would be the trial and Max was right, she'd have to go through with it, her sense of duty told her that. But despite everything she felt unreasonably sorry for Glading. How would he feel when he learned how she'd betrayed him? And if he went to prison – surely he'd go to prison – what would happen to Rosa and their daughter? The whole thing was dreadful.

Outside the winter twilight was gathering and she got up to close the curtains. Beyond the stable yard was a paddock, then a view of ploughed fields edged with the skeletons of trees above which clouds of rooks were circling.

Forty

A fortnight later Minnie sat waiting in a gloomy corridor at the Bow Street Magistrates Court, her hands clammy and her mouth dry as she stared down at the tiled floor. Today was the preliminary hearing, in preparation for the trial and she was terrified.

A click and a slight draught as the door of the courtroom opened and a low voice spoke, 'Miss. They're ready for you. Follow me, please.'

She took a breath and rose quickly, her handbag tucked under her arm. The usher led her into a light, warm wood-lined room full of faces and at her entrance a rush of murmurs started up. Minnie remembered to nod respectfully towards the judge, then kept her eyes on the usher's black garb until she found herself in the witness stand and reciting words from a printed card in a voice that did not sound like her own.

For a moment after this she allowed her eye to stray. Four men sat in the dock across the room, but there was only one she recognized. Glading was staring straight at her, his face strained and white with shock. Their eyes locked and she registered his vehemence, like a bolt of electricity, forcing her to look away. Instead she concentrated on the tall, lugubrious figure of the prosecution barrister, Mr McClure, who had risen to address her.

'Miss X.' McClure left his bench and sauntered across to hand her a folded strip of paper. She opened it and read the handwriting and for a moment was struck by fear because it was her real name that was written there and her mother's address.

There came a fresh murmur of voices from around the court. Minnie stood as straight as she could and waited.

'Miss X,' Mr McClure said again, drawing out the words as though he relished them and she regarded him nervously. 'Can you confirm that you are the person named on that paper and that you live at that address?'

'It is my mother's address, but, yes, it is me.'

'My Lord.' A man she guessed to be a defence lawyer was addressing the judge. 'I can see no reason why her name should not be disclosed if she is going to be the principal witness in this case.'

Minnie turned faint with terror and the room began to spin. It was only the promise of anonymity that had persuaded her to testify. If Glading's Russian friends knew who had betrayed him, if her name or picture was printed in the newspapers for any Tom, Dick and Harry to read, then who knew what might happen. She'd be a target of Soviet agents, or any madman with a grudge and an opportunity. It was bad enough that Glading knew her identity. She gripped the rail in front of her with whitened knuckles and stared pleadingly at the judge, who regarded her thoughtfully over his wire-rimmed spectacles.

Eventually he said, 'I disagree, Mr Collard. This case is obviously going to proceed to trial and the decision about which matters are to be withheld may therefore be deferred.'

Minnie's relief was palpable. Collard sat down, looking peeved.

McClure, for the prosecution, shuffled his papers. 'Miss X, I'd like to take you through your written statement for the benefit of the court.' He proceeded to question her about the testimony she'd submitted some days before. This described the history of her involvement with the intelligence services from her recruitment to her engagement by the League Against Imperialism, from her meeting in Paris with Glading prior to her visit to India, her employment by the Communist Party of Great Britain, all the way to the securing of the safe house in Holland Road and her long observation of Glading's covert activities.

She could not look at the defendants as she spoke for fear that Glading's expression would put her off her account, and was careful never to say anything that would reveal her real identity. It was taken for granted that the names of anyone connected with MI5 would remain a secret so there was no mention of Max or any of his colleagues.

She spoke bravely and confidently, but when she described the strain of that final evening of Glading's arrest, 'I waited and waited for him to return and I didn't know ...' She couldn't stop her voice cracking with emotion.

After she'd finished speaking and McClure resumed his seat a silence fell over the court. The judge at last looked up from his notes and fixed his gaze on the defence barrister. 'Mr Collard, have you or your colleague Mr Pritt anything to say before we move on?'

Mr Collard rose briefly and muttered, 'No, my Lord.'

Afterwards, Minnie was ushered out of a door at the back of the building where a black car with drawn blinds waited, its engine running.

'Who are you really, Miss X?'

She glanced up to see a hard-faced man with a journalist's notebook sneering at her and stepped back in shock.

'This way, miss.' A smartly dressed young man took her arm and steered her toward the car. When she slid onto the rear seat she found to her relief that her brother was there.

'Was it awful?' Richard touched her arm as the car pulled away.

She nodded, unable to speak, only to fumble for his hand and hold it tightly. She leaned back, closed her eyes and tried to master her shaking body. Voices from the courtroom played through her head and Glading's face rose up, full of hate and bewilderment. After a while the movement of the car and the smell of the leather seats became overwhelming and she raised the window blind and looked out at the passing scene until she felt better.

'Richard,' she said eventually, 'where are we going?'

'Another hotel.'

The car was heading west now, into the sun, and they were silent as they passed through Kensington and Hammersmith, past rows of brick houses with diamond-paned windows, then finally out between wintry fields.

The hotel stood in its own grounds at the far edge of a busy village. It was a converted country house, classical in style, approached by a long drive through scrubby parkland where deer roamed.

'You'll be able to see anyone coming for miles,' Richard said with a grin, 'so don't worry.'

Minnie shot him a look of distress. 'You think I'm silly, don't you? These Russians, they're ruthless.'

Seeing her face his grin vanished and he assured her that he would never think she was silly.

'They could get me, any of them. You don't know what they're like. Dangerous, Richard, they're dangerous, these Russian agents. They'll go to any lengths at all. They liquidate people with secret poisons. I wouldn't stand a chance.'

He looked concerned. 'I say, Minnie, steady on. You sound like one of those awful novels.'

'I *am* steady. None of you have been through what I have. Don't belittle me.'

Again, he apologized. Then he said, 'I have to leave you, tomorrow, I'm afraid, but Marjorie's coming instead.'

'Marjorie? She doesn't have to do that. Can't you stay?'

'Unfortunately not. But you won't be alone and Marjorie wants to come.' Minnie had revealed the facts of her secret life to her family, but instead of being impressed they'd been confused and disbelieving. News of the court case had worried them. Her mother, while concerned for Minnie, clearly thought the affair vulgar, even shaming. Still, Minnie was grateful that her sister was coming.

Minnie's room was on the second floor and overlooked the drive, which meant that she could see comings and goings, but she also felt exposed. Despite there still being light in the sky she drew the curtains and switched on the lamps, then lay on the bed and tried to rest. Later she joined Richard downstairs for a drink in the bar and then dinner. Who was paying for all this? If there was one thing she'd learned over the years it was that M-section operated on a shoestring.

'You're a celebrity now,' Richard said when she wondered aloud. He was making his way lustily through a slab of steak.

'I sincerely hope not.' She picked at her grilled fish without interest.

That night sleep would not come, though she was exhausted. She felt taut, like a bowstring pulled to its furthest extent. Only when dawn came did she remake enough of a connection to her comfortable surroundings to fall into a sleep which the maid interrupted by trundling in breakfast on a trolley.

Like a brisk gust of air, Minnie's sister Marjorie arrived before lunch in a taxi from the station. Able to leave Minnie in safe hands, Richard commandeered the vehicle to return to his usual duties in London.

'All this fuss, Minnie,' Marjorie said, as she pulled off her gloves and squinted at her own pointed face in the bedroom mirror. 'Mother's terribly worried about you. I say, you don't mind if I share your bed, do you? Some of us can't afford nice places like this.'

'I'm sure I'll sleep better with you in it. Oh, Marjorie, I'm so glad to see you.'

Marjorie's glance softened. 'You *are* in a bad way, aren't you?'

'The preliminary hearing was worse than I imagined. I didn't realize how sorry I'd feel, seeing that poor man in the dock.'

'He's not a "poor" man, Minnie. Whatever it is he's done he brought it on himself.'

'He trusted me, Marjorie, and it was awful seeing him realize that I was the one who betrayed him.'

'Let's go and find something for lunch. Breakfast was a long time ago.'

As they wandered across the thickly carpeted foyer on the way to the bar they passed an array of newspapers neatly folded on a console table. Minnie stopped to pick one up with a feeling of trepidation. When they sat down and a barman had taken their order she unfolded it and turned the pages.

The story was on page six and her eyes widened as she read the headline. *'Blonde Spy in Flat: "Miss X" Tells of Secret Life'*. She covered her mouth and forced herself to read on. *'Speaking in a low, cultured voice, blonde and pretty "Miss X", her name a secret, told Bow Street court yesterday how she was called from the provinces by the War Office Intelligence Service to watch activities in a London flat and elsewhere. Dressed in smart furs . . .'*

'Smart furs?' Minnie was horrified. 'I sound like a high-class tart!'

'Let me see.'

Wordlessly she pushed the paper across the table. Marjorie peered short-sightedly at it. 'Blonde Spy? This is you?'

'Who else do you think it is?'

'I don't know. There isn't a picture. Dear me, the print's so small.' Marjorie found her spectacles then read on, her frown deepening.

'Blonde and pretty,' Minnie murmured. 'I suppose it's meant to be a compliment, but it doesn't feel like me. And I wasn't "in furs", unless you count the trim on my coat.'

'Wait a minute.' Marjorie was a slow reader. When she arrived at the end she put down the paper and took off her spectacles.

'I didn't know about all this,' Marjorie whispered. 'Everything you've done. All these years, Minnie, and you never told us. You *are* a dark horse. Mother and I, we thought, I don't know, that you'd just been following him a bit. But it says here that you've been working with the Communists for years. Is that true, Minnie? And I didn't realize that he was giving military secrets to the Russians. Why, that's treason, isn't it?'

'I did try to explain.'

'People get hanged for treason. What you've been doing must've been terribly important.'

'And you didn't think your sister would do that?'

'Until you said, I thought you were a typist, simply a typist in London with some odd friends.'

'Communists.'

'Yes, we guessed that. But you're not a Communist, are you?'

Minnie rolled her eyes. 'I had to pretend to be,' she said

patiently. To her family she'd been plain, prickly Minnie, the oldest daughter, who couldn't find a husband and had to work for a living. Now her sister had finally discovered the truth Minnie saw all this clearly. She knew they loved her in their dutiful way, but only now had she impressed them. She sighed, sensing that Marjorie's narrow experience of life would never enable her to fully understand what her eldest sister had endured.

'It's like a film, isn't it, like ... I don't know, that one with Robert Donat. Wait till Mother reads this.'

'I'm sure the neighbours will be certain to alert her.'

Their sandwiches arrived and they ate hungrily, then Marjorie fetched copies of the other newspapers and read aloud to Minnie snatches of similar accounts of the preliminary hearing. Although the editors had followed the rules and printed no photograph of her, the salacious tone was similar in each and the more Marjorie read the more jittery Minnie became. She imagined Glading's sinister Soviet contacts reading the accounts, and Pollitt would know by now the extent to which she'd betrayed them all. He wasn't a violent man, but he must know people who were.

So when after lunch Marjorie said, 'Well, I think if it's all the same to you I'll walk down to the village to buy some hairpins,' Minnie begged her not to.

'Don't leave me alone. Please.'

Marjorie's eyes widened with concern. 'Goodness. Come with me then.'

'I can't.' It was hard to get across to her sister how frightened she felt. 'I don't know who might be out there.'

'Minnie, this is *England*.'

'You don't know what these people are like.' There would be no point in using words such as 'liquidation' or 'assassination' with her sister, who would think she was going mad.

Marjorie sighed and said she'd do without hairpins, but she insisted that they sit downstairs in the hotel lounge, despite Minnie claiming she'd feel safer in the bedroom with the curtains closed.

'I don't know how I can live like this,' Minnie groaned.

It would be several weeks before the full trial at the Old Bailey, where she'd be expected to give evidence in greater detail and be cross-examined by the defence's awful lawyers. The idea of doing this was terrifying, but so was the wait. And in the meantime there was much to prepare. Minnie's ordeal was far from over.

Forty-one

'You are the prosecution's chief witness,' Minnie's lawyer, Mr Pettit said, fixing her with beady black eyes. 'Do you realize the full importance of that, Miss Gray?'

'I think so,' Minnie said nervously. They were sitting with Max in the flat in Dolphin Square, preparing for the trial.

'If you muddle anything or contradict yourself the case may fail. It is vital, therefore, that we go through your statement to probe for weaknesses and to anticipate any lines that the defence might follow.'

'It's like a rehearsal,' Max said gently. 'Nothing to worry about.'

'I do understand and I'm sure it will be helpful.'

'Good.' Pettit sighed. 'Now, the basics. Glading and his three accomplices are charged with offences under the Official Secrets Act. These concern obtaining and trading information that might be useful to a nation that is regarded as a potential enemy. We're talking about Russia, of course. The case for the prosecution is that they stole the secret plans for a number of weapons and a book on explosives from Woolwich Arsenal, took photographs of them and passed these on to agents of the Soviet Union, et cetera and so forth. Any questions?'

Minnie shook her head.

'Do you think you ought to explain, Pettit, why Miss Gray's testimony is so important?' Max asked.

'I was coming to that.' Petitt frowned and shuffled his papers. 'Miss Gray, there is other important evidence against Glading and his cronies. Although it seems that he went to great lengths not to leave fingerprints on any photographic equipment—'

'I remember that,' Minnie broke in. 'He would wipe everything with a handkerchief.'

'Yes. But it seems that on the night that he was arrested he had to change a bulb on an arc light, that's what you said, isn't it?'

'Yes.'

'And in his hurry, he failed to wipe off the prints. These are enough to link him unquestionably to the equipment.'

'I didn't actually see him change the bulb, but he told me he'd had to.'

'Very good. The police also collected the false-bottomed suitcase that was used to smuggle the documents in and out of the Arsenal. They did, however, make a major slip. They failed to obtain a warrant for their initial search of Glading's house, so the evidence from that search is inadmissible.'

Minnie opened her mouth, then closed it again. She didn't understand why that should be. Surely if something was found, then it was found, but she supposed she had to accept that it was to do with correct procedure.

Max handed out copies of Minnie's official statement and Pettit went through it, stopping to cross-question Minnie on various points. He was keen to know her original motivation for agreeing to spy for Max and she spoke confidently about that, having brooded on it for so long. 'I wanted to do something useful for my country. I felt that I had the right skills to offer.'

Petitt paused to make a note before moving on. Although she'd been careful in the statement not to mention the gruelling mental agonies that she'd been through during the long period of her spying activities, he alighted upon her explanation of why she had left her post as Harry Pollitt's secretary.

'I gather that you hadn't been well and that this is why you left.'

'Yes, that's right. It had been a very stressful period for me.' Her voice cracked as she spoke, causing him to look at her fiercely.

'A stress you feel still, I take it,' he said shrewdly.

'Well, yes, I ... I'm much better now, but it's difficult to forget. There were times as a spy when I really was under terrific pressure. The time I visited India is an example.'

'Yes, Max here has told me about that. A young lady travelling there on her own. Very plucky indeed. I also gather that you spent some time in the Hospital for Nervous Diseases in Bloomsbury.'

She glanced at Max, who would not meet her eye, then

looked back at the lawyer. 'I didn't think that it was important to mention that.'

'You were right not to enter it in your statement, and we must do everything we can to keep it out of court.' Pettit wagged his finger. 'Your nervous state is exactly the weak point in your account that we must keep from the jury. It would enable the defence lawyer to question your judgement and that, I'm afraid, would discredit your testimony entirely. Who else knows about your, er, breakdown?'

'You mean ... I see.' A wave of panic washed over her, but after a moment she recovered herself and tried to think clearly. 'Harry Pollitt knew. I think Glading must do, although we didn't ever discuss it.'

'I see. This then, must be the central pillar of our work together over the next few weeks. On it the fate of the whole case may depend.'

Forty-two

14 March 1938

The opening day of the full trial came at last. With her hat brim pulled down to hide her face, Minnie was led past the crowds up the stone steps of the imposing court building and entered an echoing marble-floored atrium. She stared around at its soaring ceiling, ornate mosaic arches and, beyond, a staircase of monumental grandeur.

To the world she hoped she appeared poised and confident. She'd dressed as smartly and elegantly as she could that morning, wearing once more the coat with the fur trim that had so excited the newspapers. She was as prepared as she could ever be and determined to play her part well. The last gruelling six years of her life had led up to this moment, and she'd need every last drop of courage for her performance.

The thought of facing Glading again and laying out before this man who had thought she was his friend the full details of her betrayal would be the hardest thing Minnie had ever had to do. Behind her elegant and confident façade she was quaking with fear.

After a short wait in an ante room, she was shown into the crowded oak-panelled courtroom. Once again, a murmur of interest went up from the public gallery at the sight of the now famous 'Miss X', then the judge called order and there was silence as she took her place in the witness stand. Was Max up in the gallery, silently supporting her? He'd said he would be, but it wasn't possible to see. He'd be discreet, anyway, and sit out of sight. It helped to imagine him there. After she'd read the oath she dared glance at the dock where Glading and the others sat glumly in a row. Glading stared fixedly ahead and would not look at her and she was relieved.

'Miss X.' It was time now to concentrate on McClure, the prosecution lawyer, as he took his chief witness once more through her account.

She was aware of the intense hush as, guided by his prompts, she described in more detail than at the preliminary hearing in the Bow Street court that she'd been recruited as an agent, how she'd come to know Glading, built his trust and become his accessory. Because she had thoroughly rehearsed all this, she described it fluently. Speaking to this fascinated audience she understood what a thrilling story it must sound. At last she had her chance to explain herself to the world and, painful though it was to lay her life bare in public, she felt it to be a validation of herself and all that she'd endured.

'I was asked by Harry Pollitt and Percy Glading to be a courier.' She managed to cover her visit to India in a few factual sentences, without mention of the terrible mental agonies she'd undergone there. Then came the tricky bit: her reason for resigning her post as Harry Pollitt's secretary. 'The work was very hard … I found it too great a burden …' She breathed in, gripped the edge of the stand for support and ploughed on. 'I resigned my post because I found the work a great strain … It was all … all …' She was falling apart.

'Take your time, Miss X,' McClure said encouragingly.

She looked at him, startled back into reality, then nodded and straightened. *You must be clear and consistent and not stumble.* Max's voice sounded in her mind.

It was when Collard, one of the defence barristers, took his turn to cross-examine her that Minnie ran into trouble. He was trying, as her team had warned, to undermine the impression she'd given of having good judgement.

'Would you say,' Collard asked, his eyes gleaming, 'that you react well in situations of great stress?'

'Generally, yes,' she replied.

'What do you mean by generally?'

She wished she had simply said yes. *You must not appear uncertain.*

'I mean that I remain calm and sensible and make good decisions.'

'And yet in your own words you "found the work a great strain". Do you agree?'

'Yes, but—'

'Yes or no, Miss X.'

'Yes, I did find the work a great strain.'

'Could I therefore put it that you did not in fact always "remain calm and sensible and make good decisions"?'

'I ... I did remain calm. As for good decisions, I believe I managed the situation sensibly by seeking less stressful employment.'

'Yes, I can accept that answer.'

How very generous of you, she wished she could tell him.

'However, I have been party to other evidence that I believe relevant to the case. Evidence that suggests that you have not always been calm and sensible.'

Minnie felt faint. It must be her spell in hospital he was alluding to.

'Miss X. Did you or did you not spend several days in the Hospital for Nervous Diseases in July 1935?'

'I did, but ...'

'And why was that?'

'My workload had become so heavy that I needed a short period of rest.'

'Could it be said that you suffered a nervous breakdown?'

'Not at all. I was in hospital for several days, then enjoyed a holiday away with my family. After that I returned to London and found less onerous employment.'

The judge broke in. 'This so-called evidence is of a delicate and confidential nature and I do not believe it has bearing on the case. Carry on.'

Relief flooded through her. Collard continued his probing, but an expression of weariness had entered his voice. He moved on to the photographic sessions that had taken place in the house in Holland Road and tried to persuade the court that the mysterious Mrs Stevens had been solely responsible for the copying of the plans and the onward transmission of the copies.

'Mr Glading was in the room all the time on these occasions,' Minnie asserted, 'and on the first occasion you mention I gave the copies to him myself on her instructions.'

At this point Collard said he believed that her memory had become muddled. 'I contend,' he said, 'that you were continuing to live under "great strain" and that this affected your judgement.'

'It did not,' she said hotly.

'But you don't deny that you were living under stress.'

'Anyone would in that situation, but the stress was not sufficient to affect my judgement.'

Once again she knew he was hovering dangerously around the subject of her mental stability and again she felt herself go faint.

'Do you need to sit down, Miss X?' Was it so obvious?

'No,' she managed to say.

'Would someone fetch Miss X some water.'

'I don't need any,' she said between clenched teeth.

'Very well.'

She wondered if her ordeal would ever end.

When she was finally dismissed she left the stand as gracefully as she could, but her instinct was to flee. As she passed Glading he met her eye and his look of hatred was like a kick in the gut. Outside, she sat weakly in the little sitting room with her eyes closed, sipping water with a shaking hand.

*

Later in the day, as she sat sightlessly turning the pages of a magazine, the guard on the door spoke her name.

'You're free to go.' Quickly she rose and left the room, her heart beating with nerves. In the atrium she found Richard buttoning his overcoat. He hurried across and embraced her.

'It's over, Minnie' he said. 'Guilty. They're all guilty except that chap Munday. Not enough evidence, they've let him go.'

A shiver went through her. She could hardly take it in. 'Richard!' she whispered.

'It's over, Minnie. You've done it. You were marvellous!'

The relief was incredible.

And now the atrium was filling with people, strangers staring curiously and pointing her out. Her lawyer spoke briefly to congratulate her, but she hardly took in what he said. Where was Max? She couldn't see him. And then she did. He was speaking animatedly to a man she didn't know, then he looked up and their eyes met and he flashed her his charming smile. She expected him to come across to her at once, but instead he became lost in the crowd surging out of the building. She hung back in fear. Outside there would be the press to face, flashbulbs, intrusive questions. She turned in blind panic, looking for Richard, but couldn't see him now.

'Miss, this way.' A young policeman with a sympathetic face had appeared at her elbow, then Richard returned. Together they escorted her to a rear entrance and straight into the safety of a police van. Its doors closed, they moved off, sitting in tense silence as they passed out into the street, the van carving a slow path through the noisy crowds. She thought of Glading and wondered if he would have to face them on his way back to some bare cell. It wasn't rational to feel sorry for him, but nevertheless she did.

The telephone call from 'Captain King' came that evening as she was sitting down to dinner with Richard at the hotel near Hyde Park where they'd stayed the previous night. The receptionist showed her into a tiny sitting room with a desk and a telephone. The room smelled overpoweringly of lilies from a vase on a stand, which put her in mind of the hospital room.

She sat at the desk and lifted the receiver. 'M, it's me.'

'How are you?'

'Tired, I've never felt so tired. But thankful, too.'

'I must apologize about earlier. I was buttonholed by a chap I used to know. I looked up and you'd gone. We got our verdict, Minnie, that's the important thing. I can't thank you enough. You surpassed yourself.'

'Thank you. I—'

He was not to be interrupted. 'The sentencing is to be the day after tomorrow. You'll need to attend in case you're called. I can't be there, unfortunately. Something's cropped up.' The sound of his voice was coming and going. A barking dog could be heard in the background and then a rustling noise. Suddenly his voice came steadily again. 'Sorry. The sentencing, yes. If Glading's not taken off the streets for some considerable time I'll be disappointed. I wait eagerly to hear the news. Well, that's all, really. I simply wanted to congratulate you.' His voice was fading once more.

'Wait, please. What will happen to me now?'

'What will happen? Life can return to normal for you,

that's what'll happen. It's what you wanted, isn't it? We'll meet up for a drink sometime, you and I. Or lunch. Yes, lunch, to celebrate. I'll be in touch. Magnificent job. It's quite a coup for both of us. You may have a well-earned rest, my dear. A little holiday, perhaps.'

After he rang off she replaced the receiver with a sense of unease. Max was already drifting away from her. She swallowed against threatening tears, then gathered her handbag and stumbled off to find Richard.

A broken night was followed by an abrupt awakening. When Minnie came downstairs, sluggish, to breakfast, she was drawn irresistibly to the day's newspapers, fanned out on the side table outside the hotel restaurant. Hitler's Anschluss of Austria dominated the headlines, but inside she found all she feared. '*Miss X describes capture of spies . . .*' one heading blazed. '*Blonde secret agent calls Guilty!*' cried another. She picked up this particular paper with trembling hands.

'Minnie, no.' Richard's stern voice came from behind. He closed the paper, took her arm and steered her into the restaurant. 'Not today. Give yourself a rest.' As they were shown to a table he whispered. 'Two more days to get through and it will be over.'

'You're right, I suppose.'

'Let's go for a walk in the park after breakfast. A bit of fresh air will do you good.'

And a walk would keep her away from the newspapers. She sighed, but agreed.

By the time they returned to the hotel mid-afternoon, the

morning papers had been replaced by the evening ones and the headlines inside had moved on to a nasty domestic murder.

Soon it will be over, she thought as she went to bed that night.

Two mornings later, Minnie made up her tired face carefully then selected a beige blouse and a mid-blue suit for her final act on the public stage. Glading and the two associates who had been found guilty with him were to appear in court for sentencing. It was, she thought as she studied her reflection, the right look, neither too bright nor too funereal. She had to be there outside in case, but with any luck she wouldn't be needed.

At the Old Bailey, while the court was in session, she sat and waited in the same small room, turning the pages of the same old magazines and trying to stay calm. Every time she glanced at her watch the hands did not seem to have moved.

Finally there came a gentle knock and an usher appeared in the doorway. 'Would you like to follow me, miss?' She rose too quickly and the magazine fell to the floor. 'Leave it, please, miss.'

When she entered the courtroom, she was momentarily dazzled by winter sunlight and a tremor of voices filled her ears. Where was she to go? The witness stand? There was no one to guide her. Then the judge spoke.

'Miss X.'

She blinked and moved slightly until she could see his grave face clearly. He removed his spectacles and regarded her in a kindly fashion.

'I've invited you here to tell you that I think you're a young woman possessed of extraordinary courage. You have done a great service to your country.'

'Thank you,' she breathed. 'Thank you,' but her words were drowned by a patter like the sea rattling over shingle or the wind rustling the trees. It took her a moment to realize that it was the sound of applause. It grew louder, until it filled her ears. Somebody cheered. She stood stunned and blinking, utterly overcome.

Back in the witness room, Minnie almost gave way to tears. It was a struggle for her not to unravel, but by the time Richard came to collect her a few minutes later she'd recovered herself, dabbing eau de cologne on her aching temples.

'You're a heroine,' her brother said with a grin and hugged her.

'Never mind that. What did the judge give Glading?'

'Six years' penal servitude. Hard labour to you and me.'

'Hard labour?' She had only imagined prison and was struck by horror. The idea of Glading, pale and slight, stone-breaking in all weathers. The poor man. 'What have I done?' she whispered, dismayed.

'Minnie! It was treason. He knew the risks.'

'I thought it would be prison, simply prison.' She could not stifle a sob.

'He doesn't deserve your pity.'

'I can't bear to think of it. And his poor wife, and the child.'

'He isn't even married to Rosa, Minnie. Didn't you know? He has a wife still living.'

She stared at her brother in disbelief. Was there no end to Glading's secrets?

'What now, Minnie? Back to the hotel for lunch?'

'No, Richard,' she said, 'Somewhere quiet and anonymous. Then I want to go home.'

A puzzled frown crossed her brother's face. 'I thought you said you wouldn't stay in Holland Road.' They'd agreed that everything there belonging to her should go into storage until she'd found somewhere new in London to live.

'I meant Edgbaston, silly. I want to go home and see Mother.'

Forty-three

'You're wanted on the telephone, Minnie,' her mother announced. 'A Miss such and such, I didn't catch the name.'

Minnie put down the novel she'd been trying to read. A week had passed since the trial, a difficult week because even safe in Edgbaston she hadn't been able to sleep or to settle and there simply wasn't anything to do at home.

'Hello?'

'Miss Gray? I'm M's assistant. I'm ringing to see when you might be free for lunch. Are you coming to London in the near future?'

Happiness spread through her. Lunch with Max. 'I can do, with pleasure.'

They arranged a day a week hence and the afternoon before, the girl rang again when Minnie was out shopping and left a message. 'The Ritz, one o'clock, table booked in the main restaurant in the name of Mr Harper,' her mother told her.

She frowned. Who on earth was Mr Harper and why was he joining them for lunch?

Minnie was fairly sure she hadn't been followed, but looked quickly behind as she entered the pink and gold glory of the great hotel. Downstairs in the powder room she checked her face in one of the many mirrors and remembered the last and only time she'd come here. It had been after she'd broken up with Raymond and become so ill with her nerves. She'd decided to give up her work as a spy, but Max had bought her a cocktail and tried so charmingly to persuade her to continue. She wondered what he would say to her today after their triumph and her spirits rose.

She walked back upstairs and past the Palm Court, glancing at the tables just in case, but there was no one of foreign appearance sitting morosely over coffee, or anything else to evoke concern and her footsteps lightened as she continued across the acre of carpet to the restaurant. This lunch would be a celebration of the successful result of her hard work, but a small, ridiculous part of her wondered if Max would suggest something else she could do for M-section. Nothing as stressful as the last few years, no, she wouldn't go through that again for anything, but perhaps she'd deign to accept a small role somewhere she wouldn't be recognized. Maybe that was the reason this other man, Harper, was coming along. She was intrigued.

She was surprised and disappointed, therefore, when she announced herself at the desk and the maître d' showed her to a table laid only for two. The man who rose from his seat to greet her wasn't Max, but a tall, heavily built stranger of a red-faced, well-lunched appearance, with a small moustache.

'Miss Gray,' Mr Harper said, shaking her hand. 'It's a privilege to meet you. A very great privilege.'

'Thank you,' she murmured and took her seat. After Harper ordered drinks, she ventured, 'I think I may have misunderstood. Won't M be joining us?'

'Unfortunately he has been called away, so the pleasure is all mine.'

She stared at him in disbelief, but Harper quickly moved on. 'Now, Miss Gray, this lunch is to say thank you. We are all very grateful at the Ministry for your work over the years and particularly for your performance during the recent, ah, legal proceedings. I wasn't there myself, but I'm told that it was masterly. A splendid result, Miss Gray. Now, here come our drinks and we should order our meal, yes indeed.'

There was a long pause while Mr Harper discussed with the waiter the tenderness of the steak dish on the menu and the age of a particular bottle of wine and made a show of being shocked that Minnie, whose appetite had suddenly deserted her, only wanted consommé and a little grilled sole. The disappointment of Max's absence had taken all her pleasure in the day.

Why, she thought, as she gulped her gin and tonic, hadn't he come, or at least let her know? Surely it wasn't for security reasons. If she wasn't frightened to come here, she felt with growing fury, why should he be? It wasn't fair.

Their first course arrived and she did her best with Mr Harper as he talked about his gout and the problems with staffing they were experiencing in the department since they were starved of funds. 'We're hoping this recent success will make a real difference,' he said, his face growing redder as he finished his martini and started on red wine. 'Not only have your efforts delivered invaluable knowledge of the workings of the Communist Party in this country and the links of certain individuals to foreign powers, but you have secured the conviction of several men whose activities threatened national security. Now we can demonstrate that we're of real use it will transform perceptions. Mark my words, it'll be men like us – and a woman or two, of course – who will prove to be of crucial use should there be another war in Europe.'

Minnie felt she ought to glow with pleasure at this praise, but instead it made her crosser. 'I'm only glad to have done my bit,' she said, crumbling a piece from her roll.

'You must be relieved that it's all over. Glad to return to civilian life, eh? A young woman like you, I expect you have plans.' His eyes twinkled benevolently.

'I don't know what I shall do,' she told him, truthfully. 'I was wondering if the department might have something else for me.'

'I'm afraid that would not be possible. Ah, is this our main course? Oh dear, I hope you don't find the fish to be a mistake.'

She gazed at the great slab of meat on his plate, oozing blood into the gravy, and looked down at the gently steaming sole and wished she was hungry. She waited for the vegetables to be served then picked up her knife and fork.

So that was that. A clean break. She slipped a morsel of fish into her mouth. It tasted comfortingly of salt tears and butter. Perhaps that would be the reason why Max hadn't come. He probably thought he was being kind. Yes, that would be typical of him. But it didn't feel kind, it felt like being dumped.

During the rest of lunch Mr Harper questioned her in a way that was at the same time gentle and as sharp as a surgeon's knife, stripping her of her knowledge and her techniques as a cashiered military officer might be stripped of his sword and epaulettes.

At the end of the meal, over coffee, he harrumphed and reached into an inside pocket from which he extracted a slim brown envelope. 'This is from the department in recognition of your service,' he said gravely. 'Put it away in your handbag, that's it. Now the bill. I must get back to the office. Some of us have work to do, you know.'

Out in the foyer Minnie thanked him politely for the meal and they parted. She watched his portly figure shamble away. In the downstairs haven of the powder room she took out the envelope and inspected its contents. It was a cheque, written out in an old-fashioned copperplate hand. £500. Her eyes widened at the generous sum. It was nearly four years' wages, she calculated. Enough to set her up again very comfortably. She slid it back into the envelope and stood there, feeling flat.

The door opened and she hastily thrust the envelope inside her handbag, but it was no one sinister, only a young, elegantly dressed girl with fair hair. The girl gave a sweet smile before entering one of the stalls. *Calm down*, Minnie told herself as she adjusted her hat and set off on her long journey home.

*

Near the underground station, Minnie stopped at a news-stand to buy an evening paper. As she waited for the grizzled old man to pick out some change a strapline on a magazine caught her eye and she frowned. 'I'll have a copy of *Time* as well,' she told him.

She rolled up her purchases and waited until she was safely on the Birmingham train before she dared to read the maga-zine. The article was supposed to be about her, but the whole thing bore such scant relation to reality that it felt like reading about someone else, a character in a novel or a film, perhaps. *'A sample of the tempting sort of bait successfully used to catch spies by His Majesty's Government has now been on view in London's ancient, soot-blackened Bow Street Police Court for several weeks, officially tagged "Miss X".'* The Old Bailey, not Bow Street – the inaccuracies were appalling – but it was what came next that upset her more. *'This slim, bob-haired blonde . . . arrived curvesomely sheathed in clinging black, kept shifting her handsome fur piece with the sinuosity of Mae West as she testified before a bug-eyed judge.'*

She sat back against the seat in disbelief, unable to read on. The British press had been bad enough, but *Time* magazine . . . The whole of America would be reading this rubbish. And this was how they would think of her, not as an intelligent, dutiful young woman, but as some glamorous sex-bomb. Her disbelief melted away and she prickled with anger. All the quiet, meticulous bravery of the past six years for which the judge had praised her had been dismissed. Instead she was portrayed as a siren, a femme fatale, as though there could be no other model for a female spy. Minnie closed her eyes against the pain.

The train rattled on. Two young married women sitting opposite were discussing the shortcomings of a mutual friend. Their silly gossip was briefly distracting, until the phrase, 'she'll never get a husband if she behaves like that' nettled Minnie. Was this all that conventional people thought about, that a woman was nothing without a husband? What would these women think of *her* if she showed them the magazine? That Miss X was a glamour girl who would never attract an honest man. Despite her anger she allowed herself an ironic smile. That these ladies would connect Miss X to the ordinary-looking young woman sharing their carriage was as unlikely as snow in summer.

The train banked sharply and the magazine slipped off the seat. Minnie bent to pick it up. It had been an odd day, she mused, eyeing the headline again with distaste, and she felt low. The awful lunch – well, the Ritz and the food hadn't been awful, but Mr Harper certainly was. Even if she'd liked him, though, he hadn't been Max. Then there had been the matter of the pay-off. Not the money itself, that was welcome. It was the manner of it. She had no job, nowhere to live and she was broken-hearted.

Yes, it was the way the whole thing had been done. Like a shutter coming down. *We've wrung you out like an old rag and now we don't need you anymore. Thank you and goodbye.* Again, Minnie brooded over Max's absence. Perhaps he really had got a cast-iron excuse, a meeting he couldn't miss, a trip he'd been forced to make. She was comforted by the thought. *Perhaps he didn't, though,* a voice whispered in her mind, a nasty whining voice she knew of old. *He'll be in touch,* she told the voice firmly. She and Max had been too close for him to forget her.

What if he isn't? the voice persisted. She dug her hands into her coat pockets and squared her shoulders. She had a cheque for £500 in her bag and a new life before her. What that was to be she didn't know yet.

The train slowed as it arrived into Birmingham's big, busy station. *It'll work out,* she told herself fiercely as she gathered her possessions. *I'll make it work out. I have to.*

Forty-four

November 1940

The air raid was underway when Minnie left home at nine-thirty for her night shift at the ambulance station. Plane engines droned from somewhere up ahead and the grim old streets of Notting Hill were lit up sporadically by the flames of incendiary bombs while searchlights turned the skies into a giant light show. As she stumbled along, wet snow stinging her face, the weak beam from her torch picked out rubble, the sparkle of broken glass and at one point a black crater in the pavement into which she almost fell.

Eventually she reached her destination, a walled yard off a side road where several ambulances painted with white crosses glinted in the darkness. She hurried past them down a short slope and pushed open a door in a low, utilitarian brick building to be welcomed into cheerful yellow light.

'Look what the wind's blown in!' a girl's light voice said.

'Hello to you, too, Fliss. Phew!' Minnie pulled off her

gloves, brushed sleet from her eyelashes, and blinked until her surroundings came into focus. A makeshift office with an old sofa, a table and basic kitchen facilities. Three lively faces, one male, two female, looking up at her.

'How's the North Pole, Gray?' Cooper, an amiable burly man of forty, was sitting on a stool at the kitchen worktop, a popular newspaper spread open before him.

'The polar bears send love. Nobody been called out yet?'

'Not yet.' Fliss's eyes gleamed in her pointed face. 'Sounds busy out there, though.'

'Getting that way. Any tea in the pot, Bluett?'

Bluett, a short, compact young woman with wiry hair, put down her knitting to peer into the teapot on the wooden crate that served as a side table and frowned. 'Stick some hot water in this, please, dear Cooper?'

'Hang about.' Cooper plonked a kettle on the little gas burner.

'Evening, Mr Warren,' Minnie greeted a tall angular man with a lantern jaw who was emerging from the back room. The station leader nodded at her. 'Better get yourself ready quickly, Gray,' he said in his low, soft voice. Despite the stern expression he always wore, she found Vic Warren a kindly man. He never lost his temper, and treated everyone the same.

While the kettle boiled Minnie hurried into the back room, where she pulled on work trousers and boots. She was adjusting the strap on her tin helmet when the sounds of explosions grew suddenly closer and she paused to listen. *Somewhere a few streets away*, she thought.

'Poor devils,' she remarked when she returned to the

others. She clasped a steaming mug of tea in both hands and they were all silent for a while, wincing at the boom of the bombs and the answering rattle of the ack-ack guns.

The door opened with a blast of cold air and the final two of the new shift entered.

'Hurry up, all of you,' Warren called.

Soon, what with everyone clambering about and the kettle on the boil again, the station began to feel pleasantly warm. Cooper set out some old mattresses and blankets on the floor for later, but the explosions were getting closer still and the atmosphere was too tense for anyone to contemplate a time for relaxation. Then a huge crump sounded terrifyingly near, causing the whole building to quiver. Everyone froze. Minnie watched a teaspoon slide across the worktop and clatter onto the floor.

Shortly after this the wall-mounted telephone started to ring. Warren stepped across to snatch up the receiver.

'Here we go,' Bluett murmured and rolled up her knitting. Warren turned towards them, his brow furrowed as he listened to the voice on the line.

'Right away,' he said into the telephone and replaced the receiver.

'Incident at Westbourne Park. Gray, you take Fliss. Cooper, go with Bluett.'

There was a shuffle of activity as the four of them collected up helmets and other paraphernalia and stepped out into the sleet.

This is what I was made for, Minnie thought as she edged her vehicle out of the yard and into the street, following the faint beam of its dimmed headlights, and headed towards the main road. She drove as fast as she dared, turning the wheel sharply to dodge fallen masonry and the odd unexpected pedestrian as the vehicle wove round bends and shot across junctions, with Fliss, terrified beside her, urging her to 'Slow down, for goodness' sake!' But she only obeyed when curtains of dust hung in the air or settled on the windscreen, obscuring her vision.

It was the urgency she liked, the buzz it gave her. Fliss had nothing to worry about because Minnie always remained steady, watchful, completely in control. With the street signs all taken down she'd had to learn the geography of the area. Even so it kept altering under the brutal artistry of the bombs.

Minnie had volunteered to train as a driver after the government appeal went out some months before war broke out. She'd seen learning to drive as a new challenge, a welcome change from her current job of secretary to the managing director of a shoe company. She'd been right about the pleasure of a challenge. She'd loved the exercises in the dark, careering through country woods, avoiding obstacles, and later, driving more carefully through the London streets. She'd had to learn to maintain the vehicles, too, and practised lifting loaded stretchers into the backs of the ambulances and up onto the top shelves, the trainees using each other as dummies. There had been first-aid drills, but they were fairly rudimentary. The whole exercise had filled a gap in her life, made her feel useful and important again. It was as though she'd been numb inside since the trial and the brisk pay-off from MI5, and now she could feel again.

War came as expected, but Minnie hadn't been needed for most of the first year because hostilities took place abroad. Then two months ago the Germans began to blitz London and every trained volunteer was required, in Minnie's case twice a week. If the overnight shift was busy she slept it off the following morning and went in to work at lunchtime. Her boss simply had to put up with it. Somehow everyone managed.

On nights like these she felt fully alert, as she had at the high points of her spying days, giving her all to the task in hand. *I matter*, she always felt. There were low points, too, when the tragic sights she witnessed overwhelmed her. She tried not to brood, but to live moment by moment and this helped keep her worries in check.

And there were worries a plenty. Two and a half years of Glading's six-year sentence had passed. Not a day went by without her thinking of him, and wondering when he'd be released. Suppose they let him out early? Would they warn her first? And the nub of it, would he come looking for her?

Tonight, as they drew near to Westbourne Park underground station, the air smelled of burning rubber, and clouds of dust clung to the windshield. The area was busy with emergency vehicles and uniformed figures moving purposefully. Here and there onlookers gathered, parents clutching sleepy children, a man comforting a big woman in a gaping overcoat who sat on the kerb weeping.

'There,' Fliss said urgently, pointing to a blue glow down a side road, marking the site of the incident. Minnie turned the wheel, taking it slowly, feeling it in her bones when the undercarriage scraped on rubble or the wheels scrunched glass. At one point water drummed on the bonnet from a spouting pipe.

Suddenly there was a distant explosion and the sky lit up, revealing a scene that was now familiar to her, but each time uniquely distressing. Helmeted firemen combing hills of broken masonry that had once been houses. The shapes of two bodies on the pavement, the faces shrouded by a single ragged curtain. A man in a warden's uniform squatted to tuck a coat round a motionless patient, a woman, Minnie saw, before darkness fell once more. She halted the ambulance so that its headlights fell on the injured woman, leaped down and went to help while Fliss fetched a stretcher out of the back.

'She caught the blast,' the warden murmured to Minnie. Most of the woman's clothes had been blown off and her naked skin looked livid and raw. Her eyes were closed, but she made little moans with each shallow breath. She would die of shock if she wasn't kept warm. Fliss shook out a blanket and the three of them managed to roll her onto the stretcher. They loaded her into the ambulance and Minnie checked that she was comfortable while Fliss discussed with the warden, whose face was black with dirt, if they should wait in case there was anyone else for the hospital, but it was decided that, no, they should go. Cooper and Bluett would be along in a moment, they were sure, and drive the bodies to the mortuary once the paperwork was complete.

Minnie listened to them talk and thought the man sounded familiar, but everything was distorted by the noise and the urgency of the situation and her brain refused to make links.

Only later, as they left the hospital having deposited their patient and began the journey back to the ambulance station, did scenes from the last hour start to replay through her mind. Their last sight of the warden, caught in the head-lights as he turned away. She didn't know him after all, but something about him had reminded her of her old boyfriend Raymond, the timbre of his voice, the shy friendliness. Later, when she lay in bed in her Notting Hill flat, listening to the milkman's whistle and the clank of the milk churns, she fell to thinking about it and was visited by a terrible sense of loss.

For years, she'd tried not to dwell on Raymond. After learning of his marriage, she'd put the matter behind her, though not without some anguish. 'Why are you telling me this?' she'd snapped at her mother for mentioning the birth of his child – 'a sweet little boy, apparently' – and Mrs Gray had stuttered, 'I thought you'd want to know,' and threw her an expression of such pity that Minnie felt rage and frustration wash over her. She had run upstairs, thrown herself on her bed and burst into violent tears.

Mrs Gray learned her lesson, because if she ever bumped into Raymond's mother after that she did not tell her daughter and Raymond was shut once more behind that door in Minnie's memory.

Several nights later, she and Fliss were called to an incident that was even more tragic. The bomb had fallen on a back garden near an Anderson shelter where an entire family had been sleeping. The young mother, in her dressing gown, was hysterical. They sat her in the ambulance and tried to calm her. 'I went back into the house to fetch some cough linctus for the baby,' she sobbed. 'They'll get them out quickly, won't they?'

'They're doing their best,' Fliss said in her most soothing voice.

Minnie said nothing as she helped the woman sip tea from a flask. She'd spoken to one of the firemen. From all accounts the back of the house had collapsed and mounds of rubble had to be shifted to get to the shelter underneath. 'It don't look good,' the fireman had muttered.

Neighbours offered to take charge of the young mother, but she refused to go with them, so they all stayed waiting until one by one the bodies were brought out, the father first, then two children and finally the baby, a pitiful heap of rags. The woman's screams filled the night. She tore herself from Fliss's grasp and ran to them. Minnie watched in horror as she moved from one little body to the next before she was caught by the rescuers and taken away to a nearby house.

Minnie stared at the boy and felt such compassion that something made her kneel down and wipe the dirt from his face. It was otherwise unmarked. He was young, five or six, she thought, because he had lost his baby chubbiness. He reminded her of her youngest nephew, but then a picture from further back came to her unbidden; Eddie, her brother, who had died, and all the sadness of her far-off childhood rolled back in. Minnie touched this child's cheek a final time, then rose and turned away. Later, when they loaded the shrouded bodies into the back of the ambulance, they worked in silence. Then she drove slowly and carefully to the hospital mortuary as though the battered old ambulance were a hearse.

On the way back to their station in the early hours of the morning, Fliss said, 'Sometimes I don't think I can do this anymore,' and when Minnie glanced at the girl she saw tears glinting on her cheeks.

'It's bloody awful,' Minnie agreed.

'The poor mother—'

'Don't.'

'Do you think ... one can ever recover from something like that?'

'I suppose some people do.'

'I wouldn't be able to. Ever.'

Minnie could not think what to say. All over London scenes like tonight had played out, in other cities, too. In other countries in this war and all through history mothers had lost children and children their mothers. And many, she supposed, had picked themselves up and gone on, somehow, despite their grief. She thought of her own family, the loss of Eddie and how badly the tragedy had damaged her father, while her mother had been more resilient. Had survived the death of her husband, too.

Finally, she said, 'We don't know how strong we are until things happen to us.' Fliss was very young still and had not seen much of life until now. It was different for Minnie. She knew she could survive things, or at least the sort of things that life had so far thrown at her. But the wounds were still raw.

Had she been good enough? Most of the time she was able

to rationalize that, yes, she had, but she knew the effects of almost seven years leading a double life would never leave her. She'd betrayed people who had trusted her, and had felt bitterly betrayed in her turn. Most of all by Max.

He had never contacted her again.

Tonight had made her think, though, how far she'd come. She was her own person now. No need to rely on anyone else for strength or reassurance. So much that she'd learned from Max had been valuable, but he'd dropped her when he didn't need her anymore. Now she realized that she didn't need him. She was free.

Forty-five

January 1944

A frosty winter's evening and the streets were emptying of crowds. Minnie was glad to enter the warmth of Holborn underground station. She'd stayed late at work in order to catch up with correspondence and longed for the piece of bacon she'd kept back for her supper and the chance of an early night. After the Blitz had ended she'd stood down from the ambulance driving and expected to sleep better, but she couldn't stop herself waking in the night and lay restless. Any strange sound and she'd freeze with fear before realizing that it was only the swish of a petticoat slipping off a chair or the creak of the curtain rail in a draught.

Tonight the escalator wasn't working and she trod carefully down the steps into the depths of the station, twice stopping to glance round when she heard impatient footsteps behind. Both times it was simply someone in a hurry. Lately she'd become jittery as a result of a letter she'd received.

During the last few months she'd been acutely aware that Glading's sentence would soon be completed. The prospect of this terrified her. Suppose he came after her? She'd given herself a good talking to about the likelihood – Glading was not a violent man – but this hadn't helped, not really. It was true that she'd been safe so far – she'd never even heard from Harry Pollitt – but perhaps this would change. It wouldn't take much sleuthing on Glading's part to discover her new address. She still lived near Holland Park because she liked the area and it was convenient. The latest flat was several streets away from her previous addresses, but still in good reach of the underground station. Glading or one of his Russians might reasonably start by hanging around there in the hope that he'd see her. Or suppose they managed to track her down at the hockey club?

She'd decided that if she knew definitely when he was going to be released it would help. Three months ago she'd taken matters into her own hands and had written to Mr Harper who'd taken her for lunch at the Ritz all those years ago. The reply was commendably swift. He'd made enquiries and so far as he knew Glading was expected to serve his full sentence of six years, which, as she rightly said, would mean he'd leave prison in March. He'd let her know if he heard otherwise. For a while she'd been able to relax a little but now that Christmas was over and Glading's release date was fast approaching, she'd begun to feel fearful again. Harper's letter made no mention of police protection after Glading's release. It simply urged her to be watchful.

The westbound platform was nearly deserted. She must

just have missed a train. There was no indication when the next one would be, but everyone was used to that. So much of life in wartime was about waiting without knowing how long something would take or indeed if it was worth waiting for. Queues formed at greengrocers' at a rumour of oranges or onions only for the item to run out by the time you got there, if it had existed in the first place. Trains and buses might be promised, but never turn up. Minnie sighed and tapped her foot, wondering how long she'd have to wait for supper.

She felt rather than saw a man a few feet away looking at her. Out of the corner of her eye she assessed him. Blue uniform with an officer's stripes; thank heavens, no dark besuited Russian. Her own age, possibly. She turned her head and gave him her coldest stare, but instead of looking sheepish or moving away as men usually did in her experience, he smiled. It was a friendly smile and she liked the way it lit up his eyes. Not English, she thought; he lacked that grey guarded look. She tossed her head to show she wasn't interested and pretended to concentrate on a shabby advertisement for a health drink pasted on the wall on the further side of the track.

'Excuse me, lady,' his voice came, rich and warm. American, probably. 'Do you have the time on you?'

She fumbled with her sleeve. 'Half past seven.'

'Thank you. It looks like I'll miss my connection. Just my luck.'

She nodded politely, but her frostiness failed to put him off.

'There's nobody official to ask. Do *you* know when the next train's due?'

'I'm afraid not.' She wished he'd go away and leave her to her thoughts. Even though he seemed attractively wistful. And she liked the rich timbre of his voice. She wondered what he was doing on his own and couldn't stop herself asking, 'Where are you going? Maybe a bus would be better.'

'Paddington station. I'm staying with a buddy in Reading tonight. Is there a bus from here?'

'Probably.' Despite herself Minnie met his eye. There was something about him she liked, a boy-next-door quality that reminded her of Raymond. Good-looking. Deepset blue eyes that crinkled when he smiled. A soft, tender mouth, a tanned face, out of place in England in January. He wasn't tall, instead about average, and he held himself confidently, his feet planted apart as though at ease on a parade ground.

'If you go up to the street and turn . . .' she started to say, but just at that moment the slightest of breezes brushed her face and lifted her hair, bringing with it a smell of hot rubber. A distant rumble could be heard, which grew louder. 'Here we are,' she cried, and they stood together and watched the train rush in.

It squealed to a halt and he waited for her to step on first, then asked if he could sit with her.

'I suppose so.' She tucked the skirt of her coat out of the way and he sat on the bench beside her. As the train moved off he put out his hand. 'My name's Sam. Sam Stanley, Canadian Royal Air Force.'

Canadian, of course, the blue uniform. 'I'm Miss Gray. Minnie.' She looked down at his hand as she clasped its steady warmth. His jacket sleeve had slid up and her eyes widened in surprise, then she laughed.

'Do I amuse you?'

'You asked me the time just now, but you're wearing a watch!'

'You've rumbled me,' he declared without shame. And then both of them were laughing.

She was intrigued by him now. 'Are you really going to Paddington? Or have you made that up, too?'

'I certainly am, except ... Well, Miss Gray, this might sound impertinent, but I haven't had any dinner and if you don't have any plans, what would you say to us getting off soon and finding one of your Lyons places?'

'There's one near Oxford Circus. Yes, let's do that. I was only going home.' Minnie spared no further thought for the bit of bacon. She felt light and free, because after all the grimness and the duty she was able to do something fun on a whim. And she liked him, this man, which was odd because she knew nothing about him. He was looking appraisingly at her, but respectfully, too, so for once the attention made her feel good rather than grubby and self-conscious. Her mother's voice sounded a warning in her head, but she ignored it. A meal in a Lyons Corner House could hardly be dangerous. Yes, she'd do it.

The Lyons was busy, warm and cheerful, and a band was playing. There were three main dishes on the menu. Minnie chose steak and kidney pie and he a hotpot, which, he said reminded him of home.

'Tell me about home,' she said, taking a sip of lemonade

and he described tenderly a small town called Lindsay in Ontario with a main street wide enough to turn a coach-and-four in. It was set on a river amid beautiful lakes and he told her about fishing as a very young man, and the wild deer roaming the land that his family farmed. Minnie said that it sounded idyllic. 'It's warm and humid in summer,' he said, 'but gets cold like here in January February time.'

He was excited to hear that she played hockey. 'Why, ice hockey, that's our national sport, you must know that. I follow the Leafs, that's the Toronto Maple Leafs, have you heard of 'em? There's a guy from Lindsay plays for the team, Joe Primeau, Gentleman Joe, folk call him. I wonder if he still does.' Sam appeared wistful again. 'My, time does pass. Four years I've been away. I'd never been outside Ontario before and now I've travelled across Europe.'

'Where have you been?' she wanted to know.

'All over. France, Greece, Italy.'

She listened to his experiences at the fall of Crete and the invasion of Sicily then mainland Italy, saw pain cross his face as he described the loss of comrades at Salerno.

'I've been to France, but nowhere else much. Except India.' As soon as she said it she was plunged into memories of that awful time. 'I didn't like it.'

'Where did you go there? I have a buddy who went to Bombay.'

'I was in Bombay for several weeks at the beginning of monsoon.' The terrible heat, the fear. 'It was to do with a job I had. They needed a courier.'

'Sounds like you hit the wrong season. It was magical to

my buddy. All that life and colour and the people coming from every side. Never seen anything like it, he said.'

'It was extraordinary, I'll say that, but I was glad to get home again.'

'I don't know when I'll get home. We're hanging around waiting for instructions again. What about you?'

'I'm a secretary.'

He asked her about her work and Minnie talked happily enough about the shoe business, running the managing director's office, the pressure they were under because they were supplying boots to the services, though, like everyone, he knew not to ask too many questions.

Instead he said simply, 'You never think about all that, do you? Where everything comes from, the uniforms and stuff. War is like some huge machine.'

They'd finished eating now and the nippy cleared their plates away. They sat for a moment in companionable silence, waiting for the apple crumble they'd asked for. He felt in his inside pocket for his wallet. She watched him extract a couple of photographs, which he laid on the table between them. They were creased, with furry edges as though he'd handled them many times. One was of a family with several children and a farmhouse in the background. Sam pointed out his mother and father and himself, the eldest, he said. The second print was of a pretty young woman with a mass of dark curly hair and an intelligent face. He hesitated, then said, 'This is Naomi, my fiancée.'

Minnie felt a twinge of disappointment and looked up to see that his eyes were watchful. She touched the portrait with her finger and opened her mouth to say that Naomi was lovely, he must be very happy, but he stopped her by placing his hand over hers.

'She was a nurse, Minnie. When war came she wanted to help, came to London, but she was killed in a raid. It was in November 1940. I got the news on Christmas Eve. You can imagine what kind of Christmas that was.'

'I ... I'm so sorry. You're right. I can only imagine. How long had you known her?'

'We'd met at a dance a couple of years before the war. She was from a nearby town but had cousins in Lindsay. I'd never met anyone before I'd wanted to marry. When you've known girls all your life, they seem ordinary. She was different. Always wanting to get away, do something with her life.' He shook his head. 'Maybe she wouldn't have said yes if we hadn't been going to war, I don't know. A farmer's wife. Can't see her having settled for that.' He smiled sadly.

He was still holding Minnie's hand and she felt warmth and steadiness flow from him. Then their pudding arrived and he fitted the precious photographs back into the wallet. He picked up his spoon, then put it down again.

'I won't say I'm over Naomi exactly, but it feels nice to be with a beautiful girl again. Have you ever been married?'

'No. I ... came close to it once, but it wasn't to be.' Minnie told Sam about Raymond and the holiday that she'd missed with him which had led to him meeting someone else.

'You're not an ordinary girl, I knew that at once,' he said, in between mouthfuls of apple crumble. 'That girl's special, I thought when I saw you, and I can't let her get away.'

'What rubbish.' Minnie licked custard from her spoon and grinned happily.

'I'm serious. A beautiful girl with spunk. That's what I thought.'

'Next you're going to tell me I remind you of your mother.'

'You're kidding me, aren't you?'

They stayed, talking, until Sam finally said that he ought to be leaving if he was to reach Reading that night, but before they parted he asked her if she would go out with him the following evening and did she like dancing. The speed of this request took Minnie's breath away.

'I don't usually go out in the week,' she said with a frown. 'And I can't remember when I last danced.'

'Then it's time you did. And I'm sorry, I can't wait and take things slow. I'm due back at base in three days' time. Please come, Minnie Gray. I promise you a great evening.'

Laughing, she agreed. How could she not when he looked so pleading.

Forty-six

Minnie had never been to the Hammersmith Palais before, but Sam had plenty of times, he said, and as they waited in the queue outside he described how a guy had told him it had been a tram shed until after the Great War, after which it had become a dance hall, then an ice rink, before being renovated for dancing once more.

'It still feels like a tram shed,' she said, when they'd finally gained access to the vast, high-ceilinged space inside. She had to speak loudly into his ear to be heard above the jazz band and the chattering crowds and he took the opportunity of her closeness to put his arm round her waist and draw her onto the polished floor.

'You look beautiful,' he murmured as they danced cheek to cheek.

'Oh, rubbish,' she said automatically, but managed to add, 'I mean, thank you.' She'd tried hard to look nice tonight, unearthing a fitted blue frock she'd had made before the war that emphasized her figure, and had made herself up carefully, scraping the last bit of carmine out of an old lipstick case.

He lifted his head to look at her. 'You don't like compliments, do you? I've noticed that. You should do, you know, because I meant it. You are beautiful. I think so anyway.' He pressed her to him briefly and she breathed in the clean, salty smell of him.

'Thank you.' She grinned sheepishly. 'I do believe you.' Because he made her feel beautiful in a way no one ever had before.

The music became sultry and slow. She laid her head against his shoulder, where it fitted exactly, and they drifted about together under the sweeping lights. It confused her that although she had only met Sam yesterday, this felt so right. She was no naïve young thing now and knew she must take care, because really she knew nothing about him, and yet some deep instinct told her he was a good person.

The music changed again, this time to something vivid and joyous, and Sam upped their pace and swung Minnie round and she cried out with the thrill of it. He was a good dancer and she managed not to step on his toes and soon she was laughing and breathless.

After several fast numbers she pronounced herself to be exhausted and now he became solicitous. 'Let's go and find a drink and something to eat,' and he led her off to the restaurant. There they found a table overlooking the dancefloor where they sipped cocktails and ate club sandwiches. They swapped information about their families and about things they enjoyed doing, films they'd both seen, books they'd read. Sam liked adventure stories, especially Jack London, and spoke so enthrallingly about *White Fang* being about the extremes that humans could be driven to that Minnie became determined to read it.

The meal over, they danced some more. After a couple of slow numbers when they'd turned together in silence, she with her head on Sam's shoulder, she felt him gently stroke her cheek and she closed her eyes and brushed her lips against his hand. Sam whispered, 'You're so gorgeous,' into her ear, and his warm breath made her prickle with pleasure. When the music changed again and Minnie said she'd danced enough and ought to go he took her hand and asked very tentatively if he could see her home. 'I won't come in, if you don't want me to, but I'd like to see you're safe.' She stared into his bright eyes and her longing answered his and she nodded. They collected their coats and went out into the star-studded night.

Minnie's latest flat was on the second floor of a five-storey purpose-built block, its fittings all clean lines and geometric shapes. She'd liked the brand-newness when she chose it and being higher felt safer, while still being able to view comings and goings in the residential street. When, true to his word, Sam kissed her cheek and said goodbye, asking if he could see her the following day, she relented and asked him in.

'Are you sure?'

She nodded, but as she led him up the stairs, she marvelled at the irony of what she was doing: *I usually take such care yet here I am, inviting a complete stranger into my home because I feel I can trust him.*

Once inside the flat she closed the curtains and darted about, switching on lamps and pouring drinks while Sam studied the family photographs on a bookshelf and asked her about the people in them. Then they sat together on the sofa, but she kept a distance from him. She was grateful that he respected this.

'There's no picture of your daddy.' So he had noticed.

'He was killed in the last war,' she said, dully. 'I suppose I have a photograph somewhere. We weren't close, you know.' Little by little she found herself unburdening herself to this kind man with the expressive blue eyes that seemed to see right into her.

'I desperately wanted to prove myself, even though he wasn't there anymore. Isn't that ridiculous? There I was, living at home, working as a typist and wondering when life would begin. I felt so bored and restless. And then an opportunity came and I took it. Sam, I'll tell you the whole story if you like, but there's a risk. You might not like me so much afterwards.'

'Try me.'

'I'm serious. I'm not what you think I am.' And she told him from the beginning, how she'd been approached at a garden party, how Max had recruited her, the long story of her meticulous work for him, the excitements and the low points that had put her under such strain. And finally the story of giving the evidence at the trial, her feelings of guilt for betraying Glading and the betrayal by Max that she endured in turn. So much of it was public knowledge now that she didn't think it wrong to tell him.

After this she went to a drawer in the sideboard and drew out an old envelope full of newspaper cuttings and laid them out before Sam on the coffee table. 'That's what they wrote about me. All these lies. They made me feel cheap.'

'I never knew about this case,' Sam murmured as he fingered the cuttings, a frown on his face. Then he shook his head.

Beside him, she waited anxiously. Was she right, that he despised her now? Had she spoiled his impressions of her? If she had, he'd be like all the others, but she would bear it. She'd known worse.

But when he looked up at her, his eyes were full of sympathy and something else, awe.

'That judge was right. You were brave, Minnie. What a woman you are.' He opened his arms to her and she fell easily into them and he hugged her tight. And now, finally, she wept. It was such a comfort to have told someone, to have her story accepted, to be understood.

'Don't cry, don't cry.'

'I can't help it,' she sobbed. 'They're not bad tears, they're good ones. Oh, Sam.'

He found a handkerchief in his jacket and she dried her eyes and then he leaned and kissed her mouth. 'My beautiful spy,' he said, smiling. 'Minnie, my beautiful spy.'

'Don't,' she gasped. 'You'll make me cry again.'

So he kissed her properly this time, and she kissed him back, and soon they were in a tumble of clothes and cushions until Sam stopped and pulled back and looked at her, smiling. 'I ought to go now,' he said gravely.

'Do you have to?'

'Yes, I think I should. But I'll see you tomorrow. May I?'

What could she say, but 'Of course.'

After he'd gone she rinsed the glasses then went to the bathroom where she was shocked to see her red-rimmed eyes and ruined make up. All her doubts set in. How could this man find her attractive? *But he does,* she told her reflection. *And he knows all about you now.*

She lay awake for ages, wondering why she'd told him, why she'd trusted him, a man she'd known for little more than a day. She'd heard of love of first sight, but had never believed in it. Is this what had happened to them? There was something about him that was familiar, that felt like coming home, and his openness made her trust him. *You silly girl,* a voice inside her hissed, *think of all the men who've let you down, starting with your father. Why should this one be any different?* She didn't know, but she badly wanted to try, that was all. Everybody deserved love. Why shouldn't she have it, too? Even if it was only for a little while, because he'd be gone soon and maybe he'd be killed and she'd never see him again.

All the following day, as she made telephone calls and typed correspondence Minnie thought about Sam and counted the hours away. When she left the office at five he was outside, waiting for her. His face lit up when he saw her and she felt the curious eyes of her colleagues on her as she slipped her arm through his. It was a new thing to see Miss Gray with a boyfriend and they'd tease her about it on Monday. She didn't care what they thought, for he made her happy. He'd spent the day seeing London with other officer buddies. She'd taken Saturday morning off so they'd have the whole weekend together. They'd have to make the most of every moment, he told her wistfully, because he was to rejoin his unit on Monday morning.

How much pleasure could two people who enjoyed each other's company wring out of two days together with the possibility hanging over them that they'd never see one another again? Sam treated her with old-fashioned courtesy and returned to his hotel on the first night, but by Saturday evening it was harder to part.

The day had been exceptionally cold and snow was forecast. They'd passed the time shopping and in cafés and had dinner in an Italian restaurant near Covent Garden, where they'd lingered and the waiter, succumbing to Sam's friendly charm, brought out a dusty bottle of Chianti. The man grew misty-eyed as he poured the ruby wine and spoke about his homeland and his family's farm, now a battleground, so that after he tactfully withdrew an air of seriousness fell upon them.

They sipped the glorious wine and Sam reached for Minnie's hand. 'I've had such a wonderful day. I cannot believe we only met a few days ago. Minnie, do you feel the same?'

She nodded, her eyes fixed tenderly on his.

'Do you promise not to laugh at what I say next, because I'm serious. Minnie Gray, would you think of marrying me? I mean it. It's not only because I'm going away. It's ... You're the girl I want. Now you're laughing and I asked you not to, Minnie.'

'Oh, Sam. I'm not laughing at you. It's the situation. Everything's upside down, isn't it? You must admit it has its funny side.'

'I suppose so.' He looked forlorn and it touched her heart.

'I didn't think I'd find someone before you came along. And now it's happened and it seems so hurried and … businesslike.'

'I know it's a hurry, I can't help that, but if it's romance you want, I can be romantic.'

And right in the middle of the restaurant he got down on one knee, took Minnie by the hand and said, 'Minnie Gray, you're the most beautiful girl in the world and I love you like crazy. Will you do me the honour of becoming my wife?'

Minnie gave him her other hand and smiled. 'That was the most wonderful proposal, Sam,' she whispered. 'And yes, the answer's yes.'

Once again adventure called and she would follow. Marrying a man she'd just met had every kind of risk attached, but she'd learn to love him, she believed she would. And he'd want to return to Canada. Canada. The more she thought about it in the days that followed the more deliriously free she felt. When the war was over they would go to Canada and she could throw off the fears of the future, Glading, Max, the memories of the past, and start a brand new life.

Couldn't she?

Epilogue

Ontario, June 1955

Minnie typed the final sentence then glanced at the clock on the mantelpiece. She didn't have long. Quickly she freed the paper from the typewriter and shrugged on her cardigan while scouring the article for errors. A flick or two of her pen, a crossing out, a substitution. There, it was done. Just her byline to add at the bottom, 'Sylvia Pagett', stupid really, but Sam had begged her to use a false name. 'My wife can't be seen to work. The whole of Lindsay will think I can't support you.' She understood. Lindsay was a small town with small town values. She'd found life far from easy here, but at least she'd felt . . . safe. Too safe sometimes, she thought, checking her neat brown curls in the mirror. She folded the article into an envelope and addressed it to the editor, then snatched up her keys. And smiled, thinking of what lay ahead.

The old Ford rattled over potholes as Minnie drove into town and up the main street. She pulled up outside the offices of the Gazette and leaped out, leaving the door open and the engine running. Inside *she greeted the receptionist, handed her the envelope and hurried out, throwing a 'Must rush, Monique, the children . . .' behind her.*

The sun dazzled as she swung the car round and set off in the direction of the school. The kids would be miserable if she was late and she was late too often, but she always knew how to cheer them up. There they were, the pair of them, waiting alone by the picket fence outside the school, the boy corralling ants in the gutter with a stick. His little sister watched, dwarfed by the satchel strapped across her chest. They looked up as their mother approached with a toot of the horn, their faces accusing.

She slowed the Ford to a halt, leaned across and pushed open the passenger door. 'Sorry, darlings.' They tumbled over one another in their rush to climb in and take possession of the biscuit tin.

'I want a maple cream, leave me a maple cream,' her daughter cried.

'There are plenty there,' Minnie soothed. 'Shut the door, that's it. Are we ready for some fun?' Her eyes twinkled and the children perked up. 'Yes,' they cried in unison, spraying crumbs.

She couldn't help it. Every now and then she needed it to counter the restlessness. It was like an addiction, her 'fix' of danger. Sam hated it, warned her against it, but she didn't care. It was the closest she dared go to the edge. Minnie revved the engine and the car shot off, heading out of town, but not in the direction of the farm. Instead she chose a little-used road that petered out after half a mile or so into a dirt track that ran parallel to the railroad. There they waited with the engine ticking over, watching and listening with the windows wound down and all around the quiet grass waving in the breeze. It wouldn't be long now.

Minnie heard it first, the chugging of the goods train. 'Right on time,' she whispered, sitting up ready. The children tensed and their eyes grew round with excitement.

As the train drew near Minnie sounded the horn and waved. The train whistle blew in answer. 'Ready, kids?' she cried, revving the engine and crashing the gears. 'Ready,' they shouted.

'Go!' She stamped down the accelerator and the car leaped forward. So did the train. Side by side they raced, the train and the car, faster and faster, engines straining, first one pulling ahead, then the other, the old Ford sending up clouds of dust. The children squealed with fear. Minnie screamed, too, but with utter joy. This was it, the mad rush of adrenaline, the desire to win. Faster and faster went the old car, straining and belching out smoke. And then the dirt road ran out as it always did and Minnie braked. The train pulled ahead, its whistle blowing in triumph as it chugged away into the distance, billowing smoke.

Minnie and her children panted and laughed. She turned the vehicle round and headed for home.

It was over, but there was always next time.

Author's Note and Acknowledgements

A Beautiful Spy is a work of fiction inspired by the story of the real life Olga Gray (1906-1990), who spied for Maxwell Knight of British Intelligence during the 1930s and whose brave and meticulous work was crucial in bringing Percy Glading to justice for treachery in March 1938. I have endeavoured where possible to follow the known facts, but the demands of fiction being such as they are, am guilty of some simplification, the alteration of names and of copious use of my imagination where there were gaps or conflicts in my knowledge.

The following books were particularly important to my dramatization of Olga/Minnie's life: *Spooks* by Thomas Hennessey and Claire Thomas, *M: MI5's Greatest Spymaster* by Henry Hemming, *The Man Who was M* by Anthony Masters. The Bishopsgate Library proved a useful resource for information about London in the 1930s as did material from the National Archives.

I am hugely grateful to Paul Willetts, author of *Rendezvous at the Russian Tearooms*, for generous advice about sources, period language and much else; to Karen Pegg and her husband William for providing their atmospheric house in Le Gers for what turned out to be not at all a quiet writing week in the summer of 2019, to my husband David for editorial suggestions and numerous cups of tea. Thank you to His Honour Roger Shawcross, for his advice on the courtroom scene. Thanks to my project editor Alice Rodgers, and copyeditor Sally Partington. Thanks as ever are due to my wonderful agent Sheila Crowley at Curtis Brown Literary Agency and her colleagues, and to my marvellous editor Suzanne Baboneau at Simon & Schuster together with her team. I am so fortunate to be published by them.

Rachel Hore